He hated war, but if the Yankee bastards were going invade Texas, he'd fight them to the death...

The Yankee lieutenant crashed down on top of Shane. Pain radiated through Shane's back. Locked in a deadly draw, he rolled onto his side and fought nose to nose with the officer. The bastard pulled Shane's Walker Colt from his waist and aimed the barrel. The fluted-steel chamber clicked empty.

Shane grabbed the saber blade and pointed the tip toward the lieutenant's gut. Responding with an ear-splitting rebel yell, Shane rallied his strength and thrust the saber into the lieutenant's stomach. Blood spilled down the blade and oozed across his fingers. The Yankee bastard gasped and coughed but kept on fighting.

Shane plunged the three-foot saber deeper. Filled with pent up hate and rage, he drove the curved blade through the lieutenant's abdomen until the hand guard could go no farther. The officer's body went limp. His eyes rolled back into his head and his warm breath expired against Shane's cheek.

Shane slid his saber free and climbed to his feet. He dragged the lieutenant through the cave like a butchered animal. As he stacked his bloody remains with the rest of the Yankee swine, a soldier lurked outside.

Scavenging the pockets of the dead, Shane took two pistols, an eight-inch knife, and chewing tobacco. Sergeant Rufus Beavers stepped into the cavern with his pistol drawn. His eyes widened. Looking up from his bounty of plunder, Shane placed a flask of gunpowder and a handful of cigars inside his shell jacket.

"Holy Jesus, McLean!" Rufus lowered his gun and waved his campaign hat over the mass of twisted bodies. "There's ten dead men in here."

At fifteen, Frank "Shane" McLean covets a commission in the Texas Rangers. With the shadow of civil war on the country's doorstep, he uncovers a dark family secret. His God-fearing father Kirby is an Illuminati henchman and hired assassin for the secret society. Kirby is responsible for the death of a renegade Freemason with ties to Governor Sam Houston. A staunch Freemason and secret Illuminati, Houston hires bounty hunters who kill Kirby in front of his wife and son.

Shane begins a violent life of revenge for his father's death and as a member of Terry's Texas Rangers in the Civil War. The battles of Shiloh, Antietam, and Gettysburg leave him wounded and emotionally scarred, while his inner demons cry for vengeance.

Quest for Vengeance is the first in an action/adventure series detailing Shane's lifelong pursuit to punish the men who made him a widow's son.

KUDOS for *Quest for Vengeance*

In *Legend of Shane McLean, Quest for Vengeance* by Ian Mclean, Shane McLean is a sixteen-year-old farm boy who witnesses his father's murder and vows to exact vengeance on the killers. With the Civil War breaking out, Shane joins the Texas Rangers, thinking that will be the best way to find and destroy his father's murderers. The first book takes us through the early years of the war and the beginning of Shane's search. The story gives us a chilling glimpse into life as a Civil Was soldier in a time of lawlessness and desperation, with very little real justice available. It's a page turner. I can't wait for the next one in the series. ~ *Taylor Jones, Reviewer*

Legend of Shane McLean, Quest for Vengeance is the story of one young boy's quest to avenge his father's brutal murder and his mother's assault at the hands of men who believe they are above the law based on their positions in the military. Only sixteen at the time of the attack on his family, Shane soon joins the Texas Rangers, believing this is the only way he will ever find his father's killers and exact his vengeance. But things don't work out quite like he planned. Once in the military, Shane must follow orders and finds he has little time for personal quests. He also discovers that war is not the glorious adventure he imagined. Instead it is a cruel and merciless struggle of death, horrific injuries, and appalling living conditions, with very little justice to be had for anyone. *Legend of Shane McLean, Quest for Vengeance* is the well-written first installment of what promises to be an incredible series. My heart ached for Shane in his struggle to bring to some kind of justice the heinous bullies who destroyed his family in a time when most justice was enacted through the barrel of a gun belonging to a victim rather than a law-enforcement office. ~ *Regan Murphy, Reviewer*

ACKNOWLEDGEMENTS

I would like to thank my family who encouraged me throughout this project: Mom and Dad, I love you more than you'll ever know; to my beautiful wife, Peggy, thanks for the motivation; to my brother, Shane, you've always been there, and I hope I did Grandpa Vern's stories justice; to my children, Mason, Alexandrea, Lance, I leave this legacy to you.

To my dear friends and colleagues who inspired me throughout this project, I couldn't finish this without you.

A special note of thanks to Duaine and Nancy Lowstetter, Todd Moehlig, Roger Paulding, Joe Walker, Ty Lucas, Genia Goulet, Sandy Jarka, Dean Krantz, and Karen Momanaee.

LEGEND OF SHANE MCLEAN

QUEST FOR VENGEANCE

Ian McLean

A Black Opal Books Publication

GENRE: HISTORICAL FICTION/CIVIL WAR THRILLER

LEGEND OF SHANE MCLEAN ~ QUEST FOR VENGEANCE
Copyright © 2016 by Ian McLean
Cover Design by Jackson Cover Designs
All cover art copyright © 2016
All Rights Reserved
Print ISBN: 978-1-626945-62-3

First Publication: NOVEMBER 2016

Published by Black Opal Books **http://www.blackopalbooks.com**

DEDICATION

Mason, Alexandrea, and Lance, Daddy wrote this story for you. Hope you enjoy Legend of Shane McLean, Quest for Vengeance *as much as I did writing it.*

PREFACE

For the Reader

The legend of Shane McLean was a closely guarded secret, passed down to adult family members by my grandfather Vern F. McLean.

I feel obliged to advise the reader that Grandpa Vern was a notorious storyteller, known to take liberties with the truth. In 1984, I visited him at his home in San Diego. What I learned inspired me to write my first book *Quest for Vengeance*.

☙❧

Chula Vista, California, December, 1984:

"My father was murdered on Valentine's Day." Grandpa Vern's arthritic hands picked at the lock of a dusty old Hutchison chest. "For the sins of his father Shane McLean."

A past Grand Master of the Chula Vista Lodge, Grandpa Vern kept his *work* within the secret society hushed and rarely talked about his grandfather. What I'd learned about Shane McLean came in outlandish stories from my own father.

"Fighting and killing's in our blood. We're descendants of the Scotch-Irish Clan MacLean—the most vicious clan in the Scottish Highlands." Vern opened the cedar chest and took a seat in his high back Victorian chair. "Since I was six, I've lived in fear of being killed."

The bitter scent of mothballs seeped from the old strong-box. Covered in Masonic allegory, the chest contained a Freemason thirty-third-degree apron and a stack of black and white photographs. *Dodge City Peace Commission 1883* etched in the corner of a photo caught my attention. The original picture is in the Smithsonian museum and contains lawmen, Wyatt Earp, Bat Masterson, Sherriff Charlie Bassett, and legendary Frank "Shane" McLean.

"I guess you're old enough to hear the real family story." Vern grabbed an unfiltered Camel cigarette from his shirt pocket. "Shane McLean killed over fifty men." Grandpa cupped his hands around his Zippo and inhaled until the to-bacco came to life. "Listen to me. Most of 'em were killed during the war—so don't judge Shane until you hear his story."

I cherished Grandpa Vern and loved his incredible sto-ries. An 1873 Colt .45 revolver protruded from the Masonic half apron in the strongbox. The Peacemaker was wrapped in a tooled holster and nearly the length of my arm. Wanting to learn about Shane, I eagerly handed Vern the stack of old photos.

"Shane looks so young in this picture." Vern sighed and pulled the Dodge City Peace Commission photograph clos-er. "He's seated on the front row next to Wyatt." His tobac-co-stained finger pointed out a wiry lawman in the photo. "Shane was in his sixties when I knew him."

I'd heard stories but didn't believe him. "Grandpa Shane knew Wyatt Earp—really?"

"Did more than know him. Shane saved Wyatt's life in Dodge City." Vern's eyes narrowed. "He was an elite Texas Ranger during the war. Showed Wyatt how to shoot like a guerrilla fighter and even taught him to gamble and chase women." His raspy voice sharpened. "Shane had been trained to kill since he was seventeen."

"Sounds like a snake oil story." I kneeled at my grandfather's feet. "How come nobody has ever heard of him?"

"Shane had enemies. He's a widow's son, like me." Vern flashed his Masonic ring. "Spent his life hunting down a gang of men who'd murdered his father. He also performed *righteous work* for a secret society known as the Order of Illuminati." He rubbed his thumb over an Owl of Minerva embroidered on the silky half apron. "We've kept his story in the family because that's what Shane wanted. To this very day, I fear his enemies and for your safety."

The chaos in my childhood started to make sense. For as long as I remember, my dad kept a loaded shotgun in his closet, and my family moved like gypsies. By the age of eighteen, I'd lived in California, Canada, Pennsylvania, Texas, and spent time with relatives in Michigan.

A nervous feeling settled in my stomach. "Why are they still after us?"

"Shane was part of a blood-feud that started before the Civil War. His violent past scared the hell out of people." Vern inspected the chamber of his six-shooter. "When Shane told someone to keep quiet, they did—or he'd shut them up." He handed the Peacemaker to me and took a long drag on his cigarette. "That's another reason why we only talked about Shane with adult family."

"His gun's heavier than you'd think." I aimed Shane's revolver at the wall. "It's nearly the length of my arm."

"Longer the barrel, the straighter the shot." Vern leaned back in his chair. "When I was your age, I thought Shane's war stories and accounts of robbing banks and trains with Jesse James was a bunch of hogwash. Until he took me prospecting with Wyatt Earp along the California-Arizona border." His eyes widened. "Back in '25 I mined gold with Wyatt in Vidal."

"Did you find any gold?" I wanted to believe Grandpa Vern's story but sought the truth. "I thought Wyatt was dead by then?"

"No gold that day, but I heard some amazing stories."

Vern shuffled through the photos and stopped at a family portrait taken outside his Colorado cabin. "I've known Wyatt since I was a boy. He'd stop by our home with his wife Josie and visit Shane for hours." His voice softened. "Until the gang of bounty hunters showed up and murdered Daddy."

I wanted to ask Grandpa Vern about the murder but was too afraid. His father was shot and killed in front of him. At the age of six, Vern's mother sent him into the haunted woods to get Shane.

Grandpa Vern wiped his eyes and got choked up. His voice trembled. A Chula Vista motorcycle policeman and rodeo performer, he was tough as leather. I'd never seen him so emotional.

"After Daddy's death, Wyatt helped move our family to San Diego." Vern held up a picture of himself wearing his police uniform on his Harley Davidson motorcycle. "That's me back in the 'twenties. I patrolled the streets with Shane's gun." He eyed the Colt .45 in my hand and grinned. "When I pulled that Peacemaker from my holster, I never had any problems."

Vern snubbed out his cigarette. "I tracked down several of Shane's associates, Bat Masterson, Texas Ranger Lieutenant Sam Maverick, and Brushy Bill Roberts, whom you know as Billy the Kid. What I discovered changed my life."

Fishing in his flimsy shirt pocket for another smoke, Vern turned cold and his voice cracked. "It's been seventy years since my father's murder. The memory of my mother's cries still haunts me—*They shot Fredrick right in front of the children*." He tossed a cigarette in his mouth and reached for his lighter. "Wanna hear a story like that?"

"Yessir."

Grandpa Vern puffed on his cigarette and stared off into the distance. His cold blue eyes narrowed. As he recalled that awful day, I watched the old man become a frightened boy of six. The cold-blooded murder of his father changed him forever.

ↄ৯ↄ৯

Howard, Colorado, Valentine's Day, 1914, in the words of Vern McLean:

I hid behind my pregnant mother in the doorway of our cabin. My father Fredrick cradled my infant brother. Outside, four armed men stood in ankle-deep snow and a model T Roadster glistened in the moist mountain air.

A man with a thick gray beard stepped forward. "Shane McLean, you murdering coward! Come out. We know you're in there." He shook the snow off his black slicker and flashed his pistol. "Come outside and show your face."

Fear shot through my veins. Grandpa Shane was at his cabin, a mile deeper in the woods. Daddy shoved Baby Pete into my arms and grabbed a shotgun from above the doorway. As he peeked out the window, I feared we would all be damned to hell. Wind gusted outside our cabin.

"Send Shane out here!" The assassin's voice deepened. "Get moving or we'll burn this damn shack to the ground."

Momma's eyes narrowed. "I told you fools, Shane don't live here!" She slammed and bolted the solid wood door. "Vern, take your brother and hide behind the bed."

Even at six years old, I didn't need to be told twice. My little sister Aurora sat alone at a table and colored Valentines. While Daddy clung to the thick log wall, Momma grabbed her hand and raced toward the bed. Aurora panicked and dropped her box of crayons. Red and white wax pastels rolled across the wood plank floor. Since I could remember, we lived like hermits due to Grandpa Shane's violent past. Daddy refused to abandon his father.

Mother blamed his stubborn Scotch-Irish clannishness. He would get angry and tell her. "Blood is blood—and blood comes before all else."

The gray-bearded assassin lifted his lantern. "Fred, I ain't here to harm your family. But I'll kill every last one of them if you don't send Shane out now."

Daddy cussed and rammed the butt of his shotgun against the log wall. A picture of Jesus fell to the floor. My throat tightened and heart pounded in my chest. Fearing we'd all be killed, I cradled Baby Pete in my arms and huddled behind the bed with my mother and sister.

"God save us!" Daddy shook his head and stared across the cabin. "Amy, they ain't going away empty handed. I got to give myself up."

Mother pointed toward Shane's cabin on the hillside. "How much longer do we have to endure your father's penance? We're suffering for his sins." Her voice choked. "Your children come first."

"I'm sorry, honey." He sighed and lowered his head. "Didn't think they'd find us out here in the mountains."

"If you're innocent, go and take those men to Shane's cabin." She covered Aurora's ears. "He brought this damned feud on us. Let him deal with those killers."

Daddy shook his head. "I was with Shane the night he burned down the Masonic Lodge."

"Damn it, Fred! You've put everyone in danger." Her tone turned spiteful. "For what? Your bitter old drunken father."

"Listen to your mother," he said to me. "Help her take care of your sister and brother." He approached from across the room. "I'll be leaving for a while." He pushed the hair from my face and lifted Baby Pete from my arms. "Vern, you'll be the man of the house."

I sensed he didn't intend to come home. A gun blast rang out. The door frame splintered. Fearing for my life, I ducked and dropped to the floor at Daddy's feet. As he handed Baby Pete to Momma, she sobbed and wiped her cheek. Her puffy red-eyes dripped with tears.

"Fred!" The assassin's voice screeched like a pesky blackbird. "If you don't come out here, I'm gonna turn your shack into a bonfire."

Daddy wheeled around and unbolted the door. "I'm coming out, Ivey!"

I climbed to my knees and chased after my father. As the door swung open, an icy breeze drifted through the cabin. Four men dressed in long black coats stood shoulder to shoulder in the snow. The outlaws carried guns and looked like wicked scarecrows. Daddy slowly raised his hands. Stepping toward the doorway, he looked over his shoulder and smiled at me. His deep-blue eyes pieced my heart.

"Lock it, Vern!" He stepped onto the porch and slammed the solid-wood door shut. "Don't shoot me, Ivey. I'm unarmed."

I didn't want to let Daddy down and raced to slide the bolt into the doorframe. Silence filled the cabin. A porch board creaked. As he stepped into the snow, I rushed to the window and glanced outside. His tall silhouette moved toward the lantern light.

"Last chance, Shane!" Ivey brandished his pistol and shouted into the cabin. "Save your son and come out now."

Momma pushed me aside and shouted through the window. "Shane don't live here!"

"That murdering son-of-bitch is around here somewhere." Ivey placed the barrel of his gun to my father's head. "Where in the hell is Shane?"

"In your mother's bed!" Daddy's voice echoed into the cabin. "Leave us alone. Y'all started the damn killing when you murdered Shane's father in Austin."

"Kirby McLean was wanted for murder—dead or alive. We did the State of Texas a service." Ivey turned toward his men and laughed. "Governor Houston and the Freemasons paid us well for that job."

"That's a barefaced lie and you know it!" Daddy spat in the assassin's face. "Damn you, William Ivey!"

Ivey leveled his gun at Daddy's head. "All of you McLeans are no good killers!"

A six-inch flame exploded from Ivey's pistol. Tissue exploded from Daddy's skull. While the blasted echoed into the cabin, he remained on his feet. I flinched and covered my head. My ears rang like church bells.

Daddy wobbled and collapsed to his knees. As his bloodstained head landed in the snow, Mother cradled Baby Pete and screamed. Gunpowder drifted toward the cabin. The murder played in my mind like a slow-motion picture.

Ivey wiped the spit from his face. "Spread out and look for Shane. He's around here somewhere." He stepped over Daddy's body and motioned toward the woods. "Be careful—bastard has no remorse. He'll shoot you dead in a second."

While his men rushed off in different directions, Ivey approached the cabin. Mother stepped away from the window and grabbed my hand. As she led us toward the bed, Aurora cried. The sound of breaking glass shot through the cabin. A lantern crashed through the window, spilling kerosene on the floorboards. Fire raced across the room.

"Woman!" Ivey stared through the broken window pane. "I know Shane's around here. That no-good coward can watch his family burn."

Flames shot toward the metal roof. As smoke filled the cabin, Aurora covered her eyes and cried. Her wax crayons melted to the floor. Six months pregnant, Mother grabbed Aurora's hand and dashed around the fire with Baby Pete clinging to her hip. I struggled to see through the smoke. Red and yellow flames glowed inside the cabin.

"Vern!" Mother's voice shrieked. "Over here, Vern. Come to the door."

Smoke and kerosene burned my nostrils. Waving through the thick black smoke, I spotted Momma with my brother and sister. She unlatched the deadbolt and pushed the door open.

"You gotta go and warn Grandpa Shane. Tell him what these monsters did." She stood in the doorway and pointed into the darkness. "Can you do that?"

Smoke poured out of the broken window. I couldn't believe Mother told me to go alone. She never let me step foot in the haunted woods and the bad men were still outside. Blood drained from Daddy's head.

An outlaw's voice echoed from behind an evergreen tree. "I don't see him, Boss. Ain't nobody in that cabin but a pregnant woman and three little kids."

"Keep your eyes peeled. That son-of-a-bitch is around here," Ivey shouted from the porch. "Probably watching us now."

A second outlaw approached from the rear. "I knew McLean was a damn hard case, but I never thought he'd let his own women and children burn. He's got no soul."

Ivey stepped off the porch and sloshed through the snow. "Shane killed my father and my crippled brother." His tone sharpened. "I want him dead."

"Run, Vern!" Mother pushed me out the door. "Run and lead those men to Grandpa Shane's cabin."

I swallowed my fear and leaped off the porch. Guided by moonlight, I ran by Daddy's bloodstained body and dashed past the outlaws into the woods. While I headed to Grandpa Shane's cabin, lantern light trailed in the distance. The perilous fifteen-minute trek through the foothills of the Twin Sister Mountains ran along a fast-flowing stream. Shane lived deep in the forest. Hiding from his violent past, he seldom went to town or entertained company.

Gunfire rang out in the forest. While my home went up in flames, I dodged low limbs and jagged rocks and ran as fast as I could. My lungs burned and toes stung with frostbite. A snow-covered roof pierced through the trees.

"Grandpa Shane, let me in!" I leaped onto his porch and delivered the awful news. "Grandpa Shane, they shot Daddy."

A match light appeared through the window. As I pounded my fist against Shane's door, the deadbolt slid open. The door creaked and my heart raced. Candlelight shimmered inside the cabin.

Shane pulled me inside. "What's going on, Vern?"

My throat tightened and I struggled to speak. Shane was a shadow of his former self. Bent with age, the Civil War hero struggled with a limp wrought by years of living on the run. His piercing blue-eyes and handsome face was framed by wrinkled cheekbones. Gunfire rang out in the dark.

"They shot Daddy!" I choked out the words. "Mother says to come right now."

Shane stood in his doorway and scanned the woods below his cabin. A bright orange glow resonated from my home in the valley. Petrified by fear, I clung to Grandpa Shane's leg and closed my eyes. The image of my pregnant mother, brother, and sister lying side by side in the snow ran through my head.

Shane rushed to a dusty cedar chest at the foot of his bed. "Close the door, Vern!"

I slammed the door shut but couldn't lock the deadbolt. As I turned for help, a strange woman climbed out of Shane's bed. Wrapped in a bed sheet, she rushed out of the candlelight and lit a cigarette. I'd never seen her before. Lifting the lid to his cedar chest, Shane pulled out his 1873 Colt .45 Peacemaker and tied a black neckerchief over the inch-wide scar around his neck. His wrinkled face tightened into a cold dark stare.

"I promised your mother *The Feud* was over." Shane's voice deepened. "God, I hope she can forgive me. Let's go, boy. It's on again."

And the legend began...

CHAPTER 1

Raised up Tough

Shamrock Ranch, McLennan County, Texas, 1860:

*F*orgiveness and compassion are noble virtues for the righteous. Vengeance belongs to God.

Comanches raided a settlement along the chalky limestone banks of the Bosque River. While the hot midday sun beat down, armed horsemen kicked up dust on the horizon. Frank "Shane" McLean looked up from a page of Shakespeare's *Othello* and sulked. Banished to the porch of his family's log cabin, he tracked the silhouettes of two riders in a field of bluestem grass. His mother Margaret dropped a dish in the kitchen.

As the dust cloud grew closer, she made a startled cry. "Get Pa's gun!" Margaret poked her head out of the doorway. "Banditos robbed the Jensen home last week. Killed Misses Jensen and her two children."

"What?" Shane twisted in his rocking chair and eyed his mother. "You didn't tell me? I'm old enough to know."

Frustrated by his secretive parents, he closed his book and sought protection. Strangers couldn't be trusted. His father Kirby kept a Big Colt Walker in the kitchen hutch.

As he retrieved the huge six-shooter, the horsemen steered toward the cabin and rode through a yellow clump of Indiangrass. Startled doves flew into the sky.

"Better take that gun to Pa. He'll know how to handle 'em." Margaret grabbed an old Springfield musket stored above the doorway and her voice trembled. "Hope he's still out back. Mister Pierson needed his help."

Intending to prove his manhood, Shane didn't need his aging father. "Pa better stay away. They might rough him up." His eyes strained to track the horsemen. "He'd bless 'em while they rob us. I won't let that happen."

Margaret covered her mouth and sighed. Shane stepped outside to investigate. Friends or foes, he opened the cylinder of his revolver and checked the gunpowder. Sweat dripped from his brow. Talk of secession and war with the North turned God-fearing men against each other. His mother cocked the flint-lock hammer of her model 1822 Springfield.

A lanky rider rose in his saddle and politely waved. His left hand dangled by his gun holster. When the dust cleared, Shane recognized the horseman's upright posture.

Seventeen-year-old Jerry Ringo and his kid brother Jimmy lived on a neighboring ranch. Shane used to play stickball and marbles with the Ringo brothers. They'd gone to Sunday school together until their mother died.

"Thought y'all were highwaymen out to rob us." Shane tucked his six-shooter behind his belt. "Haven't seen you since the funeral last year. What brings you around?"

Lean and country strong, Jerry reined up beside the hitching post. "Comanche attacked a cabin near Tonk Crossing. Mister Pierson's getting a posse together to hunt 'em savages down."

"Pa's a man of God. He won't let me join you." Shane looked to see if his mother was listening. "Old coot ain't got the heart to kill Indians."

"Freemasons are sponsoring the Fourth of July shooting match tomorrow in Waco." Jerry turned in his saddle and motioned to his thirteen-year-old brother. "Jimmy and I need your father to take a look at our shooting skills."

"Pa's in the animal pen. But I ain't asking him for nothing." Shane shook his head. "All he does is nag. Told me to read the *Bible* with Ma 'cause I took too long feeding the hogs." His tone sharpened. "Sick of him telling me what to do. I ain't a child no more."

"At least he's not a drunkard like my daddy." Jerry rested a thumb on his hand-tooled holster. "Since Momma died, Franklin can't escape his inner demons."

Shane didn't want to pry. Rumors swirled around church about Mr. Ringo's violent temper and battle with alcoholism. A veteran of the Mexican War, Franklin had been a regular at mass until Mrs. Ringo died giving birth to Baby Johnny. "Living here ain't no better." Shane declared, venting his frustration. "Senator Erath stopped by the other day and got into an argument with Pa—left without spending the night. It's hell living in the backwoods with *Bible*-thumping parents."

"You should join the US Army with us and see the country." Jimmy turned to hide his face. "I hate living out here in Crawford. Soldier's life gotta be better than this."

Shane noticed Jimmy had a black-eye and his temper flared. "Did Franklin do that?"

"No! No! No! Daddy didn't hit me." Jimmy steadied his horse and motioned to his big brother. "Ask Jerry—it was an accident. I ran into a door last night."

Shane eyed Jerry with contempt. "You can't let him do that. Jimmy's just a kid."

"It won't happen again. We hid Daddy's whiskey." Jerry brandished his father's Army Colt. "When he passed out last night, I took his gun."

"Don't be mad, Frank. It was my mistake." Jimmy covered his swollen eye. "I told him to quit yelling at Baby Johnny. It wasn't his fault Momma died. God needed her up in heaven."

"He's just lonely." Jerry placed his finger to his temple and formed his hand into a pistol. "Put his gun to his head and threatened to shoot himself."

Glass shattered inside the cabin. Jerry wheeled around and scanned the perimeter. As he aimed his Colt toward the doorway, Shane searched for his overzealous mother. The four-foot barrel of the old Springfield stuck out of the entry.

Jerry pushed his scraggily red hair under his straw palmetto. "Doctor says Daddy's melancholy, Misses McLean. It'll pass with time."

"I read 'em books you give us, Misses McLean." Jimmy's voice cracked. "Lern't 'em math tables too."

"Then speak proper English." Margaret stepped into the daylight and glared through the doorway. "I promised your dying mother, I'd see to your schooling. Don't make me a liar." Her stern voice cut like dagger. "*There is no darkness but ignorance.*"

Jerry eyed Shane and shrugged. "We didn't ride over here for sympathy—tomorrow's your birthday."

"Come on, Frank." Jimmy leaned forward in his saddle. "Tell Kirby you're gonna compete in the shooting contest with us. First place gets a hundred dollars and a fancy Bowie knife."

Shane wished it was that easy. Born on Independence Day in 1844, he could legally drink, vote, and get married. But his devoutly religious parents wouldn't approve. The Village of Waco had a reputation for violence and boasted a wicked red-light district.

"Pa already sent me to the cabin this morning 'cause of my attitude." Shane feared soliciting something frivolous when there was work to do. "I'll ask when he's in a better mood."

"Ask him now." Jimmy nodded at his big brother. "Jerry's been practicing. Bet he wins that shooting contest. Second place pays twenty-five dollars." His mouth tightened into a smug grin. "Third place's all yours."

Shane scoffed. "If Pa lets me go, I'd beat both of you."

"Tell him to chaperone us." Jerry pulled his Mississippi rifle from a saddle holster. "Maybe, he'll pay our two dollar entry fee. We'll ditch him and go squire girls."

"I ain't going to Waco with that Holy Roller." Shane didn't want to court females with his father around. "He'll make us stop and pray at every church on the way. Big cities make old people nervous."

"Kirby's old-fashioned, but he ain't afraid of nothing. He fought with Sam Houston during the revolution." Jerry placed his Mississippi rifle across his shoulder. "That makes him a war hero."

Shane laughed at the outrageous notion. His father didn't have the stomach to kill. Kirby had been a priest in Gotha and claimed to be a stone mason, when he could find work.

"Pa was an advisor during the revolution and just a scout during the Mexican War. Probably ran at the first sound of gunfire." Shane removed his sweaty palmetto hat. "Momma orders him around like a child." His shoulder-length hair fell into his eyes. "Kirby ain't a real killer like your father. How many men did Franklin shoot...three or four?"

Jimmy held up a handful of fingers. "Daddy killed a man in Tennessee—a Negro down in Wharton County—and three Mexican soldiers during the war." He turned to follow Jerry to the animal pen. "Ask your pa to go with us or I'll do it for you."

A pig squealed. While a breeze brought the foul stench of hogs, Shane begrudgingly joined his friends. Eager to hold his pet piglet Daisy, he rounded the cabin and locked eyes with the affectionate brown babe. He'd slept with the furry critter at his feet all winter. Daisy slipped under the broken cedar post gate.

"Don't say anything to Pa about us squiring girls in Waco." Shane pulled a carrot from the garden and dropped to a knee. "Here piggy, piggy. Over here, Daisy."

"I ain't saying nothing to him." Jerry glanced toward the cedar post pen. "Your old man scares the daylights outta me."

Kirby wrestled a ravenous four-hundred-pound hog from the feeding trough. Lean and exceptionally fit, he stood an intimidating six feet, four inches. Shane ignored his father and dangled a carrot in front of Daisy. The cuddly pet piglet leaped into his open arms.

"*Shaneee!*" Kirby's Irish brogue rolled off his tongue. "Come fix this gate. We can't afford to lose any more animals."

Shane hated the ethnic sobriquet. The nickname identified him as a lowly Scotch-Irish immigrant. He preferred his more American birth name, Frank.

"I tried to help you this morning!" Shane couldn't let go of an earlier argument. "But you got mad and called me a child. Told me to do woman's chores with Ma." He cradled his pet piglet and kissed her fuzzy belly. "I ain't a kid no more."

"I said if you're gonna act like a child, go help your mother. You're the one that stormed off to the cabin." Kirby turned toward the Ringo brothers. "Shane doesn't have time for friends. He's got work to do."

"Yessir." Jimmy dropped his head. "Our daddy ain't got time for us neither."

"That's a nasty shiner, boy." Kirby wiped a splotch of mud on his cheek. "Been fighting at school again?"

"Pa, mind your P's and Q's. You're nosier than the preacher." Shane kissed Daisy's snout and tried to explain his crazy family to his friends. "He's in one of his moods— y'all better go." He was determined to go to Waco and compete with his friends. "I've got an idea for the shooting contest, but I'll wait until tonight to ask."

While the Ringo brothers turned tail and rode away, Shane worked to gain his father's good graces. He mended the broken cedar post gate, separated the hogs, and chopped wood until dusk. Instead of complaining about chores, he helped his mother hang laundry and read his nightly *Bible* scriptures without protest.

Thunderstorms boomed on the horizon. As the dark ominous clouds rolled in, Kirby oiled his Big Colt Walker at the kitchen table. Shane lit a lantern and sat across from his intimidating father.

Desperate to go to town, he waited for an opportunity to beg permission.

"You must want something." Kirby released the cylinder pin on his revolver. "Mother and I noticed a change this afternoon—a generally helpful attitude on your part."

"Do you know about that Fourth of July fiesta in Waco?" Shane jumped at his chance. "They got a circus this year with horse races and a barbecue. Freemans are sponsoring a shooting contest with a hundred dollar prize. Ringo brothers want me to go with 'em." He stared across the wood-trestle table. "It'd be a great way to celebrate my birthday."

Margaret placed her needlepoint on the fireplace. "Thought this foolishness had already been settled. Waco's dangerous." She shook her head and rocked forward in her chair. "Rustlers, murderers, and highwaymen out to rob travelers. Armed militia that support open rebellion against the Union." Her eyes narrowed. "Reverend Dahl calls the place Six Shooter Junction."

Shane hated his overbearing parents and pushed aside the family *Bible.* Rising from the table, he grabbed a ceramic vase off his mother's Scandinavian hutch and removed a key hidden inside. As he unlocked a cabinet drawer, Margaret gasped and put her hand to her mouth. Kirby's secret *Prayer Book* sat wrapped in a silky green half-apron. The black leather-bound volume had the Athenian Owl of Minerva engraved on the cover. Strange symbols and numbers filled the six-inch pages. Forbidden to view the mysterious contents, he'd taken the liberty to occasionally sneak a peek inside. But he always feared his parents would find out.

"I'm old enough to know that you go to secret meetings at the Masonic temple." Shane placed the mystic book in front of his father. "My friend Mack says you know the Freemason Grand Master and powerful politicians. Will you register me in tomorrow afternoon's shooting contest?"

Mack S. Dodd was three years older than Shane and a troublemaker. At six feet, five inches and well over 250 pounds, the mountain of a man had a larger than life perso-

na. Loud and intimidating, Mack backed up his fierce reputation with his sledgehammer fists.

"Your friend needs to hold his tongue before it's torn out
by the root." Kirby blew the gunpowder out of a chamber
and flashed his fraternal ring. "Silence is golden. There's
nothing wrong with keeping secrets."

A bolt of lightning illuminated the sky and struck a lone
post oak tree. As a limb crashed to the ground, Shane
cringed and took a seat across from his father. He'd heard
rumors of sorcery, secret passwords, and handshakes. Freemasons took a vow of silence punishable by death. The
preacher in Norse warned of Devil worship and human sacrifices at the Grand Temple. Intrigued by the secret society,
Shane didn't believe the claims of eternal damnation and
wanted to join the mystic brotherhood. But his mother for-
bade it.

Margaret grabbed a laundry basket. "Watch your
words...that was close."

Shane wished he'd kept his mouth shut. As he braced for
a stern lecture, wind blew across the Shamrock Ranch.
Horses whinnied and the musty smell of rain filled the cabin. Kirby grabbed his chest and grimaced in pain. His
breathing quickened.

"Pa's irritable heart has been bothering him." Margaret
placed the basket on her hip and headed toward the doorway. "I've got clothes on the line that needs bringing in.
Don't bother your father." Her face tightened. "You're *not*
going to Waco."

"I'll be sixteen tomorrow. Don't need your permission."
Shane knew better than to backtalk but couldn't stop himself. "I'm gonna win that shooting contest and join the army
with the Ringo brothers. Gonna get my own ranch too." His
tone turned spiteful. "It won't be way out here in the backwoods—hidden from normal people."

"Hush your mouth, boy!" Kirby slammed his fist on the
table. "You've got *no* chance to win that contest. When soldiers catch wind of the prize money they'll come in droves.

Only reason the lodge is putting up that kind of cash is so they can recruit fools like you and the Ringos into the military." His thick Irish brogue cleared into precise English. "Civil war is brewing back east. You'd do well to avoid it."

Shane intended to defend the family honor. Disgusted by his simpleminded father, he yearned to fight and save the Union. Whenever he went to town, church, or someone came to call, the topic always turned to war. Labeled Black Republicans by secessionists, he'd grown leery of ridicule from his friends and McLennan County cotton farmers.

"Remember Goliad! Remember the Alamo." Shane leaned across the table. "You might be too old to fight, but I ain't scared." He stared into his father's cold-blue eyes. "If you ain't prepared to die for liberty, you don't deserve to live in peace."

"Don't lecture me, boy! Signing up to be slaughtered like cattle doesn't make you a man." Kirby paused to catch his breath. "I fought in two wars, so you and your mother could live in peace on this ranch. I've seen the face of death. It's an awful sight." He rubbed his heart and grimaced. "Artillery ripping arms from bodies, legs split in two, grown men crying out in battle." His lower lip trembled. "You couldn't last a day in the US Army."

"Yes, I could!" Shane wished his father dead. "Can't wait to get off this backwater ranch."

"Do it! Maybe you'll appreciate your mother and me." Kirby's face turned red and a blue vein popped in his neck. "We work damn hard to keep food on this table. 'Eat the fruit of the labor of your hands and be blessed.'"

"Don't preach your old-fashioned virtues to me. I'm destined for bigger and better things in life." Shane scoffed. "Look around here. God's forsaken this place."

"If you don't like our rules, then leave. Work and pay for everything." Kirby doubled over and choked. "While you still know everything."

‿ᔆᐧᔆ‿

McLean family cabin in McLennan County Texas, July 4, 1860:

Fresh bacon sizzled in the skillet and filled the split-log cabin with a tasty aroma. While morning sun crept through the doorway, overnight rain saturated the cabin floor. Shane rubbed his eyes open and rolled out of a raw-hide laced cot. His mother cooked in the fireplace. Devout in her worship of the *Bible* and love of Shakespeare, her light Scandinavian skin was as wrinkle-free as her neatly pressed dresses. A bloodstained carving knife lay in his father's place at the table.

"Where's Pa?" Shane grabbed a seat and sipped a glass of buttermilk. "He loves pork belly."

"Your father couldn't sleep. Says his chest feels tight." Margaret approached with a skillet of crackling pork fat. "Don't know why his heart's been so irritable."

Breathing the scrumptious smell of sizzling bacon, Shane eyed the fresh blood on her apron and looked to apologize to his father. "He'll be fine. Old Coot's too tough to die."

"Don't talk about your father like that." Margaret waved her wooden spoon toward the animal pen. "Last night's thunderstorm stirred up the hogs. He's been up since dawn chasing down animals that escaped from the gate *you* repaired."

Shane took the news like a kick to the groin and hung his head in shame. He wished he'd driven the gate post deeper. As he glanced outside, the anticipation of Kirby's fierce anger ruined his appetite.

"Sows trampled the garden." Margaret wiped her brow and sighed. "Don't know how we're gonna survive without those vegetables. Happy sixteenth birthday." She dropped a spoonful of bacon pieces onto his plate and forced a smile. "Made 'em crunchy. Just the way you like."

"Sorry, Ma. I'll do a better job next time." Shane bit into his bacon and savored the flavor. "This pork belly is delicious." He spoke with his mouth full. "How come Pa didn't wake me to help round up the hogs?"

"After the way you behaved last night, he thought you'd gather your things and leave the ranch for good." Margaret's voice trembled. "Your dear father loves you more than you'll ever know. He just wants what's best for us."

"Got an odd way of showing it." Shane needed to bide his time. If only he could set out on his own. "How much damage can four hogs do? Daisy is just a babe." He covered his mouth and gagged. "Ma, you're not feeding me Daisy— are you?"

Margaret bowed her head. "I'm afraid your little piglet got stuck under the gate you repaired. Daisy drowned." Her voice dropped an octave. "And on your birthday too."

Shane yearned for Daisy's slobbery snout kisses. Thinking of her friendly manner, he choked and spit a mouthful of bacon onto his plate. How could his mother be so insensitive?

"Eat it, Frank. We can't let good meat go to waste." Margaret pointed toward an oak tree used for butchering animals. "Daisy's like any of God's creatures we use to survive."

Shane tried to be a man, but her cold indifference hurt his feelings. He didn't want his mother to see him cry. Ashamed of his childish emotions, he gulped down a mouthful of sour-tasting buttermilk and winced.

"Daisy wasn't a meal!" Shane rose from his chair and choked on his words. "She used to lick my face and kept my feet warm all winter." He wiped his cheek and headed toward the door. "Gonna see if Pa wants my help."

"Oh, Shane, I'm sorry." Margaret covered her mouth. "We can get another piglet from Mister Pierson."

Spotting his butchered piglet, Shane froze in the doorway and fought the urge to cry. Daisy dangled by her hindquarters. A tear rolled down his cheek.

"Oh—my—God!" Kirby rounded the corner with his Big Walker Colt holstered to his hip. "Grow up, son. You're too

damn old to be crying over a pet." His wrinkled face tightened in disgust. "It's sustenance."

Shane tried to control his emotions but couldn't. As he
turned away in shame, Margaret stepped outside and ran to
comfort him. Kirby threw up his hands and shook his head.

"Be nice, Daddy. It's Shane's birthday." Margaret's
voice softened. "He's always had tender feelings."

"Hell's bells, honey! He wanted to run away and join the
army last night," Kirby said in a condescending tone. "Now
he's crying over his little piglet. Is he a man or a child?" He
turned toward the horse stable. "When he's done whining,
have him fetch the musket and saddle the horses. We're going to the Ringos."

Shane took his frustrations out on his mother. "Why'd
you tell Pa? Mr. Ringo is gonna kill him."

CHAPTER 2

Dark Family Secret

McLennan County Texas, July 4, 1860:

Shane wasn't going to let his sixty-year-old father face down a mad killer like Franklin Ringo alone. Splashing through a shallow ford in the drought-stricken Bosque River, Shane carried the flintlock Springfield musket across his saddle pommel and prepared to fight. As he rode alongside his mother, Kirby charged ahead. Since leaving the Shamrock Ranch, he had a wicked look in his eyes and hadn't uttered a word. His frock coat concealed his holstered Walker Colt.

The Ringos' one-roomed cabin looked like a filthy raccoon nest. Nestled in a grove of cottonwood trees, the thatch roof leaked and the ground reeked of urine and stale whiskey.

Flies buzzed through the air. Stunned by the squalid conditions, Shane steered toward the cabin and spotted young Jimmy Ringo playing in the dirt with hand-painted lead toy soldiers. His black eye had nearly swollen shut.

"This is not how Bea wanted her boys raised." Margaret kissed her silver Luther Rose necklace and glanced toward Heaven. "She's probably looking down on us, wishing someone would help her family."

Shane brandished his old Springfield musket. "That's why Pa and me are here."

"Load the gun," Kirby said over his shoulder. "Stay here and protect your mother. You don't need to witness this."

Shane feared for his father's safety. "I'm coming with you. I can help."

"Don't cross him, Frank." Margaret grabbed his reins and halted twenty yards from the cabin. "When he gets like this, I've learned to leave him alone."

Shane glared at his mother. "Why'd you put Pa up to this?"

Baby Johnny cried out in the cabin. Margaret's face tightened. As she rushed a hand to her mouth, the frantic baby wailed like a gunshot coyote. Dirty laundry and liquor bottles littered the front porch.

"Jimmmyyy!" Mr. Ringo's angry voice echoed through the doorway. "I told you to keep this youngling quiet. I'm trying to sleep."

Leaping to his feet, Jimmy snatched a handful of toy soldiers and spotted Kirby. He tried to hide his swollen eye. Jerry rushed around the side of the cabin. Blood oozed from his lower lip. His gun holster was empty. Shane pitied his battered and abused friends.

"What are y'all doing here?" Jerry covered his injured lip and pointed toward the Shamrock Ranch. "Best be going. Daddy's not feeling well."

Kirby dismounted and tied off his horse. As he headed toward the cabin, Jerry rushed to the doorway. Spreading his arms across the wooden frame, he braced his body and blocked the entrance. Margaret grabbed Shane's hand and sighed.

Jimmy rushed to his brother's side. "Don't come inside, Mister McLean."

"My father's sleeping." Jerry refused to budge. "Franklin doesn't like to be woken up."

Half a head taller, Kirby lowered his shoulder and barreled forward. "Get out of my way.

Margaret screamed. As she squeezed Shane's hand, Kirby sliced through the Ringo brothers like a hot knife through butter. Shane listened for gunfire.

"Frank!" Jerry held his shoulder and buckled in pain. "Daddy's got a gun."

Baby Johnny wailed. Furniture crashed against the wall and broke apart on the floor. While glass shattered inside the cabin, Shane eyed the Ringo brothers and feared someone would lose their father. Margaret hummed a sweet lullaby.

"Get up, Franklin! You enjoy slapping your boys around—showing 'em how tough you are?" Kirby shouted like a madman. "Don't feel so good, does it?"

The slap of an open hand striking a skull rang out. Jimmy cringed and stepped away from the doorway. As he hid behind his big brother, a struggle and several more slaps ensued.

"Don't beg forgiveness from me, apologize to your little boys," Kirby yelled. "They've lost their mother to God's Will and their father to the Devil's drink."

A bottle broke against the wall. Pushing his frightened little brother aside, Jerry peered inside and stared in stunned silence. Shane had second thoughts about his father's past. Nobody could've come into Mr. Ringo's home and pushed him around without select military training.

"You ain't dead, Franklin!" Kirby cursed like soldier. "Get off the damn ground. Be a father to your boys. You're supposed to protect 'em."

A gunshot rang out. Fearing the worst, Shane dismounted and rushed toward the cabin. Gunsmoke streamed from the door. As he approached the Ringo brothers, Kirby dragged Franklin by the ankle. The strapping two-hundred-pound war veteran squirmed on the floor like a bullied child.

"Stop hitting me, Kirby." Mr. Ringo rolled onto his back and wiped his bloodstained mouth. "I'm gonna quit drinking—promise."

"Set an example for your boys. Find God and seek inner peace." Kirby released Franklin's ankle and flashed his golden fraternal ring. "Follow the rules of the Brotherhood."

"Don't come at me with your righteous talk. You're no better than anyone else." Mr. Ringo lifted his battered head and spit a mouthful of blood. "I've been to your secret temple in Waco. Does sweet little Frank here know about your hocus-pocus with Weishaupt's Illuminati?" He rolled onto his side and pointed at Shane. "Did you tell your son how many men you've killed for the Rothschilds?"

Kirby made a fist and grunted through clenched teeth, "It's a benign fraternity with a sacred oath of silence."

Shane had never heard of the Illuminati, but the name sounded devious. Astounded by the turn of events, he'd never seen such a wicked look on his father's face. Kirby lunged forward like a raging bull. As his cold blue-eyes tightened, Mr. Ringo covered his face and cried out. The blood-curling scream echoed off the walls.

Kirby slammed his fist into Franklin's jaw. "Nothing's wrong with secrets."

Blood splattered the floor. Kirby lingered over the body. Stepping over a shattered whiskey bottle, Shane feared his father had killed Mr. Ringo. Murder was a hanging offense. While Jerry and Jimmy stared at their father, a deathly silence lingered.

"Wake up, Franklin." Kirby tapped Mr. Ringo's blood-stained cheek. "Wake up. Margaret's gonna take care of the baby for a while."

Mr. Ringo gasped. As he rolled onto his side and spit, Shane sighed. What else could go wrong?

"Saddle up your horses. There's a shooting contest in Waco this afternoon." Kirby cradled Mr. Ringo's head. "If you hurry, I'll register all three of you."

Shane struggled to contain his excitement. As he cracked a smile, the Ringo brothers rushed outside. Kirby pulled out an eight-inch knife and whispered in Mr. Ringo's ear. Franklin's face tightened in despair.

CRICRICRI

McLennan County, Texas, July 4, 1860:

Waco celebrated the nation's independence with a big fiesta. A circus, horse races, and shooting contest sponsored by Masonic Lodge Ninety-Two peaked Shane's interest. The three-hour ride wound through forests of black jacks and prairies of bluestem grass. While Mr. Ringo recovered at home, Shane looked forward to spending the day with his friends. Flanked by Jerry and Jimmy, he rode along the Bosque River and reflected on his gray-haired father. He concluded Mr. Ringo had an axe to grind. Kirby would never be an enforcer for a devious organization like the Illuminati.

Summer drought shrank the mighty Bosque into a meandering stream. Taught to be logical and question everything, Shane rode alongside his secretive father with skepticism. As he steered along the riverbed, the Ringo brothers slowed to avoid a boulder. Kirby's knuckles dripped blood.

"Better wrap your hand in a bandage." Shane slumped in his saddle. "How'd you meet Ma? You never talk about your past."

Kirby licked his knuckles and spit blood. "Met her during a dance at Rutersville College." He glanced over his shoulder and whispered, "Mister Ringo had some damning words this morning. Some things he said are true." His eyes narrowed. "You're of age to become a Freemason, but I don't discuss the Brotherhood with non-members."

"Yessir." Shane didn't want to upset his father. "I understand. When you think I'm ready, I'd like to be invited to join." He steered toward a watery shoal and changed the subject. "How'd you get invited to a college dance down in Fayette County?"

"Before you were born, I led a squadron of militia." Kirby removed his wide-brimmed palmetto hat and fanned his face. "We chased off a Comanche war party and the school held a ball to thank the soldiers. Your mother was the prettiest girl I've laid eyes on." His wrinkled cheeks tightened into a bright smile. "She still is."

Shane shuddered at the thought. "You use to be an officer in the Texas Militia? Thought you said you were a bricklayer and priest."

"I was also a lieutenant, but I got crossways with General Houston after the war." Kirby eyed the Ringo brothers approach. "You don't believe me?"

Shane rubbed his brown bay's thick mane. "Brownie might believe your story, but I don't. Why would you give up a glorious military career?"

"I loved your mother and had *work* at the lodge. Some things are more important than fame and fortune." Kirby splashed his horse into the knee-deep shoal. "When your mother left school to marry me, her family shunned her. They'd heard rumors about my past." His tone turned to disgust. "Mister and Misses Nordboe lived in Dallas, but they still refuse to see us or even speak to Margaret."

Shane had been led to believe his maternal grandparents lived too far to visit. Since he was a child, his mother complained about not finishing college. Margaret vowed he'd attend Waco University and become somebody respectful. Shane knew even less about his paternal family. Kirby was born in Scotland but claimed to be educated by Jesuits in Gotha. The Kingdom of Bavaria and Scottish Isles were miles apart.

"How come your family doesn't come to visit?" Shane eyed the approaching Ringo brothers and whispered. "Did you get crossways with 'em too?"

"I was orphaned at age six. Catholic church in Edinburgh had my parents arrested for heresy." Kirby held out his golden fraternal ring. "This ring belonged to my father. He was a reformer allied with the Grand Lodge of Scotland. He questioned the church's doctrine and exposed hypocrisy."

"Mister McLean, Daddy says inquisitions were cruel

back then." Jerry approached with his little brother. "Did the church make him recant his Protestant faith before setting him free?"

"They were both executed. When you're suspended in the air by ropes with your innards ripped open, the pain is so horrible you'll confess to anything just to be killed quickly." Kirby shook his head. "But my father resisted until he could strike his best deal with the Jesuits." He popped the cork on his wooden canteen and took a sip of water. "He wouldn't renounce his faith unless the executioner cut off my mother's head first—with a single swing." His voice choked. "He couldn't bear the thought of her being tortured and mutilated."

Shane questioned his father's story. "People were killed for heresy?"

"Catholic Church infiltrated the Grand Lodge in Edinburgh." Kirby shrugged. "My parents weren't executed for their faith. It was my father's belief in the Order of Illuminati."

Jerry turned in his saddle. "Would you sponsor me at the Gatesville Lodge?"

"I wanna join too, Mister McLean." Jimmy nodded. "Daddy says Freemasons run the world. They control the government, banks, and organize political power." His eyes widened. "Even the Pope in Rome is scared of 'em."

"Shut your mouth." Jerry eyed his little brother. "You don't ask to join the Masons. They ask you."

"Mister McLean. Is John the Baptist's head hidden inside the Waco Grand Temple?" Jimmy steered toward Kirby. "Do they perform human sacrifices?"

"Hush before you get sacrificed." Jerry rushed his finger to his lips. "You're insulting Mister McLean with that nonsense." He waved his fist. "Knock it off, or I'll give you a matching black eye."

A gray wolf trotted through the riverside woods. Shane carried a dozen .69 caliber bullets and a leather flask of gunpowder. Highwaymen roamed the countryside. Kirby reined up beneath a hundred-foot limestone cliff. His eyes locked on the towering peak. While the Ringo brothers rode on, a silver-dollar-sized sliver of limestone whizzed past Shane's head. The chalky rock hit the riverbed and broke into pieces.

"Did y'all see that?" Jimmy's voice trembled. "A rock must've fallen off those bluffs."

Jerry grabbed his rifle. "They don't fall this far out. Someone's throwing 'em at us."

"There's Comanche up there!" Kirby yelled from the rear. "They look angry too. This is their ancestral land." He pointed to the top of the cliff. "Hope that war party doesn't attack us."

"Where?" Jimmy wheeled his horse and frantically scanned the clifftop. "Where are they? I don't see any braves."

A second rock hit the ground between the Ringo brothers. Shane sensed a ruse. Most of the Comanche were relocated to the Indian Territory north of the Red River. As he traced the rock's path back to his father, he noticed that Kirby held a handful of limestone slivers.

"Put your rifle away. Pa's throwing the rocks." Shane shook his head. "When I was a kid, he'd scare me by throwing things and blame it on wild Indians." He eyed his father and recalled another frightening game. "Be glad Pa didn't play the pumpkin trick on you."

"You still remember that?" Kirby laughed and dropped the rocks in his hand. "Pumpkin trick was your mother's idea. Her father used to play it on her to keep her out of the woods."

"Pa would carve scary faces on pumpkins." Shane shared the frightening game's cruel ruse. "He'd put a candle inside and get my mother to hide 'em outside at night, then he'd tell me some gruesome story and make me fetch him something." He shuddered at the terrifying images. "Still don't like to be alone in the woods after dark."

"Kept you from wandering off!" Kirby wiped the chalky film off his hands and gripped his reins. "Let's ride."

ฅ๏ฅ๏

Three miles west of Waco, July 4, 1860:

Vultures circled in the distance. A forest of cottonwoods lined the beautiful banks of the Bosque River. Shane hoped to register for the shooting contest before lunch. Riding along the riverbed, he planned to ditch his father in town and squire girls with the Ringo brothers.

Jimmy flared his nostrils. "Smells like a skunk's ass."

A metal object flashed behind a large juniper bush. Shane glimpsed the silhouette of a man hiding in the woods. Visions of hostile Comanche filled his mind. Sliding his old Springfield free, he squeezed the steel barrel like the handle of a battle axe and rounded a bend in the river. The decaying carcass of an escaped slave hung from a tree jetting over the Bosque. Vultures ripped flesh from the dead Negros's face and neck.

Shane peeled off from the others. Circling behind the juniper bush, he gripped his musket and prepared to attack. His heart raced. As he rode toward the stranger, evergreen branches snapped.

"Come back, Frank!" Jimmy shouted from the riverbed. "There could be Indians in there."

A Negro darted from the juniper. Escaped slaves hid in packs and killed to survive. Shane feared an ambush but gave chase. As he slowed to ride beneath a cottonwood branch, the Negro fled deeper into the woods.

"Frank!" Kirby's angry voice shot through the trees. "Get out of there."

Unable to penetrate the underbrush, Shane wheeled his horse and back tracked toward the river. A Methodist preacher in a clerical collar shirt crouched behind an oak tree. Scattered clothes and a bed roll lay the ground. Surrounded by his worldly possessions, the graybeard snatched his *Bible* and stared toward the river. The Ringo brothers aimed their guns at the impoverished camp.

"Reverend Johnson!" Kirby stood in his stirrups. "Show yourself."

The gray-bearded preacher limped out of the woods and ran his fingers through his disheveled hair. Clutching his *Bible,* he closed his eyes and prayed toward heaven. His lips rambled. Disfiguring whip marks scarred his face and neck. Shane put away his musket and steered toward the river.

"Jesus Christ is coming! Repent of your sin," Reverend Johnson said in trance like devotion. "Turn back. There's evil and insurrection in Waco. Praise the Lord." His tongue twisted verses into incoherent babble. "Jesus died for your sins—arose from the dead to save you from the fires of hell."

Kirby holstered his gun and dismounted. Grabbing his pocket *Bible,* he approached the fiery preacher with his hand raised in spiritual rejoice. Shane halted on a sandbar and worried his father would be fleeced or shamed into returning home. His brown bay whinnied and bucked. A loud hiss sounded from the watery shoal.

"Snake!" Jimmy leapt from his saddle.

A thick black water moccasin crawled across the rocks. Shane squeezed his reins and clung to his stirrups. The air smelled like a musky billy goat. His panicked horse kicked her hind legs. Tossed forward in his saddle, he slammed his face against the mare's bony neck and slithered to the ground. The vinegary taste of blood filled his mouth.

"Lookout!" Jerry pointed to the sandbar. "Cottonmouth's headed straight for you."

The four-foot water moccasin hissed and opened its white mouth. Shane struggled to gain his bearings. Fearing a nasty bite, he staggered behind his jittery horse and wiggled his front teeth. As he spit a mouthful of blood, Jimmy rushed in behind the deadly black viper.

"No!" shouted Jerry. "Don't touch it."

Fearing for his young friend, Shane stepped from his horse and lost his balance. Jimmy snatched the cottonmouth by the tail. The snake coiled and snapped at his hand. Whipping the black viper through the air, he slammed its triangular head against the rocks several times.

"What I tell you in darkness, speak ye in light." Reverend Johnson hobbled along the riverbed. "What ye hear in the ear, preach on the housetops."

"You're a fool, Jimmy." Jerry grabbed his brother's horse. "One bite from that cottonmouth, you'd been a deadman."

"I'm faster than a snake and quicker than a jackrabbit." Jimmy dangled the four-foot cottonmouth by the tail. "Gonna cook it up for lunch."

"Better watch out. It'll bite even if it's dead." Shane spit a mouthful of blood. "Got any water left?"

"I think your father knows that crazy preacher." Jerry tossed his canteen to Shane. "See those whip marks on the graybeard's neck? Someone didn't like what he was preaching." His voice softened. "Let's dump Jimmy off on your Pa and go to town on our own."

"I don't want to go to Waco with a busted mouth." Shane wiggled his loose incisors. "If my front teeth fall out I ain't got a chance of meeting a girl." He wiped a blood-stained string of drool off his chin and took a sip. "Why's that reverend living under an oak tree with an escaped slave?"

"He's an ignorant fire eater—like your abolitionist parents." Jerry scoffed. "Black Republican's been running their damn mouths and getting chased out of towns all across Texas."

"I ain't for slavery or against it, but it seems wrong to own someone." Shane intended to get his father's perspective on the issue. "Gotta think on it more." He didn't want to upset his friend and changed the topic. "Pa ain't stupid. If we leave to squire girls in Waco, he'll know I'm up to something."

"I've got an idea." Jerry wheeled his horse and shouted across the sandbar. "Mister McLean! Frank's hurt bad—needs to see a doctor." His voice filled with concern. "I'm gonna take him to town."

Eying the cottonmouth in Jimmy's hand, Kirby splashed through a puddle and rushed across the riverbed. His boot slipped in a patch of mossy limestone. As he tumbled awkwardly onto his backside, Shane cussed Jerry's half-baked scheme. Reverend Johnson approached with a look of concern.

"Damn it, Ringo! Pa thinks I'm really hurt." Shane watched his father climb to his feet and feared his furious anger. "You didn't have to worry him. He's got a bad heart." He wiggled his teeth to make his mouth appear worse. "You've took a little accident and turned it into the bloody Alamo."

"How'd I know you were such a Daddy's boy?" Jerry steered his horse away. "Your pa looks really pissed-off. I'm gonna wait with Jimmy."

Wiping his waterlogged clothes, Kirby limped forward and struggled to catch his breath. "Where'd it bite you?"

"I didn't get bit, sir." Shane dripped a mouthful of bloodstained saliva over his lips. "Cottonmouth startled Brownie. She panicked and bucked me off."

"Open your mouth." Kirby examined Shane's teeth and scoffed. "You'll be fine. Got a couple of loose teeth. It'll heal. Drink some water."

Shane turned his empty canteen upside down. "Don't have any."

"There's a big spring where the Bosque meets the Brazos." Reverend Johnson pointed downriver. "But you'd better be careful. The Booth Gang uses the water for their cattle. They don't like strangers. Chased a group of women and children out of the river this morning."

"Booth is a two-bit thief and rustler." Kirby flashed his

fraternal ring at the fiery preacher. "Part of the corruption at the Waco Lodge."

"World's gone mad. End of times is upon us." Reverend Johnson unbuttoned his clerical collar. "Secession's spreading evil like fever through Texas." He pointed to his scarred neck. "I was whipped by a mob when a farmer claimed I'd planned a slave uprising."

"You probably deserved it for spreading lies and harboring slaves." Jerry's eyes narrowed. "God works in mysterious ways." He pushed his little brother forward. "Mister McLean, I'm leaving Jimmy with you. Frank and I are gonna ride to town. We'll meet y'all at the livery."

Kirby dropped his head and appeared disappointed. Jerry's presumptuous tone made everyone uneasy. Shane feared his father's reaction.

"You're sixteen. Guess you don't need your father around." Kirby's eyes narrowed. "Stay away from strangers—and far away from the military recruiters."

"Yessir. I won't join the army." Shane couldn't believe his luck. "What time do you want to meet at the livery?"

"We'll be right behind you." Kirby approached the fiery preacher. "I'm gonna pray with my dear friend Reverend Johnson then help him gather his things. Gonna send him to do the Lord's work."

"Send him up north to Philadelphia." Jerry scoffed. "Lots of Unionists and crazy abolitionists there."

"I believe I'll send the reverend to a ranch near Crawford. "Kirby's tone sharpened. "Where three boys need the love of God and a sober father."

CHAPTER 3

Waco Masonic Lodge Number Ninety-Two

Two Miles west of Waco, July 4, 1860:

The confluence of the Bosque and Brazos flowed around sandy strips of limestone. While his father and Jimmy prayed with the crazy Methodist preacher, Shane and Jerry struck out on their own. Veering around a boulder, he heard a splash and voices downriver. A large plantation and cotton field filled with slaves lined the Brazos.

"Someone's swimming in the spring." Jerry stood in his stirrups and strained to see. "Might be girls?"

Shane wished. "Probably the Booth Gang the preacher warned us about."

Cattle grazed along the grassy bank. Riding onto a fifty-foot sandbar to get a better look, Shane spotted saddled horses and four men bathing in the river. Guns hung on their saddlebags.

The strangers sipped liquor and looked like trouble. Yearning for a drink, he grabbed his canteen and noticed cow dung floating in the water. A low hanging oak branch dipped into the river.

"Ready your pistol. There're four men up ahead." Shane pointed to a fast-flowing stream along the riverbank. "See if you can find a safe path around 'em rustlers. I'm gonna fill my canteen in the white water."

A distressed calf mooed from behind the overhanging oak branch. While Jerry withdrew a Colt Army, the branch shook and water splashed. Shane dismounted on the sandy center island. His throat ached for a drink. Grabbing his canteen, he slipped off his boots and rolled up his pants. A pair of extra-large pants draped across a chinaberry tree.

Brownie whinnied and wandered along the sandbar. The thirsty mare sunk her nose beneath the fast-flowing water. Shane waded into the rapids. As the clear water rushed over his feet, he slipped on an algae-covered rock and nearly lost his balance. A naked person in waist-deep water peered through the low-hanging branch.

"Whose goes there?" Jerry brandished his gun. "I can see you hiding in those leaves."

A foot-long crayfish with pinchers the size of fists slithered across a rock. Shane lifted his canteen out of the rapids and leapt backward. As he stumbled in the knee-deep rapids, the tree branches parted.

"Frank!" Mack Dodd's deep familiar voice put Shane on notice. "What are you doing here?"

Mack was a mountain of a man. At six feet, five inches, he was mean, intimidating, and used to getting his way. Startled by his naked friend, Shane lost his balance and tumbled awkwardly into the Brazos. His leather flask of gunpowder sank below the water.

"Thought y'all were part of the Booth Gang." Mack waded through the rapids with a baby calf cradled in his arms. "What're you doing here?"

"Damn it, Dodd! Scared me half to death." Shane slammed his fist in frustration. "Thought you were one of those rustlers."

Jerry reined up on the sandbar and laughed. Shane yanked his waterlogged bag of gunpowder out of the river. As he rolled onto his side, the giant crayfish pinched his fleshy calf. Searing pain radiated through his leg. In a fit of rage, he peeled the painful claw off his skin and tossed the spiny crustacean onto the sandbar.

"What'd you go and throw it for?" Mack placed the calf on the riverbank. "That little critter didn't do nothing—you landed on him."

"Can't save every animal you come across." Shane pointed to the inch-long claw mark on his calf and turned toward his naked friend. "Put some clothes on, you big dufus."

Jerry scoffed. "What were you doing to that baby heifer with your clothes off—trying to breed it?"

"Buzz off, Ringo." Mack splashed a handful of water. "Keep jawing and you'll be picking your teeth out of the river."

Jerry's horse sipped from the Brazos. "Hope you ain't pissed in the river. My horse is thirsty."

Mack hurled a wall of water. "Take a drink and find out."

"Knock it off, Dodd." Shane eyed his big troublemaking friend. "Did you steal that calf from those rustlers?"

"I ain't no thief. Little babe was stuck in the mud, so I freed her." Mack put his hand over his privates and motioned downriver. "Now that y'all are here to back me up, let's go chase the Booth Gang outta the spring."

Shane searched for an excuse. The rustlers were armed and appeared dangerous. Even with Mack on his side, the thought of fighting four grown men struck fear in his heart.

"I can't. My father's just down yonder." Shane pointed over his shoulder. "If he finds out I'm starting trouble, he won't register me in the Freemason's shooting contest."

"Frank and me ain't got time for your foolishness. We're gonna squire girls in town." Jerry tossed his canteen to Mack. "Fill it up. We're in a hurry."

"I'm gonna ride to town with y'all." Mack held up a silver fraternal ring. "Since I'm an apprentice at the Meridian Lodge, I'm already signed up for the contest." He filled Jerry's canteen and shook the water from his curly-black hair.

"Some pretty girls from Cliff Town passed by a while ago. Told 'em to get a good spot so they can watch me win."

Shane didn't want to be caught with his troublesome friend. Kirby wouldn't put up with a loud mouth. Mack grabbed his privates and headed toward the riverbank. As he splashed through the rapids like an excited bird dog, Shane readied to leave.

"We'll wait for you." Jerry lifted his canteen in salute. "Hope those Cliff Town girls look better than that little heifer you had."

Mack raised his middle finger. As he made a beeline toward the chinaberry tree, a gunshot rang out. Shane froze. The gang of rustlers rode four abreast toward the rapids.

"Cattle thieves!" A shirtless obese man waved a pistol. "That calf belongs to Mr. Booth. Better ride on outta here or we'll string y'all up."

Shane didn't need to be told twice. He didn't have a functional weapon or will to fight a gang of armed outlaws. *Kind words can accomplish much.*

"Make us, fat guts! We ain't scared of you." Mack stood on the riverbank in his long-Johns carrying a lever-action Henry rifle. "We ain't running like those women and children you chased away this morning."

"Frank, get over here. Those men are crazy mad." Jerry wheeled his horse. "Dodd probably stole that calf. I ain't hanging for his deeds. Let's make a run for it and return with sheriff."

"Dodd ain't no thief. They're just out to scare us." Shane grabbed his old Springfield and rushed over to Jerry. "If he says he's sorry, maybe they'll let us leave."

"That big fool ain't gonna apologize." Jerry's voice was filled with disgust. "Look at him—running around in his drawers like he's gonna kill someone. If Dodd was twice as smart, he'd still be stupid."

"We ain't afraid of you!" Mack cocked his Colt revolving rifle at the fat man. "I saved that calf from downing, and you're gonna call me a thief?" His voice deepened. "I say you're all peckerwoods."

Shane squeezed his wet flask of gunpowder and wished he'd stayed on the Shamrock Ranch. The Booth Gang rode onto the fifty-foot sandbar.

"Shut up, Dodd!" Jerry turned toward Shane. "See what I mean? The fool thinks he can whip all four 'em by himself." He slid forward in his saddle. "Lay your old military musket across my horse and aim at the fat man's chest. Maybe they'll turn tail and run."

"My powder's wet." Shane eyed Jerry's saddlebag. "Where's yours?"

"Jimmy took the rifle." Jerry shrugged. "Didn't think we'd need it."

Shane cocked his flintlock hammer and bluffed. Aiming at the fat man's chest, he placed his finger on the trigger and glared down four-foot barrel. His heart spun like a paddle wheel. The gang brandished their pistols and kept on coming.

"Spread out, men." The fat man glanced at Shane. "If these cattle thieves wanna fight, let's give 'em one."

The four armed men fanned out along the sandbar. Shane kept his musket pointed at leader's bare chest. A dingy rustler with tobacco-stained buckteeth halted twenty-feet away. He spotted Shane's empty flash pan and cackled like an evil little gnome. A horse whinnied.

While water splashed in the river, the bucktooth rustler glanced to his left and reached for his pistol. Shane squeezed his empty musket. Paralyzed by fear, he struggled to breath and prayed the rustlers would break and run. *If death hath a thousand doors, oh Lord, please open one.*

A blast of gunfire rang out. Blood splattered from the bucktooth rustler's skull. Wilting into his saddle, he tumbled backward and landed on the sandbar. His tobacco-stained teeth slammed against the rocks. A gray cloud of gunsmoke lingered above the Brazos.

Kirby rode out of a watery shoal and aimed his Big Colt

Walker at the gang. His cold blue eyes hardened. Charging through the gunsmoke, he splashed onto the center island like a demon sent from hell. The fat man glanced at his dead friend. As the rustlers banded together, a grotesque little man with a hunchback holstered his pistol.

"Put down your gun, Bud! I've seen him at the lodge." The hunchback's voice cracked. "That's Kirby McLean, a cold-blooded assassin."

"I'm a killer too, Charlie." Bud shifted his pistol around his enormous stomach. "That old man ain't better than the three of us. Bucktooth Ted was a friend of mine."

Shane feared they'd all go to jail for murder. While Jimmy stood on the riverbank with his Mississippi rifle, Mack Dodd waded into the rapids. Staring down the muzzle of fat man's pistol, Shane panicked and hit the barrel of his Springfield on Jerry's saddle. His gun slipped through his sweaty palms. The flint-lock struck a jagged rock and broke loose at the stock. As he bent to retrieve his broken gun, the hunchback's eyes widened.

A second gunshot rang out. Shane cringed and braced for impact. Bud cried out. As he dropped his pistol, the bullet tore through his hand. Blood splattered onto his cheek. Gunsmoke poured from Kirby's revolver.

"What the hell, old man." Charlie the hunchback threw his tiny arms into the air. "Quit shooting. We give up."

"Please don't kill me!" Bud squeezed his wrist and twisted in his saddle. "I've got a pregnant wife and baby at home. Show a little mercy for my family."

"That's my son you're aiming at. Don't beg for mercy when you don't give it." Kirby reined up in front of Bucktooth Ted. "Your dead friend didn't show any pity for the family he robbed and murdered in Comanche County last year."

"He didn't kill those settlers." Bud cradled his blood-soaked hand. "Ted works for Mr. Booth. He didn't deserve to die like this." His voice trembled. "You'll hear from Sheriff Twaddell."

"Shut your mouth before I put a bullet in it." Kirby aimed his gun at Bud's head. "Go get the damn sheriff. Bucktooth's worth fifty dollars in Comanche." He cocked the hammer back and extended his arm. "Rest of y'all might fetch another twenty—dead or alive."

Bud wrapped his gunshot hand in a cloth bandage. "Mr. Booth ain't gonna like this."

"Booth can claim any reward money. If there's a problem, I'll see him at the lodge." Kirby pointed to Bucktooth Ted's lifeless body. "Get your dead friend and ride on outta here while you still can."

Awed by his father, Shane worried about Mack's big mouth and searched for an excuse to explain the gunfight. Kirby held his heart and appeared sick. His pale cheeks looked like a ghost. While the rustlers tied Bucktooth Ted to a horse, Mack stepped onto the sandbar with his rifle draped across his shoulders. Shane worried about the law but feared reprisal by the Booth Gang.

"Nice shot, Mister McLean. That fat man was gonna kill Frank." Mack nodded. "I like your style—shoot first and ask questions later.

Kirby holstered his revolver. "I was aiming for his heart."

"You need to see a doctor, Pa. You look awful." Shane approached his father. "Is your heart burning again?

Kirby shrugged and wheeled his horse toward town. "Let's not tell your Ma about this."

∽∾∾

Village of Waco, Texas, July 4, 1860:

A rundown row of wooden shacks loomed on the edge of Six Shooter Junction. While a barroom piano played "Darling Nelly Gray," patrons sang the harmonious chorus, "Oh my Nelly Gray they have taken you away." Drunken men and scantily clad women spilled onto the boardwalk. Shane and his friends soaked in the noontime debauchery. Trailing behind his father, he steered toward Main Street and hoped to taste his first drink. A woman's laugh echoed in a dark alleyway.

"We're gonna have us a rip-roaring Independence Day." Mack turned in his saddle. "Rat Row is already celebrating."

Shane cringed. Pushing his shoulder-length hair under his palmetto, he knew his father wouldn't put up with loud-mouthed kids. His friends needed to behave.

"After y'all get registered for the contest, let's ditch your old man," Mack whispered. "I know where the working girls are."

Eying his father, Shane lowered his head and steered away. "Paying for a woman's an abomination. I'm saving myself for my future wife."

"Stay out of The Reservation." Kirby eyed the row of seedy shacks. "Nothing good ever happens there."

"Hell's bells, Mister McLean." Mack scoffed. "Brothers at the lodge say the girls and liquor is cheap and plentiful. I can take care of myself."

"What's said at the lodge stays at the lodge." Kirby turned in his saddle. "If you wanna go hobnobbing, ride on. But don't come around the boys."

"Sir, I wasn't planning on drinking until after I win this afternoon's shooting contest." Mack steered toward Shane and whispered. "Got a better idea."

A riverboat sat grounded on a limestone shoal in the drought-stricken Brazos. Law offices, apothecaries, mercantile businesses, and a court house lined the village square. Steering around a parked wagon, Shane thought about winning the Freemason shooting contest.

As he approached a busy intersection, Captain William Dalrymple's Texas Rangers marched in parade formation. Appointed by Governor Sam Houston, the elite company of rangers only accepted the best sharpshooters and horsemen into their ranks for the defense of the frontier.

"Watch out, Frank!" Kirby reined up in the street. "Halt for the side traffic."

A Phaeton double-buggy sped toward the intersection. Shane yanked on his reins and pushed down in his stirrups. His startled horse twisted to a stop. Tossed forward in his saddle, he snapped his chin to his chest and his straw palmetto tumbled into the street. As he leaped to retrieve his hat, the large spoke wheels kicked up a cloud of dust. The speeding buggy rolled over his palmetto. Covered in grime, he picked up his hat and slapped the crushed brim against his thigh.

"Watch where you're going, old man!" Shane waved his fist and cussed. "I had the damn right-of-way."

A red-haired girl, about his age, leaned out of the carriage. Her bright green-eyes glistened. Smitten by the girl's pretty face, he stared until her buggy sped out of sight.

"That's Mary Kelly. Forget about her." Mack gave a disapproving nod. "She's from Cliff Town and way outta your class."

"Maybe for a bumpkin like you." Shane straightened the crown of his hat and sighed. "One day I'm gonna marry that girl."

Masonic Lodge Number Ninety-Two was on the third floor of the Gothic-inspired WW Downs Building. Stabling their horses at the Waco Livery, Shane and his friends followed Kirby through the crowded downtown streets. As they approached the public square, the humid Fourth of July heat caused tensions to rise. Texas Rangers separated a mob of militiamen from a boisterous reverend and his flock of abolitionist Whites and Negros. The bitter rivals nearly came to blows on the corner of Austin Street and the Square.

Half a dozen US Army officers, wearing half-aprons embroidered in Masonic allegory, loitered outside the three-story Downs Building.

Surrounded by Mack and the Ringo brothers, Shane

yearned to join the lodge. His father stopped outside the arched doorway.

"If y'all want to join the Brotherhood, keep your mouths shut," Kirby whispered over his shoulder. "Don't draw attention to yourself while we're inside the Tyler Room."

"I know the rules." Mack flashed his Masonic ring. "I'm already a prospect. Took the blood oath at the lodge in Meridian."

"You ain't no apprentice. Where are you from?" Kirby's eyes narrowed. "How old is your father?"

"He'll be fifty-one in September." Mack shrugged. "I was born in Tennessee. Why does it matter?"

"Complete your Masonic memory work! You're from Saint John's Bethlehem. Your father's and your mother is 762." Kirby grabbed Mack and pulled him close until their noses nearly touched. "Masons aren't powerless like the Odd Fellows. Influential men serve here." His voice deepened. "This ain't a social lodge like Meridian. Open your mouth to the wrong person you might not wake up in the morning."

Intrigued by tales of sorcery and human sacrifice, Shane wondered what made the Waco Lodge unique. As he scanned the arch doorway, a woman screamed. The Booth Gang rode down Austin Street. Bucktooth Ted's lifeless body dangled from his horse.

The lobby door swung open. While Kirby shook hands with a Freemason guarding the archway, two Kansas Federal guardsmen rushed outside. The intimidating soldiers dressed in red leg gaiters looked like trouble. Trailed by his friends, Shane followed his father into the lobby. A Masonic guard with a golden ceremonial sword stood from a grand mahogany chair.

"A Mason's son is called a *Lewis*." Kirby wheeled around. "If the Tyler Guard approaches, don't shake his hand. Look him in the eye and say *mah-hah-bone*."

A large square and compass with an inlaid "G" hung above an ornately carved doorway. Shouldering past the roomful of Freemasons, Shane fell in line behind his father. As he approached the main entry, the Tyler Guard brandished his sword and blocked access.

Kirby veered toward a rear hallway. "Follow me."

The vacant corridor contained life-sized sculptures and paintings. Struggling to keep up with his father, Shane rushed through the lobby and past the contestant table. Two dozen names filled the register's list. Half of the contestants had a military title. Doubting his chances in the shooting match, he cussed his luck and headed down the corridor.

Kirby stood in front of a painting of the Egyptian Sphinx. Glancing over his shoulder, he placed a bronze skeleton key into the floor-length frame and pushed open a secret passage. The hidden doorway led to a spiral staircase. Without saying a word, Shane slipped inside the dimly lit room. Mack and the Ringo brothers quickly followed.

The thick-hazy air smelled like rosemary. Kirby locked the door. As he grabbed a candelabra and started up the iron staircase, Shane felt like he was being watched.

"Stay close." Kirby's voice softened. "They're not expecting us."

Shane wanted to know who, but was afraid to ask. Masonic allegory covered the walls. Pythagorean Theorem root numbers, three, four, five and the forty-seventh problem of Euclid were painted in three-foot effigies. As he followed after his father, the spiraling stairs appeared to climb into the heavens. Staring at an image of the goddess Virgo, he got the creeps and appeared to enter another dimension. A soft chant echoed from above.

"Think I saw a ghost," Mack whispered. "This ain't like the lodge in Meridian. Your Pa must hold a high rank in the Brotherhood." He grabbed Shane's arm. "Think he'd be my sponsor?"

"I don't know, and I ain't asking." Shane lost sight of his father. "Let's go. Don't want him to come looking for us."

The call of a cattle horn echoed through the darkness. Rounding the first level, Shane stared at a Masonic magic square painted on the wall and bumped into a brass candle-stick. Hot wax dripped onto his wrist. As he rubbed his burned skin, Mack pushed him up the staircase toward the Preparation room. The plush second level ceremonial chamber displayed a wooden altar, containing a square and compass.

"Those are the Fellow Craft Degree symbols. Working tools of a Mason." Mack stepped toward the ritual altar. "Let's see if we can find the Pillars of Knowledge."

"Get out of there! Somebody's probably watching." Shane eyed the dark middle chamber room. "You'll get us in trouble."

"Frank! Better get up here." Jerry's voice echoed down the staircase. "Your Pa's arguing with a Tyler Guard."

Shane rushed upstairs. As he pushed past the Ringo brothers, Kirby stood alone in the Chamber of Reflection. He tied a green embroidered half-apron to his waist. His Big Colt Walker had been replaced by an ivory-handled .36 Colt Special. Monuments to corn, wine, and oil hung on the walls. Twin side doors swung open. As a draft of fresh air blew through the chamber, a Tyler Guard led two distin-guished Masons through the ornate temple doors.

"Brother McLean, I'm Grand Master Taylor." The pudgy man with a thick beard motioned to his colleague. "I believe you know Worshipful Master Gurley." Taylor used a split fingered grip to shake hands while his demeanor turned contemptuous. "We ask that you not bring these 'Lewises' up the spiral stairway."

"If you'd responded to my correspondence, I wouldn't have used the Illuminati doorway." Kirby's tone sharpened. "Brotherhood replies to my letters when they need throats cut across, tongues torn out by the root, and bowels burned to ashes and scattered before the four winds of the earth."

"Leadership at this lodge has changed. They're distanc-ing themselves from your kind of operations." Grand Mas-ter Taylor stepped back. "Old ways need to stop. Your witch hunt for William Morgan tarnished President Jackson's legacy and still brings disrepute on the Brotherhood."

"Morgan Affair happened thirty years ago. Brother Jackson's reputation is secure." Kirby's voice deepened. "Old Hickory's been dead for a decade and he's still the hero of New Orleans." He adjusted his half-apron and pointed in the Grand Master's face. "Don't speak on things you don't understand. Brother Spartacus and the Jesuits wanted Morgan in Gotha. The end justified the means."

While the Ringo brothers stood in silence, Shane looked for any sign of Mack Dodd. He didn't trust Grand Master Taylor or understand the depths of his father's involvement in the Illuminati. Kirby kept too many secrets.

"I'm not under Weishaupt's delusional spell, nor do I take the Rothschild's blood money." Taylor lifted a silver medallion dangling from his neck. "I don't know what your agenda is, but as long as I'm the Grand Master, the Illuminati will not infiltrate the lodges in Texas." His eyes narrowed. "Even Sam Houston realizes the New World Order is dead."

"Houston's a fool if he thinks the Order is dead." Kirby scoffed. "The big drunk's a coward and should've been banished by the Jesuits when he failed his Brothers at the Alamo. His hands drip with the blood of Colonel Travis and Davey Crocket, along with a hundred other Masons he turned his back on."

Shouldering up to the Ringo brothers, Shane feared for his father's safety. Sam Houston boasted a fierce reputation. The sixty-eight-year-old governor notoriously dueled with his enemies and had powerful friends in Washington. A door in the rear of the chamber opened.

"Honor and integrity mean nothing to that half-crazy drunkard." Kirby grabbed his chest and paused to catch his breath. "Houston failed to come to the aid of Brother Fannin at Goliad—and disobeyed his Sacred Oath to help and assist worthy Masons."

"You'd do well to let old wounds heal." Taylor nodded. "I'll let Brother Raven know you *still* take issue with his tactic to Runaway Scrape and flee the hostilities." His tone sharpened. "Justice from Fort Leavenworth's a telegraph away."

"Don't threaten me with one of Senator Lane's Death Squads." Kirby pointed in the Grand Master's face. "You brought up the Morgan Affair, and you challenged the Illuminati's influence. I was in New Orleans and witnessed Houston and Jackson swear allegiance to the Order. Both men were vetted by the Jesuits, and both selected president of their nations." He shook his finger in the other man's face. "Don't ever question the authority of the Enlightened, or you'll face fate."

"Brother McLean, remember where you are. There's no fighting in this lodge." Worshipful Master Gurley stepped forward. "Anderson's Constitution is strictly enforced. Take it to the street if you must," he scolded Kirby. "You're wrong about Brother Raven. His tactic to Runaway Scrape saved the Revolution."

"Don't patronize me! If I intended Grand Master Taylor harm, we'd be talking over his body." Kirby dismissed Gurley with a wave of his hand. "Where's Past Master Varner or Speight? I need men with reason and logic. Not puppets of ignorance."

A bright light flashed from the spiral stairway. As a harmonious chant echoed in temple, Shane hoped for calm. His father had gone too far. Flanked by the Ringo brothers, he stood in the shadows and waited to approach. Mack Dodd still hadn't made his way to the third floor.

"Brother McLean, why the pent up hatred for Houston? We're all faulted men in eyes of the Supreme Architect." Taylor shrugged. "Brother Raven's a god-fearing family man, a worthy statesman and Texas hero, undeserving of your scorn."

"Houston ignored a directive from Rome to cut out Santa Anna's tongue." Kirby rested his thumb on his gun holster and scoffed. "The Raven's no family man. He's a drunkard, insane, and deeply depressed—ask any of his three wives."

"Not everyone has your bloodlust. Brother Santa Anna hailed the Sign of Distress." Taylor raised his hand and ceded the Masonic Hailing Sign. "Houston honored the privilege, so he could acquire the entire State of Texas without further loss of lives."

"Brother Fannin and Brother Travis didn't receive privilege from Santa Anna. Little Napoleon slaughtered everyone." Kirby clenched his teeth. "Even fellow Masons who'd surrendered."

"Better hold your tongue...Houston's here in town." Taylor scoffed. "He's running for President of the United States and judging today's shooting contest."

"We've dueled in the past." Kirby flashed his fraternal ring and stared at the Grand Master. "I'll duel with Houston again. *Cave-ne-cadas*—beware of falling from your high position."

The rear chamber door swung open. Senator George Erath wielded a blood-soaked knife. As he led a line of blindfolded and shirtless men toward the temple doors, Shane froze in place. The aspirants were bound by rope with their hands tied behind their backs. Their bare chests were stained in blood. Mack Dodd brought up the rear of the line.

Shane awaited his destiny. Staring at his blindfolded friend, his heart pounded. He'd known Mr. Erath and his wife Lucinda all his life. But that was a life before the spiritual enlightening of Freemasonry.

"Brother McLean, I'm requesting your assistance with today's rite." Erath approached Kirby with a blindfold and aimed his bloody knife at Shane. "Hoodwink the *Lewis's* eyes—before he enters the temple."

CHAPTER 4

A Texas Legend ~ Born on the Fourth of July

Waco Village Square, July 4, 1860:

Shane swore an oath under pain of death never to divulge the Brotherhood's secrets. Enlightened by his symbolic death and rebirth in the temple, he joined his friends and walked toward the shooting contest held along the grassy banks of Brazos. As he passed a group of ragtag militiamen, a squadron of elite Texas Rangers paraded down Main Street. Dressed in pristine uniforms trimmed with golden braids, the Rangers looked like gallant knights from King Arthur's round table.

"After I win today's contest, I'm joining Dalryrmple's Rangers." Mack snapped the collar on his shirt and brandished his Colt revolving rifle. "Gonna run the Black Republicans outta town."

Shane rushed his finger to his lips. "Shhh—you're gonna make trouble."

"Quit dreaming, Dodd. They wouldn't take you." Jerry shook his head. "You're too damn big for a cavalry unit."

A carriage full of Freemasons sped toward the shootout. Grand Master Taylor sat in the plush rear seat. His eyes locked on Kirby. Following the heated argument at the lodge, Shane feared repercussions from the Freemason hierarchy. His father hadn't said a word since leaving the temple. Leading the way in his Masonic apron, Kirby kept his head down and his custom .36 Special secured in his holster. A second carriage decorated in presidential-election banners rolled down the Main Street. Constitutional Union Candidate Sam Houston waved at a crowd of star-struck women.

Mack watched the carriage pass by. "Mister McLean, you gonna challenge the governor to another duel? Bet you could take him."

"What's discussed at a lodge stays in the lodge." Kirby grabbed Mack by the throat. "If you can't be trusted with a little secret, how can you be trusted with important things?"

Mack wobbled and his knees buckled. As he dropped to the ground, a two-hundred-pound woman in a floral-print blouse stopped on the boardwalk. Her chubby son hid behind her hoop skirt. Gunfire blasted from the Brazos. Embarrassed by his overbearing father's antics, Shane looked away. He'd seen enough violence and worried how Mack would react.

"Let him go, Pa." Shane motioned toward the Waco Livery. "Forget about today's shooting match. Let's get the horses and leave while we still can."

"Running from your words makes you look like a liar." Kirby stepped back. "McLeans ain't liars—you're gonna compete today."

Climbing to his feet, Mack rubbed his throat and eyed Shane. "Keep your crazy old father away from me, or I'll hit him."

৩৩৩৩

Waco Shooting Match, Preliminary Round, July 4, 1860:

Civilized Indians and pot-bellied Negros walked the streets alongside their white masters. The well-fed slaves dressed in fancy coats and expensive top hats. Shane struggled to understand his mother's abolitionist views. As far as he could tell, the African slaves appeared happy and well-cared for. War pitting Southern Whites against Northerners seemed like a waste of money and lives.

A hand-painted banner *Welcome to the Heart of Texas Shooting Match* hung between cottonwood trees along the grassy banks of the Brazos. Five hundred rowdy spectators spread out around the roped-off shooter's gallery. As the sweltering afternoon sun bore down, Shane and his friends joined two dozen contestants around the official's table.

Grand Master Taylor and a panel of judges explained the rules. Contestants had two shots to hit a flume-shaped whiskey bottle. A line was drawn in the dirt at fifty paces and a bottle was placed atop a cut log pedestal. Any shooter who shattered a target earned a spot in the finals. While the crowd tightened like a noose around the gallery, Kirby waited with Senator Erath behind the carved mahogany table.

Shane didn't trust shifty-eyed Grand Master Taylor. As contestant after contestant failed, he listened for the Freemason announcer to call his name and his confidence grew. An inborn icy calm took over. He couldn't explain the feeling, but it felt good.

The broad-shouldered announcer stood behind the official's table and examined his list of names. Dressed in a coat and top hat, he glanced at Kirby and motioned to an army captain. The inquisitive officer turned in his chair but said nothing.

"Next shooter," the announcer said with a Northern accent. "Frank Mac…cLe…ean."

Accustomed to his last name being enunciated wrong, Shane raised his musket. "I'm here, sir." He shouldered between two intimidating federal guardsmen. "Coming through."

The packed crowd slowly parted. Shane squeezed his moist leather flask and realized he'd forgotten to borrow fresh gunpowder. Turning to find the Ringo brothers, he bumped into the ornery hunchback from the river. He hoped the grubby little rustler with the grotesquely curved-spine didn't recognize him.

"Watch where you're going, boy!" The hunchback blocked Shane's path to the shooting gallery. "Didn't know they was letting kids enter this contest."

While spectators jeered, Shane turned to apologize but held his tongue. A foot taller than the hunchback, he wasn't about to cower to the combative half-man. A working girl in a low-cut dress waved her chubby arm. Her fleshy bosom jiggled in the afternoon sun. glistened.

"Leave blue eyes alone." The brunette batted her eyes and sighed. "He's just a child—fresh off the farm."

"Are there no men in this village looking for a challenge?" A contestant in a fancy white linen suit wrapped his arms around a pair of attractive female associates and scoffed. "I've travelled a thousand miles to compete with the best sharpshooters in the west and the best Waco can do is put forth kids." The flamboyant sportsman spoke with a Northern accent. "Are we competing for penny candy or cash?"

While laughter shot through the packed crowd, Mack Dodd pushed aside a militiaman and tossed his gunpowder flask to Shane. His enormous size garnered immediate respect.

The hunchback stepped aside.

"You gotta go through me first to fight my friend." Mack waved his sledgehammer-sized fist at the combative little man. "We can row now or after I win this contest. Don't matter to me."

Shane didn't need Mack to fight his battles but appreciated the gesture. A loyal friend, Mack defended animals and loved-ones with brutal force. The hunchback slipped behind the Kansas Federal Guardsmen.

"There's one real man amongst you ready to compete today." The sportsman tipped his stylish Plug hat at Mack.

"Hope to compete against you in this afternoon's championship match."

Removing his crushed palmetto, Shane wiped his sweaty face and headed toward the shooter's line. The flashy sportsman brandished his Maynard target rifle. The Swiss-style gun had an octagonal barrel and expensive Malcolm riflescope mounted on the front and real dovetails. Flanked by blonde and brunette associates, the sportsman had already qualified for the championship round by shattering a whiskey bottle on his first attempt.

"I bet five dollars that kid's old military musket won't fire." The sportsman flashed a handful of cash and addressed the crowd. "Send for the candy confectioner. I'll pay the child in rock candy and gum drops."

"I'll take your bet, mister." Shane didn't have a dime to his name. "And I'll wager another five dollars I'll hit the bottle and make the finals."

The working girl gave a sly smile and shook her bodacious chest. "Oh, honey child!" Her big red lips parted revealing a missing tooth. "If I'd known you had ten dollars, I'd sold you something sweeter than candy."

"Hush your mouth, Miss Wanda. There's children around." Texas Ranger Captain Dalrymple approached the official's table. "Somebody escort her back to the Reservation."

Shane had never been with a woman. Nor did he intend to be until marriage. Miss Wanda was old, fat, and smelled like a sow. Who'd want to be with her?

"Come with me, Wanda." The hunchback spit a mouthful of tobacco and snatched her fleshy wrist. "You're like candy to these sweet people. Get too much, you'll make 'em sick."

"Crippled little thing!" Miss Wanda waved her round fist. "Hush your mouth, or I'll straighten out that crooked back."

The sportsman tugged the lapel of his white linen jacket. "I'll take your bet, kid. If that Brown Bess fires, I'll pay you

five dollars and buy you a big bag of rock candy." He eyed
Shane's old Springfield and scoffed. "Your flint-lock's
busted at the stock."

Covering his cracked musket handle, Shane glanced at
his father and hoped he hadn't overheard. He planned to get
the musket repaired with his contest winnings.

A group of rowdy militia approached the shooter's gallery. Bud brought up the rear and looked like trouble. The
fat rustler had his gunshot hand wrapped in a cloth bandage.

"Make your side bets with someone else, Billy Bob."
Captain Dalrymple approached the flashy sportsman. "He's
just a boy. Leave him alone."

Shane appreciated the captain's concern, but he was
more concerned with his Springfield. If the cracked musket
didn't fire, he'd have to beg his father for the money. As he
toed the shooter's line, the spectators hushed. A dog barked
and a baby cried out. Placing his thumb on the loose flint-
lock, he turned toward the official's table.

Mary Kelly stood in the front row. The red-haired beauty
from Cliff Town wore a racy feathered leghorn-straw hat
and clung to her father's sleeve. Her jeweled fingers
squeezed a new straw palmetto.

"Shoot, Penny Candy Kid!" Billy Bob dabbed his forehead with a handkerchief. "Don't just stand there, shoot."

Shane stood silent and struggled to respond. Mary was
far more stunning than he'd remembered. His knees wobbled and heart pounded. Mesmerized by her perfect ruby
lips, he gazed into her bright green-eyes and knew she was
the one.

While the crowd grew restless, Mary smiled and pointed
to the shooter's line. Taking a deep breath, Shane wheeled
around and took aim at the target. The whiskey bottle
danced in his crosshairs. He squeezed the trigger and flames
flashed from the pan. Engulfed in a cloud of gunsmoke, his
ears rang. He'd won half his bet with Billy Bob Barron.

Backing away from the log pedestal, the target judge
shouted. "Miss!"

A heart-rending awe resonated through the crowd. Shane fanned the smoky air and spotted the whiskey bottle. Lowering his musket, he eyed his disappointed father and his stomach tightened in a knot.

"At least it fired." Billy Bob spoke in a demeaning tone. "Got one shot left, penny candy kid. Better make it count."

"Frank!" Kirby slipped under the gallery rope. "Bring my musket."

Angry glances spread like plague through the crowd. Shane feared his father would take his last shot and worried what others would say. He'd be humiliated in front of everyone. As he obediently approached his father, contestants looked on in disgust.

"I can see from here the flintlock's loose." Kirby grabbed his musket and examined the front sight. "Wasn't broke this morning. Did you drop it?"

"No, sir." Shane lied. "It's been on my saddle pommel all day. You must've dropped it or maybe Ma broke it. She used it when the Ringo brothers stopped by yesterday."

"Sir, my side bet's only with the kid." Billy Bob politely tipped his Plug hat. "But if you'd like to arrange something after the contest—"

"I'm not here to compete," Kirby growled, cutting off the flashy sportsman. "You must be the showman Houston hired in Baltimore last month. A professional shootist shouldn't need to hustle a sixteen-year-old."

"I'll bet you or any of these fine people gathered here today." Billy Bob paused and pandered to the crowd. "Don't matter to me where the money comes from."

"Let me challenge him, Pa." Shane snatched the barrel of his musket. "If I hit the bottle and make the finals, he said he'd pay me five dollars and buy me some candy."

"Nothing in this world's free. If you miss, you'll owe him." Kirby yanked the musket away. "He's gonna keep upping the ante until you lose." He reached behind his Masonic apron and pulled out his ivory-handled .36 Colt Special. "Use my *work* gun. It's an inch longer than a standard six-shooter. Nine-inch barrel's rifled with spiraled grooves to spin the bullet." He skillfully spun the revolver in his hand. "Shoots straighter than the musket."

Shane feared he'd drop the expensive revolver. Eying the Masonic square and compass engraved in the handle, he took hold of his father's gun. The plow-shaped handle fit snugly in his hand. His icy calm returned.

"Looks like it belongs in a museum." Shane struggled to hold the three-pound custom order Colt revolver. "It's nearly the length of my arm."

"Longer the barrel straighter the shot." Kirby warned. "Don't break it. It's one of a kind."

Shane cocked his revolver and dug his toes in behind the shooter's line. Resting the barrel over his left forearm, he focused on winning and slowly squeezed the trigger. The steel-hammer struck a percussion cap and ignited a paper cartridge in the chamber. While smoke and flames exploded from the muzzle, the conical-shaped bullet spun toward the target.

The whiskey bottle shattered. Glass rained down on the log pedestal. As applause erupted from the frenzied crowd, Mack and the Ringo brothers rushed under the ropes. Yearning for his father approval, Shane struggled to contain his emotions. He scanned the crowd and noticed Kirby shaking hands with Senator Erath. His heart warmed with pride.

Mack Dodd wrapped his burley arms around Shane's waist. As he lifted him into the air, the Ringo brothers showered him with praise. Swarmed by his friends, he accepted their congratulations but still wanted his father's approval.

Kirby tipped his hat. "Good job, son. I'm proud of you."

Shane felt ten feet tall and bulletproof. The simple words meant the world to him. His demanding father had finally taken notice.

e/ɔe/ɔ

Final Round, Heart of Texas Shooting Match, July 4, 1860:

Only five of the twenty-five contestants advanced to the championship round. Shane was joined by Jerry Ringo, two intimidating Texas Rangers, and the flamboyant sportsman Billy Bob Barron. Mack missed the whiskey bottle on both attempts and Jimmy Ringo's shots sailed high and left. While they wallowed in their self-pity, the remaining competitors gathered around the official's table. A dozen armed militiamen bullied their way past a fiery young reverend and his flock of Negros and abolitionist Whites.

Shane dreamed of winning the hundred-dollar cash prize and accompanying Bowie knife. Worth a year of soldier's pay, the fancy eighteen-inch knife weighed nearly five pounds and included a carved-leather scabbard.

Presidential Candidate Sam Houston served as an honorary official. Wearing an audacious jaguar-skin vest, the sixty-eight-year-old governor anointed Grand Master Taylor and Worshipful Master Gurley target judges. Sensing a rigged competition, Shane waited with Jerry and listened to Houston dictate the contest rules.

Each finalist had one shot to hit the bulls-eye. The Mexican peso-sized center mark was surrounded by five concentric circles drawn on parchment. Placed at fifty yards, the paper target was nailed to the face of a cottonwood log, stacked on a six-foot pyramid of timber.

Scanning the crowd, Shane gripped his father's ivory-handled Colt Special and spotted Mary Kelly's feathered hat. Her pinned-up red hair and pale white skin sparkled in the sun. A giant of a man at six foot six, Governor Houston leaned his walking stick against the official's table. As he removed his black bowler and tossed five numbered tags inside, the contestants gathered around.

"The kid picks first." Houston shook his hat and locked eyes with Shane. "Pick a good one."

Kirby and Senator Erath looked on with a group of Freemasons. Bud gave an evil smile. Lingering behind the ropes, he gestured slitting Shane's throat with his bandaged hand. Shane reached into Houston's hat. He pulled out a tag and read the number five. The coveted fifth shooter could observe the other contestants and know exactly the shot needed to win. Jerry Ringo drew third shooter and Billy Bob fourth.

A long-haired ranger lieutenant started the competition. Using a Mississippi rife, he placed the stock against his shoulder and lifted his slouch hat. The lieutenant aimed at the black center mark and fired. While gun smoke blasted from the muzzle, the target judge rushed toward the timber pyramid.

"Hit!" Grand Master Taylor pointed toward the middle of the parchment target. "Inside the first ring. Shooter's an inch from the center mark."

As spectators erupted into applause, the lieutenant swaggered toward the official's table. Flush with Billy Bob's cash, Shane munched on a mouthful of rock candy and cussed his chances. He'd have to clip the center mark to win. No one could expect to accomplish that at fifty paces.

"It'll take a perfect shot to win." Sam Houston eyed the remaining contest. "Looks like the rest of you men are vying for second place."

A scar-faced ranger sergeant headed toward the shooter's line. Carrying his Hall rifle, he licked his finger and checked the wind. As he paced behind a line in the dirt, Shane noticed a flaw in the sergeant's technique and waved over his father.

"He's too anxious," Shane whispered to his father. "Sergeant's hand is shaking. He won't do well."

"We'll see about that." Kirby nodded. "He's a friend of mine and a shooting instructor for Dalryrmple's Rangers."

A blast of gunfire echoed through the gallery. As spectators rushed forward, Shane stood alongside his father and listened for the judge's decision. Mary Kelly and her father approached the gallery ropes. A soldier with a thick mustache held her gloved hand.

"Hit!" Grand Master Taylor stepped away from the log pyramid. "Third ring. Mighty fine shot."

Shane cussed his luck. As the crowd cheered, the disappointed sergeant snatched the barrel of his Hall and stormed toward the gallery. Jerry Ringo headed toward the shooter's line. As he glanced toward a mass of excited spectators, an ear-piercing shrill rang out. Mack Dodd whistled louder than any man alive. Jerry lowered his head and grinned. Talented with a gun, he'd won all the practice shooting games on the Shamrock Ranch, unless Kirby participated. Shane had closed the competitive gap, but he'd never beaten Jerry when it mattered. He wished his friend well but not too well. He'd come to win.

"Relax and aim high. There's a light headwind." Kirby shouted a last minute tip. "Concentrated rage."

Jimmy Ringo eyed his big brother and grasped his hands in prayer. As he looked toward Heaven, Jerry leveled his Mississippi Rifle on the target. Crouching in a shooter's stance, he raised the muzzle and fired. Spectators swarmed the ropes. As men fought for a closer look at the target, Shane got punched in the ribs. His bag of rock candy spilled on the ground. The hunchback stepped back and cackled with delight.

"Hit! First ring." Grand Master Taylor held his thumb and forefinger an inch apart. "Hell of shot young man. Second place by that much."

Shane grabbed his injured side and buckled in pain. His pride had been called into question. With Mack Dodd around to back him up, he required more than an apology and squared his shoulders to fight. Nobody was going to insult him.

"Bring it on, boy!" The hunchback pulled a knife and gestured to fight. "I'll cut you to pieces and mail you to your ma."

"Let it be, Frank! You'll wind up in jail." Kirby picked up the spilled candy. "Charlie's a loner with nothing to lose. Focus on the competition." He steered Shane toward the official's table. "They don't want you to compete today."

Shane couldn't let it go. A wave of aggression shot through his veins. He blamed his fierce temper on his mother's Viking ancestry.

"You wouldn't let a half-man punch you and get away with it." Shane squeezed his injured ribs and glared at the hunchback. "He hurt me, Pa."

"If you can still breathe, you ain't hurt." Kirby headed to the opposite end of the official's table. "Watch the competition from over here. There's always someone tougher than you." He motioned toward the Kansas Federal Troopers. "Those Jayhawkers are bounty hunters, they're also the hunchback's friends."

Shane seethed like an unrepentant sinner. While he glared at the soldier's red leg gaiters, Kirby approached Senator Erath and a group of Freemasons. Jerry weaved through throngs of adoring spectators. His cheeks bubbled with joy. Second place with two shooters remaining was nothing to hang your head about.

Kissing his blonde associate, Billy Bob stepped forward and brandished his Maynard target rifle. "That's pretty good, boy. But let me show you how it's done."

Shane wished the flamboyant sportsman would fail. As he sank his teeth into a piece of rock candy, Billy Bob removed his fancy linen jacket and kissed his brunette associate on the cheek.

A group of unescorted females swooned. Holding his heart, he sighed at his admirers and worked the crowd like an unscrupulous politician. Sam Houston shook hands with the Kansas Troopers.

"Enjoying your bag of goodies, penny candy kid?" Billy Bob stopped in front of Shane. "Hope you give me a chance to win back my money. I'll wager twenty-five dollars that my mark is inside of yours." He tipped his stylish Plug hat and flashed a handful of cash. "Another fifty if either of us hits the bull's eye."

"Quit trying to hustle my son." Kirby stepped forward.

"Put your money away. He can't compete with a professional shootist."

"Just wanted to keep things interesting." Billy Bob shrugged and humbly raised his hands. "These fine people came here to be entertained. Just giving 'em a show."

Shane intended to separate Billy Bob Barron from his money. He wished his old-fashioned father would stay out of his affairs. The flamboyant sportsman was either filthy rich or really good.

As he swaggered through the crowd, an unescorted, middle-age woman, dressed in a sky blue silk taffeta gown, blushed and fanned her cheeks. Billy Bob paused and lifted her gloved hand to his mouth.

"Get a move on, Barron. Horse races are gonna start." Sam Houston pointed toward the village square. "I've got a speech to give this afternoon."

"For luck, Widow Brown." Billy Bob kissed her fingers. "Until we meet again."

Shane watched the showman work the crowd. Billy Bob had no shame. As he headed toward the shooter's line, the energized crowd hushed. Dropping to one knee, he placed his Swiss-style butt plate against his shoulder and peered through the Malcolm riflescope. His finger reached for the trigger. A baby wailed somewhere in the crowd.

"Let's give these people a show, Barron!" Kirby lifted a handful of cash and shouted. "We'll accept your fifty dollar bet...and raise it another fifty." His deep voice startled the crowd. "Can you spend Texas Treasury Notes back in Baltimore?"

"It'll spend." Billy Bob lowered his muzzle and appeared agitated. "Refresh my memory, old man." He climbed to his feet. "What did we agree to?"

"I'm betting a hundred dollars my son beats your shot." Kirby scoffed. "Surely a professional shootist like yourself can beat my son."

Shane feared the origin of his father's sudden wealth. One hundred dollars was a lot of cash. He prayed Kirby didn't borrow the money and hoped the sportsman would decline the offer.

"I'll take your bet. I'm the best there's ever been." Billy Bob threw back his shoulders and propositioned the crowd. "I'm prepared to offer a hundred and fifty dollars to any man who can outshoot me."

While spectators scanned the crowd for a challenge, Shane eyed the sportsman's stylish slim-brim hat. He wanted to impress Mary Kelly. The mob of militiamen pushed a reluctant soldier forward.

"Hundred and fifty dollars." Shane intended to strike fear in the flamboyant sportsman. "Throw in that Plug hat and it's a deal."

"Damn, kid—you're as dense as the day is long." Billy Bob snapped his head around and mumbled. "I'm trying to give you a chance."

"Wealth gotten by vanity shall be diminished." The fiery young reverend led his flock through the crowd. "Heed the Lord's word. No man can serve two masters."

Concerned for his father, Shane worried he'd run his mouth too much. He feared facing a heartless shylock who might be sent to collect his debt. The stress of the situation weighed on his mind. Billy Bob dropped to a knee and adjusted the front sight on his carbine rifle. As he peered down the thirty-two inch scope, Shane wished for a misfire or big gust of wind. A small cloud of gun smoke shot from the sleek target rifle.

"Hit!" Grand Master Taylor stepped away from the parchment target. "We've got a new top shot. Mister Barron clipped the edge of the center mark."

Shane felt the joy leave his body. While spectators erupted into applause, he figured the fix had to be in. Billy Bob leapt to his feet. Thrusting his rifle toward the sky, he swaggered toward the official's table like a game rooster.

"Relax and aim high. There's a light headwind." Governor Houston licked his finger and raised it into the breeze. "Concentrated rage."

Shane thought Houston's advice odd. His father had given Jerry the same tip. As he headed toward the shooter's line, Bud leaned over the ropes and again slashed his bandaged hand across his throat. Shane felt doomed and feared the rustler's intentions.

"Governor Houston's a fraud and hypocrite." The fiery young reverend stood surrounded by his flock. "He claimed to hold Unionist values at the Baltimore Convention but owns slaves here in Texas." He struck a phosphorus match on his thigh and held up the flame. "If Houston's elected president, the Lord will strike down upon thee with great vengeance and furious anger."

"Go back to Yankee Land!" A militiaman scolded. "We don't need no Northern preachers inciting revolt in our slaves. Negros in these parts are happy—singing and dancing a jig."

"Fire eaters like you will soon be purged from this earth." The reverend blew out his flame. "Mark my words, within the week, terror will spread like plague. Towns across Texas will burn to ashes."

A farmer with a noose motioned to a group of militiamen. "Shut your mouth, preacher man. Let's run these abolitionists outta town." His voice deepened. "Hang their Negros....before they rape our wives and daughters."

While the inflamed mob chased the terrified reverend and his flock, Shane toed the shooter's line. Leveling his custom .36 revolver, he focused on the bull's eye. Billy Bob's shot had indeed clipped the center mark. Three additional bullet holes peppered the target. The Freemason target judges upheld the Brotherhood's core values of honor and integrity.

Calm settled through the gallery. Taking a deep breath, Shane stared down the nine-inch barrel and locked in his front sight onto the bull's eye. A gunshot rang out. Startled by the blast, he nearly jumped out of his skin. His heart skipped a beat. Billy Bob stood in a cloud of gun smoke and fiddled with a Colt pocket revolver. As he slipped the tiny belly gun inside his jacket pocket, Shane cussed the under-handed tactic and tried to calm his nerves.

"Damn revolver!" Billy Bob shrugged smugly. "It's got a mind of its own."

"Mister Barron, that's a dirty trick." Senator Erath stepped from behind the official's table. "You must be worried about losing to a kid."

While the men argued, Shane closed his eyes and turned toward the target. An icy calm returned. Mental pictures of his bullet hitting the center mark filled his mind. Relying on instinct, he opened his eyes and squeezed the trigger. The shot felt straight.

Flanked by his female associates, Billy Bob folded his arms and waited on the target judge's decision. His eyes wandered from the official's table to the log pyramid. Shane felt confident he'd hit the parchment. But he was unsure if he'd struck the bull's eye. As the burnt smell of gunpowder filled the air, Mack Dodd whistled his approval.

"Miss!" Grand Master Taylor stepped from the target and shook his head. "No mark. Kid missed everything."

Shane felt like his soul had been ripped from his body. Humiliated by his performance, he waited for the smoke to clear and focused on the center mark. The same four bullet holes peppered the target.

He hung his head in shame. As he thought about how he'd repay his debt, Sam Houston grabbed his walking stick and limped toward the shooter's line. A ruckus broke out around the official's table.

While the governor approached, Shane turned away. He didn't want to be consoled. The mustached soldier led Mary Kelly away, clinging to his arm. Shane felt bitter as if he'd lost a part of himself. Senator Erath made a beeline for the target judge.

"Keep your chin up, son. You made the final round." Houston used his cane to tap Shane's shoulder. "Twenty other contestants would've traded places with you."

"Mister Taylor." Senator Erath rushed toward the log

pyramid. "I don't believe Kirby McLean's boy could miss that entire target. I'd like to inspect it."

"Come take a closer look, George. We've got nothing to hide," Taylor scoffed. "There're only four holes in the target. Our shooter clearly beat both of your Rangers and Kirby McLean's boy."

"Join me, Governor." Erath headed toward the parchment. "Let's see for ourselves."

Feeling lower than a ditch digger's shoes, Shane didn't need a closer look. He could see the same four bullet holes in the target. While Houston and a dozen curious spectators followed Senator Erath, Kirby approached with his arms folded. Frustrated by the poor performance, Shane didn't want his father to harp on his shortcomings. His eyes watered.

"Quit your damn crying. You wanna compete with men, act like one." Kirby shook his head and pointed toward the target. "Go see where your bullet hit, so we can fix what you did wrong."

"I ain't crying. I'm mad." Shane returned his father's gun. "Why'd you bet so much? We can't afford to lose all that money."

"Thought you'd win." Kirby's eyes narrowed. "Go find your bullet. It had to stop somewhere."

Shane didn't want to be around his demanding father. As he rushed to the target, a dozen men surrounded the stack of timber. A crack ran the length of the log pedestal. Grand Master Taylor peeled off the target and held the parchment to the sun. Two holes cut through the bull's eye. One hit dead center.

"Well I'll be damned." Senator Erath pushed his finger through the black mark. "Kid hit dead center."

Five bullet holes cut into the face of the log. Houston nudged the top log with his walking stick. As it rolled off the pyramid, the cottonwood pedestal struck the ground and split apart. A .36 caliber bullet lodged in the core.

"Hell's bells, Mister Taylor. Only one contestant used a

pistol." Houston peeled out Shane's bullet. "Unless you put this inside that log before the contest, the kid hit dead center." His voice deepened. "How could you make a mistake like that?"

"Mister Taylor didn't want his professional shooter to lose," Senator Erath admonished the Grand Master. "Better inform the announcer there's a new winner."

"It's an honest mistake." Taylor pushed through the spectators and called out to the broad-shouldered announcer. "Brother Spivey! Frank McLean's our champion. It was a perfect shot."

CHAPTER 5

Yellow Rose of Texas

Fireworks blasted along the Brazos River. While spectators cheered, Shane jumped with joy and looked to celebrate with his father and friends. Mack and the Ringo brothers climbed inside the roped-off gallery. Billy Bob cussed and smashed his Maynard target rife against a log. The thirty-two-inch scope broke free of the rear sight and struck his cheek. Storming off toward the river, he shouted expletives like a madman, throwing his rifle into the Brazos.

"That was a hell of a pistol shot." The ranger lieutenant pushed his hair beneath his slouch hat and approached to shake Shane's hand. "Have you thought about joining Dalrymple's Rangers?"

"Yessir!" Shane knew his father wouldn't approve but didn't care. "My friend Jerry Ringo wants to join, too."

"We've got positions open for both of you." The lieutenant pointed toward the official's table. "Let's meet after the award ceremony. Better collect your prize money and that fancy Bowie knife before Governor Houston walks off with it. He's offered to purchase the knife for a hundred dollars."

The crowd around the mahogany table swelled to several hundred. Shane struggled to keep his composure. His heart raced and his face beamed with pride. Walking alongside

Houston, he finally gave his father a reason to be proud of him. He'd won the hundred dollar cash award and Bowie knife. But the hundred and fifty dollar side bet with Billy Bob felt sweeter. Scanning the crowd for his friends, he yearned for someone special to spend it with. The hunchback and Bud leaned over the ropes, making gestures of cutting their throats.

"That's the best pistol shooting I've ever seen." Sam Houston handed Shane the leather scabbard containing the Bowie. "Could've used a crack shot like you during the Texas Revolution. What's your name?"

A shade over six-feet tall, Shane stared the giant of a man in the eyes and proudly proclaimed. "Frank McLean, sir. I'm from Crawford in McLennan County."

"State of Texas needs champions like Frank McLean to keep our nation together." Houston grabbed Shane's wrist and raised his arm in solidarity. "I'll need everybody's support in this fall's presidential election." He tugged on his jaguar-skinned vest and proclaimed. "Union as it is, Constitution as it is."

"Go back to Austin, Yankee lover!" a soldier shouted. "You Know Nothing Whig!"

The governor appeared to have worn out his welcome. While the pro-secession crowd jeered, Shane wanted to collect his prize money and leave. He feared mob rule. His father and Senator Erath approached with Billy Bob.

"Hold out your hand, Frank." Houston licked his finger and counted out the $100 cash prize in three-dollar bills. "Three, six, nine, twelve dollars—smile big for the voters."

While the money piled up in his hand, Shane grinned from ear to ear. The mass of humanity closed in. Fearing he'd be robbed, he squeezed his cash as his eyes searched for a familiar face. Senator Erath extended his arms and tried to hold back the rowdy crowd.

"Seventy-five, seventy-eight, eighty-one, eighty-four dollars." Houston eyed Kirby and paused. "Sir, you look familiar. Did you serve in the War of Independence?"

"Yessir, General. We fought together at San Jacinto." Kirby flashed his Masonic ring and his wrinkled cheeks tightened. "We also dueled six months later at Washington-on-the-Brazos."

"Kirby McLean." Houston's voice trembled. "Thought you were dead."

A female voice rang out. "Go home, Governor Houston! Take that dreadful leopard-skinned vest with you."

"Ma'am, this ain't leopard-skin—it's jaguar." Houston wheeled around. "Leopard's change their spots. I've always been pro-Union."

A group of army officers and Freemasons pushed through the crowd. The governor handed Shane the remainder of his cash. As Shane stuffed his money into a side seam pocket, a woman screamed. Two men threw punches in the street. While federal troopers whisked Houston away, Shane pulled out his Bowie. Cut off from his father, he covered his side pocket of money and glanced into the crowd.

A bearded man in a Masonic apron approached with a pair of Texas Ranger officers. Spectators tumbled to the ground. The Mason grabbed Shane's arm.

"I'm Counselor Speight. Better come with us for your own safety." The attorney steered him behind the ranger officers. "Captain Harrison, tell your brother to take us to a saloon, so we can discuss business."

Shane yearned to join the Texas Rangers and taste his first drink of whiskey. While he looked to escape the madness, the Harrison brothers rammed their way through the mob. A fat man with a lapel covered in ferrotype campaign buttons tumbled to the ground. Shane squeezed his pocket full of cash. Stepping over the portly politician, he ducked under an outstretched arm and caught his boot on the man's election pin-covered lapel. His knee buckled and struck the ground. Trapped inside a mass of bodies, his sense of direction blurred.

A strange hand tugged at his pockets. Daylight appeared ten feet away. Peeling the strange fingers off his pocket,

Shane pushed forward and broke free. As he stepped from the rear of the crowd, Kirby yanked him by the neck and his head snapped sideways. His collar tightened around his throat like a hangman's noose.

"My son fights for no one." Kirby's voice deepened. "He's off limits, JW. Respect my wishes."

"Freedom takes blood and sacrifice, McLean." Counselor Speight shrugged. "You and your son will be called upon to defend Southern sovereignty. *Deo Vindice*—do your duty to God, our vindicator."

"That time ain't now. My son's not joining your militia." Kirby pushed Shane toward town and protected his backside. "He's attending Waco University to study law."

Shane shrugged. He didn't want a career in law. He wanted adventure and planned to join the rangers. Attending college while the rest of the country fought a war was cowardly. As he turned to protest, the portly politician with a lapel of iron-plate ferrotype buttons limped toward Kirby.

"Sir, I'm Counselor Coke. Studying law is admirable, but right now we need men like your son to protect the Southern way of life." Coke attempted to pin Sam Houston's election button on Kirby's lapel. "The governor will appreciate your vote for president."

"Your cause ain't my cause." Kirby slapped the ferrotype button away. "Houston couldn't even win his own party's support last month in Baltimore."

"Leave him alone, Richard." Senator Erath returned Coke's pin. "McLean has a different agenda. Let's go have a smoke at the Square."

While his father and Senator Erath headed toward town, Shane looked to celebrate with his friends. He glanced over his shoulder and spotted Bud and Charlie. The rustlers turned into an alleyway. Kirby stopped in front of a bakery.

"Gotta pick your fights. I can't keep protecting you." Erath pulled an eight-inch cigar from his pocket. "You've offended Grand Master Taylor, militia officers, attorneys, and now the Big Drunk knows you're alive." He extended a cigar and box of matches. "Houston's gonna have Senator Lane send a death squad to hunt you down. We don't need Kansas-style violence in Texas."

"If Houston convinces Lane to send his Jayhawkers after me, I'll deal with it." Kirby placed a cigar to his lips. "I've known the Grim Chiefton since Monterrey. He's looking for favor in Washington, not Austin."

Shane feared they'd show up at the Shamrock Ranch. "Is a death squad from Fort Leavenworth gonna kill our family?"

"If Lane's paid enough, he'll send his men anywhere." Kirby struck a match on his trousers. "He's already sent Jayhawkers to Washington to protect Lincoln."

Erath spit in the street. "I've seen a couple here in town with Houston."

Shane eyed the Senator's fancy cigar. "Sir, may I have a smoke?"

"That's up to your father." Erath pulled a bundle of cigars from his chest pocket. "Tobacco is good for you. Opens the lungs and calms the nerves."

"You're sixteen. Do what you want." Kirby exhaled a thick cloud of fragrant smoke. "Don't tell your mother."

A wide-eyed baker stared out his window. Wiping his hands on his flour-stained apron, he spotted Kirby and rushed outside. Three soldiers approached along the boardwalk.

Shane accepted a cigar from Senator Erath and placed the uncut end in his mouth. Striking a matchstick against his thigh, he attempted to light the tobacco. The flame burned out. While he struggled to light another match, Kirby greeted the baker with a secret handshake.

Shane wanted to learn more about his father. "Why'd Pa get in a duel with Sam Houston?"

"Houston broke his sacred oath—every Freemason knows that." Erath cupped his hands around Shane's cigar. "Take deep breaths until the tip burns cherry red." His eyes glanced toward Kirby. "Santa Anna is a rogue Mason. Pope in Rome sent orders to Houston to cut out Little Napoleon's tongue."

"Thought Santa Anna's Catholic?" Shane yanked his unlit cigar from his mouth. "They can't be Masons."

"Bite off the tip before you try to light it." Erath pointed to the end of the leafy cigar and eyed Kirby. "You haven't told Frank anything?"

"Less he's illuminated, the more likely the Order will leave him alone." Kirby whispered to the senator. "Forty years of loyal service to the Jesuits has left me burdened with enemies. Don't want that life for him."

Kirby performed the secret society's righteous work. Indoctrinated by radical rationalism, he enforced the inner cabal's strict vow of silence. Since the age of twelve, he'd been trained to kill and pledged allegiance to a New World Order.

Shane bit the soggy tip off. "If Pa dueled with Sam Houston outside Cole's store, how come they're both alive?"

"Your father's a merciful man." Erath stepped onto the porch of the bakery. "Houston knew he'd face the shame of a Masonic trial for his failure to execute Santa Anna. He had a death wish and demanded they settle their differences on the lawn outside the store."

While the soldiers approached, Shane lit his cigar and inhaled until the tobacco came to life. A thick flume of smoke filled his lungs. His throat burned and his eyes watered. Attempting to hide his inexperience, he turned his head and coughed. The burning red tip of his cigar brushed against his cheek. Pain shot through his face. As he rubbed the hot ashes, a bow legged soldier with mutton chops stopped to laugh.

"You'd better learn how to smoke. Puff a cigar, never inhale." Erath shook his head. "There were a dozen officers at the pistol duel. Half had family or friends murdered by Santa Anna. They wanted blood. They blamed Houston's Runaway Scrape for their ravished property and missing livestock."

The soldiers moved on without incident. Shane puffed away on his cigar but didn't inhale. A woman passed through a cloud of aromatic smoke. Her face tightened. As she held her breath and waved her hand in front of her nose, Shane glanced at his father. Kirby shook hands with the baker and bid goodbye.

"As I remember the duel, Houston shot first. Struck your father through his side at twenty-paces." Erath nodded at Kirby. "Bullet passed straight through. Helps to be blessed with the luck of the Irish."

Shane felt warm and started to sweat. His head was light and stomach queasy.

The boardwalk appeared to sway. He took a long puff on his cigar to calm his nerves. Attempting to hide his bout with nausea, he nodded at the senator and pretended to listen.

"Kirby is the best shot I've ever seen with a gun. When Houston realized he'd only injured him, the general dropped to his knees and hailed the Masonic High Sign of Distress."

Shane recalled seeing half-a-dozen scars on his father's back and torso. Kirby claimed he'd been hurt at work or fallen from his horse. At the time, he didn't question their origin. The scars and stories sounded authentic.

"You look pale, Frank." Erath exhaled a cloud of smoke in Shane's direction. "Better save the rest of that tobacco for later. It'll make you sick if you ain't used to it."

Shane felt dizzy and put down his cigar. His breathing quickened. Vomit rose in his throat. The senator cocked his head with concern.

"I'm fine, sir." Shane fought the urge to puke and looked to his father. "You missed a free shot on Sam Houston?"

"I've never killed anyone who wouldn't have killed me." Kirby flashed his fraternal ring. "I didn't have permission."

"It was a duel." Shane turned to reason with the senator. "Who needs permission? I'd have shot him. Wouldn't you?"

"If Houston challenged me, he'd be a dead man." Erath

nodded. "His secretary Albert Sidney Johnston begged your father not to kill a Freemason Brother. Kirby relented, but Houston had been shamed." His tone sharpened. "Twenty-five years later, neither of them can let him be."

"Houston's ankle was injured from the Battle of San Jacinto. He had no business in a duel." Kirby dumped his cigar ashes in the street. "At that time, it was the right thing to do."

Lucinda Erath approached her husband with a welcoming smile. "There you are, George. You were supposed to meet us for lunch thirty minutes ago." Her eyes locked on Kirby. "Bring Margaret and Frank and join us for dinner. There's plenty of food at the restaurant."

"Thanks for the invite. But Margaret's at home taking care of the neighbor's baby." Kirby pointed to the bakery. "Owner's a dear friend of mine and he's offered us a free lunch."

Gunshots rang out along the Brazos. While Waconians celebrated the Fourth of July, Shane survived his bout with nicotine poisoning and took a seat in the bakery alongside his father. They sampled a smorgasbord of sweet meats and mouth-watering desserts. Plates filled with generous portions offered a delicious slice of heaven. Sausage, brisket, strudels and pies covered the table.

"With this prize money, I can attend Waco University and become a lawyer like Counselor Speight." Shane gauged his father's reaction. "But I'd like to save my money and put off school for a year, maybe join the Dalryrmple Rangers?"

"You'd break your mother's heart." Kirby put down his fork and leaned across the table. "Don't follow my path in life. An education will take you further than a gun. It'll open your mind to reason and logic. You'll gain control over weak-minded men." He pulled Shane close and kissed his forehead. "Don't disappoint your mother."

The uncharacteristic display of affection and kiss felt awkward. Thanks to Margaret's efforts, Shane could read, write, and perform arithmetic. He didn't want to disappoint her. Raised with dignity and discipline, though, he knew his parents cared deeply, even if Kirby didn't always demonstrate it.

"'A pen is mightier than a sword.'" Shane eyed his father's custom .36 revolver. "Unless a fight breaks out—then I'd rather be holding your Colt."

"Guns control a few men. Knowledge and fear of God control the masses." Kirby pushed aside a plate of apple pie. "Those African slaves laboring in cotton fields are forbidden to read and write. Poor souls have been taught God created 'em to work for Whites."

Dancing dogs, juggling clowns, and circus tightrope walkers paraded around the village square. A group of drunken college kids distributed political leaflets. The well-dressed students shouted support for Sam Houston. Shane scanned the rowdy crowd for Mack Dodd and the Ringo brothers. Hoping his friends were still sober, he cut into a slice of apple strudel and savored the sweet taste.

"Horse races must've ended." Shane looked to change the subject. "Hey, Pa, if you were an orphan, how'd you get so wise?"

"I was educated by Bavarian Jesuits and taught logic by a professor of cannon law. Knowledge isn't just in formal school." Kirby stared out the window. "French mercenaries loyal to Robespierre taught weaponry and hand-to-hand combat."

Shane rolled his eyes. The story sounded farfetched. A ruckus broke out in the crowded street. Fists flew and men rushed to join in. Bodies piled up. Political leaflets scattered through the air. A tall Texas Ranger with a pristine blue uniform dragged a bloodstained student from the heap of humanity.

An elderly man in an Odd Fellow fez hobbled to the bakery window. "Damn kids, disturbing the peace."

Kirby stared into the street. "Are your friends out there?"

Shane glanced outside and pretended to look. "Don't see

'em. They're probably still at the horse races."

Mack Dodd peeled himself off the pile and climbed to his feet. A head taller than any man in the crowd, he dusted his shirt and swigged from a bottle of whiskey. The graceful ranger heroically wrestled two more battered students from the fracas. Their bludgeoned faces and disheveled hair looked like they'd been through hell. Angry bloodstained students shouted obscenities at Mack.

"Save the Union!" A young man in a fancy black suit and vest suit stepped into the bakery. "Abolish slavery. It's against God's will." He approached with a stack of political pamphlets. "A vote for Sam Houston is a vote to end slavery."

"No, it won't. Houston owns a dozen Negros." Kirby dismissed the businessman with a wave of his hand. "Learn about his politics before you go spouting off at the mouth."

"Sir, I respectfully disagree." The clean-shaven businessman placed a pamphlet on the table. "You need to read this." His eyes dropped to Kirby's allegory-covered apron. "My uncle's a Mason. What's that Owl of Minerva mean?"

Kirby crumpled the pamphlet into a ball. "It means peace and quiet. Scram."

"Sir, can the governor count on your vote this fall?" The businessman un-crumpled his pamphlet. "Texas will be a separate nation again."

"I don't support Know Nothing Whigs. Houston was rejected at the Baltimore Convention for lacking the very convictions you claim he holds." Kirby tore the pamphlet in half. "If he had a lick of sense, he'd put a Northerner like Stephen Douglas on his ticket. They'd win the national election in a landslide."

"You're ignorant, old man." The young businessman stepped back and shook his head. "Houston's never been a Know Nothing or a Whig. He'll abolish slavery without a war with the North."

"Learn your history, boy!" Kirby's thick-Irish brogue cleared. "Someone's been lying to you."

Traffic on Main Street slowed to a crawl. While the Texas Ranger led three bleeding students toward the porch,
Mack pounded his chest like a mindless baboon. Looking to
leave, Shane spotted Bud and Charlie through the bakery
window. The rustlers paused and pretended to scan the
crowded street.

"I need a towel and a basin of water." The ranger dashed
through the doorway. "Three college kids are bleeding.
Some bear-sized man beat 'em all up."

"You ain't fooling anyone." The businessman pointed to
the embroidered Owl of Minerva on Kirby's apron. "I've
studied the Ancient Athenians and recognize the badge of
the Illuminati."

"You don't know what you're talking about. There's no
such thing as an Illuminati." Kirby rammed his eight-inch
knife into the table. "It's been outlawed for fifty years in
Bavaria."

"They've established their New World Order here in
America." An elderly man wearing an Odd Fellows Fez
stood from his table. "Illuminated men wrote the Declara-
tion of Independence and the Bill of Rights to keep this
country free of the oppressive Old European World Order.
Ben Franklin, Paul Revere, Thomas Jefferson, and John
Hancock were part of a secret within a secret—the Illuminati." He limped toward the businessman. "They believe God
created all men equal. Monarchies and religion divides people. This country was founded on Illuminati principles."

"Taxation without representation, separation of church
and state, and freedom of religion are Christian principles."
The ranger pointed his finger in the gimpy Odd Fellow's
face. "I'll fight you or any Black Republican Yankee who
wants to take my guns and liberty."

"Odd Fellows don't want your guns. We're a social society." The elderly man shrugged. "America is the world's
beacon for liberty. We work with the Masons to keep out
the wealthy European investors conspiring to bring Old

World Order, state-controlled religion, and censorship to our country."

"Sam Houston's a member of your secret society." The businessman waved the torn pamphlet in Kirby's face. "Why don't you give him your vote this fall?"

"There's no inner cabal, no secret within a secret, and no Illuminati." Kirby paused to catch his breath and grasp his heart. "That's all nonsense."

"Let's go, Pa. You're white as a ghost." Shane peeled his father's knife out of the table. "We've got to get you to the doctor."

The elderly man tipped his fez. "Hope you feel better, sir."

Grabbing his father's arm, Shane pushed the businessman aside and headed toward the porch. The square overflowed with festive townspeople.

"Damn, fire eater, slavery is evil," the young businessman shouted through the doorway. "Better give Houston your vote or God will punish you."

Shane didn't dignify the words with a response. Kirby grabbed his irritable heart and broke out in a cold sweat. Helping his father along the boardwalk, Shane shouldered through the crowd and locked eyes with Bud. The fat rustler stood with Freemason announcer Spivey. As the broad-shouldered announcer blocked the way, a pack of chatty women walked outside the general store. A thin lady covered her mouth and screamed.

Hoping to avoid an altercation, Shane wheeled around and led his father in the opposite direction. "Now I understand why you don't like crowds." He steered Kirby toward an apothecary shop. "Let's find a doctor and get you some medicine."

"I've got a meeting with Charles Goodnight back at the lodge. We need cattle for the ranch." Kirby rubbed his chest and struggled to keep up. "'Healthy people don't need a doctor, those who are sick do.' Take me down a quiet alleyway."

Shane looked to see if they were being followed. "You sure told those people in the bakery."

"I used to get my Irish up over little things." Kirby shrugged. "But I'm older and wiser now."

Heading down a dark covered alleyway, Shane disagreed. His sixty-year-old father killed a man, shot another in the hand, and slapped around Mr. Ringo. Shane wondered if his mother Margaret knew her husband was an Illuminati henchman.

"Your mother's Lutheran faith maintains owning another man is an abomination." Kirby stopped beside a stack of wooden crates. "Others' faiths point to the scriptures and claim it's what God intended. Slavery's been around since Moses freed the Jews from Egypt."

A rail-thin man stumbled into the alley with a bottle of whiskey. As the drunkard staggered closer, Shane pulled his new Bowie knife from its leather scabbard. Gripping his eighteen-inch blade, he turned to protect his father. The drunk hit his forehead against an overhanging crate and crumbled to the ground. Shane put away his Bowie and stared at the motionless man.

"Damn foolish, Paddy." Kirby scoffed at the Irishman. "Wealthy Northerners hire Scotch-Irish off the boat for ten cents a day. Work 'em in their factory until they drop dead or drink themselves to death. Don't cost 'em a thing. Every time a healthy African slave dies, it cost his Southern master at least a thousand dollars. If an Irishman gets injured or complains about wages, there's a dozen more fresh off the boat to replace 'em."

"I'd rather be a Paddy than an African. At least you could walk off the job without fear of a bounty hunter tracking you down." Shane eyed his father. "If Sam Houston's illuminated, why won't you vote for him?"

"I'm not a US citizen." Kirby leaned against a crate and wheezed. "If you intend to vote in this fall's election, you need to use your mother's maiden name of Nordboe." He looked toward the street and flashed his fraternal ring. "I've got enemies and keep my name and residence closely guarded. Sorry, but that's the way it is."

"Don't matter, Pa." Shane understood how registering to vote made his father vulnerable to his enemies. "Just wanted to know why."

"I've gotta go to the lodge and meet with Charles Goodnight. Need to refresh our herd with cattle from his ranch in Palo Duro." Kirby pulled twenty dollars from his pocket. "Go pay the baker for the food we ate."

"Thought lunch was free?" Shane sensed a rouse but took the money. "We didn't eat twenty dollars' worth of food."

"Nothing's free in this world, except the Lord's blessing." Kirby stared down the alleyway. "I've got *work* to do. Go get your friends and meet me at the livery in a half hour."

Stepping over the Irishman, Shane rushed out of the alleyway and leaped onto the crowded boardwalk. The village square bustled with wagon and pedestrian traffic. As he headed toward the bakery, a two-hundred-pound lady in a hoopskirt veered into his path. Her young son held a toy train. Shane rammed into the distracted woman's stomach. Knocked off balance, he spun like a top and collided with a group of chattering women. His straw palmetto fell off his head.

The fat lady landed on her skirt and rolled onto her back. As her fleshy thighs parted and flashed her cotton pantalets, Shane regained his footing. Horror filled his mind. Her skull slammed against the boardwalk and clothes tumbled from her shopping bag.

"I do declare? Your mother raise you in a barn?" A slender blonde covered with jewels rubbed her injured shoulder. "Watch where you're going, child."

"Yes, ma'am." Shane shuddered. "Sorry, ma'am. I'm not use to big crowds."

Blood dripped from the fat lady's head. Her startled son dropped his train and wobbled backward. While curious townspeople circled around, Shane felt embarrassed by his carelessness. Scrambling to gather her things, he dropped to his knees and prayed Mack Dodd and the Ringo brothers didn't see the accident. They'd surely tease him all the way back to the Shamrock Ranch.

The Texas Ranger knelt alongside the fat lady. "Someone get the doctor." He lifted her bloody head and examined the inch-wide gash. "Ma'am, you'll need a few of stitches to close the wound."

Shane hoped he wouldn't get a citation or tossed in jail. As he looked to assist, the chivalrous ranger cradled the woman and stemmed the bleeding with his handkerchief. Bud and Announcer Spivey approached along the boardwalk.

"I'm all right, sugar plum child." The woman lifted her head and struggled to sit up. "Neither of us was watching where we were going." Her eyes locked onto the Texas Ranger. "Had I known two handsome men would come to my aid, I'd have fallen a lot sooner."

Shane sighed and felt thankful. Reassured by her cheery disposition, he knelt by her side and returned her shopping bag. Bud and announcer Spivey headed into the dark alley. The broad-shouldered announcer had a pistol tucked behind his Masonic apron.

A female voice called out. "You shoot better than you walk, Shane McLean!"

Shane snapped his head around. As he scanned the street, his heart skipped a beat. Mary Kelly picked up his filthy palmetto hat. Her bright green-eyes pierced his very soul. Surprised that Mary knew his nickname, he hoped she hadn't seen him knock down the fat lady.

"My poppa said he'd never seen someone outshoot Texas Rangers, at least not with a pistol." Mary flipped her red hair and batted her eyelashes. "Wouldn't have believed it unless he'd seen it with his own eyes." She pointed over her shoulder. "Poppa bought you a new Palmetto to replace the one he ran over."

"He didn't have to go and do that. I won a Plug Ugly hat today." Shane couldn't stop staring at her perfect face. "Just gotta collect it from a man."

"Poppa wants to meet you and so does Davis." Mary smiled. "I snuck away to tell you to come to the circus." She stepped back. "But don't tell 'em I told you to come."

Shane didn't want to deal with her father. "Who's Davis? Is that your brother?"

"Be a gentleman and escort me back to the circus." Mary offered her elbow. "I'll tell you about Davis." She glanced at the fat lady and her voice trembled. "Is that poor woman gonna be all right? You nearly killed her."

"Hope so. She's a really nice lady." Shane slid his hand down Mary's arm until their hands clasped. "How'd you learn my name is Shane?" His hip brushed against her side. "Nobody calls me that except for family."

"Your big friend, Mack Dodd, told me." Mary rubbed his cotton sleeve and blushed. "He was with two brothers who never spoke a word. Are they mutes?"

"No, ma'am. They talk just fine." Shane laughed at her assessment of the Ringo brothers. "When Mack's around, it's hard for anyone to get a word in."

Clinging to Mary's arm, Shane spotted the top of the circus tent and slowed his gait. He gazed into her green-eyes and savored every extra step. Mack and the Ringo brothers would never believe they'd come together.

"I've got to get back. Poppa's probably looking for me." Mary released his arm. "Could you come to Sunday mass in Cliff Town?"

"I'll be at church in Norse with my parents. But I'll ride over afterward." He grasped her gloved hand. "Now, who's Davis?"

"He's an old man of twenty-five. Poppa promised me to him." She frowned and looked away. "I don't love him. I wanna choose my own husband."

Shane searched for a private place to share his feelings. "Well, I think you're beautiful."

"Mack Dodd told me you're gonna join the Texas Rangers with him." Her big green-eyes widened. "I'll be of marrying age next fall."

"Dodd's a big oaf! I've got money saved and land set aside for a cabin on my family's Shamrock Ranch." He stroked a horse's fluffy mane and led Mary between a pair of covered wagons. "I'm gonna study law at Waco University."

"Oh, Shane. I don't wanna marry that old man." She sighed and fell into his arms. "Promise you'll come for me."

Shane caught Mary with both hands. As he felt her slender hips through her cotton dress, the old slave song "Yellow Rose of Texas" played in a saloon. A team of horses kicked up a cloud of dust in the street.

"Mary Kelly! Your father's looking for you." A middle-aged woman peered between the wagons. "Davis is with him."

Shane released his hands from Mary's hips. As he leaned against the wagon, Mary kissed his lips. She quickly pulled away and glanced at the nosey woman.

"Goodbye, Misses Kettler." Mary shook her head. "If you see Poppa, tell 'em I'm on my way."

While the woman turned away, Shane closed his eyes and longed for Mary. Her sweet taste lingered on his lips. A businessman dressed in a Masonic apron rushed through the street.

"I've gotta go. Poppa's gonna be angry." Mary's soft voice choked. "Promise me you'll come to Sunday mass."

"I'll be there." Shane struggled for the right words. "'Parting is such sweet sorrow.'"

"You read Shakespeare?" Mary's eyes widened. "Me, too."

The drunken Paddy staggered out of the covered alleyway. His clothes were saturated in blood. As he collapsed in the street, a woman screamed. Soldiers rushed into the alley. Fearing for his sickly father, Shane grabbed Mary's hand and looked to help. A white barn owl flew past the soldier's heads. The ominous bird of prey flapped its four-foot wings and soared to a neighboring rooftop.

Shane approached the panicked Freemason. "Sir, what happened in the alley?"

"It's terrible. Two people are dead." The frightened man gestured his fingers across his neck. "Their throats were slashed. Brother Spivey's tongue is torn out by the roots and his guts are sliced open."

Mary Kelly fell into Shane's arms. "Who could do such a thing?"

Shane knew. A chill shot down his spine.

CHAPTER 6

Sins of the Father become Sins of the Son

Texas State Capitol, March, 1861:

Eight months after winning the Heart of Texas Shooting Match, Shane had grown two inches and stood well over six-feet tall. His piercing blue eyes were framed by high-cheek bones and shaggy brown hair. He'd cleared land on the Shamrock Ranch for a future cabin and kept Mary Kelly in his daily thoughts and prayers. His father kept his dealings in Waco secret.

Talk of Civil War spread like wildfire. Men argued politics and fought over perceived slights. While US General Twiggs surrendered the Army of Texas to the Confederates, Unionist Governor Sam Houston hired protection and refused to relinquish the governorship. Austin teetered on rebellion.

Hoping to impress Mary with a stylish black bowler, Shane borrowed a buckboard wagon and drove his parents to the state capitol to shop for a new hat. The two mule team labored on the three-day trip to Austin. Confederate army recruiters swarmed the capital square. As he passed the Fifth Military District Building, a small squadron of federal guardsmen loitered in the street. Sent from Fort Leavenworth, the Jayhawkers carried pistols and shotguns. He wished his father allowed him to carry the custom .36 Special. Kirby kept his *work* gun at the lodge in Waco.

"Don't stare at those soldiers. You'll give 'em a reason to stop you and learn your politics." Kirby grabbed the reins. "War's on the country's doorstep."

"Kirby McLean!" A Jayhawker colonel staggered into the street, swigging a bottle of whiskey. "Ain't seen you since we whipped Santa Anna down in Monterrey."

"Hog Johnson." Kirby halted the two-mule team. "You back in Texas to return Santa Anna's cork leg?" He greeted the beady-eyed colonel with a Masonic handshake and his thick Irish brogue rolled off his tongue. "It'd look mighty good on a pedestal in the capital building."

"Nope, we left Little Napoleon's leg back in Springfield." Johnson's words slurred. "Last I heard, Sergeant Rhodes is charging folks a nickel a piece to see it. You know why we're here." He released Kirby's thumb on the knuckle grip and his disposition darkened. "I've been asked for us to *silence* another rogue Mason."

Shane didn't trust the beady-eyed colonel or his federal guardsmen. Eying a silver Masonic pin on Johnson's lapel, Shane recalled a similar square and compass badge hidden inside his mother's hutch. As he glanced at Johnson's Jayhawkers, a sinewy sergeant with deep-acne scars gave a wicked stare.

"Ought to be getting along, gentlemen." Margaret cleared her throat and grasp Kirby's arm. "We've got errands to run."

Johnson folded his arms. "Better keep an eye on your pretty wife—lots of lonely men around here."

"She's well cared for, Colonel." Kirby peeled back his frock coat and flashed his .44 Colt Walker. "I've been loyal to the Brotherhood. Keep that in mind if you take any of Sam Houston's blood-money."

Tipping his tall Hardee hat, Johnson backed away. "I'll take that into consideration, old friend."

Kirby steered the mules down Congress Avenue. "If

you're gonna come looking for me, I'll be at the lodge."

Shane wondered why his father didn't put the quietus on the beady-eyed colonel. Margaret lifted her Lutheran Rose necklace. As she kissed the silver-cross pendant and whispered a short prayer, Colonel Johnson swigged his bottle of whiskey.

"Honey, your friend's a drunkard." Margaret drew inspiration from her love of Shakespeare. "'Tis better to be vile than vile esteemed. Good riddance.'"

"You're wrong about that. Hog's no friend of mine." Kirby snapped his head around. "He's a god-damned bounty hunter."

"Follow the Lord's example." Margaret leaned toward Shane and whispered. "Don't make enemies like your father. Steer clear of sin and the Devil's Nectar."

Swarmed by rabid army recruiters following the shooting contest in Waco, Shane yearned to take his first drink. As he shrugged off his mother's warning, a fistfight spilled onto a saloon porch. Austin bars overflowed with wicked men and hard-spirited liquor. Kirby slowed the mules and steered around a rowdy crowd. The brawl ended with a whiskey bottle smashed over a soldier's head.

"Talk of war's got everyone on edge." Kirby stared at a group of federal guardsmen loitering outside the Missouri House Bar and Saloon. "Damn Yankee stragglers. Maybe we should leave town and return another time."

"We promised Shane a new bowler to court Mary in." Margaret eyed the soldiers and sighed. "But if you'd prefer to shop later—"

"I'm gonna see about getting a saddle for an old roan Mister Pierson wants to sell us." Kirby parked the wagon outside Sampson and Hendricks Haberdashery. "Son, escort your mother into the store." He handed Shane the reins and stepped out of the wagon. "Keep a close eye on those soldiers. I don't trust 'em around her."

Accompanying Margret inside the three-story haberdashery, Shane spotted a short-brimmed bowler in the storefront window. The black bowler looked like the Plug hat he'd won from Billy Bob. Parting company with his mother, he doubled back down the aisle and tried on the stylish hat. The sinewy Jayhawker sergeant with a pitted-faced shopped in the rear of the store.

"What do you think, Ma?" Shane placed the stylish bowler on his head. "Will Mary like this one?"

Margaret read the price tag and frowned. "Five dollars? You don't want her to think you're a Jim-dandy." She placed a more modest Plug hat on his head. "This one's only two dollars. Stand up straight, so I can see your eyes." Her face beamed with motherly-love. "Slim brim makes you look even more handsome."

Shane kissed her cheek. "If you say so."

"Move your wagon to a side street, boy." A balding store clerk shouldered up to the sergeant. "I've got a delivery coming."

Shane feared leaving his mother alone.

"I'll be fine. Go move our wagon." Margaret pointed outside. "If your father's still around, tell him I'll be a moment." She held a blue prairie dress to her blouse. "Can't make up my mind on a color."

Shane handed the clerk two dollars and locked eyes with the spying sergeant. "I'll be back shortly."

While his mother shopped for a dress, Shane parked the buckboard wagon on a side street and headed back toward the haberdashery. Festive music blared from the Missouri House Bar and Saloon. Wanting his first drink, he stared over the saloon's bat wing doors and adjusted his new hat. A militia officer in a Masonic apron rushed out of the bar. As he headed across the street to a general store, Shane sauntered inside. A dozen patrons filled the two-story saloon.

A tinny old piano belted out "Dandy Jim of Caroline." Slipping past a table full of Johnson's Jayhawkers, Shane elbowed between two men and gazed at a busty blonde barmaid. His eyes dropped to her satin corset. Distracted by the attractive blonde's fleshy bosom, he bumped into a federal guardsman. While he thought about apologizing, the red-haired Jayhawker slammed his shillelagh on the table and wiped whiskey from his lapel.

"Damn fool!" The soldier aimed the two-pound knob of his walking stick at Shane. "Watch where you're going, boy."

As the piano music stopped, three men looked up from their card game. Soldiers carrying shotguns rushed from the rear of the saloon. Dressed in red leg gaiters and yellow trimmed uniforms, the intimidating Jayhawkers circled around. Unarmed and outnumbered, Shane looked to make amends. "Sorry, sir."

"He owes you a drink, Red." A stocky soldier seated alongside his twin brother scoffed. "Don't let that damn pig farmer waste your hard earned money."

"Stop it, William Ivey. It was an accident." A brunette put down her tray of drinks and rushed across the saloon. "He's just a boy, Red. Leave him alone. I'll get you another drink." She kissed the angry soldier and fell into his arms. "Let me make it up to you."

"Get outta here, stupid kid." William Ivey elbowed his twin brother. "Go down to the damn candy shop. Let us men drink in peace."

"You and Lawrence better not start more trouble." The brunette turned to scold the Ivey twins. "Deputy Thompson's been in here once today."

Shane thought about walking out, but he'd come for a drink and intended to get one. While the brunette fetched a bottle of whiskey, he turned his back on the despicable soldiers and bellied up to the bar. Staring into the ornate wall mirror, he noticed the barmaid's shapely backside and wondered what it would be like to be with a woman.

"Those federals have been nothing but trouble since they arrived from Fort Leavenworth." The blonde barmaid shook her large bosom and mumbled under her breath. "Someone with guts needs to run them out of town."

Shane had the fortitude but lacked the means. The better part of valor was discretion. Even if he wanted to start a gunfight against six federal guardsmen, his musket was in the wagon and Kirby had the Colt Walker.

"My name's Luanne. Come join me in my room." The blonde flashed an inviting smile and motioned upstairs. "I'll show you a good time, blue eyes."

Flattered by the proposition, Shane tapped his foot to the piano music but intended to remain pure. Thoughts of Mary Kelly halted his wandering eye. He wanted his first time with a woman to be special.

"Thanks for the offer, but I've promised to be faithful to a girl back home." Shane shook head. "Being with someone you care about makes it a hundred times better."

"Luanne, you've got the wrong kind of sweets for that kid." A soldier with shoulder-length hair glanced up from his cards and winked. "But I'll stop by later for some."

"I'm done with you, Buck." Luanne shook her head. "You still ain't paid for last night."

Shane smothered a laugh.

"Think it's funny, boy! Quit eyeballing me." Buck placed his cards on the table. "Get outta here before I run you out."

"I'm sixteen and I got eight bits in my pocket." Shane turned his back on the table of soldiers. "Give me a whiskey, barkeep."

"Y'all leave my paying customers alone." The bartender picked up a shot glass. "You want top shelf or regular rot gut?"

Shane didn't know. Angered by the vile soldiers, he glanced into the bar mirror and spotted a painting of the Owl of Minerva on the wall. His father had the same image engraved on the ivory-handle of his .36. The bartender lifted an unlabeled bottle from under the counter. Juggling a jigger high in the air, he caught and filled the shot glass in one spectacular motion.

"Put a peppermint candy stick in it, barkeep." Buck

leaned back in his chair. "Bet a dollar the little momma's boy can't shoot it and keep it down."

"Knock it off, Buck!" The bartender slid the jigger of whiskey across the bar to Shane. "Two-bit whiskey will knock you on your ass just like the expensive stuff—but for half the price."

Glancing over the second floor staircase, a Jayhawker lieutenant with gold loop earrings pulled up his pants. Two drunken women clung to his body. As he adjusted his suspenders over his long johns, the barmaids giggled.

"Private Davidson, find Colonel Johnson and inform him there's a situation in the saloon." The lieutenant gave Shane a wicked stare. "Tell him to hurry."

As a young soldier peeled out of the saloon, a chair screeched across the floor. William Ivey rose from the table and aimed his shotgun at Shane's head. The festive music stopped. Staring down the double-barrels, Shane froze in place while his body trembled in fear.

"Boy, you've been told by several men to get the hell outta here." William Ivey motioned to the doorway. "Go tend pigs with your no good father while you still can."

"Put your shotgun away!" A man in a cabinetmaker's smock stood from a corner table. "Senator Lane sent you men to Austin to help protect Unionist settlers, not start trouble."

"Sit your ass down, Hannig! These are the United States of America." William Ivey glared at the cabinetmaker. "This ain't no damn Bohemian beer garden. Talk to me like that again, I'll blow your damn head off. Ignorant immigrant."

"Amen, William." Lawrence nodded at his twin brother. "These damn foreigners need to learn their place here in America."

"Huuurrahhh!" Buck tossed back his hair and leaped from his chair. "Look what just arrived."

While the Jayhawkers turned toward the batwing doors, Shane grabbed his shot glass and tossed his whiskey into his mouth. It tasted like fire. Placing the empty jigger on the bar, he choked down his liquor and gagged. Why the hell did anyone drink this stuff?

"Shane McLean!" Margaret stood in the doorway with her hands on her hips. "Does your father know you're in here?"

Shane winced and his throat burned. As he struggled with whiskey's aftertaste, Margaret stepped farther inside the saloon. The look on her face could slice rawhide. Three Masons rose from a neighboring table and rushed toward the rear door.

"Told you men McLean's got a pretty wife." Buck pushed his chair aside. "Seen her in his wagon when the Colonel Johnson was talking to him."

"This is federal business." Red slammed his shillelagh on a table and chased the crowd outside. "Bar's closed. Scram."

While patrons scattered, Buck eyed Margaret with an evil smile. A woman cried out from the upstairs balcony. Shane slipped his Bowie from his scabbard. Fearing for his mother, he stepped from the bar.

"Hold it right there, boy." William Ivey aimed his shotgun at Shane's chest. "We're gonna take your mother to the back and show her a real *good* time."

"Where's your father? Freemasons got a five-hundred-dollar bounty on his head." The Jayhawker lieutenant spit a mouthful of tobacco juice at a spittoon and wiped his grimy chin. "I aim to collect it."

Buck snatched Margaret's hand. "Stop squirming...you sweet little thing. Come lay with me on the sofa and be my darling."

"I seen her first." William Ivey ran his eyes up and down Margret's body. "That's a right pretty woman."

"You Ivey twins gotta wait your turn." Buck wrapped his arm around her neck and grabbed his crotch. "There's plenty of her to go around."

"Stop it, .you heathen devil!" Margaret wiggled free. "I'm a Christian woman."

Grabbing her collar, Buck yanked her close and scoffed. "I'm a lonely man in need of a fresh religious woman."

Margaret fought back and her blouse tore. As she twisted, her bodice popped open and a breast fell out. The soldier's eyes widened. Struggling to cover herself, she bent at the waist and grabbed her ripped cotton top. Her voice trembled with fear.

Outnumbered eight to one, Shane clenched his Bowie and shook with rage. He wished his father was here. Staring down the barrel of Ivey's shotgun, his stomach churned. Kirby would never let this happen.

"Watch out, Buck!" Lawrence Ivey shouted across the room. "She'll sink her teeth into you."

"Don't you dare bite me, woman." Buck slapped her face and forced his hand down her blouse. "You like it rough, huh."

"Stop it! Police are on their way." Margaret yanked his fingers from her breast. "I'm a married woman, you son-of-Satin."

"To hell with the police, we're friends of the governor." Buck kissed her mouth and dragged her toward a Rosewood sofa. "Let's smooch it up before your husband gets here."

Margaret spit in the soldier's face. Buck wiped his cheek and slapped her mouth. Shane couldn't take any more. Ignoring the shotgun aimed at his head, he picked up an empty jigger and tossed it at Buck's head. The glass sailed high and shattered against the wall.

"Bastard!" Shane rushed at the table of Jayhawkers. "Get your hands off her."

William Ivey slid his foot into Shane's path. Tripping over Ivey's boot, he tumbled forward and his new hat rolled under a table. His forehead struck a metal spittoon. Tobacco juice spilled onto the grimy saw-dust floor and stuck to his cheek. As he pushed himself up, the wooden stock of a gun slammed into his skull. Blood oozed through his scalp. The room spun and everything twisted into black and gray.

Margaret screamed. Lifting his face out of foul spit, Shane blinked and his head throbbed. His eyelid was caked in thick blood. Through blurred vision, he spotted his mother stretched beneath Buck on a sofa. The long-haired soldier dropped his pants to his knees and buried his lips against the flesh of her neck. Pinned against the three-seat settee, she choked and squirmed.

"Stop!" Margaret's voice trembled. "Get off me—you're the Devil."

Buck squeezed her throat. As he worked his hips between her thighs, Shane crawled forward. Blood dripped along the bridge of his nose. The room wobbled and the gang of Jayhawker's drifted in and out of focus. Fighting her attacker, Margaret lifted her hips off the settee and twisted her body. Buck pressed down on her chest. His red leg gaiter dropped onto the floor. Three soldiers rushed to be next in line.

Margaret screamed. Her Lutheran Rose necklace broke and fell between the sofa cushions. Turning his head, Shane wished it would end. He closed his eyes and prayed for divine intervention.

The blast of gunfire reverberated off the walls. Lifting his battered head, Shane strained to see through the gun smoke. His nostrils flared from the acrid smell of black powder. Buck lay motionless across Margaret's chest. Blood oozed from a dime-sized hole in his skull.

"Get away from my wife!" Kirby stepped between the bat wing doors. "I'll kill every last one of you sons-of-bitches."

Shane sighed and thanked God for his father. While the Ivey twins froze at the table, two soldiers faded into the gun smoke. Margaret pushed Buck's lifeless body to the floor and covered her bare chest. Kirby stared down the barrel of his Big Colt Walker. His cold blue-eyes bulged with demonic fury.

"Mister." A soldier pulled his pistol. "You killed my—

A second shot blasted from Kirby's revolver. The soldier staggered backward and crumpled to the floor. Shane wanted to stand with his father. Lifting his chest off the ground, he struggled to rise but his battered body gave out and collapsed.

"Goddammit, McLean." The Jayhawker lieutenant stepped from a fat barmaid and glanced at Buck's dead body. "Colonel Johnson warned us you were a gutless cold-blooded murderer."

Kirby wheeled around and fired a round between the officer's eyes. The bullet passed straight through his head. Blood sprayed the carved staircase. As the lieutenant dropped dead on the steps, the barmaid screamed and rushed back upstairs.

Kirby fanned the room with his revolver. "Who wants to be next?"

"You can't shoot all four of us, old man." William Ivey called out from a card table. "You ain't got enough bullets."

"Wanna find out, boy?" Kirby cocked the hammer on his gun and took aim at Lawrence Ivey. "I'll start by shooting your twin." His voice deepened. "I'm taking my wife and son and leaving town."

A shifty-eyed soldier with a shiny Colt Dragoon stepped from the rear of the saloon. "You killed three federal soldiers, hog farmer." His left hand hovered inches from his holstered gun. "Colonel Johnston will hunt you down and hang you before sunset."

"Don't make him mad, Lefty. Wait for the others to get here." Red shook his head. "He's worth five hundred dollars—dead or alive."

Margaret leaped off the sofa and headed toward the doorway. Stepping around the blood-stained bodies, she covered her eyes and turned away.

Lefty snatched her arm. Using her as a shield, he pulled Margret close and placed the barrel of his Dragoon against her temple.

"You ain't leaving, old man. At least, not upright." Lefty

scoffed. "I wanna find out for myself why Sam Houston makes such a fuss about you."

"Shoot him now, Lefty! Don't duel him fair in the street." Red pointed his shillelagh at the dead lieutenant. "Since Richardson ain't around to collect, I ain't sharing the Freemason's reward money with Colonel Johnson."

"Can't collect if you're dead." Lawrence Ivey stood from the table. "Wait 'til the colonel gets here with the rest of the squadron."

Kirby backed toward the doorway. "Release my wife and son. I'll fight you in the street."

"Your son's an accessory to murder, we'll keep him." Lefty's face tightened. "He'll hang for murder just as soon as I'm done killing you."

"If my family ain't out here in thirty seconds, I'll be back to kill every last one of you sons-of-bitches," Kirby's voice deepened with resolve. "Clock's ticking!"

CHAPTER 7

Murder on Congress Avenue

Missouri House Bar and Saloon, Austin, Texas, March, 1861:

Traffic ceased and townspeople scattered. While the Ivey twins dragged Shane out of the saloon, Kirby waited to duel Lefty in the street. Margaret pushed through the bat wing doors and fought with the red-haired Jayhawker. Her ripped blouse revealed scratches on her throat. Weak from his beating, Shane struggled to remain conscious and offered little resistance. His bloodstained face scraped against the grimy floor.

"Leave us alone!" Margaret cried out. "We haven't done anything to you."

"Your husband's a killer. That's why Houston and the Freemasons put a five-hundred-dollar bounty on his head." Red waved his shillelagh in her face. "Shout your mouth or I'll beat you with this here stick."

Lawrence Ivey dropped Shane on the porch. As he kicked his battered body, Lefty pushed through the doors and grabbed his Colt Dragoon. Red slapped Margret's cheek.

Kirby squared his shoulders. "Touch my wife again and I'll kill you."

"Bold words for a dead man." Red released her arm. "We'll see how tough you are when Lefty's done with you."

Margaret crumbled to the porch and buried her face in her hands. While Kirby stood alone in the street, Lefty closed the cylinder of his Dragoon and nodded at a soldier outside the general store. Stepping off the porch, he stopped ten-feet from Kirby and squared-off.

"McLean, Governor Houston says you're a dangerous man." Lefty dropped his hands. "I say you're a two-bit liar—and killer!"

An eerie silence lingered in the air. Forfeiting the battle of wills, Lefty reached for his gun, but Kirby drew quicker. A six-inch flame blazed from his Big Colt Walker. The .44 caliber bullet pierced Lefty's heart. As he spit blood and crumbled to the street, a shotgun blasted from the general store.

Shane pushed a clump of blood-soaked hair out of his face. His father shuddered and dropped to his knees. Shot through the spine, Kirby fell forward and his pistol slipped from his hand. Buckshot peppered his lower back. Margaret cried out.

"McLean ain't dead—keep a gun on him." The sinewy sergeant with acne scars lowered his shotgun. "He's still moving."

Shane cussed the Jayhawker spy. "Bastard!"

Kirby crawled forward. As he struggled for his revolver, the sergeant stepped into the street and approached cautiously. Flanked by two soldiers, he kicked the gun toward the saloon. The Big Colt Walker skidded across the dirt and came to rest in front of Shane.

An old man leaned out of an upstairs window. "Yankee Back shooter! Go home. You're all murderers."

"Stand back!" The sergeant shouted at a group of curious men. "This is federal business."

Kirby rolled onto his elbows and dragged his legs helplessly. Eyeing his father's gun, Shane rallied his strength and looked to kill the bastards. As he pushed himself off the porch, a boot slammed into his ribs and forced him back down.

William Ivey shouted. "Stay still, boy or I'll spilt your skull open."

"Get the police!" Margret cried out from the porch. "Is there no justice in this town?"

"They'll thank us for killing your husband." The sergeant motioned to the Ivey twins. "Leave the kid alone and get over here. We'll deal with him later."

William and Lawrence Ivey leaped off the porch and lifted Kirby to his knees. As they ripped down his shirt and spread his arms like a martyr, blood oozed from his wounds. The sinewy sergeant cracked an eight-foot bullwhip. Broken glass and metal shards were sadistically woven into the plaited tip. As the sergeant stepped behind Kirby, Shane closed his eyes.

"I'm Sergeant James Lauderdale with the Frontier Guard. This man's a killer, a cold-blooded assassin who just shot down four federal soldiers." The sergeant raised his whip. "He'll pay for his crimes with a flogging and hanging."

Shane cussed the lying bastard. Sergeant Lauderdale intended to murder his father. Kirby never killed a man who didn't need killing. He'd shot his way into the saloon to save Margaret when Lefty challenged him to a duel.

Lauderdale snapped his whip across Kirby's back. A frenzy of lashes ensued. The plaited tip tore through his flesh. Blood and chunks of skin splashed through the air like rain. Shot through the spine, Kirby buckled in pain but never cried out.

"Keep him up straight!" Lauderdale paused to wipe a splotch of blood from his cheek. "Let this town see how Jaywalker Justice deals with killers."

Margaret cried out. Shane feared he'd be next. Lacking the strength to muster a fight, he lay on his stomach and wished the gang of Jayhawkers would go away. His father's back was a bloody mess of sliced muscle and tissue.

Kirby struggled to speak. "Frank, take care of your mother. Don't leave her alone, son."

"Please—someone help us." Margaret pulled on her disheveled hair. "For the love of God—please help us.

"Quiet down woman or you'll be next." Lauderdale shook his blood-soaked whip. "Your husband's getting what he deserves."

Lawrence Ivey wiped the blood from his hands with a dirty laugh. "I've slaughtered swine that didn't bleed this much."

Kirby collapsed onto the dirt and grime of Congress Avenue. While Margaret buried her face in her hands, Shane feared the bastards had killed his father. A wave of hatred pumped through his veins. Eyeing his father's Colt, he climbed to his feet and stumbled into the street. Red stepped off the porch with his shillelagh.

"Look out, Frank!" Margaret shouted.

Red rammed the two-pound knob into Shane's skull. Blood splattered onto the grimy street. Shane's vision blurred. His knees buckled as his cheek struck the ground.

"Damn it, Red. You tore the kid's head wide open." William Ivey laughed. "Where can I get me one of them skull-splitting clubs?"

While the gang of Jayhawkers strutted like game roosters, death felt like a welcomed reprieve. Blinking in and out of consciousness, Shane stared at his father's mutilated body.

Vomit rose into his throat. His mother clung to a porch post and sobbed. With her torn clothes and disheveled hair she looked like a mad woman.

"Bring McLean's kid to me. He's an accessory to these murders." Sergeant Lauderdale stroked his blood-soaked whip. "He'll hang for his crimes."

"No!" Margaret pulled back her hair. "He's only sixteen."

The Ivey twins dragged Shane across the street. Placed on his knees, he closed his eyes and prepared to be whipped. He focused on Mary Kelly and hoped it would help him endure the pain.

"Ain't so full of yourself now, boy?" William Ivey slapped Shane's cheek. "Lift your head up and take your whipping like a man."

Lawrence Ivey spit in his face and cackled. "Should've stayed outta your father's business."

Grubby tobacco juice dripped down the bridge of Shane's nose. He stared at a Masonic pin on Sergeant Lauderdale's lapel. The silver square and compass badge appeared identical to the one worn by Colonel "Hog" Johnson.

"Finish him off, Sarge." William Ivey shouted. "Let's tie him to horses and quarter him."

As the sergeant reared his whip high in the air, Shane closed his eyes. The plaited tip wrapped tightly around his throat and ripped through his flesh like a saw. Pain radiated through his body. Lauderdale jerked his whip.

"You're not gonna believe this, Sarge." William Ivey pointed at Kirby. "That old pig farmer's still breathing."

"You're a liar!" Lauderdale wheeled around and his eyes narrowed. "Bastard just won't die."

Kirby gasped and crawled forward. Lauderdale dropped his whip and rushed over to the Ivey twins. As he snatched William's shotgun, Shane freed his neck and tossed the lash aside. Gripping the three-foot barrel of his shotgun, the sergeant swung the wooden stock into Kirby's skull. Chunks of brain spilled onto the street.

"McLean ain't breathing now!" Lauderdale pointed the bloodstained stock at the Ivey Twins. "String the murdering bastard up and drag him through the streets until his limbs fall off. I'll take what's left to the governor's mansion and collect our reward."

"Stop it, you *bloody* fools!" A young lawman with an English accent rushed through the street. "That man's already dead."

"Deputy Thompson, this man killed three federal soldiers. It's out of your jurisdiction." Lauderdale pointed at Shane. "His son's gonna hang for conspiracy."

"We'll see about that." Deputy Thompson turned toward the boardwalk. "Here comes Counselor Fort."

A bearded attorney hobbled into the street. "Sergeant Lauderdale, we got Constitutional laws in this town. Even if you and your troopers choose not to follow them."

"Shut your mouth, De Witt! I don't need no clubfoot lawyer preaching to me." Lauderdale scoffed. "Go back to your law office. Let real men settle this with an honest fight."

Counselor Fort's eyes narrowed. "Shooting a man in the back ain't an honest fight."

"You're out of line, soldier!" Colonel "Hog" Johnson shouted at Red. "Release that woman. Your orders were to wait for my arrival." He headed toward Sergeant Lauderdale. "This matter was to be kept private and handled at the lodge."

"Sir, we didn't have a chance. McLean barged into the saloon shooting like a wild Indian—killed four of your men and Lieutenant Richardson." Lauderdale shouldered between the Ivey twins. "We were just defending ourselves."

"Houston ain't gonna pay for a cold-blooded killing like this." Johnson turned toward the governor's mansion. "This man has friends in town." His voice trembled. "They're gonna come looking for you with a rope."

"Sir, I didn't think about his friends." Lauderdale eyed Kirby's mutilated body. "He's a killer. I was just protecting myself."

"You shot him in the back and whipped him to death in front of his wife and kid," Counselor Fort scolded the sergeant. "That ain't self-defense—not even in Texas."

"That's enough, De Witt. This is federal business." Colonel Johnson wagged his finger. "Stay out of it."

"This federal tyranny won't last." Counselor De Witt Fort pointed at the state capitol. "Legislature's meeting to secede from the Union. I'll make certain our senators know what your federal guardsmen perpetrated on this good man and his family." His face tightened. "Mark my words, Houston and his kind will be run out of Austin by the end of the month. You'd better hightail it outta here sooner."

"Is that a threat, Counselor? Better mind your manners when addressing an officer." Johnson squared his shoulders. "I'm headed to the governor's mansion. I'll make certain to express your threat on Houston's life."

The club foot attorney clamed up tighter than a fat lady's corset. While Deputy Thompson whisked the counselor away, Shane feared the gang of Jayhawkers would get away with murder. Sergeant Lauderdale, Red, and the Ivey brothers banded together.

Counselor Fort shrugged. "I'm sorry, sir. General Twiggs left for Corpus Christi, thought it be best if you joined him before the truce ends."

"I'm here to protect Sam Houston. Texas is under federal jurisdiction until a vote to secede passes." Johnson eyed Sergeant Lauderdale. "Round up the men while I settle this damn mess you've left with the governor."

"Yessir." Lauderdale headed toward a row of cavalry horses. "Are we returning to Missouri or Fort Leavenworth?"

"Louisiana. I've got unfinished business in Natchitoches." Johnson glanced at Kirby's blood-soaked body and shook his head. "I've gotta find an undertaker willing to take on this mess."

CHAPTER 8

Sworn Vengeance

Shamrock Ranch, McLennan County, Texas, March, 1861:

*V*engeance is mine, I will repay, sayeth the Lord. Shane refused to eat and struggled to sleep. He felt responsible for his father's murder. Struggling to hide the pain, he wished he'd listened to his mother and never gone into that damn saloon. The shame tore him up inside. No promise of forgiveness or preacher's sermon would bring back Kirby. His mother's Norwegian hymns helped pass time during the wagon ride home. Determined to reap vengeance on the men responsible, he sought a punishment no lawman or judge could provide—the satisfaction of watching his father's killers suffer in death at his hands.

Deep ruts in the road shook the buckboard wagon. Swatting a fly gnawing on his bloodstained neck, Shane wished the pain would go away. His bandaged head pounded like a hammer. Kirby's coffin cracked open and the stale odor of death seeped out. Attacked by a swarm of hungry insects, Shane brooded over his father's dying words and pondered. Should he pursue a path of vengeance or take care of his mother?

News of Kirby's passing flooded the Shamrock Ranch with mourners. Mack Dodd and the Ringo brothers helped dig a grave under a post oak tree on a hill overlooking the cabin. Margaret struggled to keep her composure. Overcome with grief, she didn't want a lengthy graveside service and advised the preacher to keep the noontime eulogy short. Mary Kelly and her family were absent from the ceremony. Shane wondered if Mary's father thought his family too low-class to attend?

Following a meal of beans, syrup, and cornbread, guests formed a line to offer condolences. Shane stood beside his mother and greeted well-wishers with a forced smile. While Jerry and Jimmy wound through the line, Mr. Ringo graciously offered his sympathies. Clean and sober, he held Baby Johnny in his arms.

"Kirby helped turn my life around." Franklin extended his hand. "I've quit drinking and haven't missed a church service." His voice choked with sincerity. "If there's ever anything the boys and I can do—we're just over yonder."

"Those Jayhawkers beat the hell outta you." Jerry pushed his father along. "Better start eating, Frank. You look gaunt."

"They need to be hung for what they done to you." Jimmy's eyes narrowed. "Me and Jerry will ride with you to Kansas and hunt 'em down. Just say when."

Shane appreciated the offer but intended to hunt the bastards on his own. A four-horse team pulled a Phaeton double-buggy toward the gravesite. Hoping Mary and her family arrived late, he strained to see inside. Jerry stared at the fancy carriage.

"Ya'll seen Mary today?" Shane shouldered up to Jerry. "I was hoping her father would bring her—at least for the service."

"Excuse me for saying this, but Mister Kelly don't want Mary courted by you." Jerry's voice choked. "You're poor and an immigrant's son. Not to mention your family's reputation."

Hoping this friend was wrong, Shane lowered his head. The four horse team halted behind a row of wagons and four men in half-aprons exited the carriage. A group of veteran soldiers who served with Kirby during the Texas Revolution greeted the Masons. Saddened by Mary's absence, Shane felt like he'd lost another close family member.

"That wound's gonna leave a permanent scar around your neck." A ranger sergeant with a thick dark beard pointed to Shane's throat. "It's a sad day when a man can't take his family into town without trouble. If we don't go fight Lincoln in the east, he'll invade Texas and take everything we hold dear." His voice deepened. "Frank, have you thought about joining Captain Thomas Harrison's Rangers?"

Kirby rested in a casket ten feet away. Shane didn't want to hear political talk, especially at his father's funeral. He'd met his intimidating neighbor but couldn't recall the sergeant's name. The soldier had a square and compass pin on his lapel. Looking to gage his Masonic knowledge, he stepped away from his mother and extended his hand.

"Sir, I aim to join the rangers, but not today." Shane shook the sergeant's hand and whispered a secret word. "*Mah-hah-bone.*"

"Greetings Brother McLean, I'm Rufus Beavers." The Mason placed his thumb on Shane's knuckle. "Helped your father with *work* at the Gatesville Lodge. You're truly a widow's son, like Hiram Abiff."

Impressed by the sergeant's knowledge, Shane responded with a higher-level handshake. When Brother Beavers couldn't reciprocate, he released the sergeant's hand and eyed the group of uninvited Masons. Sergeant Beavers turned toward his pregnant wife.

As the group of Masons approached the gravesite, Margaret covered her mouth. Shane wondered if he'd broken a sacred oath. Concerned for her safety, he squeezed the handle of his Big Colt Walker.

Sergeant Beavers presented his wife. "This is Louisa. I intend to protect her from Yankee invaders by any means necessary—"

"Frank, don't get any foolish ideas." Neighbor John Pierson said, cutting off the sergeant. "Your ma's not over your father's passing. She'll need you here, not fighting some rich man's war in Virginia." He gave Rufus Beavers an evil look. "An eye for an eye makes the world blind."

Mrs. Pierson eyed Shane's throat and cringed. "Your neck looks awful, Frank. What kind of people do such things to a kid?"

Uncomfortable with her concern, Shane lifted his collar and covered his injured throat. "Sergeant Beaver, keep me in mind to join the Harrison Rangers. I aim to kill as many Yankees as the Lord allows me to."

"That's what I wanted to hear from a Worthy Brother." Sergeant Beavers placed his arm around his wife and flashed a Masonic Horned Hand sign. "If a crime is committed against you, it's up to you and your family to care of it."

Shane didn't reciprocate the sinister hand sign but intended to leave home as soon as he obtained a good horse. He demanded justice but his battered body demanded recovery. Like a deadly plague or pack of rabid dogs, Sam Houston, Colonel "Hog" Johnson, and the gang of Jayhawkers needed to be eradicated from the face of earth.

"Before your father borrowed my wagon, he paid in full for my best mare." Mr. Pierson approached. "I'll bring the black bay over in the morning. She's big, strong, and fearless."

Caught off guard by the generous offer, Shane cocked his head. "Pa told me that he was only thinking about buying a horse from you. It was an old mare too."

"You're the man of the house now." Mr. Pierson picked up his young son and placed him on his broad-shoulders. "Kirby was a friend mine. As far as I'm concerned, the horse is paid for."

"Thank you." Shane appreciated the gesture. "I'll need a good horse to get even with those Jayhawkers who murdered Pa."

Mr. Pierson snapped his head around. "You can't gun down a squadron of federal troopers. You'll get yourself killed and break your mother's heart," he whispered in Shane's ear. "If you leave her alone on the ranch, she'll never forgive you."

Shane respected the advice but couldn't lead a peaceful life on the ranch while his father's killers ran free. A clannish desire for vengeance ate his soul. He couldn't escape the grotesque images of his father's tortured body. Flashbacks of the Ivey twin's cruel laughter and the crack of Sergeant Lauderdale's whip echoed like demons in his head

A week after the funeral, Shane still had no appetite and struggled to sleep. He etched a death list in his mind. Waking early in the morning, he grabbed the family's King James Bible and decided to avenge his father's murder or die trying. Margaret turned in her bed.

"Ma!" He sought the strength to tell her he was leaving. "Are you awake?"

"For the last hour. I've listened to you toss and talk in your sleep." Margaret sat up and cast aside her covers. "I know what you're gonna say, and the answer is no. I've already lost your father." Her voice trembled. "Can't bear the disappointment of losing you, too."

"Old Testament says an eye for an eye. I'm gonna do the Lord's work and cut out both eyes from those soldiers." He placed the Bible on her bedside table and scripted his words carefully. "Like the good book says, I'm gonna punish those men."

"Don't exploit God's word for your selfish reasons. I've already forgiven 'em." She climbed out of bed and reached for her flannel robe. "You promised your father you'd take care of me." Her voice choked. "You're going to be somebody, Shane. You're attending Waco University in the fall."

"My heart ain't into books. Every time I close my eyes, I hear the Ivey twins laughter." He expected her to be more understanding. "I wake up and go to sleep thinking about killing 'em. I see 'em besmirching your sacred person."

"Stop it, Shane! You sound like your father. Look where it got him." She pointed toward Kirby's grave. "You're not leaving this ranch. That's final."

"I can't go to university when those men are running free." He didn't care what she wanted. "You know people are gonna talk. I'm not a craven or a coward."

"What happened to your father keeps me up at night. but I deal with it through God. Thought that's what you've been doing." She sobbed into a black handkerchief. "What about me, Shane? Have you thought about me? I can't run this ranch with you."

"John and Peggy Pierson are just over the hill." He leaned over to hug her neck. "Look how many people showed up for Pa's funeral. They'll help you."

"It's not the same as family." She pushed him away and walked toward the kitchen. "Most of them came for the free meal."

"Ringos would help you." He followed her over to her Scandinavian hutch and took the black cloth out of her hand. "They'd do anything for us."

"Is that who put you up to this?" She spun around and wagged her finger. "Those Ringo brothers are nothing but trouble."

"Pa didn't raise a gutless son. You know what he'd do if he was still around." He realized he'd never get her consent. "'Cowards die many times before their deaths.'"

"Don't quote Shakespeare at me. You're headstrong for vengeance." Her face tightened. "Damn it, Frank!"

Shane had never heard his mother curse. Standing beside her hutch, she choked and broke into tears. He feared he'd pushed her too far.

"I'm sorry, Ma." He tied the black neckerchief around his injured throat and looked to make amends. "I've gotta hunt those damn Jayhawkers down. If they show up at the ranch, they'll kill both of us."

"You don't know that." She caught a sob. "I can't stop you, if you want to get yourself killed. Mister Pierson can dig your grave right next to your father." Her bottom lip quivered. "If you're seeking for my blessing, you won't get it."

Looking to hide the embarrassing scar around his neck, Shane tied her handkerchief around his throat and turned to leave. "I never expected it. Be home in a week. Ten days at most."

"If you must go—wait." She lifted a ceramic jar off her hutch. "I've got something for you."

A cool breeze blew through the early morning air. Shaking a key from the jar, Margaret unlocked the bottom drawer of her hutch and removed a golden tasseled half apron. Shane recognized the embroidered Owl of Minerva. His father's ivory-handled .36 Special dangled from the folded apron.

"This gun belonged to Pa. One of his Freemason Brothers gave it to me at the funeral." She handed the custom revolver to Shane. "Said you used it during the shooting contest in Waco."

Shane hadn't seen his father's *work* gun in nearly a year. The rifled nine-inch barrel spun the bullet allowing for a straighter shot. An icy calm settled his vengeful soul. As he rubbed his thumb over the engraved square and compass, Margaret sprinkled flour on the counter to prepare biscuits.

"I don't know who's after us, but you should have your father's gun for protection." She picked up a rolling pin on her hutch. "Pa had enemies—and bitter rivals like Sam Houston."

Shane squeezed the ivory-handled revolver. "Was Pa a cold-blooded killer like those Jayhawkers claim?"

"Your father was a decent man with a good heart." Tears welled in her eyes. "For us to judge him isn't fair. The Lord will do that."

A gust of wind blew open the front door. Shane slammed it shut and bolted the entrance. As his mother rolled out biscuits on the hutch, her tears fell into the dough.

Kirby's dying words echoed in Shane's head. '*Take care of your mother.*'

❧❧❧

Crawford, Texas, September, 1861:

Shane had had a change of heart. Six months after his father's murder, he remained on the Shamrock Ranch. The decision felt like a cowardly black mark on his proud Highlander ancestry. Wanting answers or a deadly resolution, he needed to know who conspired to murder his father. Was a bounty on his head and was his mother in danger?

On a humid September morning, Shane woke early and planned to attend church in Cliff Town with Mary Kelly. Seeking the spirited salvation his mother so wanted for him, he packed his pocket Bible and placed his father's revolvers in his saddle bag. Never again would he be without a gun. As he slipped out to the barn, Vengeance whinnied. The black Appaloosa appeared ready to do her master's bidding.

Shane arrived at the small Norwegian settlement of Norse. While the morning sun rose above a rocky vista, three heavily-armed horsemen rushed out of town. Fearing an attack, Shane reached for his pistol and headed for high ground. One of the riders dangled his left hand by his holster. He recognized the man's upright posture.

"Frank!" Jerry Ringo's voice rang out. "Wait for us."

Shane wheeled Vengeance around. Mack Dodd and the Ringo brothers approached. Carrying knives, pistols, and shotguns, they appeared ready to fight.

Mack reined up. "Mister Pierson said you'd be heading this way. War broke out in Virginia. Captain Harrison's mustering a company of rangers to fight for the Confederacy."

Shane didn't want to kill Yankees in a faraway land. He intended to hunt down his father's killers by himself. Armed with his six-inch Bible, he wanted to be left alone, so he could pray with Mary and her family. He turned to Ephesians 6:12 for guidance, "Our struggle is not against flesh and blood, but against the spiritual forces of wickedness. "

"Quit babbling hollow scripture." Jerry Ringo turned in his saddle. "Come on, Frank. Ride with us to Waco and join Thomas Harrison's Rangers."

"War'll be over in three or four months. You'll miss all the fun." Mack shrugged. "See the country on the government's dollar and kill a few Yankees."

Joining the elite cavalry regiment sounded tempting. Shane feared disappointing Mary and breaking the explosive news to his mother. Margaret would never approve of him fighting for the Confederacy.

"I can't go with y'all." Shane struggled for an excuse. "My family is Unionists. Gonna pray with Mary at church this morning."

"Damn you're a hard case, Frank." Mack shook his head. "Can't you see? Mary's father doesn't want you around her? Says you should go off to war." His tone sharpened. "Ask, Ringo."

Jerry tucked his scraggily red-hair under his palmetto. As he looked away, Shane realized Mary's father wanted him out of the picture. He'd promised her to an older well-established gentleman. Shane hoped to change Mr. Kelly's mind.

"Ringos are afraid to tell you the truth, but I ain't." Mack steadied his horse. "Mister Kelly doesn't think you're good enough for his daughter. That's why Mary missed your pa's funeral." He shrugged and pulled out a six-shooter tucked in his waist. "Come on, Frank, join the rangers with us, and we'll stop by and tar and feather that old coot on the way."

Jerry brandished a knife. "While we're at it, let's ride to Huntsville and slit Governor Houston's throat. Big drunks got it coming for sending Lane's death squad after your father."

"We can't kill Sam Houston. Every Texas Ranger in the

state will come after us." Shane fought the urge to punish his father's killers. "We could stuff a pillow over the bastard's head when he's sleeping."

Mack nodded. "Now you're talking."

"Don't know how I'd tell my mother I'm running off to war." Shane sought spiritual guidance. "Gotta pray about this with Preacher Dahl."

"That gutless talk might impress old ladies at church. But it makes me wanna puke." Mack shook his head in disgust. "War'll be over by Christmas. Don't tell your Ma nothing. Write her a damn letter." His voice trembled. "Come on, let's ride!"

CHAPTER 9

Harrison's Texas Rangers

Cameron, Texas, September, 1861:

Shane succumbed to his friend's pressure and left to join the war. Due to the late start, they missed Captain Thomas Harrison's call to muster in Waco and tracked the elite company of rangers south to Wilderville and on to Cameron. Rows of saddled cavalry horses lined both sides of Main Street. While a handful of Negros fed and wiped down the animals, Shane rode toward a small wooden courthouse and spotted a balding gentleman in a sky-blue officer's uniform. He'd met Captain Harrison and his brother James following the shooting contest in Waco, but wasn't sure of his identity outside the Masonic lodge.

"See that old man reading a newspaper?" Shane turned in his saddle and pointed to the courthouse bench. "Is that Captain Harrison?"

Mack nodded and steered toward Captain Harrison. Sergeant Rufus Beavers stepped out of the courthouse. The bearded soldier had attended Kirby's funeral with his wife Louisa.

"Brother Harrison." Mack flashed his Masonic ring and quickly dismounted. "It's me, Brother Dodd from the Masonic lodge."

"So it is." Harrison folded his paper and stepped into the street. "You men come to join my company? I'm looking for soldiers who shoot like Daniel Boone and ride like a Comanche."

"Yessir. We'd like to join your rangers." Mack towered over the captain and greeted him with a thumb-on-the-knuckle Masonic handshake. "We've followed y'all from Waco to Wilderville, Marlin, and Cameron."

"You men got money? This is a select company." Harrison pulled a tin flask emblazoned with Masonic allegory. "You're too damn big for cavalry. Y'all need to apply for infantry with my brother James in Waco."

Shane didn't have money for a bribe. "Sir, we brought our mounts, pistols, and knives. We're signing up to kill the Unionist invaders, but we'll only do it from horseback."

Harrison sipped his flask. As he wiped his mouth, Shane waited for a response. The Ringo brothers dismounted.

"Captain Harrison, sir." Sergeant Rufus Beavers holstered his gun. "These boys are my neighbors from Crawford. They're what we're looking for." He pointed at Shane. "That's Kirby McLean's boy. He won the shooting contest in Waco last year."

Harrison eyed Shane's ivory-handled revolver. "That gun belonged to your father."

"Yessir." Shane dismounted. "Gonna use it to kill the men who murdered him."

"That was an unfortunate situation. I'd advise against stirring up old grudges." Harrison shook his head. "There's a lot you don't understand. Governor Houston was forced out of office days after Kirby's murder." He placed his hand on Shane's shoulder and whispered, "Let it be, Brother McLean. Houston's been shamed. He'll die in Huntsville penniless."

"I'm gonna slit the bastard's throat." Shane pulled his prized Bowie from a scabbard. "With the knife he awarded me before he'd conspired to have my father murdered."

"You don't know that for sure. Kirby had enemies." Harrison stepped back. "You've got evil in your eyes and vengeance in your heart. Better check yourself."

"Sir, we haven't met Colonel Terry's quota for cavalrymen yet." Rufus approached the captain. "He'll break up the company if we don't arrive to Houston with at least a hundred men. Let me train these boys. I'll turn 'em into Confederate Killing Machines."

Shane heard horrific tales of Yankees massacres. If the heathen devils invaded Texas, they'd rape woman and kill children. Drown babies in their mother's blood. If Colonel "Hog" Johnson and his Unionist Jayhawkers were any indication, the terrible stories of Yankee atrocities had to be true.

"Since Sergeant Beavers vouches for y'all, come with me." Harrison tossed his tin flask to Mack and headed toward the courthouse. "Drink up, while I'll cuss you Crawford Boys into the rangers."

The nickname Crawford Boys had a ring to it. While Mack sipped from the ornate flask, the Ringo brothers abstained. Their father's fight with alcoholism kept them temperate and sincere teetotalers. Harrison took a seat behind a cluttered desk. As he fumbled through a stack of papers, Mack belched like a bloated cow. The air reeked of rotten eggs. Shane snatched the whiskey from Mack's hand and took a sip. The flask was nearly empty.

"I've killed Indians along the Peace River with Sul Ross and rescued Cynthia Ann Parker from the Comanche. But I ain't never seen sharpshooting like that contest last year." Harrison lifted a quill pen off his desk and shook his head. "Dead center mark at fifty paces—and with a pistol."

Shane struggled to hide his pride. "It was a lucky shot, sir."

"Bet Frank could do it again." Jimmy stepped forward. "On horseback—at full gallop."

"I'd like to see that." Harrison removed a volunteer parchment from the disorganized stack of papers. "Gather around, men. President Davis and Robert E. Lee requested a regiment of elite Texas horsemen join the fighting in Virginia."

Shane recalled a colonel at Camp Verde by the same name. "Lee used camels in the West Texas Desert."

Mack staggered forward. "I ain't fighting Yankees on the back of a camel."

"Hush your mouth, soldier." Harrison dipped his pen into an ink well. "Lee accepted a general's commission in CSA." His pen dripped onto a parchment titled *Confederate States of America ~ Texas Enlisted.* "We're leaving for Camp of Instruction in the morning."

Shane returned the empty whiskey flask. "Sir, where do I sign?"

"Give me a moment, son." Harrison raised a finger and scribbled on the parchment. "Your father kin to Wilmer McLean? War in Virginia started on the McLean Plantation."

Kirby had talked about an uncle, who was a major in the Virginia Militia. Shane wanted to guard his family name. Intending to do wicked things to evil Jayhawkers, he didn't want his deeds traced back to the Shamrock Ranch.

"Sir, you know my father had enemies." Shane flashed the Owl of Minerva engraved on his ivory-handled Colt Special. "I'd appreciate the Brotherhood's privilege of secrecy."

Harrison nodded and scribbled a random name on the roster. As he stood from the desk, Mack and the Ringo brothers stepped up and joined under aliases. The budding recruits shouldered up and waited to be sworn into the rangers. "Raise your right hand." Harrison read from a parchment. "Repeat the Oath of Service after me."

እንፈ

Camp of Instruction, Houston, Texas, September, 1861:

Shane and the Crawford Boys joined ninety expert

horsemen from Central Texas and headed to Houston for training. Riding through heat waves and heavy downpours of rain, they arrived on the marshy banks of Buffalo Bayou. Regimental Commander Colonel Benjamin Franklin Terry mustered ten select companies from across the state into his Terry's Texas Rangers. The wealthy sugar planter from Fort Bend County bucked military tradition and allowed the soldiers to elect their officers.

Mosquitoes infested the marshland. Bivouacked along a swampy bayou, Shane and his friends were placed in Company A and trained in risky high-speed horse maneuvers. Houston's streets were overrun by Texas Rangers. While the daring soldiers competed in acrobatic feats of gunmanship, pretty girls lined the boardwalks fueling their competitive fire. Daily drills and inspection brought the sporting games to a halt.

A bugle call *To Assemble* echoed down Main Street. The inspection was the third of the day and soldiers were whipped for the slightest code infractions. Shane trotted Vengeance toward the flag-bearing Guidon color guard. Flanked by the Ringo brothers and trailed by Mack, he spotted the inverted Bonnie Blue flag leading the parade. The ranger line of march stretched three city blocks. A subsequent call *To Fall In* hastened his pace.

"Damn it, Frank! I can't remember what these bugle calls mean." Mack struggled to maneuver his horse into formation. "Drill and inspection, that's all we ever do."

"Quit your bitching. Ain't seen you miss a single Mess Call." Shane spotted a group of junior officers. "You're gonna get us all flogged.

Mack rubbed his stomach. "If I'd known Harrison was gonna drill us five times a day, I'd never voted him major. I came here to fight not assemble for inspection all damn day."

"Better shut your mouth. Harrison's with 'em." Shane cringed. "If he hears you talking like that, he'll whip your lard ass for insubordination."

Mack steered his brown bay into formation. "Major Harrison looks pissed off."

"Fall in...closed order. Eight abreast...Poinsett formation." Harrison cracked his horsewhip across the back of a late arriving private. "Don't make me late, soldier. Governor Lubbock's leading the regiment in parade."

Shane realized his life no longer belonged to him. He was the property of the Confederate States of America. The army told him when to get up, when to eat, when to go to bed, and everything in between. Disobey orders and there'd be hell to pay.

Throngs of Houstonians lined the boardwalk along Main Street. A sixteen-member brass band played the awe-inspiring tune of "Dixieland." As a thunderous drum roll set the ranger parade in motion, Shane rode atop Vengeance in precise procession. Dressed in new brown trousers and a pristine cotton shirt, his chest swelled with pride. Hundreds of girls clad in their Sunday finest flashed smiles and waved white handkerchiefs. The boardwalks swayed like a flock of fluttering butterflies. Savoring the glorious call of duty, Shane wished Mary Kelly could see him and hoped the fighting in Virginia would last.

Three days and eighty miles later, the pomp and pageantry continued in the city of Beaumont where an even larger and more fanatical crowd packed the downtown square. The ranger line of march stretched for a half mile. Appreciative citizens greeted the soldiers with ladles of fresh water and baskets of warm biscuits. Shane and his friends arrived at the ship docks eager for the three-day voyage to New Orleans. He'd never been on a clipper and looked forward to the sea adventure.

"Look what I found." Mack approached with an eighty pound bloodhound. "Gonna name him Lucky."

"Damn fool. You can't take a big dog like that on a boat." Jerry shook his head and grinned. "Unless it's gonna be dinner."

Shane led his horse toward the stables. As he shouldered

through the crowd, Sergeant Rufus Beavers approached with an angry scowl on his face. Sweat dripped from his brow.

"Don't bother unpacking." Rufus spit a mouthful of tobacco. "Major Harrison gave me orders to bring the officer's horses overland to New Orleans."

"That's a bullshit duty! I wanna ride on the high seas in a ship." Jerry shrugged. "They can't make us."

"Quit complaining. You signed up for the army." Mack kissed his bloodhound's mangy head. "Besides you'd get sea sick."

"I'm pissed off too. I don't wanna ride through miles of swampland." Rufus glared at Jerry and scoffed. "Go tell Major Harrison you don't wanna take the officer's horses. I dare you."

Shane and the Crawford Boys joined a dozen rangers on the overland trip to New Orleans. Sandy swamps and water-logged marshes slowed the week-long ride. Provisions ran out twenty-miles east of Lake Charles, Louisiana. Surviving on wild rice and berries, soldiers foraged the land for food and supplies. Shane craved fresh meat. He thought about eating one of the officer's horses, but feared he'd be shot.

While the Ringo brothers tended to the horses at camp, Mack took his hound dog and tried his luck fishing in a watery marsh. Shane joined Sergeant Rufus Beavers on a hunt for wild game. Setting out on foot, he brought his old Springfield musket and borrowed a Mississippi rifle. The swampland appeared void of animals. An hour into the hunt, Mack cried out. His hound dog Lucky barked.

Fearing his friend was in trouble, Shane rushed down the waterway with Sergeant Beavers in tow. Four white-tailed deer grazed in a rotting rice field. A majestic twelve-point buck chewed on a rice patty. While Rufus froze in his tracks, Shane grabbed his Springfield and carefully primed the pan, so he wouldn't miss the seventy-five yard shot. The thought of a thick venison steak made his mouth water.

"Watch the master at work." Rufus took aim at a big

buck in the middle of the herd and scoffed. "Try your luck with one of those doe up front."

Shane knew Rufus wanted to crow about his kill back at camp. The meat would provide enough sustenance for the men to reach New Orleans. Obeying Sergeant Beaver's orders, he crouched into a shooter's stance and took aim at a thick-shouldered doe. His spur caught on a cypress knee-root. As he tumbled out of control and struck the ground, a gunshot rang out. His flint-lock musket misfired. The animals scattered.

"Damn fool, you made me miss!" Sergeant Beaver's cussed. "If you cost us dinner tonight, I'll flog your ass from here to the bivouac."

Pulling his custom .36 Special from his holster, Shane rolled onto his side and extended his revolver. The thick-shouldered doe darted in front of his sight. He squeezed off a round and hit the animal through her neck. As the deer crumbled to the ground, a second doe sprinted toward the bushes. Lying on his side, he grimaced and aimed at the startled animal. The spooked deer leaped over a green patch of rice paddies.

Waiting for the fleeing doe to cross into his sights, Shane fired. The deer's hind legs buckled. As she crawled forward, the majestic twelve-point buck sprinted for cover. Aiming for the heart, he squeezed off his third shot, striking the big buck through the chest. The animal tumbled head over hooves and collapsed onto the rice field.

Gun smoke lingered in the air. Shane spotted the wounded second doe limping toward the bayou. His thoughts drifted back to Kirby's final tortured moments. Cocking the hammer, he leveled his .36 and squeezed the trigger. The doe dropped and melted into the ground.

"Holy smokes, Frank. You shoot like Davey Crocket." Rufus approached with his Springfield. "Three kills in ten seconds—with a pistol." He rubbed his thumb along the cracked flint-lock. "Why'd you bring this old military musket? It's useless for a horse-mounted ranger."

"It belonged to my Pa. Thought I might need it." Shane glanced toward Heaven. "Reminds me of the good times when we use to hunt and fish along the Bosque."

"It ain't right what those Jayhawkers did to your father." Rufus returned the cumbersome four-foot musket and headed toward the bayou. "I didn't know Kirby well, but I know he loved you." His voice softened. "After you won the shooting contest, he bragged to everyone at the Gatesville Lodge."

Shane had believed he'd never be good enough for his father. His throat tightened and eyes welled up. Touched by Rufus's kind words, he looked away and didn't want his friend to see how much he missed Kirby.

"Nothing's been the same without him." Shane sniffed and fought back tears. "Pa didn't tell me he loved me, but he didn't need to. I knew he did." His voice choked. "We didn't go hungry when he was around."

"You'll be all right. Crawford Boys are gonna stick together." Rufus wrapped his arm around Shane's shoulders. "When we return from the war in Virginia, I'll join Mack Dodd and the Ringo brothers, and we'll hunt those bastards down."

"Thanks, but they're dangerous men. Hired assassins from Senator Lane's Brigade." Shane sloshed through ankle-deep water and headed toward the bayou. "You've got a wife with child on the way."

A loud splash echoed deeper in the swamp. Shane carried his Springfield to a tangled mass of reeds overlooking the water. He whispered the "Lord's Prayer" and tossed his father's musket into the bayou.

"Doubt many of Johnson's Jayhawkers are still alive." Rufus approached with his head down. "Colonel Irwin and his Missouri Ruffians killed Hog Johnson and most of his men outside Kansas City."

"When did the son-of-bitch die?" Shane felt cheated. "I never heard that. I've been praying for his well-being."

"Calm down, Frank. Thought you wanted Colonel Johnson dead." Rufus shook his head and stepped back. "It was Dodd's idea not to tell you. He was worried you'd turn tail and go back home when you found out."

"I ain't sorry the bastard's dead, but I wanted to kill him." Shane grabbed his Bowie and eyed the thick-shouldered doe. "Let's gut these deer."

The Ringo brothers rode out of the swamp and set out across the rice field. An eight-foot alligator dangled from Jerry's saddle. As they approached, Shane noticed Mack's knife stuck in the gator's skull.

"We've got dinner!" Jimmy offered up the toothy beast. "Dodd killed it with his bare hands."

"I ain't eating that nasty gator." Rufus cringed. "Get it outta here. Frank shot three deer."

Shane glared at Jerry. "Why in the hell didn't you tell me Colonel Johnson was dead?"

"I was gonna tell you when we got to New Orleans." Jerry pulled Mack's knife out of the gator. "Dodd threatened to whip anyone who told you."

"Where's that big fool? Upset because he killed a gator?" Shane worried about his animal-loving friend. "Somebody needs to tell him to quit pouting every time an animal dies."

"Dodd's sitting by himself in those tall reeds." Jerry pointed a quarter mile down the bayou. "Alligator ate his dog he found in Beaumont. Lucky wasn't lucky after all."

ɁɔɁ

New Orleans, Louisiana, September 1861:

Following a ten day trek through the swamps of Southern Louisiana, Shane and the Crawford Boys arrived in the Crescent City. Drunken Terry's Texas Rangers paraded around the French Quarter in fancy ten-gallon hats and flamboyant bear-skin chaps. Uncertain of his time left on earth, Shane reveled in the posh saloons and celebrated life like there was no tomorrow.

The Confederate War Office sent a telegram requesting the Texas Eighth Cavalry serve in Kentucky, instead of Virginia. While most of the men complained about the change in orders, Shane saw it as an opportunity. Kentucky bordered Missouri and the murderous Ivey twins resided in the bloody Border War state. Riding by train and horseback, the Texas Rangers arrived in Central Kentucky and bivouacked outside the town of Oakland at Camp Johnston. The men of Company A took on the name Prairie Rovers and launched covert operations against the enemy.

Soldier life was difficult and demanding. Desertions and floggings for insubordination occurred daily. Scouting behind enemy lines, one wrong turn or foolish decision meant instant death or capture. Shane lived in constant fear of attack. In six weeks of service to the Confederacy, he'd yet to kill an enemy soldier.

Incessant rain turned the road to Union-held Jamestown into mush. While the two warring nations fought to flip the neutral border state of Kentucky, Shane and the Crawford Boys served as scouts for Colonel Cleburne and the Fifteenth Arkansas. Serving as an advanced guard, Shane patrolled atop Vengeance, armed with his father's revolvers. Five US cavalrymen picketed the Jamestown Turnpike.

Mack Dodd reined up. "Yankee videttes—half mile ahead!"

Flanked by the Ringo brothers, Shane sensed his first kill and broke away from Major Harrison and the rest of the Prairie Rovers. As he charged down the rain-soaked road, Yankee cavalrymen wheeled around and raced back toward Jamestown. Gunfire rang out in the roadside woods. A bullet buzzed past by Shane's head. Mack and Sergeant Rufus Beavers joined the pursuit.

Shane pulled his Colt Special and spurred Vengeance after the fleeing Yankees. His powerful black Appaloosa splashed mud through the air. Death lingered at any moment. Racing up a long incline, he charged down the turn-pike and closed within fifty yards. Two Yankee videttes split off into the woods. Mack and Sergeant Beavers gave chase.

Gunfire echoed through the trees. Hunting down the three-remaining videttes, Shane pulled ahead of the Ringo brothers by twenty horse-lengths. Vengeance slobbered and panted. Shot after shot erupted in the roadside woods. A soldier cried out. Somebody's darling would not be coming home to their family.

The fleeing Yankees crested the hill and escaped down the other side. Shane sensed an ambush. Leaning forward in his saddle, he peered down the turnpike and spotted fifty US cavalrymen at the bottom of the hill. A bullet struck the ground between Vengeance's hooves. He wanted to stay and fight but the numbers weren't in his favor. Major Harrison and the rest of the Prairie Rovers were a mile away.

A volley of gunfire blasted from the squadron Yankee cavalry. Shane steadied Vengeance and returned fire. The Ringo brothers halted on his flanks and fired until their re-volvers clicked empty.

"There's too damn many!" Jerry motioned back down the turnpike. "Let's get the hell outta here. We gotta warn Harrison and rest of the men."

While the Ringo brothers fled back toward Company A, gun smoke drifted through the trees. Shane scanned the roadside woods for any sign of Mack and Rufus. Shots rang out in the rear. If they were dead, the Yankees could charge him at any moment.

Unable to claim his first kill, Shane raced down the turn-pike toward Harrison and the Prairie Rovers. As he rounded a bend, Sergeant Beavers and Mack rode out of the woods. Rufus look like he'd seen a ghost.

Slowing his horse to a trot, Shane wondered how his friends escaped unscathed. "Keep moving. There's fifty US Cavalry headed this way. Damn Yankees got away from me."

"Dodd killed one and I winged the other." Rufus shook his head. "I would've finished mine off, but Dodd shot him in the back of the head."

Mack had two confirmed kills. Stunned by the news, Shane felt like a failure. He wanted to be the first of his friends to kill the enemy.

"Good hunting, Dodd." Shane steered alongside his friend and attempted to hide his disappointment. "Two kills. Captain King will wanna make you a lieutenant."

"I know, right! I'm a pretty damn good shot." Mack's excited voice cracked. "Didn't think it would be so easy. I'm ready to kill some more of 'em sons-of-bitches."

Major Harrison led the squadron down the Jamestown Turnpike. Parading four-across in Poinsett formation, the intimidating Prairie Rovers stretched the width of the road for a quarter mile. Harrison raised his hand and halted the company of rangers. Shane loaded his custom .36. The Ringo brothers halted in front of the flag-bearing color guard.

"Sergeant Beavers, ride back to Colonel Cleburne and tell him we've encountered a large enemy force outside Jamestown." Harrison's voice cracked. "We're falling back."

"Major Harrison, sir." Rufus protested. "Men want to fight. Sir, General Hardee's orders were to attack the enemy."

"Our orders are to attack only if the enemy is not too great in force." Harrison turned in his saddle. "Squadron against squadron isn't my kind of odds. We're falling back."

"I ain't retreating, sir!" Mack brandished his pistol. "Rangers don't run from a fight. I didn't ride all the way to Kentucky to turn and run in the face of the enemy."

"You'll do as you're told, soldier!" Harrison's eyes narrowed. "That's an order."

Shane didn't want to be flogged for Mack's insubordination. As much as he wanted to stay and fight, Harrison was right. The odds weren't in their favor.

"Don't go around half-cocked, Dodd. You heard the major." Shane steered his horse toward Mack. "It's not a pitched fight."

"You're jealous I killed two Yankees before you got one." Mack scoffed. "We took the same oath. Kill or be killed. Never surrender."

Three Prairie Rovers broke formation. In a show of support, they surrounded Mack and looked ready to fight. A smug veteran ranger with a week's razor stubble made a fist.

"Dodd and me are following Major Harrison's orders." Shane wanted to slap the grin off the bastard's face. "If you know what's good for you, you will too."

"We ain't retreating, Major. You can't make us." The soldier pointed his middle-finger at Shane. "I didn't know Harrison had a Parlor Soldier."

Shane lost control of his emotions. Since his father's murder, he refused to be a silent victim. Yanking his reins, he rammed Vengeance into the cocky bastard's horse. The tan mustang whinnied. As the soldier tumbled forward, Shane grabbed his middle-finger and twisted until bone snapped. The ranger squeezed his hand and cried out.

"That's enough, soldiers!" Harrison charged forward. "We're pulling back to the Fifteenth Arkansas. That's an order." He waved his whip at Mack. "Disobey and you'll be shot."

CHAPTER 10

Mammoth Caves

Cave City, Kentucky, November, 1861:

W
ord of the Jamestown retreat spread through Company A like dysentery. While frustrated Prairie Rovers labeled Shane a toadying subordinate, Major Harrison was branded with the cowardly nickname Jimtown Major. Nobody dare say it to his face. Mack Dodd and Sergeant Beavers paraded around the bivouac like Roman Gladiators. As Mack proudly recounted his death-defying shootout, Shane secretly envied his friend. He coveted his first enemy kill.

The Texas Eighth Cavalry camped in the woods surrounding Cave City, Kentucky. The world-famous Mammoth Cave and Hotel was abandoned by war weary tourists months before. Low on war supplies, the Confederates commandeered the three-hundred mile cavern system to provide an endless supply of bat droppings to make saltpeter, a key ingredient in gunpowder. Assigned to a work detail, Shane shoveled guano in a dark torch-lit cavern, hundreds of feet below the ground. Highly-soluble ammonia gasses made his eyes water and left his clothes saturated with a foul stench.

"Master McLean—sir." A Negro cave guide with a thick

beard approached with a grease-oil lamp. "Enemy cavalry in the area. Major Harrison wants to see you, sir."

Shane stretched his aching back. "How many Yankees did the scouts report?"

"Don't know, sir." The slave aimed his lamp toward the surface. "I'm supposed to get you outta the cave, sir."

"Stop talking and get to work!" The duty sergeant approached through the dim light. "McLean, five lashes will shut that mouth of yours."

"Don't be mad, master. It be me, Mat Bransford, master." The slave held the light to his thick-beard. "I'm to bring Master McLean to the hotel porch. Major Harrison and Captain Wharton be waiting for him."

"Don't lie to me, boy." The duty sergeant waved his horsewhip. "I'll hurt you—real bad."

Shane wondered what the officer's wanted. Captain John A. Wharton led the rival Archer Grays of Company B. He was wealthy plantation owner from Brazoria County, Texas and his uppity men dressed like it. Outfitted with stylish grey uniforms, Wharton's Rangers were the best dressed company in the regiment and hated for it.

"Can't keep officers waiting, Sarge." Shane tossed his shovel into a wheelbarrow and followed Mat into the darkness. "See you up top."

The dark cavern walls widened to a hundred-feet. Wading through ankle deep water, Shane followed the Negro through a maze of hanging stalactites. Icicle-shaped stalagmites protruded from the mouth of the cave like razorback incisors. Water dripped onto his head. As he stared through the darkness, green eyes moved along the cave wall. Startled by the eerie eyes, he slipped on the damp limestone floor and grabbed the back of Mat's jacket. The silhouette of a demon-like creature crept behind an odd rock formation.

"This place gives me the creeps." Shane steadied his feet and attempted to calm his nerves. "You ever see bears in here?"

"Yessir, master. Bears and lots of wolves be getting in here." Mat shined his lamp at the cave floor. "Venomous spiders and snakes be scaring me more. Kill ya dead in minutes."

A tingling sensation ran down Shane's spine. He couldn't see his boots in the darkness and his socks were soaked. Slithering around a large limestone stalagmite, he reached into his pocket for a lucky charm. As he squeezed the wooden St. Patrick Shamrock in the palm of his hand, a ray of daylight crept through the mouth of the cave.

"I whittle these charms for friends." Shane handed his carved shamrock to the Negro guide. "They're good luck. My father claimed Saint Patrick chased all snakes and scorpions from Ireland."

"Thank you, master." Mat held the shamrock to the sky and nodded. "Master, nobody ever give me something so nice. You're good with the knife."

The rumble of horses echoed through the air. Shane said goodbye and headed toward the Mammoth Cave Hotel. Spotting a porch full of ranger officers, he hoped Mack and the Ringo brothers hadn't started trouble at camp. Horse hooves shook the ground. As he turned to investigate, a group of scouts raced toward him. Stepping out of the way, he recognized the lead rider and raised his hand to halt.

"Lieutenant Gordon." Shane waited for his friend to slow. "How many Yankees are there?"

"There's about a hundred US Cavalry camped in the wheat field." The lieutenant flared his nostrils in disgust. "Take a bath, McLean. You stink like a skunk's ass."

While the scouts headed toward the stables, Shane brushed his dingy frock coat and ran his sleeve under his nose. The stench of ammonia made him gag. Self-conscious about his foul odor, he approached a group of officers on the hotel veranda. Major Harrison stepped off the porch. As he extended his hand, Captain Wharton and his junior officers circled around.

"This is Private McLean." Harrison shook his hand and

nodded toward the officers. "He's one of the Crawford Boys I've been telling you about. Frank's the best shot in Company A and I'd dare say the entire Texas Rangers."

"I've got a special assignment for a couple of sharp-shooters." Wharton ran his eyes up and down Shane. "Captain King's been wasting you. He's got you wearing rags and shoveling shit in a cave. I treat my men like soldiers. My Archer Grays are the best trained, best fed, and best paid company in the regiment." He pulled out a wad of cash and peeled off ten dollars. "Here's back pay." He handed Shane the money and peeled off forty more. "Prove you're the best and join Company B. Let's kill Yankees together."

Since he'd signed up with the Harrison Rangers, Shane hadn't seen a cent. His only loyalty was to his friends. While in Houston, Harrison accepted a promotion to major and left Captain King in command. King ruled like a monarch with an iron first.

"Yessir." Shane accepted Wharton's bribe money with no regrets. "I've been itching to kill a few of them damn Yankees."

"That's what I wanted to hear, son." Wharton handed Major Harrison a bottle of whiskey and handful of cash. "Thomas, I've no interest in advancing my career in the military. Let me take our plan to attack the enemy's camp over to Colonel Terry. Ben and I are friends back home."

Harrison shook his head. "Colonel Terry left for a meeting with General Hardee in Bowling Green. Gonna have to get approval from Colonel Lubbock."

"That's even better. Lubbock's here in camp." Wharton snapped his head around and flared his nostrils. "Private McLean, I can smell you from here. Clean yourself up and wash those filthy clothes. I need to be escorted to Lubbock's tent." His face tightened. "Half of that money's for Jerry Ringo. Go get him. Be outside my tent in twenty minutes."

Shane saluted. "Yessir."

The Terry's Texas Ranger bivouac stretched a half mile,

covering a lush field of bluegrass while extending into the rocky hillside woods.

Shane knew better than to make Wharton wait and ran toward the Green River. Commandeering a bar of lye soap, he kicked off his worn out boots and jumped in fully-clothed. As he scrubbed his body and clothes, the cold November water stole his breath.

Shane shared a CSA-issued dog tent with Jerry Ringo. Dodging tree branches and waist-high rocks, he drip-dried on the way to camp. As he passed through two rival companies of rangers, soldiers smoked pipes around campfires and cleaned their weapons. Taking a short cut, he darted behind a large cedar bush and ran into a broad-shouldered ranger, urinating with his head down. The grizzled veteran had an eye patch on his scarred face.

"Watch where you're going, boy!" The intimidating ranger shook the urine off his hand. "Devil takes the hindmost."

With the clock in his head ticking down, Shane ignored the soldier's slight and rushed through the woods. Captain Wharton's wasn't the type of officer to keep waiting. As Shane arrived at the hillside bivouac of Company A, Jerry rested on his stomach inside their shared dog tent. His wool-socked feet dangled outside.

"Get your lazy ass up!" Shane wiggled Jerry's toe through a hole in his sock. "Captain wants us to escort him over to Colonel Lubbock."

"Don't touch me." Jerry jerked his foot inside the tent. "Captain King can kiss my ass. I hate that bastard."

"We ain't taking orders from King no more." Shane waved the fifty dollar wad of cash in front of his face. "Starting tomorrow we're serving with Captain Wharton in Company B."

"Really?" Jerry sat up. "What's that uppity bastard want with us?"

"Wharton's paying us to join his Archer Grays." Shane dropped a ten dollar note into the tent and pocketed the rest of the money. "Get a move on it. I don't want to keep him waiting."

"Holy molly, ten whole dollars." Jerry's eyes widened. "I ain't seen this much money since you won the shooting contest in Waco." He popped his head outside and grinned like a royal prince. "Bring my boots?"

"I ain't your daddy." Shane spotted a pair of worn out Jefferson boots covered in the mud. "Wharton's got a special duty for us. We're finally gonna kill Yankees." He tossed the grimy boots into the tent. "This what you're looking for?"

"Damn it, Frank! You play around too much." Jerry flicked a smudge of mud off his chest. "You got dirt on my jacket. I can't meet Captain Wharton looking like this."

"You look like a soldier. Wharton won't even notice." Shane took a jab at his friend. "An ugly damn soldier."

"Look who's talking. You look like a vagabond tramp who bathes in the river." Jerry scoffed. "You're pants are too small, you've got holes in the knees, and you're wearing the same yellow-stained pitted up shirt you bought in Houston. But that ain't the worst of it." He paused and shook his head. "I probably shouldn't tell you this, but you're a damn laughing-stock. Nobody wants to hear your stories about Mary Kelly." His tone sharpened. "She doesn't love you and never will. Everyone knows it, but you."

"You're wrong!" Shane fought the urge to punch his friend. "I'm not gonna be late listening to your cock and bull stories."

"Don't be cross at me. You cast the first stone." Jerry grabbed his boot and scoffed. "I said what everyone else is afraid to say."

"You don't know what you're talking about." Shane turned and headed downhill. "I'm leaving. You can be late and explain to Captain Wharton why you made him wait."

Shane ignored his rude friend and slipped into the woods. Attempting to walk and dress, Jerry hopped on one foot and struggled to keep up. As he lost his balance and stumbled to the ground, Shane dipped beneath a leafy branch.

Captain Wharton and his Archer Grays bivouacked in the field of bluegrass. Winding through the maze of underbrush, Shane spotted three rangers tossing knifes at the face of a log. Jerry rushed to Shane's side. A dozen men circled around and bet on a winner.

"That's Company F's bivouac. Don't go down there." Jerry's voice deepened. "Lone Star Rangers are a bunch of cocksure assholes."

Shane intended to apologize for storming off. As he followed Jerry down the hillside, the opportunity never materialized. Ducking under a low hanging branch, he stepped out of the woods and scanned the rows of white A-frame tents. Soldiers cooked on campfires and clothes hung on rope lines. A large, square officer tent overlooked a blazing bonfire.

"This way, Ringo. Captain Wharton's a generous man." Shane planned to ask the friendly captain if Jimmy and Mack Dodd could also join Company B. "You'll like Wharton a lot more than Captain King."

Jerry nodded. "He pays good."

Shane recognized a junior officer standing guard outside Wharton's tent. As he approached, two Negros servants brushed a spare captain's uniform on a hanger. The junior officer guard poked his head inside and promptly returned to his post. The tent flap swung open.

"Stand at attention!" Wharton stepped outside and shook his head. "Salute when you meet an officer. You men look like the devil." His eyes narrowed. "I don't tolerate insubordination in my ranks."

Shane threw back his shoulders and snapped his hand to salute. His heart raced. A Negro servant dropped his brush and picked up a knee-high cavalry boot. As he spit-shined the fine leather top, Jerry looked like he'd seen a ghost.

"Don't eyeball me, Private." Wharton inspected a tear in Shane's frock coat. "Take pride in your dress even if you've paid for your clothes." He pushed a finger through a hole in Jerry's collar. "Get a housewife from supply and stitch this up. If you can't sew, learn how. I don't tolerate the sin of sloth." His face tightened. "I'm not your momma, soldier. She's in Texas.

Jerry's mother was dead. Stunned by the captain's change in demeanor, Shane stood firm and felt obliged to speak up. Wharton was more of a tyrant than Captain King.

"Wipe that smirk off your face." Wharton stood nose to nose with Jerry. "I'm forming a squadron of Elite Escorts to serve as my personal scouts. You ever kill a man, watch him bleed out in front of you?" His tone sharpened. "You ever seen the face of death? Bodies contorted in every conceivable position? War means fighting, and fighting means killing."

"Yessir, I've seen men shot down all around." Shane tugged on the black neckerchief hiding his disfigured neck. "My father was murdered in front of me by Unionist Jayhawkers." He revealed the fleshy inch-wide scar hidden underneath. "I ain't afraid of dying nor killing the enemy."

"That's what I wanted to hear, Ranger." Wharton stepped back. "Major Harrison had kind words about your father. Sorry for your loss." He motioned to his junior officer. "Corporal Mimms, take these soldiers to the supply wagon. Fit 'em with new uniforms, cavalry boots, and anything else they deem necessary. We're off to see the colonel." His eyes focused on Shane's scarred neck. "Give Frank use of my new Henry Rifle. I'd like to see what he can do with a repeater."

While dusk settled on Eighth Texas cavalry bivouac, Shane and Jerry escorted Captain Wharton through the rows of white tents. Dressed in a pristine jean-wool uniform and stylish knee-high cavalry boots, he felt like a million bucks. As he paraded Wharton across the encampment, rangers halted their activities and stood in salute. A grease oil lantern hung outside a Colonel Lubbock's tent.

"Wait here until I call for you." Wharton stopped outside

the square tent. "The colonel's been sick. He may not be up for a meeting."

Two saber-wielding guards stood posted along the doorway. While Wharton stepped inside, Shane couldn't believe his good fortune. Admiring his stylish shell jacket, he couldn't wait to ride into Cave City and make a photo to send to his mother and Mary Kelly.

"Colonel Lubbock, sir. My men are in need of a fight." Wharton's deep voice reverberated through the canvas tent. "There's too much tension around camp. We need to attack the enemy. Sir, I'd sure like a crack at that Yankee Cavalry."

"I'll tell you the same thing I told the other officers." Lubbock covered his mouth with a handkerchief and coughed. "Soldiers need a swift kick in the ass, more drill and inspection."

"Yessir. But they'll also need combat experience. General Sherman's mustering a large army in Louisville." Wharton pleaded. "When the Yankees march south, I don't wanna put untested soldiers up against superior numbers."

"You'll do as you're ordered, Captain. We're the righteous in this war. I've got confidence in my rangers. They'll fight to the death." Lubbock paused. "What's this plan you've concocted with Major Harrison and why isn't he here to explain it?"

"Sir, I've already consulted Major Harrison. He's provided me with two sharpshooters to burrow in trees and pick-off their officers," Wharton said. "Yankee soldiers will be running around, looking for someone to give orders."

Waiting outside Lubbock's tent, Shane didn't like the plan. His special duty sounded like a suicide mission. At seventeen, he wasn't ready to die for God and country.

"Cut the head off the snake. It's underhanded, but I like it." Lubbock cleared his throat. "How'd you get these men to volunteer for such a dangerous mission?"

"They're right outside, sir. I took 'em off work detail and gave 'em uniforms." Wharton's tone sharpened. "Major

Harrison assured me they're both loyal and dedicated to the Southern cause. One of the men had a father murdered by Jayhawkers. He's on the warpath. I'm looking forward to giving him my rifle and turning him loose on the enemy."

Lubbock demanded. "Bring these men inside."

"Yessir." Wharton stepped outside. "Ringo, McLean, get your asses in here."

Shane led Jerry inside. Having been berated earlier by Wharton for not saluting, he stopped in front of Colonel Lubbock and immediately raised his hand to his head. As he stood at attention, Lubbock glared across a flimsy table and wiped his nose with a linen handkerchief. A thick goatee covered his mouth and chin.

"Rest, Rangers." Lubbock folded his handkerchief. "State your name and where you're from?"

"Frank McLean, sir." Shane exuded confidence. "I'm from Crawford in McLennan County."

"You're Kirby McLean's boy, aren't you? I was in Waco last year, when you outshot Colonel Dalryrmple's Rangers." Lubbock shrugged. "Does Kirby know you're up here fighting?"

"Sir, my father was murdered by Union scum. That's why I joined the rangers." Shane spoke in a calm deliberate tone. "I intend to take as many souls as the Lord sends my way."

"I applaud your convictions. Let's hope our Lord Jesus Christ's in a vengeful mood." Lubbock glanced at Jerry. "Name and town, soldier."

"Jerry Ringo, sir." He mumbled. "I'm from Crawford too."

"Speak up, soldier." Lubbock leaned forward. "This mission requires your dedication and sacrifice. Death's a shot away. Do you trust Frank with your life?"

"Yessir." Jerry nodded. "He's the best shot I've ever seen. I trust him like a brother."

"When bullets start to fly, you'll need faith in each other." Lubbock tugged at his whiskers. "Gotta trust the man fighting next to you will do his job, otherwise you'll both end up dead."

Shane had a bad feeling in his stomach. Compelled by duty and honor, he wanted to refuse the mission but feared being labeled a coward. He'd come a thousand miles to kill the enemy and return home a war hero like his father.

"Captain Wharton, let's use your battle plan. We need to convince General Sherman and the Yankees that our forces in Kentucky are strong." Lubbock stood from behind the flimsy table. "Send these two killers out in the morning. I'll lead Company A from the east, we'll catch the enemy in crossfire."

"But sir, you've been ill." Wharton cocked his head. "Are you up for an attack?"

"Don't be a glory hog." Lubbock saluted. "You're dismissed, Captain."

Shane stepped forward. "Colonel Lubbock, sir. How'd you know my father?"

"I fought with Kirby back in the Texas Revolution and was at Cole's Store when he made General Houston beg for his life." Lubbock coughed into his hand. Your father was a brave and principled man." Lubbock paused to wipe his nose on his sleeve. "Get a good night's rest. We've got a squadron of Yankee cavalry to vanquish."

"Yessir." Shane saluted and stepped outside.

Campfires illuminated the night sky. Struggling to find his bearings, Shane breathed in the smoky air and feared he could be dead in twelve hours. The special duty weighed heavily on his mind.

"Watch your step." Jerry headed into the darkness. "Dodd's cooking his spicy chili tonight. Let's get to camp before it's gone."

While a breeze swept the sweet smell of sizzling meat through the bivouac, Shane followed his nose and led Jerry past a group of festive soldiers. His stomach growled for a cup of spicy chili. Mack Dodd cooked better than most women. During the journey from Houston to New Orleans, he came across a beautiful island plantation in the swamps of Iberia Parish Louisiana. Petite Anse Isle sat on a salt dome surrounded by fields of cayenne peppers and man-eating alligators. The plantation cook made hot sauce so good, a few drops could season an entire pot of chili.

Winding through rows of tents, Shane glanced at the moon and caught his boot on a staked picket pin. His barbed spur snapped the rope. As he stumbled forward, the center pole collapsed.

"Goddammit!" an angry voice shouted from under the canvas. "I'm gonna kill somebody."

Shane laughed to himself and rushed toward the hillside. Nothing looked familiar in the dark woods. Red and yellow flames flickered a hundred yards ahead.

"Ringo, stick close to me. Think our camp's over there." Shane glanced over his shoulder but couldn't see his friend. "Jerry, get up here."

Nobody replied. Passing beneath the canopy of a tree, Shane heard laughter from soldiers seated around a campfire. A sap-covered branch brushed against his cheek and scratched his eye. The pain stung like a bee. As he cussed and blinked, tears welled and his temper raged.

Intending to rip down the branch, Shane grabbed the leafy limb with both hands. As he twisted the branch and shook the tree, a creepy sensation tickled his skin. Pain shot through his index finger. Fearing he'd been bitten, he released the tree and clenched his throbbing hand. A brown spider crawled between his knuckles. While the branch swung backward, he shook the eight-legged arachnid to the ground.

"Goddammit!" Jerry's angry voice rang out. "You hit me in the balls."

"Sorry, didn't know you were behind me." Shane rushed to help his friend. "Something bit me on the finger—think it's a wolf spider."

Grabbing his groin, Jerry dropped to a knee and mumbled. "Good. I hope it kills you."

"I said I'm sorry, Ringo." Shane turned to leave. "Don't have to be such a baby about it."

Clouds rolled in and blocked the moonlight. While red hot ambers floated into the night sky, Shane headed toward the campfire. A dozen rangers sat on logs circled around the flames. Tired and irritable, he searched for a familiar face but didn't recognize anyone. Smoke burned his eyes and flared his nostrils. As he approached, the rangers carefree laughter ceased. An eerie silence lingered.

"I smell horseshit!" A pint-sized ranger eyed Shane's approach. "Lookie here, boys, we got us one of Wharton's Elite Escorts."

Shane wasn't in the mood to argue. "Where's Company A?"

"Where're your manners, pretty boy?" The stocky-little soldier climbed to his feet. "All you high-falutin Company B bastards think you can waltz into another man's camp." His voice turned serious. "There's twelve of us and only one of you."

Shane intended to get directions. "You gonna tell me where Company A is, or not?"

"This is Company F, boy." The stocky soldier scoffed. "Lone Star Rangers don't give a *damn* about Captain Wharton or his parlor boy soldiers."

"Are you here to arrest somebody?" a voice cackled from across the campfire. "Virgil and me got friends from Waco serving in Company A."

Shane sensed movement. Needing to react, he grabbed Virgil's neck and placed his Bowie to his jugular. The stocky-little ranger stiffened.

Jerry Ringo stepped into the light with a pistol in each hand. As he cocked the hammer of his gun, rangers around the campfire froze. Shane fought the urge to slit Virgil's throat. Assigned to a suicide mission in the morning, he had little to lose and pressed down on his Bowie. The eighteen-inch blade sliced into his skin.

"Hold it!" Jerry stepped forward and fanned out his

guns. "Next man that moves gets it between the eyes."

Virgil trembled against Shane's knife. As he closed his eyes and swallowed, his boney Adam's apple bobbed. Blood dripped along the razor-sharp blade.

"Wanna live or die?" Shane squeezed his fingers into Virgil's throat. "Where's Company A?"

Virgil choked and pointed deeper into the woods. "Hundred yards east, sir."

෴

Prairie Rovers Camp, Edmonson County, Kentucky, November, 1861:

The dispute ended without a loss of life. Fearing reprisal from the Lone Star Rangers, Shane and Jerry needed a hostage and dragged Virgil into the woods. The dark underbrush provided ample cover for a getaway. As the stocky-little ranger stumbled, Shane glanced to see if they'd been followed. The spicy scent of vinegar and boiled red hot peppers filled the air.

"Smell that chili cooking?" Shane sized up Virgil's chin. "Take a whiff."

As the cocky little man lifted his nose, Shane rammed his fist into Virgil's jaw and tossed his body into the bushes. Jerry led the way to camp. A twenty-five-pound Dutch oven hung on a tripod over the flames. While half a dozen Prairie Rovers slurped cups of chili, Mack Dodd stirred the pot with a cast-iron ladle.

"I'll get your cup and spoon." Jerry headed toward their shared tent. "Make sure Dodd doesn't eat it all."

Officers received the best cuts of meat. Mack offered to cook, so he could steal a few choice pieces for himself. He picked over the remains of slaughtered animals like a surgeon. Nothing went to waste. Deer heads, hooves, bones, hearts, intestines, and even brains were boiled into his chili.

"Where have you been, Frank?" Sergeant Rufus Beavers raised a spoon in salute. "Dodd's outdone himself. This is the best chili I've ever tasted."

Shane ignored the question. He didn't want to tell his friends he'd switched to Wharton's Company B. If he survived the mission, they would figure it out on their own.

"Take a sip of the broth." Mack extended a ladle of boiling chili. "Where did you get that fancy uniform?"

Looking to change the subject, Shane sipped the chili and nodded. "It's tasty. Hope Mary can cook this good." He spotted an eyeball floating in the ladle and sighed. "What's this?"

"Damn it!" Mack's face tightened. "I was saving that for Ringo."

"Put it in Jerry's chili." Jimmy Ringo approached with a couple of soldiers. "He'll flip out mad."

Sergeant Beavers scrapped the bottom of his chili with a spoon. "Dodd might be the better cook, but I'd bet Mary's the better kisser."

Shane nodded his approval. "Yessir."

"I don't know about that." Jimmy scoffed. "I overheard Dodd's horse bragging to the other mares at the stables that he's got soft lips. Dodd's right popular with farm animals."

"Sheep are scared of him," a big-nosed soldier joked. "When Dodd comes to town, they all run away."

"Ha. Ha." Mack's smile disappeared. "Not funny!" He waved his sledgehammer-sized fist. "Shut your mouth, or I'll cock your hat and straighten that big nose of yours."

Jerry approached the campfire in his new uniform. As he peered inside the Dutch oven, Mack dipped his ladle and covered the eyeball in boiling chili. Shane braced for a fight and looked to diffuse the situation. Mack had been stealing food for weeks, but nobody dared confront him. He was the biggest, toughest, and meanest son-of-a-bitch in the company, maybe the entire regiment.

Mack lifted the cast-iron scoop out of the chili. "I've been saving this special for you."

Jerry extended his cup. "Better not be watered down."

"Let me flavor it for you." Mack farted on the ladle and laughed. "Eat up, peckerwood."

Jerry squared his shoulder to fight. "Damn lard ass!"

"Let it be. It's just a joke." Jimmy grabbed his brother's arm. "Dodd's gonna kill you."

"I'll put a damn cap in his big ass!" Jerry ripped his arm free. "My number is up tomorrow, so I really don't give a damn."

"Hey, Ringo!" Mack tossed the ladle of boiling chili in Jerry's face. "Have seconds, pie eater."

Scalding juice dripped from Jerry's chin. As he doubled over in pain, the eyeball rolled down his chest and tumbled to the ground. Mack howled with laughter.

"That's enough, Dodd." Shane stepped between his friends. "Don't waste good food."

Mack dipped his ladle back into the pot. As he pretended to toss the boiling chili, Jerry ducked down. Stopping in his upswing, Mack poured the contents down his throat and belched. Jerry charged forward. Fearing they'd all face company discipline, Shane held Ringo back.

"Let him go, Frank." Mack raised his leg and farted. "Maybe I won't spit in your chili next time."

"You're demented! Better keep your eyes peeled to-night." Jerry backed off and turned to leave. "I'm gonna slit your damn throat."

While Jimmy escorted his angry brother away, Shane worried about Mack's safety. Jerry didn't mince words. If he said he'd slit your throat, he meant it.

While the camaraderie around the campfire died down around midnight, Shane helped Mack washed the Dutch oven and headed off to bed. He hoped the bad blood between his friends had subsided and climbed into his tent. As he nudged Jerry to the side and spread out on his bed roll, a cool breeze chilled his body. He gazed at the stars and dozed off to sleep.

"Wake up, Frank! Wake up." Jerry's panicked voice rang out. "Wake up."

Shane blinked. A hand shook his shoulder. Horrifying visions of Sergeant Lauderdale, Red, and the Ivey brothers lingered in his mind. Yanked forward and backward, he grabbed his Bowie and rolled onto his side.

"Put the knife away. You're having a nightmare." Jerry fell back onto his side of the tent. "You were tossing around and cussing in your sleep, calling out for your pa."

A hoot owl sounded a loud ominous *oo-awe*. Shane hadn't thought about his father in days but constant nightmares were an inescapable reality. He sat up and struggled to catch his breath. His spider bite throbbed.

"Sorry, I'll try not to wake you." Shane scratched his swollen finger and rolled over. "That goddamn special duty's got us both on edge."

"Something's wrong with you, Frank. Those ain't normal dreams." Jerry's voice cracked. "You've got the Devil inside. Better see Parson Bunting in the morning."

"I don't need no damn preacher." Shane stared off into the woods. "Ain't nothing in me but the good Lord's blessing."

Mack's angry voice shouted from a neighboring tent. "Shut the hell up! I'm trying to sleep."

Revelry trumpeted from the company bugler. Exhausted and homesick, Shane hadn't slept an hour. His father's killing played itself over and over in his head. He wished he could forget that awful day. But he'd never forgive the men responsible. The simple life of the Shamrock Ranch seemed a lifetime ago.

"We've got a long day, Ringo." Shane hoped it wouldn't be his last. "Let's get breakfast. I wanna find that Union bivouac before the shooting starts."

A serving line formed alongside the charred remains of last night's campfire. Shane grabbed two deer sausages, a buttermilk biscuit, and a cup full of grits. The home-cooked meal soothed his nervous stomach. As he joined the Ringo brothers around a half-burned log, Captain King made his way through camp. The tyrannical leader of Company A sipped coffee and locked eyes with Shane.

"Private McLean, a little bird told me you got into a scrap last night." King frowned tossed his coffee on the ground. "Damn bitter coffee." His eyes narrowed. "Are you some kind of hard case?" Rangers over in Company F said you gave Virgil Yarborough quite a scare—made him piss his pants."

Shane didn't trust the captain and kept his mouth shut. He feared anything he said would be twisted and used against him. He'd rather take his chances at ranger tribunal with Colonel Lubbock sitting in judgment.

"Frank and me got lost last night and stumbled into Company F." Jerry shrugged. "Virgil got cross with us, so Frank got a little rough with him."

"You boys can plan on shoveling bat shit in caves...all day." King scoffed. "Virgil showed up at Doc Weston's tent with a three-inch gash across his throat. Took a dozen stitches to sew up his neck." He grabbed Shane's wrist and examined his spider bite. "By the look your hand and bloodshot eye, I'd say Virgil did a number on you."

"Captain King, sir." A courier from Wharton's Elite Escort approached with a Henry repeating rifle. "Privates Ringo and McLean are to start reconnaissance for Colonel Lubbock immediately."

"What are you two doing talking to the colonel?" King shook his head. "Lubbock's only spoken to me a couple of times."

Jerry threw back his shoulders. "Colonel Lubbock asked to speak with us."

"Are you gonna arrest us, or let us get on with Lubbock's scout?" Shane didn't plan on returning to Company A. "I don't give a damn."

CHAPTER 11

Rebel Yell

Edmonson County, Kentucky, November, 1861:

Shane and Jerry rode north in search of sharpshooter positions to attack the Union encampment. A brisk autumn wind cut through his new jean-wool jacket trimmed in red-braiding, and a sense of hopelessness set in. He thought about skipping his special duty and heading for Missouri to hunt down his father's killers but feared being labeled a deserter. War would be over by spring planting. As he passed by the Mammoth Cave, Mat Bransford ran from behind a tree and waved his arms. The Negro cave guide had his wooden Shamrock charm tied around his neck.

"Master McLean, 'em Yankees you be asking about yesterday is five miles yonder in a field." Mat pointed down the railroad tracks. "If ya'll need a place to hole up, there's a cave south of the Yankees' camp." His teeth chattered from the cold. "It's one way in and one way out."

Shane tipped his new slouch hat and his hair fell past his shoulders. "Like your charm necklace, Mat."

"Yessir, master." The slave kissed his wooden Shamrock. "I ain't seen no snakes today, master."

"That's because they're all underground trying to stay

warm." Jerry rubbed his gloved hands together. "Only Yankees live in this cold weather. I'd still be farming back home in Texas."

The rolling hills of Kentucky sustained vast forests of oak, maple, and birch trees. Splashed with blazing reds and muted yellows, the lines and contours of the fall foliage looked like an Impressionist painting by Monet or Renoir. Shane wanted to sight in Captain Wharton's repeating rifle, but the covert mission required silence. As he steered Vengeance toward the Yankee encampment, a herd of white-tailed deer sipped from a spring. His mouth watered for fresh venison.

"Is that the cave the slave was talking about?" Jerry pointed to a shrub covered opening at the base of a hill. "I can't feel my toes. Do we have time to go inside and warm up?"

Shane shook his head. He wanted out of the cold but needed to find a position to fire on the Union camp. Colonel Lubbock and Captain Wharton planned to arrive within the hour. As he glanced down the fifty-yard gully leading to the cave entrance, an idea popped into his head.

Shane reined up. "Stay here with the horses. I'm gonna look inside."

"You ain't the boss of me. I'm going inside with you." Jerry's warm breath condensed into steam. "I'm freezing to death out here."

A gust of cold air blew from the north. Shane led Jerry through the five-foot entrance and lost traction on the damp limestone floor. Slipping and tumbling backward, he landed in a pool of icy groundwater and grabbed his tailbone. Pain radiated through his aching ass.

"Goddammit!" Shane rolled onto his side. "Watch out, Ringo. Damn rocks are slick as butter."

"Want me to fetch Doc Westin?" Jerry treaded lightly through the entrance and joked. "It's open season on you."

Shane climbed to his feet and shook his trousers. "My pants are soaked."

Sunlight crept fifty-feet into the cave. While the constant fifty-four-degree temperature warmed his bones, Shane descended into the bowels of the cavern and looked for a place to hole up. The walls widened and icicle-shaped stalactites hung from the ceiling. A musty odor filled the air.

"This place gives me the creeps. Don't try and spook me." Jerry leaned against a stalagmite pillar. "Smells like a root cellar."

Hurrying toward the rear, Shane slipped behind a large boulder and waved his arm. "Ringo, can you see me?"

"I can't see nothing. It's pitch black back there." Jerry pulled his pistol and made his way through the cavern. "I swear, Frank. If you jump out at me, I'll shoot you."

"Hush your mouth, Ringo! You'll wake one of these black bears." Shane halfheartedly joked. "Hear 'em snoring?"

"There ain't no bears back in here—is there?" Jerry backtracked toward the exit. "Let's get the hell outta here."

Leery of enemy pickets, Shane and Jerry stayed in the thicket as they rode north in search of the Yankee encampment. His hands and feet ached from the cold. Approaching a large red oak, he tracked the ground for fresh boot-prints and scanned the area for sharpshooters. The sound of Yankee officer barking orders to his men reverberated through the trees. Spotting blue uniforms in a decaying wheat field, Shane rushed his finger to his mouth.

"I can see 'em bastards through the bushes." Shane leaned forward and strained to see. "Green eyed monsters."

"What do they look like?" Jerry stood in his stirrups. "Are they mean looking? Think we can whip 'em?"

"I'm gonna climb the tree and get a better look." Shane handed his reins to Jerry. "Tie off the horses and bring the rifles."

The US Cavalry camp loomed a fifty yards away. Shane counted five rows of pup tents and dozens of soldiers. As he climber higher, the Yankees odd vernacular grew clearer. A group of enemy officers sat around a campfire. The devils-in-blue smoked cigars, sipped coffee, and engaged in light-hearted conversation. Two Parrot Rifles guarded a trampled path through the woods. The ten-pound artillery cannons protected the camp's perimeter and a row of saddled horses.

Perched above the enemy camp, Shane had never killed a man but that was going to change. His thoughts drifted to vengeance. The unsuspecting officers would pay for what those Unionist Jayhawkers did to his father. While he waited for Colonel Lubbock and the rangers to arrive, the crack of Sergeant Lauderdale's whip echoed in his head. He imagined the Ivey twins' humiliating laughter and relived the bone-jarring pain of Red's notched shillelagh. The sound of a mockingbird chirped.

"McLean! I found you." Sergeant Rufus Beaver's voice echoed into the tree canopy. "You're easier to track than a three-legged man."

Shane grabbed a branch and dropped to the ground. "Shhh. Yankees are fifty yards away. You trying to get us killed?"

"I chirped like a mockingbird to get your attention, but you were asleep in the tree." Rufus steadied his horse. "You left tracks plum across the county. What're you and Ringo doing in that cave?"

"We was looking for a place to hole up." Jerry approached with Wharton's fifteen-shot Henry rifles. "We wanted you to find us, old man."

"Balderdash! You're mad I found y'all." Rufus shook his head. "I'm the best tracker in Central Texas."

Shane released the lever lock. "Did you come to help us pick-off the Yankee officers?"

"Hell, no! I ain't as foolish as you young bucks," Rufus shrugged. "Captain King sent me to tell you don't start shooting." His voice turned to disgust. "Colonel Lubbock ain't coming. He's sick."

Shane felt duped. "Where's Captain Wharton and Major Harrison? This was their idea."

"Wharton and the Archer Grays are thirty minutes away,

but the Jimtown Major's already here." Rufus pointed over
his shoulder. "He's been sipping his medicine all morning
and itching for a fight."

Shane turned to climb back up his tree. "Wharton better
get here, before Harrison gets so drunk he charges the enemy all by himself."

Fifty Yankees guarded the encampment. While Union
patrols roamed the countryside, Shane and Jerry burrowed
in neighboring trees and waited on Captain Wharton's arrival. Equipped with his eighteen-inch Bowie, two pistols,
and a repeating Henry rifle, Shane kept surveillance on the
enemy officers. Vivid memories of his father's last breath
churned in his head like a powerful locomotive. His inner
demons awakened. Burrowing in the tree, he squeezed his
sixteen-shot Henry rifle and fought the urge to scream. A
Yankee Major placed a cigar in his mouth and approached
the campfire.

Sunlight reflected off Jerry's rifle. The Yankee Major
pointed toward his position. Forced to act, Shane aimed his
gun at the officer and squeezed the trigger. As the stock of
his rifle kicked into his shoulder, the major grabbed his
chest and tumbled into the fire.

Shane snatched an overhead branch and steadied himself. Watching the enemy burn in the flames, he ejected the
.44 caliber cartridge from the chamber and looked toward
Heaven. His first kill left him empty. No regret. No remorse. That bastard had it coming.

Cocking down on his lever action rifle, Shane whispered.
"That's one for you, Pa."

While soldiers ducked behind tents and dove for the
ground, Jerry fired a shot from his tree. Shane searched for
a colonel or general to kill. A young lieutenant stepped into
his V-notch sight. As he shot the clean-shaven officer
through the chest, gun smoke lingered in the air compromis-
ing his position.

Yankee cavalrymen grabbed their weapons and rushed
toward their horses. Five artillerymen wheeled a Parrot Ri-

fle around. Staring through his sights, Shane hunted for valuable enemy officers like a hawk circling prey. Soldiers rushed to form a firing line on the edge of camp.

A Yankee captain in a campaign hat crouched behind a chair. As he sipped coffee, two junior officers dutifully shielded his backside. Leveling his sights on the captain's yellow-tasseled hatband, Shane wrapped his finger around the trigger and squeezed. Blood splattered high into the air. The headshot instantly killed the captain. His lifeless body slumped to the ground. His stunned subordinates stepped back and wiped off chunks of skull and brains. "To Assemble" trumpeted from the bugler.

Yankee cavalrymen gathered in the rear. Whiles the enemy mounted their horse, Jerry Ringo fired his second shot. An Artillery lieutenant approached the Parrot Rifle with his saber pointed in Shane's direction. Five artillerymen worked to load the cannon. As they stepped back, a bone-rattling boom shook the ground.

Gun smoke drifted across the field. The ten-pound cannon ball shot through the tree canopy. Shane looked for Major Harrison and the main ranger attack. Where the hell were Captain Wharton and the Archer Grays? They could've walked here by now.

The Artillery lieutenant charged through a cloud of gun smoke with his saber raised. As he turned to direct fire, Shane shot the bastard through the cheek. The .44 caliber bullet ripped his skull open like a snapped sausage.

Jerry shouted from the neighboring tree. "Damn, Frank! You killed him good."

Cocking his lever-action handle, Shane lowered his rifle and glimpsed the bloody remains. The gory picture of death chilled his bones. In thirty seconds time, he'd claimed four souls, stealing the officers from their family and friends. His mother Margaret could never know what he'd done.

A second blast boomed from the cannon. As the high-pitched shriek of the incoming missile grew louder, Shane squeezed his rifle barrel and braced for impact. The smoldering barrel burned his fingers and slipped from his grasp. While Wharton's gun fell to the ground, a ten-pound cannon ball struck the trunk of his tree.

Stunned by the shocking reverberation, Shane lost balance and tumbled out of the tree. His head smacked a branch. Flipping head over heels, he crashed to the ground like a ragdoll and landed face down in a puddle of mud. A volley of musketry ripped through the woods.

"Help me, Frank! I'm stuck." Jerry's panicked voice rang out. "Yankees are coming."

Shane spit a mouthful of blood. While leaves and splintered branches rained from the canopy, Jerry hung upside down fifteen-feet in the air. The leg of his pants caught on a tree branch.

Jerry cried out. "Hurry, Frank!"

Shane grabbed his Bowie. Leaping to his feet, he placed the eighteen-inch blade in his mouth and scaled the trunk of Jerry's tree. Two dozen Yankee cavalrymen moved into formation. As he cut his friend's pant leg free, "To Charge" trumpeted from the bugler. Jerry fell through the branches and slammed against the ground.

"Frank, I've been shot." Jerry wiped his blood soaked head. "I can't see."

While the squadron of Yankee cavalrymen charged across the wheat field, Shane jumped out of the tree and noticed a three-inch gash in Jerry's hairline. Blood drained down his forehead.

"Get up." Shane yanked his friend off the ground. "If the damned Blue Bellies catch us, they'll kill us."

Jerry staggered forward. "Help me to my horse. I'm dizzy."

"Goddammit, Ringo! They're gonna cut us to bits." Shane tore a piece of his shirt. "Hold this on your head and get moving." He grabbed Jerry by the seat of his pants and dragged him to the horses. "We've gotta get to the cave."

A bullet whizzed past Shane's head. He couldn't fend off two-dozen enemy soldiers. Not by himself.

An ear-splitting rebel yell reverberated through the field like a pack of wild dogs. "Yeee...hawww!"

Major Harrison led fifty Prairie Rovers out of the woods. Converging on the Yankee camp, the rangers sounded like a pack of angry mountain lions. Jerry climbed into his saddle. He coughed, gagged, and heaved. Vomit sprang from his mouth.

Shane spotted Wharton's Henry rifle on the ground. He couldn't return to Company B without the gun. Two dozen Yankee cavalrymen headed straight toward him.

"Save yourself, Frank." Jerry wiped a chunk of salt pork off his chin. "Leave me here—to die."

"Shut up and hold on! I ain't leaving you." Shane rushed to retrieve Wharton's rifle. "Keep your damn head down." He mounted Vengeance and grabbed Jerry's reins. "We've got to get to that cave."

While Major Harrison and the rangers attacked the Union encampment, Shane led Jerry through the woods. Steering the horses around trees and low-hanging branches, he hoped to lose the squadron of enemy cavalrymen. As he rode through the sunken gully, Jerry held onto his saddle with both hands. His blood-soaked-face looked like a butcher's table.

Shane reined up in front of the cave. "Can you walk?"

"I'll try." Jerry climbed down from his horse and covered his mouth. "Think I'm gonna vomit."

Gunfire raged in the battlefield. Jerry took a step toward the cave and his knees buckled. Shane rushed to help his injured friend. Vengeance whinnied.

Placing Jerry's arm around his neck, Shane caught a whiff of his breath. "Damn, Ringo! You smell like rotten cheese." His stomach churned. "Breathe the other way."

"What'd you expect?" Jerry stopped and gagged. "I've been spewing my guts."

The shiny flash of a saber reflected through the woods. Shane bent down and threw his shoulder into Jerry's stomach. As he lifted him off the ground and headed for the cave, Jerry choked and coughed. His chin dug into Shane's spine and vomit spewed down his new shell jacket.

"Damn it, Ringo!" Shane rushed into the cave and felt vomit drain into his trousers. "Turn your damn head next time."

The sound of galloping hooves echoed through the gully like a violent thunderstorm. Shane rushed toward the rear of the cavern. As he placed Jerry behind a chest-high bolder, a rattlesnake slithered away into the darkness. Wiping vomit from the crack of his ass, he dug his fingers into his cotton drawers and flipped a handful of chunks on the ground. His hand smelled like rotten cheese.

"I gotta get the Henry rifle and hide the horses." Shane stared into the deep dark cavern. "If a bear wakes up, breathe on him."

Cradling his bloodstained head, Jerry curled his knees to his chest and sighed. "Do they really eat people?"

"Only if they smell blood." Shane worried his wounded friend would go to sleep and never wake up. "Don't pass out on me. Bears gnaw flesh down to the bone." He placed Jerry's Army Colt in his hand and headed toward the exit. "If I don't make it back, shoot first and ask questions later."

Sporadic gunfire echoed in the distance. Peering out of the cave, Shane spotted two-dozen Yankee cavalrymen riding down the gully. Vengeance stood twenty-feet away. As he eyed the Henry rifle in saddle holster, a bullet ricocheted off the limestone entrance.

A soldier shouted in a Northern accent. "Lieutenant Jones, those rebel bushwhackers are holed up in the cave."

Shane raced to retrieve the repeating rifle and a handful of precious cartridges. As he approached Jerry's Appaloosa, a bullet landed between his knee-high boots. Vengeance was too far away. He grabbed Jerry's shotgun and a box of buckshot. While a gust of wind ripped through the frozen ravine, the Yankee cavalrymen stayed in battle formation. Pulling his Colt Special, he retreated toward the cave and fired at the enemy until his revolver clicked empty.

"You men upfront, dismount and go inside. Kill those bushwhacking cowards." The Yankee lieutenant barked. "Bring their damn heads to me."

Shane rushed toward the rear of the cave. Jerry lay in his vomit, his fingers gripped tightly around his Colt. As he lifted his wounded head off the cave floor, blood drained from his bandaged skull.

Stepping behind the boulder, Shane loaded the twelve-gage shotgun with buckshot. "Yankees are pissed we killed their officers."

Jerry closed his eyes and rolled onto his side. Four Yankees appeared in the sunlit entrance. The soldiers clung together and crouched with pistols drawn. As they crept into the cavern, Shane placed his thumb on the hammer of his double-barrel shotgun. Leaning against the boulder, he held the wooden stock to his shoulder and pulled the hammer back. The metal spring on both triggers clicked. His mind raced. If he fired at the Yankees, he'd face an irate enemy with vastly superior numbers.

The soldier shouted. "Give yourselves up!" "Surrender your weapons, and you can return home."

Shane knew better and wrapped his fingers around both triggers. He'd killed four officers. The Yankees wanted revenge. As the soldiers moved forward, he squeezed. A two-foot stream of gunfire blazed from the muzzle and lit up the cavern. Double-ought shot tore through flesh and bones. As the ear-splitting blast reverberated off the cave walls, the Yankee bastards crumbled to the limestone floor. A young soldier grabbed his side and flopped like a fish on a trawl line.

"Please, someone help me," the panicked boy cried out. "I'm bleeding out real bad. Please—I want my momma." His dying voice waned. "Oh Lord—Momma, please—"

Shane handed his shotgun to Jerry. "Load it."

Gun smoke lingered in the cave and blocked the sunlight. While the dying boy cried out for his mother, Shane pitied the poor bastard. His heart wrenched with each sob.

Scanning the entrance, he wanted to comfort the young soldier but didn't know how. Killing the evil enemy didn't provide the vengeful satisfaction he'd prayed for. His quest for blood and revenge only brought more pain and sorrow.

"Pull Private Galloway out of the cave," the angry lieutenant shouted. "If you see that bushwhacking murdering son-of-bitch, kill 'em."

"They're gonna hang us for what we done." Jerry returned the loaded shotgun and his voice trembled. "That lieutenant done said .he wants our heads."

"They'll torture us first." Shane spotted the enemy outside the cave. "Slow painful death ain't no way to die. I won't be taken alive."

Two soldiers entered the cave and picked over the bodies. As they lifted a dead man's leg, Shane aimed his shotgun. His heart wasn't into killing. Unable to escape, he felt doomed. The thought of taking his own life crept into his mind.

"Private Galloway bled out, Lieutenant." A soldier crouched over the contorted bodies. "They're all dead, sir. Damn rebel trash—murdered all four of 'em."

Shane felt bad and lowered his shotgun. "Get the bodies. I won't shoot."

The soldier snapped his head around. "You'd better not be lying, you rebel scum."

A third soldier stepped into the cave. "Goddamned Texas Rangers are a bunch of murderers. Let's get 'em."

Shane feared he'd lose control. Threatened by the enemy soldiers, he got mad dog crazy and fired both shotgun barrels. The two men crumbled to the cave floor. A third limped outside. Return gunfire ricocheted off the cave wall.

"Lying rebel scum!" the Yankee Lieutenant shouted. "You're gonna hang for murder."

Struggling to see through the smoke-filled cavern, Shane dropped his shotgun and rushed to the jagged limestone wall. The acrid smell of gunpowder lingered in the cave. His eyes itched and his nostrils flared. Running out of ammunition, he grabbed his Big Walker Colt and prayed he could hold on until help arrived. As he moved toward the sunlight, six dead soldiers lay strewn across the rocks. Blood splattered the ground and stained the groundwater. Horrific images of his father's mutilated body rushed through his mind.

"Billie Yanks are goddamned murderers!" Shane glanced outside and shouted like a lunatic. "I'm gonna kill every damn one of you sons-of-bitches."

Yankees were spread out across the fifty-yard gully. Staring down the barrel of his Colt, Shane couldn't kill them all. A sense of helplessness hung over him. Stepping over the dead soldiers, he took aim at anyone in a blue uniform and fired until his chamber clicked empty. Bodies littered the ravine.

A piercing rebel yell rang out in the woods. Sergeant Rufus Beavers led a dozen Prairie Rovers down the gully. Splitting into two lines of attack, the rangers rode on opposite side of the ravine and mowed down Yankees like cattle in a slaughterhouse. The enemy scattered.

A half dozen enemy soldiers fled toward the cave. Led by the Yankee lieutenant, the retreating soldiers fired at the rangers. Return gunfire rang out like the Fourth of July. Shane backtracked over the dead bodies. Out of bullets, he tucked his Big Walker Colt behind his belt and raced toward the darkness. Three blood-stained soldiers stumbled into the cave.

"Get down, Frank!" Jerry stood behind a boulder with his shotgun aimed at the entrance. "Lying Yankee bastards."

Shane dove behind a stalagmite. A yellow-flame exploded from the muzzle and lit up the cavern. The enemy soldiers spiraled to the ground. Jerry lowered his shotgun and collapsed. His blood-soaked skull slammed against the limestone floor.

A celebratory rebel yell rang out in the gully. As the boisterous Texas Rangers cheered their victory, Shane rushed to help his wounded friend. As he cradled Jerry's blood-soaked head, water dripped from an icicle-shaped stalactite. Pondering the senseless deaths, he watched Jerry's chest rise and fall and prayed for forgiveness.

"Thank you, Frank." Jerry opened his eyes. "You whipped 'em Yankee bastards good."

"Hell's bells, Ringo. You shot half of 'em." Shane pressed down on Jerry's bandaged head. "You've dripped blood everywhere."

"Sure would like to see the look on Mack Dodd's face when he finds out we killed all those officers." Jerry closed his eyes and sighed. "Bet he'll be foaming at the mouth."

"Don't you up and die on me." Shane whistled for Vengeance. "I'm gonna get the horses and a fresh bandage for your head. We've gotta get you to Doc Westin."

Sergeant Rufus Beavers and the Prairie Rovers celebrated in the gully. Shane made his way toward the exit. A shiny metal object shimmered in the shadows. As he turned toward the flash, the Yankee lieutenant charged out of the darkness with his saber overhead. The barrel-chested officer brandished his three-foot blade.

Out of bullets, Shane braced his feet and thrust his arms. He locked onto the lieutenant's wrist with both hands and fended off the razor-sharp blade. The officer rammed into him. Knocked off his feet, Shane tightened his grip on the lieutenant's wrist and landed wildly on his back. His head slammed against the limestone rocks.

The Yankee bastard crashed down on top of Shane. Pain radiated through Shane's back. Locked in a deadly draw, he rolled onto his side and fought nose to nose with the lieutenant. The officer pulled Shane's Walker Colt from his waist and aimed the barrel. The chamber clicked empty.

Shane grabbed the saber blade and pointed the tip toward the lieutenant's gut. Responding with an ear-splitting rebel yell, Shane rallied his strength and thrust the saber into the lieutenant's stomach. Blood spilled down the blade and oozed across his fingers. The Yankee bastard gasped and coughed but kept on fighting.

Shane plunged the three-foot saber deeper. Filled with pent up hate and rage, he drove the curved blade through the lieutenant's abdomen until the hand guard could go no farther. The officer's body went limp. His eyes rolled back into his head and his warm breath expired against Shane's cheek.

Shane slid his saber free and climbed to his feet. He dragged the lieutenant through the cave like a butchered animal. As he stacked his bloody remains with the rest of the Yankee swine, a soldier lurked outside.

Scavenging the pockets of the dead, Shane took two pistols, an eight-inch knife, and chewing tobacco. Sergeant Rufus Beavers stepped into the cavern with his pistol drawn. His eyes widened. Looking up from his bounty of plunder, Shane placed a flask of gunpowder and a handful of cigars inside his shell jacket.

"Holy Jesus, McLean!" Rufus lowered his gun and waved his campaign hat over the mass of twisted bodies. "There's ten dead men in here."

CHAPTER 12

Texas Trojan Horse

Camp Johnston outside Oakland, Kentucky, January 1862:

Six weeks after Shane killed a dozen enemy soldiers in the cave, epidemics of disease ravished the Texas Eighth Cavalry like the great plague eradicated half of Europe. Fever, measles, and respiratory infections left Tennessee Valley hospitals overflowing with sick and dying rangers. Regimental namesake Colonel Benjamin F. Terry died on the battlefield and Colonel Lubbock succumbed to typhus. Their untimely deaths elevated Colonel Wharton to regimental commander and left the Texas Rangers in desperate need of officers.

Shane survived his special duty, but the emotional toil lingered. Both ashamed and proud of killing the enemy officers, he felt uncomfortable sharing the horrific details. His friends would never understand. Fearing for his eternal soul, he prayed for forgiveness and hoped God would absolve his actions.

The Texas Eighth Cavalry spent Christmas and New Year's away from home. Camped in the woods, Shane and the Crawford Boys had never experienced prolonged cold weather. His frostbitten nose and fingers burned. As he warmed his feet around a communal fire, a foot of snow covered Central Kentucky. Regimental Commander Colonel Wharton approached with an eight-inch cigar. Mack and the Ringo brothers lowered their profile and pretended to be busy.

"Private McLean." Colonel Wharton halted beside a hastily-built snowman with a button nose. "We need to talk. Walk with me."

Fearing another special duty, Shane climbed to his feet and cussed under his breath. "Yessir."

"We've lost half the officers to death, disease, or desertion." Wharton handed Shane a cigar and headed toward a snow-capped evergreen. "You fight with enthusiasm and a daring fervor. Men respect that in their officers. Grab a Lucifer." He extended a box of matches. "Major Harrison put your name up for promotion. He wants the men to vote on it tonight."

Preferring the Spartan life of a partisan ranger, Shane didn't want to be confined or obligated by the chain of command. The rise to officer required proper war etiquette and maintaining a code of procedures. He wanted to bide his time until he could ride into Springfield, Missouri, and punish his father's killers.

"Sir, I'm seventeen. Some of these men are twice my age." Shane struck a matchstick across his thigh and lit the cigar. "I wouldn't feel right ordering 'em around."

"We all gotta sacrifice, boy. I nearly died last month from the measles, and I'm here leading the regiment." Wharton's face tightened with disgust. "Lieutenant McNeal quit today. I need good officers who'll stay with me."

Shane tugged on his black neckerchief. "Sir, with all due respect, a private in the Texas Rangers is equal to any officer."

"You'll do as you're told, Ranger. That means leading the men." Wharton spit in the snow. "Pick a couple of men from your company and report to me. You're gonna scout an enemy supply depot."

Shane chose Mack and the Ringo brothers and rode north

to Hart County, Kentucky. The reconnaissance cut through snow-covered forests and wound around rocky hilltops. Icicles dangled from his frothy beard. Halting on the crest of a hill, he spotted a wood-staked fort guarded by Union soldiers. As he dismounted to stretch his aching back, a team of six horses led a supply wagon out of a storehouse. The hundred-foot depot stockpiled crates of guns, munitions, and victuals.

"I'd love to see the look on Wharton's face, if we returned to bivouac with a wagon of provisions." Shane rubbed his cold gloved-hands together and mulled over how to gain entry. "How many Yankees are guarding the front gates?"

"Too many to count." Mack scoffed. "Why don't we get the Ringo brothers to ride down and ask 'em to let us in?"

"Why don't you shut your big mouth?" Jimmy hit Mack in the back with a snowball. "Jerry and me are hungry."

"Frank, don't get any wild ideas." Jerry shook his head. "Wharton wants us to scout the fort and report to him—not attack it."

Mack rubbed his stomach and sighed. "Think they got corned-beef in any of those crates?"

"Gotta get inside that storehouse to find out." Shane scanned the fort and his mouth watered. "Bet there's more food, guns, and supplies than we could carry."

"Don't be a fool." Jerry scoffed. "Dead men can't eat."

While the canvas top wagon rolled toward the front gates, Shane chomped on a cigar. He intended to raid the wagon. Ten troopers from the Second Indiana escorted the supplies.

Shane turned to his second in command. "Jerry, how many guards do you count?"

"Four riding in front and four in back." Jerry moved his finger from trooper to trooper. "Wagon master and the shot-gun guard make ten."

"There's only nine, you idiot." Mack sat regally in his saddle and scoffed. "Four leading and four trailing plus a driver and shotgun guard. Eight and two makes *nine,* Fool!"

Shane swallowed a laugh. Instead of correcting his temperamental friend's arithmetic, he mounted Vengeance and let the argument play out. A snowball struck Mack's chin.

"You're the fool! There's ten!" Jimmy stepped behind his big brother. "You need to learn how to add."

Yanking off his wool mittens, Mack counted on his fingers. As he got to ten, he grimaced and recounted. The Ringo brothers cackled and awaited an apology. Shane knew Mack well enough to know they'd never get one.

"It don't matter. Me and Frank don't need your help." Mack shrugged. "We can whip nine, ten, or a dozen Yankees by ourselves."

Charting a course ahead of the supply wagon, Shane led his friends down the snowy hillside. The cold wind chilled his bones. As they rode through a forest of evergreens, Shane scouted for a site to ambush the supply wagon. Mack struggled to keep up.

"Where in the hell is Dodd?" Shane felt responsible for his friend's well-being. "Is he saving another starving animal?"

Jimmy shook his head. "He stopped to take a piss."

"Goddammit, I'm in charge." Shane worried his friends didn't respect his leadership. "I'm planning an ambush. He needs to ask me before wandering off."

"You oughta flog his big dumb ass, show him who's in charge." Jerry's eyes narrowed. "He thinks it's him."

Shane dreaded his volatile friend's temper. Mack rarely followed orders and responded to threats with aggression. He bitched about all officers.

"I can't flog him for taking a piss." Shane shrugged. "When Dodd gets here, I'll set him straight."

Jerry scoffed. "You're afraid of him."

"Shut your mouth. I ain't scared of him." Shane took exception to Jerry's words but had more pressing business. "Give me your damn rifle and hide in the brush. Yankees gotta come this way. When they pass by, you'll attack the rear guards with Jimmy." He pulled his Enfield carbine rifle out of a saddle sling and pointed at a boulder towering over the trail. "I'll take out the wagon master and shotgun guard from above."

While the Ringo brothers waited in the roadside thicket, Shane tied Vengeance to a hillside bush and unloaded a pair of rifles. As he sat in the snow, perched behind a waist-high boulder, the supply wagon rounded a bend in the trail. Mack Dodd charged out of the woods with his pistols blazing.

The Second Indiana Troopers leading the wagon spread into a Poinsett formation. Shane rushed his rifle to his shoulder and locked his V-shaped sight on the wagon master. As he squeezed the trigger, a .58 caliber Minnie ball ripped through the bastard's skull. Brains sprayed the white canvas top.

The dead wagon master fell backward and landed inside the canvas top buckboard. Shane felt nothing. Leaning his Enfield against the boulder, he was hardened to the sight of death. The nameless faceless soldier was just another kill.

While Mack attacked the four troopers leading the wagon, the Ringo brothers rode out of the bushes like a pack of hungry dogs. The soldiers in the rear scattered. Taking control of the reins, the shotgun guard whipped the team of horses.

Shane reached for his Mississippi Rifle. As he banged the barrel against the boulder, the gun misfired. A bullet ricocheted off the boulder and struck his boot. His big toe burned like fire. Gathering his guns, he cussed and hobbled over to Vengeance. Blood oozed through a dime-sized hole in his boot. Mack and the Ringo brothers chased the troopers into the surrounding thicket.

Shane couldn't let the supplies get away and spurred Vengeance onward. Pulling his custom Colt Special, he charged down the snowy trail and closed in on the wagon. Round after round of gunfire blasted in the rear. As he moved alongside the driver, the broad-shouldered trooper's jaw fell open. Cocking the hammer, he extended the ivory-handled revolver and sent a bullet screaming through the bastard's open mouth.

The trooper went limp and rolled out of the wagon like a barrel of Kentucky whiskey. As he hit the ground, the speeding wheels crushed his torso and split him in half. The wagon caromed out of control.

A forest loomed fifty yards ahead. Blinded by leather bridles, the six-horse team veered off the trail and sped toward a massive evergreen. The wagon reins dangled from the hitch.

Needing to halt the spooked team or risk losing the precious supplies, Shane pulled Vengeance alongside the horses and slipped his gunshot foot out of the stirrup. Snow and clumps of slush splashed into his face. As he vaulted onto the back of a horse, the massive evergreen loomed twenty yards away. Holding onto a leather bridle, he lunged for the reins and clutched leather. Gunfire blasted deep in woods.

"Whoa!" Shane stepped down on the hitch and yanked hard. "Whoa horses—whoa."

The supply wagon rolled to a stop seconds from impact. Shane dropped to the ground and struggled to catch his breath. Three riders appeared on the horizon. Fearing for his safety, he reached into the wagon and grabbed the guard's double barrel ten-gauge shotgun. As he aimed the English percussion gun down the trail, one of the riders sat upright. His left hand dangled by his holster.

"Don't shoot, Frank." Jerry shouted.

Mack Dodd and the Ringo brothers approached on horseback. As they steered around the crushed trooper, Mack stared at the gory scene and shook his head. His pudgy round-face tightened in disgust.

"Wagon wheel tore the poor bastard in two." Mack drew an imaginary line across his stomach. "Blood and guts are spread like wildflowers in the snow."

Eying the bloodstained rear wheel, Shane wished the trooper would've surrendered. He'd have let the bastard live. A gunshot rang out in the distant woods.

"Bastards are still sniping at us." Jimmy scanned the surrounding thicket. "One second they fight, next second they turn and run into the brush." His voice trembled. "Damn Yankees don't fight fair."

"Quit your bitching, Ringo." Mack reined up behind the wagon. "I killed three of 'em and Jerry killed two. If you had the guts to kill, you'd get a taste for Yankee blood like Frank and me." He dismounted and headed toward the wagon. "What's for lunch? I'm starving."

"I only killed one, wounded the other trooper in the shoulder." Jerry turned in his saddle and stared into the hillside woods. "Be on the lookout. There's three or four still out there."

"Hide the wagon, take *only* what you can carry back to the bivouac." Shane contemplated the twenty mile journey to Camp Johnston. "Highway back to Bowling Green is swarming with spies and troopers."

"Balderdash! I risked my life for these supplies." Mack popped his head from the rear of the wagon. "There're cases of food, kegs of gun powder, and who knows what else in here. If we ride into camp with this wagon of supplies, we'll be hailed Pirates of the Brush." His lips smacked on an applesauce cookie. "I ain't gotta listen to you, Frank."

"Shut your damn mouth! He's in charge." Jerry turned in his saddle. "You'll do as he says. We ain't risking capture just so you can feed your fat face."

"Damn you, Ringo!" Mack spit a mouthful of cookies. "If you wanna fight, get off your high horse." He squared his shoulders and tightened his ten-inch hands into monstrous fists. "Let's row, .you little red-haired leprechaun."

"Stand down—both of you!" Shane didn't need Jerry to fight his battles. "We'll hide the wagon and come back for the supplies later."

Jerry pulled his Army Colt. Ignoring Shane's orders, he wheeled his horse and leveled the barrel at Mack. His eyes narrowed and his freckled-face turned red.

Shane had never seen Jerry so angry. Quarrels and harsh

words between friends occurred daily, yet the arguments rarely reached the point of a gunfight. Insubordination needed to be punished. His leadership lacked authority. Tugging on his black neckerchief, he had to react decisively but feared a potential bloody outcome.

"I told you to stand down." Shane aimed his revolver at Jerry's head. "If you shoot him, I'll put a bullet between your eyes." He cocked the hammer and counted, "Three...two..."

"Goddammit!" Jerry lowered his pistol. "This ain't over, Dodd!"

Mack looked like a scalded dog but couldn't keep his big mouth shut. "Real men fight with their fists. Cowards pull pistols."

Jerry wheeled his horse and holstered his gun. As he rode away, Shane, filled with rage, confronted Mack. His heart pounded and his mouth watered. Standing toe to toe with his defiant friend, he spit orders like a fiery sergeant. Mack slumped.

"Wharton put me in charge of this scout. If you got a problem following my command, take it to the colonel." Shane pushed his finger into Mack's chest. "You *will not* take a piss, chase after stray animals, or sneak attack the enemy without my permission." He balled his hand into a fist and fought the urge to swing. "I've got the mind to shoot you right here, right now. Don't ever cross me again." His lips foamed with spit. "I'm your friend, but I won't tolerate disrespect."

"Sorry, Frank." Mack wiped saliva from his cheek. "I don't get why you're mad at me. I killed three of 'em Yankee guards."

"You're reckless!" Shane slapped Mack's cheek, hard. "Always jawing, talking back, and getting crossways with people." He slapped Mack's head twice more. "One of these days you're gonna pick a fight with the wrong man." His voice choked. "You wanna try me? I'll fight you right now, tough guy."

Holding his battered jaw, Mack shook his head and spit blood. "I ain't fighting you."

"Don't you ever talk back to me again, or I'll cock your hat!" Shane had a change of heart. "If you wanna risk capture by the Yankees, so be it. I was trying to save your hide." He grabbed the dead wagon master by the heels and pulled. "Go get a uniform off those dead troopers you killed. We've got a wagon to escort."

The wagon master's blood-soaked head struck the wooden bench. A disgusting thud sounded from his skull. As he landed in the snow, his neck contorted at an awkward right angle. A pocket Bible tumbled from dead soldier's pocket.

Shane turned his head and squirmed. Blood stained the pearly white snow. Seeking intercession from above, he removed the trooper's blue coat and prayed for forgiveness.

"It was you or him, Frank." Mack shrugged. "Kill or be killed."

Slipping on the dead soldier's coat, Shane recited the Gospel of Luke. "'Hail Mary, full of grace…'"

"You were right. Let's ditch the wagon." Mack stepped back. "If the Yankees catch us in their uniforms, they hang us as spies."

"Better not let 'em catch us then." Shane yanked off the soldier's pants. "Tell the Ringo Brothers to drag that split-open trooper into the bushes and hide the body."

The twenty-mile journey to Confederate Camp Johnston cut through heavily-contested Hart County, Kentucky. Jerry and Mack buried the hatchet and made up. Riding atop Vengeance, Shane led the plundered wagon toward the Louisville-Bowling Green Highway. He asked Mack to drive the six-horse team and ordered the Ringo brothers to act as rear guards. They dressed like US cavalry but behaved like court jesters. Long spells of silence were interrupted by bouts of laughter and spiteful teasing.

Wearing a bloodstained captain's uniform, Mack poked his head around the side of the wagon. "You Ringos look good in Yankee blue. Sure y'all ain't spies for Lincoln?"

"Knock it off, Dodd." Shane didn't want the teasing to escalate. "How'd you end up with an officer's uniform?"

"I killed the bastard, so I got first choice of his duds." Mack pushed his finger through a bullet hole in his lapel. "If I gotta be a damn Lincoln Lover, I might as well be an officer."

Jimmy veered toward the bushes. "Go boil your shirt, Captain Billie Yank."

"Damn, Ringo, you're stopping to pee again?" Mack mocked. "Better not squat this time. A lonely soldier happens by and see those bird legs, he'd mistake you for a woman."

"Kiss my ass, Dodd." Jimmy dropped his trousers and shouted over his shoulder. "You look thirsty. I'll bring you a mouthful of yellow snow."

"If you bring it around me, I'll rub your face in it." Mack steered the six-horse team toward the highway. "You're the reason I prefer animals to people."

The echo of war drums sounded in the distance. Approaching an intersection with the Bowling Green Road, Shane noticed the heavily traveled highway was conspicuously void of traffic. The intimidating drumbeat made his heart race. General Carlos Buell and the Union Army of Ohio were supposed to be in Louisville. He needed to get word to Colonel Wharton and the Confederate Army at Fort Donelson.

"Hey, Dodd!" Jimmy raced alongside the wagon and hit Mack in the face with a snowball. "Eat up, Peckerwood."

"Goddammit, Ringo!" Mack wiped the snow from his cheek. "There'd better not be piss in it."

"Stop and listen! Hear those drums?" Shane feared capture by an enemy patrol. "Yankees are marching south through Munfordville. Their advanced guard is probably five minutes away."

"We can't fight an entire squadron." Mack's eyes widened. "What do we do with this wagon? There'll catch us if we run."

"That's why you should've listened to Frank and ditched it in the woods." Jerry wheeled his horse. "We'll be strung up by nightfall."

Shane pointed to a narrow path through the thicket. "Get this wagon into the woods—double quick."

Wheeling the team around, Mack raced the wagon between giant cedar trees. As he drove up the wooded hillside, branches snapped on the rigid canopy. Leafy debris littered the roadside. Horse tracks and wagon ruts marked the snowy pathway like a giant X on a treasure map.

"Take my horse and help Dodd hide the wagon with brushwood." Shane handed his reins to Jimmy. "I'm gonna cover our tracks."

While the sound of horses clamored down the highway, Shane swept the snow with a cedar branch and headed thirty yards into the woods to join his friends. His heart pounded in his chest. Hidden behind an evergreen, he prayed the approaching Yankees would ride on without incident.

A squadron of advance guards appeared on the horizon. Waiting in silence, Shane stared down the highway and fed Vengeance handfuls of oats to keep her calm. The troopers stopped in the intersection and spread out.

"Keep moving! General Buell's right behind us." A cavalry officer peered in Shane's direction. "Be on the lookout for rebel bushwhackers."

While the advanced guard rode on, a chill whipped through the air. Forty-thousand Union troops from the Army of the Ohio blanketed the roadway. The Yankee line of march stretched for two miles. Shane grabbed his Enfield and watched in disbelief. Where had Lincoln found so many men willing to die for federal tyranny? The poor soldiers must've been duped by Godless generals.

"We'll camp out in the woods." Shane didn't want to risk capture on the open road. "Don't build a fire."

"Ain't gotta tell me, twice." Mack stared at the imposing Yankee line of march. "I won't even snore tonight."

The rumble of horse-drawn wagons lasted deep into the

night. Officers carried torches and soldier sang patriotic huzzas. Perched in a tree on night watch duty, Shane snacked on a handful of crackers and rubbed his sore eyes. He longed for home. The two-hour duty gave him time to mull over his future. Staring into the stars, he reflected on Greek history, inspired by the mythical story of Troy and the Trojan Horse.

"Frank! Get some sleep." Mack Dodd sloshed through the snow and darkness. "I've got duty until dawn."

Morning light shinned through the trees. Snow covered the ground. As a prism of red, blue and yellow rays crept into his eyes, Shane tossed a blanket to the side and sat up in the buckboard wagon bed. The Ringo brothers slept at his feet. The soft chirp of a song bird gave the false impression of a peaceful winter wonderland.

Mack slept at his post. Dressed in a bloodstained captain's uniform, he slumped against a tree and snored like a drunken banshee. His thick fingers wrapped snugly around his six-shooter.

Shane scanned the woods for any sign of the enemy. Stepping around a keg of gunpowder, he jumped out the wagon and decided to teach Mack a lesson. This dereliction of duty put everyone in danger.

"Get your lazy ass up!" Shane slipped the gun out of Mack's hand and thumped him on the skull with the butt of his pistol. "One of these days you're gonna make us all sorry."

"Damn it, Frank! That hurt." Mack rubbed his injured head. "What did I do?"

"Don't you ever fall asleep on duty again." Shane tossed Mack's gun at his feet and headed toward the wagon. "Get moving and help me hide the rest of supplies."

"Why are we leaving the supplies? Federals are moving south toward the Cumberland River." Mack grabbed his gun and climbed to his feet. "If we wait a day and go slow, they'll be gone." His teeth chattered. "We could make Camp Johnston with the wagon and all the supplies."

"When the Army of Ohio marches through Bowling Green, they'll burn the Eighth Texas bivouac to the ground." Shane leaned against a keg of gunpowder and looked for something to eat. "Stack the crates under that cedar bush. We'll come back for them, later."

Mack shrugged. "What's your plan, Frank?"

Cracking the lid on a crate of corned beef, Shane tossed a couple of cans to Mack. "Make a fire and warm up breakfast. I'll tell you a story about the Greek city of Troy and the Trojan Horse."

"I don't give damn about Greek history." Mack's eyes narrowed. "Don't care about American history neither. I'm hungry."

"Three-thousand years ago, Greeks entered the city of Troy by offering a giant wooden horse as a gift." Shane grabbed his Bowie and sliced open a can of corned beef. "The wooden statue was a ruse. Greek soldiers were hidden inside. When everyone went to sleep, the soldiers snuck out and opened the city gates."

"That's the dumbest story I ever heard. Everyone knows not to accept gifts from your enemy." Mack shook his head. "Where's the pretty damsel in distress?"

"Ringo and me are gonna dress in these Yankee Trooper uniforms and return the wagon to the supply depot except it'll be full of gunpowder and rigged to explode." Shane joked. "Since you like pretty girls, you'll dress as Helen of Troy."

"That ain't gonna work. I ain't dressing as no girl, and I ain't risking my hide." Mack folded his arms. "I'm staying here and guarding the food."

"You'll do as you're told, Private." Shane only half-joked. "You talked me and the Ringo brothers into joining the rangers. You're gonna fight this war—even if it takes all spring. Sooner we whip the Yankees, sooner I can ride to Springfield and kill the Ivey twins." He pulled his Colt and aimed at Mack's big mouth. "Start hiding these crates or you won't have a hide to risk."

e/oe/o

Union Supply Depot, Hart County, Kentucky, January 1862:

The supply wagon was packed with two kegs of black powder and rigged to explode. Shane and the Crawford Boys masqueraded as Yankee Troopers and drove their Texas Trojan Horse back to the Union fort. Midday sun illuminated the snowy countryside. Protected by Mack out front and trailed by the Ringo Brothers, he steered the rolling firebomb toward the twin gate towers.

A guard with fiery red-hair approached the wagon. Eying the bloodstained canvas top, the inquisitive guard glanced at the Ringo brothers and lowered his bayonet. Shane nervously whistled "Yankee Doodle."

"Halt! Where're the rest of your men?" The guard cocked his head. "How come there's only four troopers protecting this wagon?"

Scratching his beard, Shane sought an answer. "General Grant said it himself. Four good Yankees could whip a dozen Johnny Rebs."

"We got a problem, soldier?" Mack wheeled his horse and turned to the guard. "There're kegs of gunpowder in this wagon and rebel sharpshooters in the woods. One spark from a bullet and it'll look like the Fourth of July." His voice deepened. "You'll be blown to bits so small your momma couldn't recognize you.

"No problem, sir." The inquisitive guard saluted and nodded toward the tower guards. "Pull through, sir. Magazine is in the rear."

The wood-staked gates swung open. Impressed by Mack's uppity demeanor, Shane tipped his campaign hat and snapped the driving reins. As he steered the exhausted six-horse team inside, the guard stepped back and appeared intimidated.

"Yah!" Shane rolled his Texas Trojan Horse through the gates. "Yah...Yah."

The Ringo brothers halted outside the log storehouse and dismounted. As they opened the twin doors, Shane pulled the team of horses to a stop and waited for Mack to untie Vengeance.

They backed the wagon inside.

"Park it by the wall." Shane pointed toward a row of barrels labeled explosive. "Hurry. We don't have a minute to waste."

"Y'all ain't going anywhere!" A supply sergeant with a handful of inventory papers hobbled around a stack of crates. "Unload your wagon, first."

Shane balked at the sergeant's order. The wagon was packed with brushwood kindling and rigged to explode. As he glanced toward the rear, Mack stepped away from the horses.

"General Buell took all my extra men to attack Fort Donelson." The sergeant limped on his wooden peg leg and pointed toward the Cumberland River. "I ain't unloading this wagon while you namby-pambies do diddly squat." He eyed Mack's shoulder badge and saluted. "Captain, sir. I'm sorry, sir."

"At ease, soldier. I've been known to run my mouth at times." Mack eyed Shane and smirked. "Private McLean can unload the wagon by himself, He needs the extra duty."

Grabbing a crate, Shane gave Mack a go-to-hell look. "Yessir, Captain Dodd." His tone sharpened. "I'll get right on it, sir."

Vengeance whinnied. While the Ringo brothers waited outside with the horses, the sergeant inspected Mack's bloodstained uniform and cocked his head. Shane reached into his scabbard and grabbed his eighteen-inch Bowie.

"Sir, I don't recall a Captain Dodd in the Army of the Ohio." The sergeant turned skeptical. "Come to think of it…why are you returning supplies earmarked for the march to Tennessee?"

Mack stuttered. Sweat dripped down his forehead. As he fumbled for a response, Shane circled behind the peg leg

Yankee. His fingers squeezed the leather and brass ultra-strong handle.

"What company do you command?" The gimpy sergeant hobbled forward. "Why does your collar got dried-up blood?"

Shane lunged forward and wrapped his hand around the bastard's mouth. As he slashed his throat, blood spurted into Mack's face. The sergeant's peg leg buckled and his inventory papers fell to the ground. Shane tossed the lifeless body to the side.

"Goddammit, Frank! You didn't have to slice his whole neck open." Mack wiped his bloodstained cheek. "I was gonna talk our way outta trouble."

Peering into the wagon, Shane eyed a pile of brushwood kindling and struck a match. "Get the hell outta here!"

Mack bolted out of the storehouse like a renegade Comanche. Shane tossed the burning match into the rear of the wagon. As he turned to leave, Mack charged back inside. Flames blazed around the powder kegs.

Mack shouted. "We can't blow up the horses!"

Shane forgot to release the six-horse team. Grabbing his Bowie, he bent to cut the leather harness. Fire raced along the rigid canvas top.

"Go, .it's gonna blow!" Shane grabbed the wooden hitch and sliced the straps. "I'll bring the horses."

Smoke poured from the storehouse doorway. Leaping onto a bareback steed, Shane charged the tangled team toward the front gates. As he attempted to steer the blinded horses, a trooper with his arm in a sling stood in the way. Unable to escape the charging team, the panicked soldier froze.

"Whoa!" The trooper's eyes widened. "Whoa!"

Trailed by Mack and the Ringo brothers, Shane clung to the tangled bridle and braced for impact. The thousand-pound animals trampled the soldier. The grotesque thud of hooves sent a chill down Shane's spine. Guards stationed around the gate towers turned toward the commotion.

The stunned soldiers fumbled for their muskets.

A red ball of fire exploded from the storehouse. Launched forward on his steed, Shane struggled to stay upright and felt the air leave his lungs. His side burned like fire. Debris rained from the sky. Guards scurried for cover. Shane reached around his back and spurred the team of horses toward the gates. A splintered chunk of wood lodged between his ribs. As Shane exited the fort without firing a shot, the red-haired guard grabbed a musket and climbed to his feet.

"Grant was wrong!" Shane aimed his six-shooter and squeezed off a round which hit between the soldier's eyes. "An entire squadron of Yankees can't whip four rangers."

CHAPTER 13

Ghost Rider

Kentucky/Tennessee Border, February, 1862:

In the weeks following the Texas Trojan Horse incident, Shane and Wharton Rangers employed guerilla-style hit and run tactics on the Union Army. The surgical strikes on the enemy's overextended supply lines provided a bounty of provisions and slowed federal progress into the Tennessee Valley. While the Union Army of Ohio marched toward Fort Donelson, Confederate sympathizers evacuated the neutral state of Kentucky. The highway to Nashville overflowed with desperate families.

Shane and the Crawford boys rode in parade formation with the Texas Eighth Cavalry. Patrolling along the Kentucky/Tennessee border, he steered Vengeance behind the Guidon bearer while the rangers protected the mass retreat south. A woman dressed in rags stepped off the roadway. Her two small children sat atop a raw-boned mule.

"I beg of you, Colonel." The woman turned and revealed her swollen battered face. "Can you spare something to eat for my younglings?"

Wharton raised his arm and the quarter-mile-long line of march halted. Shane took pity on the poor woman and her kids. Flush with provisions from the looted supply wagon,

he reached into his saddlebag for a box of applesauce cookies. The battered woman wiped her bruised cheek and
pulled her son from the saddle. As she cradled him in her
arms, the exhausted mule neighed. A little green eyed girl
with blonde tangled-hair climbed down the beast of burden.

"Squadron of Yankee Jayhawkers took over Tiny
Town." The woman pulled her frightened daughter close.
"They murder Southerners and take liberties with the ladies.
My husband's away fighting for the Confederacy." Her
voice choked. "A Jayhawker with a shillelagh forced us out
of our home, said I'd provide comfort to the enemy."

Shane tugged on his black neckerchief. The very sound
of the word Jayhawker made his skin crawl. He prayed Sergeant Lauderdale, Red, and the Ivey twins were still alive.
The Incarnate Yankee Devils needed to be exterminated. No
matter the cost.

"I was beaten for taking a basket of food from our
home." The woman caught a sob and approached Colonel
Wharton. "Sir, when I showed a Jayhawker there was only
enough for my younglings to eat. He beat me with his shillelagh. I had to keep still and pretend to be dead before he'd
stop." She wiped a tear from her bruised cheek and kissed
her son's forehead. "Thoughts of my babies kept me alive."

Shane recalled the red-haired Jayhawker who'd split his
head open in Austin with a shillelagh. Adrenaline pumped
through his veins. Starving children and beating women was
an abomination. God-fearing men didn't behave like that.
Her story hit a nerve and opened old emotional wounds.

"Colonel Wharton, children gotta eat." Shane struggled
to contain his anger and approached the woman with a box
of applesauce cookies. "For you and your younglings,
ma'am."

"Thank you, sir. Bless your heart." The woman blushed
and crouched beside her daughter. "Tell the nice soldier
thank you, Jane."

"Thank you, mister." The green-eyed girl pushed the
tangled blonde hair out of her face. "God bless you."

"Men, this is why we must endure the hardship. To fight the scourge of heathen Yankees." Wharton shouted to the Guidon bearer. "Lead us north to Tiny Town."

The ranger line of march wheeled around on the highway. A supply wagon backed into a snow bank and got stuck. Shane knew the desperate woman and her children needed more sustenance. He also knew where to find it.

"Dodd!" Shane pointed to Mack's haversack. "Give me that corned beef you've got stashed away."

"I only got a couple cans left." Mack reached inside the leather bag and whispered, "Better not let the colonel see you feeding civilians. He'll cut our rations in half."

Shane feared his animal-loving friend was right. As he waited for Wharton and his officers to ride off, the woman huddled with her starving children.

Mack dismounted and slipped the cans to Shane. Grabbing a bag of horse oats, he looked over his shoulder and approached the family's raw-boned mule. Jerry Ringo shook his head. "Don't look at me like that. Poor ole girl's exhausted." Mack fed the starving mule a handful of oats and kissed her lathered nose. "She'll fall over dead if she don't eat."

Shane approached the desperate woman. Punching open the lids with his Bowie knife, he dropped to a knee and extended the embalmed-beef to her little daughter. The girl's green eyes widened. As he brushed the frightened child's blonde hair with his fingers, Mack stepped back and stood at attention.

"Be good and listen to your momma." Shane missed his simple life on the Shamrock Ranch. "Help her take care of your little brother."

"McLean! Wharton wants to see you." Sergeant Beavers approached with a scowl on his face. "Says if you got extra food he's got an extra special duty for you.

ꙮ

Todd County, Kentucky, February, 1861:

Shane and the Eighth Texas camped in the snow-covered woods five miles east of Tiny Town. Struggling with his inner demons, Shane woke from a nightmare in a cold sweat. The battered woman and her children weighed on his mind. Colonel Wharton ordered him to ride into the Yankee occupied town to scout their defenses. Thirsting for vengeance, he had a different agenda and intended to dole out justice from the barrel of his guns. "The righteous shall rejoice and wash his feet in the blood of the wicked."

Shane rose early and skipped breakfast. The crisp morning air made him feel alive. Dressed as a civilian, he hid an armament of weapons inside his wool sack coat. Two Army Colts, three knives, and his father's revolvers were placed inside additional pockets sewn into the lining. As he headed toward the stables, a group of rangers warmed themselves around a communal fire. The cheerful soldiers smiled and waved good morning. They were unaware of the hell he intended to unleash.

"McLean, how are you this fine morning?" Parson Bunting rose up and offered his Bible. "Come share a blessing with us."

If things went bad, Shane wanted to be right with God. "Yessir, Parson."

"You look troubled. Remember, we're God's chosen people." The ranger chaplain handed over his *Bible* and warmed his fingers in the fire. "You're a Christian soldier. Killing heathen Yankees is performing the Lord's righteous work." He kissed a wooden cross and prayed toward Heaven. "We've gotta cleanse the earth of the wicked, so the God-fearing can live in peace."

With *Bible* in hand, Shane felt reassured and cherished his duty to God and Country. As he prayed for salvation, a weight was lifted from his shoulders. Devil be damned. He felt sure he'd prayed enough to enter the Lord's kingdom.

"Pardon me, Parson. I need to get this ranger on the

road." Colonel Wharton approached with a full bottle of whiskey. "Remember what those Jayhawkers did to you and your family—death before dishonor. Righteous shall inherit the earth." He took the *Bible* and placed the Devil's drink in his hand. "Drink up, McLean. If we don't stop 'em here, they'll go to Texas and finish the job."

Shane swigged his whiskey and nodded his approval. The colonel had a way with words that rallied his fighting spirit. He'd ride to hell and back for Wharton. *Take all the heads off the people and hang them up before the Lord.*

"Yankees are pure evil, wicked to the core." Wharton shook the *Bible*. "Don't let down the women and children of Texas. The hopes of the Confederacy ride with you."

High on Biblical scripture and whiskey, Shane headed toward the stables to prepare Vengeance for the scout. He was at peace with what he had to do. As he cut through camp, Major Harrison drank coffee outside his tent. The Jimtown Major's stare shook Shane's confidence.

"Cheer up, McLean! We're gonna raid Tiny Town." Harrison toasted his coffee. "There'll be lots of killing today." He eyed Shane's half-drunk bottle. "Ain't it a little early to be drinking whiskey?"

"Ain't never too early, sir. It's cold this morning." Shane drank to forget his problems. "I'll be hunting 'em damn Jayhawkers."

"Remember you're only to do reconnaissance. Wharton wants to lead today's raid." Harrison extended his coffee cup. "Better put a little shot in here. Its cold outside."

Tipping his palmetto, Shane spiked Harrison's coffee and sloshed through the snow toward the stables. A row of saddled horses stood hitched to a rope along the tree line. While slaves wiped down the horses, Shane placed a leather feeding bag in front of Vengeance and swigged a mouthful of whiskey. A peaceful calm settled on the ranger bivouac.

Mack's deep voice rang out. "Frank, Wharton's been looking for you."

Startled by his friend, Shane shuddered and snapped his

head around. "I've already spoke with him."

"You don't have to yell. I'm standing right behind you."
Mack folded his arms. "You used to smile and be fun to
hang around. I'm worried about you, Frank."

"I've got a lot to think about." Shane extended his ten-
gauge percussion shotgun. "Take it. Wharton wants me to
look like a farmer. Can't ride into town with a gun like this
straddled to my pommel.

"Keep it. Farmers need a gun." Mack reached for the
whiskey. "You shouldn't drink so much."

"Who are you to talk? You drink more than me." Shane
yanked his bottle away and scoffed. "Thought you were my
friend."

"I know what you're gonna do. I can see the evil in your
eyes. You can't kill 'em all." Mack's voice was choked with
concern. "You're drunk. I'm telling Wharton to send me
instead of you."

"I ain't drunk. I'm only taking the edge off." Shane
rushed to mount Vengeance. "Don't wanna think about it."
His words slurred and foot missed the stirrup. "Sometimes,
I don't wanna remember what I'm gonna do."

cↄeↄ

Tiny Town, Kentucky, February, 1862:

Shane headed out on his own. Winding along a wooded
hillside trail, he cut through a snow-covered holler and prepared to unleash his fury. The three-block town sat nestled
in a narrow valley between majestic knolls. As he rode
down the hillside, two saber-wielding Union sentries guarded Main Street. A handful of stores, three saloons, and a
hotel lined the boardwalk. Leaving his fate in the hands of
God, and his Colts, he pushed his shoulder-length hair behind his palmetto and whispered a short prayer.

"Lord, I ask for your forgiveness for the things I'm about

to do." Shane felt doomed and tossed his empty whiskey bottle into a snowdrift. "And for your help."

Half a dozen enemy cavalrymen ate breakfast on the hotel's steeple portico. A dozen more meandered along the icy boardwalk. Dressed in a plain wool sack coat, Shane slipped his hand into his coat and approached the sentries posted in the street. His finger rested on the trigger of his Big Colt Walker. As he hunted for his father's killers, fifty US Cavalry horses lined the street.

A barrel-chested sentry leveled his saber. "What's your business, Secesh? We don't want your kind in town."

Shane ignored the derogatory name and belched whiskey. His double-vision blurred. As he pulled Vengeance to a halt, the second sentry flared his nostrils.

"Smells like whiskey. He's already drunk." The soldier's face tightened. "These damn Southerners are animals, a scourge on decent society."

Shane felt threatened. Scanning the enemy, he pulled his Big Walker Colt from his sack coat and fired a bullet into the sentry's forehead. The bastard crumbled to the street. Blood stained the snow. The other sentry's mouth fell open. Fanning his revolver, Shane sent a bullet through his forehead. A woman stepped out of the hotel and screamed.

Gun smoke lingered in the air. Steering around the dead men, Shane hunted for Jayhawkers along the boardwalk. Whiskey clouded his judgment. The moral line between right and wrong disappeared. He shot a portly soldier in the chest and killed three more eating breakfast under a steeple portico. Panicked soldiers banded together on the hotel porch. As he grabbed a pair of Army Colts from his sack coat, terrified soldiers held the lobby door shut. A bottleneck ensued on the porch. The trapped soldiers herded together beneath the portico. Squeezing off round after round, he cut down the Yankee swine in a double-fisted blaze of gunfire. Butchered bodies stacked up on the porch like a Chicago slaughter house. A bullet whizzed past his head.

Vengeance snorted and foamed at the mouth. Struggling

to see through the gun smoke, Shane glimpsed a soldier with red-leggings and wheeled his horse around. A lanky sergeant with a beard darted behind a row of cavalry horses. Visions of Sergeant James Lauderdale and his blood-soaked whip raced through his mind.

Soldiers ran down the boardwalk and ducked into doorways. Shane switched to his .36 Special. He'd planned to kill the Jayhawkers responsible for Kirby's murder with the ivory-handled revolver. As he hunted for the sergeant, adrenaline shot through his veins. The Yankee bastard slipped behind a spotted Bay horse. His red yarn leggings stood out like a wolf in a hen house.

The row of cavalry horses stretched a city block. Aiming beneath the spotted Bay, Shane fired a bullet into the sergeant's ankle. The bastard squeezed his foot and cried out.

"I give up! Don't shoot." His high-pitched voice cried out. "Awe!"

The Yankee sergeant needed to suffer for whipping Shane's father to death. Seeking Highlander clan-justice, Shane shot him through the hand to hear him scream in agony. Blood dripped off the bastard's fingertips. As Shane watched him bleed, he shot him in the other ankle to see if he'd beg for his life. The tortured soldier squeezed his red-legging and tumbled to the street.

A terrified woman on the boardwalk shrieked. Grasping his wounded ankle, the sergeant rolled onto his back and screamed like a child. As he turned his head, Shane realized he'd tormented the wrong man. Jayhawker Sergeant James Lauderdale had deep acne-scarred cheeks.

Shane cocked his revolver and took pity on the tortured sergeant. The poor bastard needed to be taken out of his misery. Leveling the barrel, he squeezed the trigger and put a bullet between the soldier's eyes. Glass shattered from a second-story hotel window.

"Starving children! Beating women!" Shane stood in his stirrups and spun his six-shooter in his hand. "Where's the Kansas Fifth Jayhawkers?" His soul filled with hate. "I'm gonna come back and shoot everyone one of you sons-a-bitches."

A bullet struck the snow between Vengeance's hooves. Shane steered his black Appaloosa toward the hotel. Tracking the shot to a second-story window, he spotted a sharpshooter in red long-handle underwear lower his rifle. As he charged Vengeance out of the soldier's line of sight, five shirtless Jayhawkers armed with pistols stepped out of the saloon. The half-dressed troopers stood barefoot on the icy porch.

"What in the hell's going on?" A bare-chested lieutenant with a distinct double-chin crouched in a shooter's stance. "Put your gun down, boy."

Shane scanned the town and looked to escape into the surrounding woods. High on whiskey, he couldn't recall how many bullets remained in his gun. While he wheeled Vengeance toward the hotel alleyway. Startled troopers scattered and returned fire. Turning in his saddle, he took aim at the chubby lieutenant's head.

A second blast shot from the hotel window. Vengeance rolled onto her hind legs and whinnied, a bullet lodged in her shoulder. Shane eyed the sharpshooter and charged his wounded horse down Main Street. As he steered toward the hotel, he glanced up and fired into the second-story window. The sharpshooter grabbed his side and tumbled through the shattered pane. His body rolled onto the steeple portico and landed in a snow bank.

Shane steered Vengeance toward a fifty-foot alleyway. As he passed by the hotel portico, the wounded sharpshooter twitched and lifted his head. Shane aimed his six-shooter and put a bullet between the bastard's eyes. Bullets whizzed past his head. Charging out of the alley, he felt nauseous and burped a mouthful of whiskey.

A Yankee trooper poured a bucket of water into an icy trough. Staring down at the terrified soldier, Shane leveled his revolver and felt sorry for bastard. As he charged up the hillside, gunfire blasted from the rooftops.

Colonel Wharton and the Eighth Texas Cavalry converged on Tiny Town. Flying the Bonnie Blue flag, the rangers rode down Main Street and attacked in a hail of gunfire. Blood-curdling rebel yells echoed into the hillside. While Yankees begged for quarter, Shane changed out of his civilian clothes and reloaded his pistols. He prayed his father's killers were among the prisoners. Yearning to interrogate the soldiers, he looked forward to finding out.

Blood drained down Vengeance's front leg. Shane opened his saddlebag and grabbed a sewing kit. As he dug his finger into her gunshot shoulder, Vengeance whimpered and kicked the ground. Sporadic gunfire rang out from Tiny Town. Removing a .36 caliber bullet, Shane stitched up his horse and headed to back down the hillside. Main Street looked like hell.

Blood splattered the snow and splashed the windows. Dead bodies littered the street like prairie dog mounds. While rangers ran in and out of buildings, searching for the enemy, gunshots rang out like the Fourth of July. Shane looked to avoid reality with a bottle of whiskey. An acrid smell of black powder filled his lungs.

Rangers dragged and stacked bodies on the hotel porch. Shane steered around the Yankee sentries he'd slaughtered on his way into town. As he glanced at the dead men, Jimmy Ringo approached on foot. A broad-shouldered sentry lay motionless with his eyes wide open. Blood clotted around his ear.

"Frank! Colonel Wharton's pissed off." Jimmy rushed down Main Street shaking his head. "Did you do all this?"

"No!" Shane didn't want to remember. "Maybe a couple of 'em."

"Damn it, Frank. These soldiers are from Indiana." Jimmy's voice trembled. "If this is what you do to Hoosiers, I'm afraid to see what you'll do when you find those Jayhawkers that killed your Pa."

Scanning the boardwalk, Shane craved whiskey and a drink for Vengeance. "Is there water around here?"

"Maybe at the hotel, but there's a dozen Yankees holed up inside." Jimmy shrugged. "There's a dead soldier floating in the water trough out back—shot between the eyes."

Steering his horse around the dead sentries, Shane eyed a line of thirty prisoners seated in the street. Gunfire rang out from the hotel. Colonel Wharton surrounded the building with three-dozen rangers. Confederate sharpshooters lurked on rooftops.

"That's him." A gray-bearded man with a black-eye limped off the boardwalk and pointed a bottle of whiskey at Shane. "That's the man who rode into town and killed those soldiers. Disappeared through an alleyway like a ghost."

"You don't know what you're talking about." Shane searched the dead soldiers for any sign of his father's killers. "Get over here, graybeard. Bring that whiskey with you."

"I'm a Southerner. Who you looking for?" The old man tugged on his chest-length beard hobbled into the street. "Yankees been beating and murdering Confederate sympathizers."

Shane dismounted. "Can you identify the soldiers who've been doing the killing?"

"Yessir, I sure can." The graybeard's voice slurred. "Those two soldiers in the middle killed a store owner in town."

Colonel Wharton's angry voice echoed down Main Street. "If the Yankees won't come outside and surrender peacefully, torch the damned hotel! Shoot any soldier who resists."

Sergeant Rufus Beavers and a dozen rangers guarded the prisoners. While Wharton ordered his men to light torches, Shane pulled out his Big Colt Walker and eyed the row of enemy soldiers.

"Any of you men serve in the Kansas Fifth, out of Fort Leavenworth?" Shane snatched the graybeard's bottle of whiskey and took a swig. "Any of you son-of-a-bitches serve in Lane's Brigade, under the command of Colonel "Hog" Johnson?"

The terrified Union soldiers remained tight lipped. Shane spotted a trooper in red cotton leggings and struggled to contain his rage. As he fought the urge to shoot all the lying bastards, Sergeant Beavers pistol whipped a smirking prisoner. The solder crumbled to the ground and grabbed his bloody skull.

"Damn it, Frank. They're afraid you're going to kill 'em." Rufus whispered. "You can't let 'em know how mad you are. Nobody's gonna talk."

Shane didn't care. The enemy needed to be killed—without quarter. A torch landed on the hotel portico. As fire raced across the roof, screams rang out from the burning building.

Shane tugged on his black neckerchief. "Any of you men been to Austin, Texas? I need to know where to send your body."

A Jayhawker lieutenant protested his displeasure to Sergeant Beavers. "Sir, you can't let my soldiers burn up in the flames. Those are good Christian men in the hotel."

"Sit down, Lieutenant!" Shane recognized the double chinned officer. "Tell your men to keep their hands on their heads or they will be shot."

A cloud of smoke blew down Main Street. The prisoners got restless. While fire raged in the hotel, Jerry Ringo waved his hand and approached through the haze.

"Sergeant Beavers!" Jerry rushed forward and pointed over his shoulder. "Colonel Wharton gave orders to shoot any prisoner who gets out of line."

Rufus nodded. "I heard him."

The Yankee lieutenant stood in protest. "I demand to speak with Colonel Wharton."

"Sit down and shut your pie hole, Lieutenant!" Rufus squeezed the handle of his Dragoon. "We've got reports of war crimes against you and your men."

"Killings in this town were done in accordance with federal law. They harbored the enemy." The lieutenant refused to sit and broke into a haughty smirk. "You can't fault my men for following the law."

The prisoners cheered their support. "Tell it like it is, Lieutenant."

A gunshot rang out like a bell. Pulling his Colt Special, Shane rushed past Rufus and grabbed the lieutenant's throat. As he placed his pistol to the officer's temple, the lieutenant's smirk disappeared.

Shane pressed the muzzle against his skull. "Where in the hell is Colonel Hog Johnston and the Kansas Fifth?"

"Colonel Johnston died last year in the Battle of Morristown." The lieutenant choked. "Best I know, Kansas Fifth is in Springfield, Missouri."

Filled with hate, Shane didn't trust the Jayhawker lieutenant. Thick smoke clouded his vision as he heard horrific screams from the burning hotel. People ran frantically along the boardwalks in fear. Rufus turned his back and looked away. Tugging on his black neckerchief, Shane released a year's worth of pent up rage and squeezed the trigger. "Lying Yankee bastard!"

The lieutenant brains exploded from his skull. As he dropped to the street, the rowdy prisoners fell silent. Shane wasn't finished with the Yankee trash.

"Goddamn right, McLean!" Rufus shouted through the haze. "Kill a few more of these lying bastards."

Shane waved over the graybeard. "Identify the soldiers who killed civilians."

"Kill 'em all, Frank!" A ranger cheered his support. "Let God sort 'em out."

The graybeard turned and pointed toward a third trooper seated at the end. "Those two men murdered a store owner in town. That tall one shot a ten year old boy and his father."

A heavy-set woman stepped out of the general store and pointed at the trooper on the end. "That soldier murdered my husband—in front of our children."

"Rufus, bring me that child killer." Shane pointed his gun at the shifty-eyed soldier. "Makes me sick to look at him."

Sergeant Beavers dragged the tall trooper from the end of the line and placed him on his knees in front of Shane. The child killer trembled and cried at Shane's feet. Terrified prisoners stared in silence.

"Please, don't kill me. I was drunk." The trooper kissed Shane's boot and begged. "For the love of God, please show mercy."

Ignoring the eleventh-hour repentance, Shane placed the barrel of his Colt to the bastard's head. The man closed his eyes and his body stiffened. Tears rolled down his cheeks.

Jerry Ringo shouted. "Shoot him, Frank. Let's kill all these sons-of-bitches."

Seeking revenge more than justice, Shane squeezed the trigger. Blood splattered through the air and splashed his face. As he licked his lips, the vinegary tang stuck to his tongue. Prisoners watched in horror. Approaching another murderer, Shane jammed the barrel of his gun against the soldier's head and squeezed the trigger. His father's gun strangely misfired.

"Forgive me, sir." The terrified soldier fell to the ground and cried out. "I've never been to Texas."

Sergeant Beavers yanked the soldier to his feet. "God forgives, Frank McLean don't!"

'You're becoming no better than that gang of Jayhawkers in Austin.' Shane heard a voice in his head. It was his father's voice, he had no doubt. A trained killer and soldier, he wasn't a judge, jury, and executioner. As he holstered his six-shooter and walked away, Jerry Ringo stepped toward the trooper.

A gunshot blasted. Shane drew his gun and wheeled around. Smoke drifted from Jerry's revolver. Chunks of brain and blood stained Main Street red. The Yankee soldier dropped to the ground like a sack of potatoes.

Jerry scanned the prisoners. "Are any more of these men murderers?"

CHAPTER 14

Archer Grays

Confederate Army Field Camp, Corinth, Mississippi, March, 1862:

While Union Major General Henry Halleck ordered three federal armies to converge in the Tennessee Valley, Colonel Wharton led the Texas Eighth Cavalry out of Kentucky. The overmatched rangers withdrew to Nashville, Murfreesboro, and onto Corinth, Mississippi. A strategic Southern railhead and vital water transport system along the Tennessee River, the Tennessee-Mississippi border town mustered Confederate armies from across the south.

Thick clouds of rain blocked out the afternoon sun. Posted in the woods two miles from Corinth, Shane huddled beneath a blanket capote. He'd been on duty since dawn and his bones ached from the cold. The sound of scuffed leaves put him on alert. Reaching for his .36 Colt Special, he hoped for a can of peaches or maybe Mack was going to finally relieve him from this intolerable duty.

"Dodd!" Shane stared through the misty air. "Is that you?"

"Don't shoot, McLean!" Colonel Wharton's voice rang out. "Is your name Frank or *Shane*?"

"Either one is fine, sir." Shane wondered what brought Wharton this far into the woods. "Frank's my given name, Shane's what my mother calls me."

Wharton stepped around a budding chokeberry bush. "The general wants to see you. Mack Dodd, and the Ringo brothers, too." His eyes narrowed. "Better not *mess up* and embarrass me."

Shane knew the military's two favorite words. "Yes, sir." He eased to his feet and holstered his gun. "When did General Lee arrive with the army from Virginia?"

"Not Lee...General Albert Sidney Johnston." Wharton headed toward the Eighth Texas Cavalry bivouac. "Follow me."

"Sir, my father served with General Johnston during the Texas Revolution. They were both privates." Shane saluted and hastily rushed to the colonel's side. "Johnston was Sam Houston's secretary during the revolution."

Wharton ducked underneath a tree branch. "I know the story, son. Me and Johnston are neighbors back home in Brazoria County."

Fearing his friends had gotten into trouble, Shane slowed his gait. "Sir, do you know what the general wants with us?"

"Johnston needs scouts." Wharton looked over his shoulder. "Mind your P's and Q's around the officers. Fix your hair and shave before you embarrass the regiment."

Forty-thousand Confederate troops from across the Tennessee Valley marched and drilled around Corinth. Dressed in his Archer Gray uniform, Shane rounded up Mack Dodd and the Ringo brothers. As the Crawford Boys arrived outside a mansion used by the Confederacy as headquarters, a gray-haired Negro dressed in a black waistcoat greeted them at the doorway. The servant bowed and pointed down a corridor.

"General will see you, sirs." The Negro nodded. "Please, follow me."

A Greek statue and several life-sized renaissance paint-

ings adorned the main corridor. Falling in line behind his
friends, Shane eyed a life-like nude sculpture and glanced at
the woman's bare bosom. Mack stopped and gawked like a
school boy. Looking over his shoulder, he winked and playfully groped the marble breasts.

"You damn fool!" Shane kicked Mack in the ass. "Keep
going. You'll get us in trouble."

While the Ringo brothers smothered a laugh, Shane
shoved Mack down the hallway. Opulent crown molding
and ten-foot carved doorways lined the corridor. Halting
outside the general's office, Shane looked up at the fancy
architecture and wondered how someone could live in such
opulence. His entire cabin on the Shamrock Ranch could
easily fit inside a single room.

A demanding voice echoed into the hallway. "Front and
center, soldiers!"

Excited to meet the general, Shane stepped inside the
spacious office and shouldered up alongside his friends who
stood in a tight disciplined row. His heart raced as he
snapped to attention. Standing in front of a grand mahogany
desk, he kept his head erect and eyes straight to the front.
As Shane tried to remain calm and keep his neck vertical,
Mack farted.

General Johnston strutted toward the front of his desk.
His thick sideburns were neatly trimmed and his pressed
uniform smelled of lilac soap. Shane caught a whiff of
stinky cheese.

Johnston stood nose to nose with Mack. "Are you Kirby
McLean's boy?"

"No, sir." Mack pointed a finger at Shane. "He is."

Stepping to his left, Johnston's eyes narrowed. "Kirby
know you're up here fighting on the gray line?"

Shane hadn't heard his father's name in weeks. "Sir, my
pa was killed by a gang of Unionist Jayhawkers."

"I'm sorry to hear that, son. I was at Cole's Store when
your father dueled with Sam Houston." Johnston stepped
back and sat on the edge of his desk. "It's sad when two

friends and devoted Freemasons dishonor themselves. I was the one who asked Houston to stand down."

Shane had heard a different version from Senator Erath. "Sir, my father is dead and can't defend his name. As soon as this war's over, I intend to kill the men responsible."

"That's an honorable pursuit. I wish you all the best." Johnston nodded. "Major Harrison claims you assassinated half a dozen Union officers and shot up a town full of Yankees."

"Sir, Jerry Ringo killed half those officers. These men standing with me are all great marksmen." Shane wondered if the general still held a grudge against Kirby. "I'm privileged to be riding with them."

"Humility is a good virtue, McLean." Johnston's voice deepened. "Your father would be proud to see the man you've become." He motioned to a Negro servant waiting alongside the doorway. "Jim, bring me a drink."

"Yessir, master." The servant bowed and poured scotch into a crystal goblet.

"I'm in need of some men to scout General Grant's movements along the Tennessee River." Johnston squared his shoulders and looked Shane in the eye. "It's a dangerous mission behind enemy lines—might be swarming with Yankee patrols."

Mack stuck out his massive chest. "Sir, we're your men."

"I knew fellow Texans could be counted on for bravery. Let's have a toast." Johnston shouted to his servant. "Jim, make us four scotches."

While the Negro approached with a silver tray of drinks, Shane and Mack grabbed a crystal goblet. Due to their father's struggle with alcoholism, the Ringo brothers abstained from alcohol. Johnston raised his glass. Honored by the privilege, Shane toasted with his goblet and gulped down the malt-barley whiskey. As he choked on the burning aftertaste, Mack raised his empty glass for another drink.

"That's all, men!" Johnston knocked back his shot and

pointed to the door. "You'll leave in the morning. Colonel Wharton has your orders."

                         എ

Reconnaissance along the Tennessee River, April 1, 1862:

Sixty-foot pine trees lined the rain-soaked road into Tennessee. While dark skies brought a relentless downpour, Shane led his friends deep behind enemy lines. The all-day scout left him cold and wet. Dressed in his jean-wool ranger uniform, he shivered. His nerves were frayed from the constant fear of a Yankee patrol.

Jerry reined-up in the middle of the muddy road. "Frank," he whispered and motioned toward a clearing. "Yankee pickets."

Shane dismounted and his boots sunk ankle deep into the mud. "How many?"

Staring across the clearing, Jerry held up two fingers. "Could be more. Don't know how we'll get past 'em soldiers."

The enemy pickets carried bayonet-tipped muskets and patrolled the perimeter of a peach orchard. Needing to get a closer look at Union troop levels, Shane planned to double back through the woods and kill the bastards. While sounds of a large encampment echoed through the clearing, he realized the pickets were too close to sound an effective alarm. Union General Grant wasn't prepared for an attack.

"Stay here with the horses. I'll take care of the two pickets." Shane handed Mack the reins and motioned for the Ringo brothers to wait in the woods. "I wanna lay eyes on Grant's defenses."

A Yankee picket stopped beneath a peach tree and puffed on a cigar. Aromatic smoke billowed through the blossoming branches. Cutting through a tilled field of carrots and potatoes, Shane arrived at the orchard and circled in behind the enemy soldier. As he stepped over a raised tree root, a four-foot cottonmouth slithered between his boots. His body froze and heart raced. Needing to keep his presence a secret, he grabbed his Bowie and watched the black viper coil and display its fangs. The enemy soldier puff on his cigar and stared across the field.

Shane stepped slowly away from the venomous snake. Moving to within arm's length of the enemy, he placed his hand over the picket's mouth and yanked his head back. The panicked soldier kicked and squirmed. His half-smoked cigar tumbled to the ground.

Slicing his razor-sharp blade like a scalpel, Shane gashed open the bastard's neck from ear to ear. Blood gurgled in his throat. Laying the soldier on the ground, he picked up the smoldering cigar and placed the soft moist tip to his lips. As he slowly inhaled, the cherry red tip came back to life. Blood oozed from the dying soldier's mouth. Suffering in silence, his eyes tracked Shane's movements.

Shane pulled the cigar from his lips and spit. He didn't like killing, but that's what he'd been trained to do. Since arriving at Camp of Instruction in Houston, he was ordered to *kill or be killed*. The sound of shuffling feet drew his attention.

The second Yankee picket came out of an adjacent row of peach trees. Shane risked losing his own life. Diving into a patch of weeds, he crawled behind a tree and waited for the enemy to pass. The soldier whistled "Battle Hymn of the Republic." Shane grabbed his Bowie and slipped in behind the enemy. As he closed within a couple of steps, the startled soldier wheeled around and leveled his bayonet. His razor-sharp blade sliced through the air.

Shane pounced on the Yankee like a hungry panther. Slapping at the bayonet blade, he lunged forward and stabbed his Bowie into the soldier's larynx. His index finger stung. As he sliced his knife, blood spurted out the side of the bastard's neck. The soldier buckled and crumbled to orchard floor.

Examining his blood-soaked finger, Shane licked his wound and spit the bitter-vinegary taste from his mouth. "Damn it!"

The inch-long gash exposed tissue down to the bone. Shane wiped his chin and looked for a place to hide the body. Dragging the soldier by the boots, he pulled the dead man behind a tree and cut out a piece of his shirt. As he wrapped the cloth around his finger, the faint whistle of a Mockingbird echoed. Turning toward his friends, he pressed down on his bandage and glanced across the clearing. Jerry pointed frantically to the rear.

A third picket patrolled the peach orchard. The bearded soldier had his head down reading a letter. Shane hid his Bowie in his jacket sleeve and placed the half-smoked cigar in his lips. Stepping around a peach tree, he approached the enemy with his hands in clear view.

"Greetings friend." Shane pulled the cigar from his mouth and smiled. "Do you have a Lucifer?"

The picket looked up from his letter and stopped in his track. Wiping his watery eyes, he lowered his bayonet and reached into his coat pocket. Shane rushed forward and rammed his Bowie into the soldier's stomach. Ripping the giant blade upwards, he sliced through the muscular diaphragm rendering the poor man breathless. Another Somebody's Darling crumpled to the ground.

While Mack and the Ringo brothers ran toward the peach orchard, dark clouds loomed on the horizon. Shane rummaged through the soldier's pockets for something of value. He took twelve Union dollars, a box of tobacco, and a six-inch carving knife. A picture of the dead man's wife and children lay by his side. Looking at the picture, Shane picked up the soldier's letter and read:

> *Ophelia, my dear wife, I've received your kind words. The soul left my body when you wrote to me that our young Francis had passed from fever. He was our joy. The Lord needed our charming son to*

brighten heaven, like he brightened our family. I wish
I could be home for you and the rest of the children.
Your pain and the children's suffering must be ago-
nizing. When this war is over and I return home, I
promise I'll never leave you and the children again...

Shane's stomach felt sick. Overcome by shame, he put
down the letter and thought about what he'd done. Taking a
man's life meant taking everything he had and everything
he'd ever have. He'd stolen a father from his children and a
husband from a grieving wife. God would surely sit in
judgment. Maybe he'd write the soldier's wife and ask for
forgiveness.

"Let's get a move on, Frank!" Jerry snatched the letter
out of Shane's hand. "Read it tonight by the fire. We gotta
finish this scout and report to the general."

Thunder roared through from the heavens. While his
friends hid the bodies, Shane surveyed the enemy from the
peach orchard. Twenty-thousand Yankees spread around the
Shiloh Methodist Church and stretched to infinity. An armada of US gunboats lined the Tennessee River. Paddleboats with another twenty-thousand Yankees were expected
in days.

"Jimtown Major lied!" Shane cussed his wretched lot in
life. "This damn war's gonna take a lot longer than six
months."

⸙⸙⸙

Confederate Headquarters, Corinth, Mississippi, April 2,
1862:

Shane and the Crawford Boys passed through fields of
Confederate soldiers while returning to the opulent Corinth
mansion. Ushered into a ballroom full of high-ranking officers, he stood sequestered in a row alongside his friends

and did his best to answer a whirlwind of questions about Union troop size and positions. A twenty-foot-long table divided the room in half.

"I'm impressed you made it back alive." General Johnston eyed Shane. "Is General Grant's paddleboat *The Tigress* docked at Pittsburg Landing?"

"Yessir. I saw it with my own eyes." Shane scanned the room full of officers. "Grant's army is camped around Shiloh Methodist Church."

"McLean." Johnston folded his arms. "Are you certain Buell's Army hasn't arrived?"

"Yessir, I counted three troop-transport paddleboats. When Buell arrives, there'll be an armada docked at the landing." Shane proceeded without permission. "Sir, we never once saw a Union patrol away from the river. Grant ain't expecting us to move in this rain." He looked around the table for a dissenting face. "We should surprise the Yankees before Buell arrives with reinforcements."

Johnson turned toward his officers. "Now that I have confirmation Grant's at half-strength, prepare your men to march north in the morning."

While the officers argued over artillery positions and troop levels, Shane stood still and waited to be spoken to. Mack smirked and playfully slapped the back of Jimmy's head. A clean-shaven artillery colonel from Georgia glared his disapproval.

"Quit running your mouth, soldier!" the artillery colonel shouted at Mack. "Wipe that smirk off your face. Don't patronize me, Texan."

Turning to his little brother, Jerry rushed his finger to his lips. "Shhh!"

The colonel pointed toward a large map on the table. "Where were their pickets posted?"

Mack gulped and motioned to Shane. "Sir, Frank killed the pickets we came across."

"Sir, their guards are too close to their main troops to sound an effective alarm." Shane offered his opinion. "We should sneak attack. They'll never expect it."

"You're dismissed, soldiers." General Johnston saluted. "You men could've served in Napoleon's Old Guard. I'll send word to Colonel Wharton—Texas Eighth Cavalry will be my personal vanguard."

Shane snapped to attention and followed his friends out of the war room. The supreme compliment made him beam with pride. Mack slowed in front of the nude Greek statue. Halfway down the fancy corridor, he paused and glanced over his shoulder. The Ringo brothers headed toward the exit. Shane feared his large but simple-minded friend would do something stupid, and he rushed to leave.

"Wait up, Frank." Mack's eyes narrowed. "Who in the hell is Napoleon?"

CHAPTER 15

Provost Guards

On Corinth Road in Hardin County, Tennessee, 5:00 p.m. April 5, 1862:

The Confederate Army of the Mississippi marched across the state border to sneak attack General Grant at the Shiloh Methodist Church. Thunderstorms roared overhead. While the incessant rain slowed the line of march, officers barked orders. Soldiers slipped in ankle-deep mud as horses hauling heavy armaments slogged along the Corinth Road. The twenty mile trek turned into a logistical nightmare.

Serving as General Johnston's advanced guard, the Texas Eighth Cavalry patrolled ahead of the main army. Painful saddle sores cut into Shane's thighs. As he steered Vengeance along the muddy road, gusts of wind blew the heavy rain sideways. Surreal thoughts of dying heroically in battle offered a welcomed reprieve from the misery of army life.

A mile south of the Shiloh Methodist Church, rain slowed to a drizzle. The Ringo brothers bobbed their heads and struggled to stay awake. Mack held his stomach and dismounted next to a juniper. Shane grew tired of his constant bitching.

Mack grimaced and rushed toward the bushes. "I've gotta go."

"What?" Jerry opened his eyes. "If you didn't eat all the damn time, you wouldn't need to crap all the damn time."

"Shut up, Ringo!" Mack raised his fist and dropped his trousers. "Or I'll shut you up."

Shane hadn't taken his boots off in a week. Exhausted from the three-day march, he wanted to eat and catch a wink before the dawn surprise attack. As he searched his haversack for something edible, Mack yanked on a juniper bush. Hornets buzzed around his head.

"Hurry up, Dodd!" Shane motioned toward a field of vegetables. "I wanna grab a root before Sergeant Beavers arrives with orders."

"Give me a break, Frank!" Mack snapped off a handful of scale leaves and released the branch. "Let me shit in peace."

A hornet's nest broke free from the branch and dropped to the ground. As the wax hive split apart, angry insects swarmed into the air. Mack let out a high-pitched holler and leaped out of the bushes. Yanking up his trousers, he ran toward the road while stinging hornets buzzed around his head. Rangers waiting in formation laughed out loud.

"Help me, Frank!" Mack swatted the air like a wild man. "Help me!"

Jerry stood in his stirrups. "Let that be a lesson. Check what's in the bushes before dropping your drawers."

Approaching the line of march, Mack pulled off his jacket and swatted the air. "Those damn hornets hurt when they bite."

Shane turned in his saddle. "Hornets don't bite, .they sting."

Scratching a tiny red bump beneath his eye, Mack mounted his horse. "Don't matter, hurts the same."

"Let's ride over to that potato field we passed through the other day." Shane moved alongside Mack. "Once the infantry gets here, they'll take it all."

Dark thunderclouds roared in the distance. Cutting through a clearing in the woods, Shane led Mack to the edge of a potato field and tied Vengeance to an oak tree. Grabbing his leather haversack, he hurried down a row and yanked tubers out of the mud by their green-leafy stems. As he filled his stomach and haversack with potatoes, Mack huddled over a patch of sprouts. The hornet sting beneath his eye had tripled in size.

"Oh my, you've got a bad red rash." Shane leaped a row of tubers to get a closer look. "You look like a Chinaman. Can you even see?"

Mack looked down at his hands. "My fingers are burning, can't hardly bend 'em."

"I've never seen a face puff-up like that. Maybe Doc Weston has something for it." Shane put a chew of tobacco in his mouth. "We gotta get back to the company before Harrison comes looking for us."

"I'm worried, Frank." Mack scratched a red rash on his neck. "My throat feels like it's closing up."

Shane spit a mouthful of tobacco juice in Mack's face. "Rub it in while I get the horses."

"Do you think I'm gonna die?" Mack rubbed the grimy juice into his swollen cheeks. Feels good. Spit in my face again."

Shane hocked up a mouthful of saliva and gleefully obliged. "Hope not. If you die, Ringo brothers would have to start cooking at camp. There'd be a revolt." He pulled out his chaw of tobacco and pressed the leafy wad against Mack's hornet sting. "Hold it on your cheek. I ain't got time to keep spitting on you."

Shane set out to retrieve the horses and entered the adjoining woods. Vengeance whinnied in the distance. Rounding the trunk of a tree, he spotted an enemy soldier rummaging through his saddlebags. The Yankee bummer removed a wad of greenbacks and a three-foot garrote rope.

Vengeance raised her snout and sniffed the air. As she turned toward Shane, the bummer yanked Vengeance's bridle and whipped her hindquarter with his hand. Shane intended to teach the thief a lesson but didn't want to alarm other enemy patrols in the area. Preparing to buffalo the enemy soldier, he pulled his custom .36 from his side holster and crept in behind the bummer. When he raised the ivory-handle to crack the bastard's skull, the snap of a twig crackled beneath his boot.

"Don't shoot me!" The bummer wheeled around and threw his hands in the air. "Please don't shoot. I didn't take anything."

Shane ignored the bummer's plea. The terrified soldier glanced up at the Masonic square and compass engraved into the handle. Dropping to his knees, he raised his arms and begged for quarter. The fellow Freemason hailed the Masonic Sign of Distress.

"Don't do it!" Mack rushed in front of Shane. "Don't kill a Freemason Brother." He shielded the bummer with his own body. "Brotherhood takes precedence over state and country."

Shane spun the revolver in his hand like a highbrow vaudevillian. As he stepped back and holstered the weapon, Mack sighed. The enemy soldier climbed to his feet and extended his hand.

"Greetings Brother." Shane put forth a token hand to determine the Yankee soldier's level of proficiency. "So mote it be, I'm a Widow's Son."

❧❧❧

One mile south of the Shiloh Methodist Church, 3:30 a.m., April 6, 1862:

Heavy rains dampened gunpowder, rendering weapons useless. An order for the Texas Eighth Cavalry to picket General Johnston's left front spread through the regiment. Shane traded his haversack of potatoes to Jimmy Ringo for a switch in duty. Taking refuge beneath a large oak tree, he closed his eyes and caught a wink before the dawn raid on General Grant's Army.

A gunshot rang out in the darkness and interrupted Shane's nap. Thinking the battle started, he forced his eyes open and reached for his Colt Walker. Second and third gunshots blasted a mere feet away. The acrid smell of gunpowder filled the misty air. Wiping the drizzle from his eyes, Shane stepped around the tree trunk and wondered who was dumb enough to discharge powder in the predawn hours before a major sneak attack?

Mack had Jerry in a headlock. "Go to hell, Ringo! You're a liar."

Sergeant Rufus Beavers and a half dozen rangers rushed into the lantern light. Looking to separate his feuding friends, Shane holstered his gun and raced toward the fight. As he veered around the hanging lantern, Mack pounded his fist into Jerry's face. Jimmy ran from his post and leaped onto Mack's back. While bodies herded together, Jerry protected his face with his hands.

"For Heaven's sake." Shane feared they'd all be arrested. "What are you doing?" Yankees are a mile away." He grabbed Jimmy's leg and pulled him off Mack. "Calm down, Ringo. Get a hold of your brother."

Jerry cussed and refused to stop fighting. Trapped in a headlock, he pumped his fists into Mack's stomach and lower back. While three rangers peeled Mack off Jerry, Jimmy latched onto his older brother's waist and pulled. Everyone tumbled to the ground in different directions.

"Cool it, Dodd." Shane stepped between his friends and sought to make peace. "What in the hell's going on?"

Mack climbed to his feet and struggled to catch his breath. He looked like he'd had enough. Jerry broke free and landed a clean right hand to Mack's chops.

Shane punched Jerry in the face and knocked him to the ground. "Damn it, Ringo. That's enough." He eyed Sergeant Beavers. "Rufus, help him keep Jerry away."

Five rangers held Mack back. He waved his fist but didn't retaliate. While Jimmy wrapped his arms around his brother, Rufus steered Jerry away.

"Ringo started it, Frank." Mack spit a mouthful of blood. "I was just following orders. Wharton said to get rid of our wet powder." His voice trembled. "Ask Wharton, if you don't believe me."

Shane examined Mack's swollen face. His cheeks were three times their normal size. Grabbing his friend by the arm, he headed toward the lantern for a closer look. Mack looked like a giant bloated china man.

"How can you even see to be fighting?" Shane motioned toward the ambulance wagons. "Did you go visit Doc Weston like I told you?"

"I didn't have time to see him." Mack raised his swollen hands under the lantern light. "My face doesn't hurt much. But my fingers are so puffy I can hardly bend 'em."

"Why in the hell are you swinging at Jerry if your hands are the size of a grapefruits?" Shane shook his head in disbelief. "Did you keep the tobacco on your face like I told you?"

Mack shrugged. "Naw, I didn't want to waste it. I chewed it instead."

Shane fought the urge to slap his friend silly. "You're a damn hard case!"

"Dodd won't listen to nobody. I told him not to discharge his powder." Jerry shouted over his brother's shoulder. "He'll give away the sneak attack and get us all arrested."

Mack scratched his red rash-covered neck. "I done told you, Ringo. Wharton said we could get rid of our wet powder."

"I don't give a shit who told you to do it! Only a fool would shoot off powder in the middle of a surprise attack." Shane grabbed Mack's arm and spun him around. "Common horse sense ought to tell you that."

Colonel Wharton approached on horseback with a pair of

junior officers. "Private Dodd, I meant for you to dispose of your wet gunpowder. Not discharge it." He carried a lantern and spoke in a concerned tone. "You men have caused a disruption to General Polk's battle plans. Our infantry are on the move."

Shane realized they were in deep trouble. Their carelessness could cost thousands of soldier's lives. A court marshal and hanging would be justified.

"Control your men, McLean!" Wharton waved his lantern in Shane's face. "Or General Polk will have my head."

Still wanting to slap his friend silly, Shane held his tongue. "Sorry, sir. I'll get 'em under control."

"It's too late for sorry." Wharton looked visibly shaken by the incident. "Be alert to the possible consequences of your actions. You can't apologize to the men killed by your carelessness."

A line of elite rearguards appeared on the edge of the bivouac. Dressed in pristine uniforms adorned with yellow-braiding and polished brass officer buttons, the Provost Guards maintained discipline and shot deserters. Shane grabbed his pistol and went on alert. The guardsmen usually patrolled the rear of the Confederate lines.

Wharton sighed and wheeled his horse toward the Provost Guards. As he prepared to fight, eight heavily armed officers circled around. The elite horsemen sat atop their beautiful mounts without a spot of dirt or blood on their immaculate uniforms. A stone-faced Provost lieutenant halted in front of Wharton. "Colonel, I've got orders to place you under arrest and deliver you to General Polk."

"Lieutenant, unless you have orders from President Davis himself, do not expect me to surrender peaceably." A lawyer and master orator, Wharton rose in his saddle and fought the accusations with a sharp condescending tone. "What we have here is some sort of miscommunication. Arresting me hours before an attack is counterproductive to our shared cause."

"Sir, your regiment's actions triggered the First Corps to

begin moving prematurely." The lieutenant brandished his sword. "Colonel Baylor informed me you might not come peacefully."

"George Baylor is a charlatan." Wharton's voice trembled. "He's a fraud, phony, and liar—and most certainly no colonel."

"Sir, I'm neither judge nor jury in this matter." The stern lieutenant lowered his saber. "Sir, will you please surrender your saber and side arm without further ado?"

An owl hooted in the darkness. While the ominous bird of prey loomed overhead, Shane admired Wharton's constitution. The colonel had been a friend to every man under his command. If Wharton gave the word, Shane would fight to the death, knowing if he did they'd all be gone to hell.

Wharton removed his old .44 Dragoon from his side holster. "Lieutenant, as you can plainly see, I don't carry a saber. Texas Rangers have no use for fancy knives."

A Provost major approached from the rear of the line. "Colonel Wharton, sir. You'll be allowed to express your grievances to General Polk in person."

"I assure you, Major. Bishop Polk is not in full control of his capacities if he ordered my arrest." Wharton threw back his shoulders and held his chin high. "Polk is averse to following imprudent orders, even more so than I."

Mack approached the demanding major. "Sir, you can't arrest Colonel Wharton. Who's gonna lead us in battle today?"

"This entire regiment is under punishment and will be banished to the rear along Oak Creek." The major's tone sharpened. "Any man refusing to obey will be shot."

CHAPTER 16

Battle of Shiloh

Fraley Field, 5:00 a.m., Sunday, April 6, 1862:

Rain hid the size and scope of the morning sneak attack. While dawn's early light reflected off the Tennessee River, eight Confederate brigades over ran a Union Division camped at Fraley Field. Hundreds of enemy soldiers were bayoneted inside their pup tents. Mack's foolish decision to discharge wet gunpowder ended with Colonel Wharton's arrest and the Texas Eighth Cavalry dismissed to the rear echelon along Oak Creek.

Volleys of musketry rang out along the mile-long battle lines. By midday, half-dressed survivors rallied around General Grant at Pittsburg Landing. Hungry Confederate soldiers stopped attacking and filled their stomachs and haversacks with a windfall of Yankee provisions.

Banished from the morning assault, Shane felt cheated by Wharton's arrest and waited in reserve alongside five hundred Texas Rangers. He sat atop Vengeance, forced to endure the humiliating regimental punishment. Eager to engage the enemy, he missed out on the grand pageantry of mass combat. Ranger officers preached the virtues of duty, honor, and the splendor of war.

Clouds of gunsmoke lingered around the Shiloh Methodist Church. Flanked by Mack and the Ringo brothers, Shane waited in the middle of the ranger line and checked the powder in his Colt Walker. A cheer rang out from the far corner of the formation. As he strained to see, a Guidon guard with a Bonnie Blue flag led a group of officers out of the woods. Texas Rangers broke into an ear-splitting rebel yell.

"Woohoo!" Mack sat regally in his saddle and spit a mouthful of tobacco juice. "Wharton's being escorted back to the regiment."

Jerry looked toward Heaven. "Am I dreaming or is this for real?"

"To Assemble" trumpeted from the company bugler. Seizing the regimental colors, Colonel Wharton rode in front of the rangers and waved the Bonnie Blue flag. Shane nodded and his chest swelled with pride.

"Gentleman, your duty to God and Country is to kill these northern aggressors." Wharton reined up in the middle of the formation and stood in his stirrups. "Texas Rangers don't run from a fight, and we sure as hell don't wait in reserve while others fight in our place."

The Yankees didn't stand a chance. Shane raised his fist and cheered his support. Equipped with three pistols and a shotgun, he felt energized by the colonel's return and intended to strike down the enemy with furious anger. As he gripped his Colt Walker, Colonel Wharton fired off a round while leading the ranger line of march toward Review Field. Marching in columns of four, the ranger parade stretched for a quarter-mile along Purdy Road.

Dark ominous clouds blanketed the roadside woods. Yankee sharpshooters hid in the surrounding trees and opened fire on the rangers. Bullets whizzed through the misty haze. Shane splashed through a watery gulch like a duck swimming in a row. Trapped inside a column of rangers, Shane clung to Vengeance and prayed to be spared from a sharpshooter's bullet. As he crested a summit, two rangers floated face down in a boggy ravine. A fiery young corporal rose in his stirrups and shouted a rousing rebel yell.

Shane steered behind the excited young officer. "Stay down!"

The young corporal's head snapped backward. His brains landed on Vengeance and splashed against Shane's face. As he tumbled off his horse, Shane wiped a chunk of skull from his cheek. The blood-soaked bone stuck to his index finger. His throat filled with sour bile. Fighting the urge to puke, he gagged and slumped in his saddle. A severed hand lingered at the edge of a boggy gulch.

Mind-numbing blasts of cannonade shook the ground. Shane felt dizzy and lowered his profile. Fearing what lay ahead on the battlefield, he closed his eyes and vomited down the side of his horse. His pomp and grandiose visions of war faded.

A barrage of twenty-pound iron missiles sailed over Review Field. While bombs burst in the air, a sea of blue bodies scattered along the roadside. An acrid smell of gunpowder lingered in the thick mist. Flanked by Mack and the Ringo brothers, Shane swore he'd passed straight through hell.

"Keep moving, Frank." Sergeant Rufus Beavers rode out of the ravine. "Battlefield is just a little farther. We're gonna whip 'em Yankees."

Colonel Wharton sat atop his horse on the edge of Review Field. As he inspired his rangers onward, volleys of musketry shot through the haze. Shane steered Vengeance toward the Eighth Cavalry battle formation in the rear. His hands shook and his throat tightened. Gory images of death littered the uncultivated killing field. Looking on in horror, he worried how anybody could survive the human butchery.

"McLean, that better not be fear in your eyes." Wharton cracked his whip and his voice deepened. "Rangers don't experience fear. They're only to be feared—that's a damn order."

Shane wondered why the colonel singled him out. Lots of men appeared scared. Brandishing his Colt Walker, he reined up in the middle of formation and waited for the bugler to trumpet the call "To Charge."

"No mercy, no quarter!" Wharton rode down the line of Rangers. "Kill the heathens where they are."

Thunder roared through the clouds and rain dropped from the sky. While Union General Sherman's Fifteenth Corps and General Hardee's Third Corps squared off in vicious hand-to-hand combat, blood splashed from bayonets. Starring across the battlefield, Shane felt doomed. He couldn't kill them all. His ears rang and heart pounded like it split through his chest. Thousands of dead soldiers lay contorted in every conceivable position.

"To Charge" sounded from the bugler. Colonel Wharton led the squadron onto the battlefield. Riding around knee-deep blast craters, Shane and the rangers attacked the far right flank of the Union line. As he steered through the maze of bodies, soldiers slaughtered each other with reckless abandon. Muskets swung like axes and eyes were gouged out. Soldiers cried out in agony.

Shane sifted through the bloody carnage. He fired at a thin soldier with a bayonet and a fat man bleeding on the ground. As bullets started to fly, his fears died down. Fighting across the field, he shot an old man in the head and a young soldier through the heart. Terrified Yankees dropped their muskets and dashed into the woods.

Colonel Wharton reined up and pointed at the retreating enemy. "Hunt the bastards down and take their cannon!"

Thick clouds of gun smoke hid the apocalyptic fight. Shane fired eighteen rounds at the enemy. All three of his pistols were empty. As far as he could see, bodies littered Review Field. Bloodstained soldiers cried out in agony. He could walk in any direction and never touch the ground.

Enemy musketry blasted from the woods. Shane forced Vengeance through the carnage. She stomped, stumbled, trampled, and whinnied. Blood stained her hooves. He feared taking his beloved horse any farther across the killing field. Pulling his Bowie, he wheeled around and slashed his way back through the fighting. As Shane looked to reload his pistols, he saw Colonel Wharton resting his leg on the pommel of his saddle. His pants were saturated with fresh blood.

Riding toward the wounded colonel, Shane motioned toward the Confederate field hospital. "Sir, you're pale as a ghost. You'd best go see Doc Weston."

Wharton didn't reply. Dripping blood from his leg, he leaned in his saddle and grimaced. A cannon ball blasted a crater in front of the colonel. As debris spiraled through the air, Wharton lost his balance and fell off his horse.

Shane dismounted Vengeance and extended a hand. "Sir, I'll escort you to the ambulance wagon."

Hundreds of soldiers lay twisted on the battlefield in a motionless dance of death. Lost in the haze of war, Shane and Colonel Wharton wandered along the rear in search of a hospital. Shane felt like collateral damage in the grand scheme of this war. A nameless and faceless soul—used to kill and be killed at an officer's discretion.

Mass confusion led entire brigades to veer off course. As an onrushing column of Georgians marched down a sunken road toward Duncan Field, Shane steered beneath an oak tree and grabbed a cloth bandage to wrap Wharton's blood-stained leg. Chased from the battlefield, he dismounted and took pity on the Fresh Fish. The Georgians were about to see the elephant.

"Fix bayonets double-quick!" an infantry major with a short stocky-frame barked. "Let's fly. Sweat saves blood."

Shane wrapped Wharton's bloodstained leg with a roll of cloth bandages. As he glanced across the battlefield, the doomed Georgia Infantrymen stepped over hundreds of dead soldiers. Union artillery opened fire.

Six massive Napoleon cannons blasted a volley of deadly canister shot. Dozens of one-pound iron balls sliced two, three, and four rows deep into the column of Georgians. Arms and legs were ripped from torsos. Blood splashed like rain through the misty sky.

While the wounded cried out and flopped on the ground, Shane turned away. The soldiers suffered horrific wounds he'd never seen before. He shuddered at the thought of dying amongst a pile of bodies and being tossed into a mass grave. His entire life was still ahead of him.

"Close the line!" The stocky infantry major grasped his bloodstained side and climbed to his feet. "Shoulder-up, soldiers. Keep marching toward the Yankee pickets."

Fresh blood spilled across the killing field. While the Georgians dutifully closed the formation, Confederate cannons blasted a barrage of return fire. The bone-rattling booms made Shane's head throb. His ears rang and the ground trembled. As he stared across the gory killing field, the infantrymen rallied together and continued their death march toward the enemy's pickets.

Colonel Wharton kept his injured leg raised on his saddle. Shane wondered what motivated the soldiers to rally in the face of certain death. A half dozen Georgians dropped their muskets and retreated. The stocky major limped toward the terrified men and fired his pistol. The bullet struck a bearded soldier in the temple. As he crumbled to the bloodstained earth, the remaining men picked up their muskets and quickly fell back into line. If there was a place worse than hell, this was it.

A volley of enemy musketry cut down every fourth soldier. Shane tied off Colonel Wharton's bandage and climbed back into his saddle. As he grabbed his Colt Special, a thunderous blast of cannonade swept across the field. When the canister fire finally ceased, not a single Georgian remained standing. Soldiers crawled through the bloodstained meadow.

Shane grabbed Colonel Wharton's reins. "Sir, we gotta keep moving and get you to a surgeon."

A second wave of Georgians rushed down the sunken road to reinforce the attack. The fresh troops marched in step to the brass band tune, "The Battle Hymn of the Republic." Paralyzed by fear, Shane rode Vengeance toward the rear and prayed for their souls. Cannon fire blasted across the killing field.

General Albert Sidney Johnston and his Confederate officers managed the battle from a hillside lookout. Perched on a sturdy bay-thoroughbred, he rode past a row of mounted officers and shouted encouragement to passing soldiers. Blood dripped from his knee into his cavalry boot. While Shane and Colonel Wharton approached the wounded general, a twenty-pound cannon ball whistled over their heads. The random Quartermaster Killer blasted a three-foot crater in front of the Confederate officers. Men and animals were chopped apart like meat in a grinder.

"Keep charging the Yankee line." General Johnston adjusted his ornate kepis hat. "Tonight we'll water our horses in the Tennessee River." He turned in his saddle and looked past Shane. "John Wharton, it's good to see an old friend. Your scouts provided excellent intelligence. I expect Grant's full-surrender before nightfall."

"Good to see you too, sir." Wharton eyed the general's blood-soaked boot. "Perhaps you should have your surgeon examine your knee. It's bleeding something awful."

"Nonsense I don't have time for doctoring." Johnston rubbed his horse's neck. "I'll summon my surgeon just as soon as fire eaters are drinking from the Tennessee River." He eyed Wharton's bandaged leg. "You should heed your own advice and visit your surgeon."

A courier from Second Corps reined-up in front of the general. "Sir, we've collapsed the Yankee flanks. But the bastards are fighting like hell in that sunken thicket. Those big cannons are cutting our men to pieces."

"Inform General Bragg that weakness will not be tolerated. He's to take that thicket before marching on to Pittsburg Landing." Johnston slammed his fist against his leather pommel. "I intend to crush Grant inside his fortifications and destroy his army's will to fight." His tone sharpened. "No matter the cost."

Wharton yanked his reins from Shane's hand. "If the

general's gonna stay and fight with a gunshot leg, I'll do the same. Report to Major Harrison and tell him to expect me within the hour."

Shane had seen too much death and lost his will to fight. His thoughts were dominated by self-preservation. Up since 3 a.m., he crossed a sunken road and searched for a place to hole up. A soldier's detached leg lay across a bloodstained rock. The gory limb made the hair on Shane's neck stand up. Disoriented by the dense tree-covered hills, he listened to rebel yells and Yankee War Whoops. He feared he'd lost his way. His thoughts drifted to the Crawford Boys. Did Sergeant Beavers, Mack, or the Ringo brothers survive?

Mist and gun smoke clouded the roadside woods. Shane rode Vengeance beside a long column of Mississippi Infantry and got funneled back onto Duncan Field. Hundreds of bloodstained Georgians lay scattered across the muddy field. A captain with thick-sideburns cussed his soldiers for refusing to charge. As he approached, Shane looked away and hoped the officer would pass him by.

"Ranger, are you separated from your company?" the Mississippi Captain demanded. "Come fight with us."

Shane looked away and ignored the brash officer. As he steered Vengeance around him, the captain grabbed Shane's leather bridle and yanked. Vengeance whinnied.

"I'm talking to you, ranger!" The captain pointed to the regiment of Mississippians. "You gonna fight with us or are you a damn coward like the rest of the Texans."

Shane took offense to the officer's uppity tone. "Sir, I ain't no coward. I came to fight and fight I will."

Soldiers leveled their muskets and set out across the battlefield. While the infantrymen picked their way over the regiment of fallen Georgians, a barrage of enemy canister fire blasted from the sunken thicket. The one-pound iron shot chopped down dozens of Mississippians. Bloodstained bodies stacked up in the field. Another wave of Mississippians rushed to reinforce the Gray line.

Human lives were cheap and plentiful. Riding atop

Vengeance, Shane patrolled in the rear of the Duncan Field. As he helped escort soldiers from the battle, dreadful cries echoed through the haze.

"Help me!" A Mississippi soldier held his innards and stumbled toward Vengeance. "I've been shot straight through."

Shane feared taking his beloved horse any farther and waited on the gut-shot man. A volley of friendly musketry barreled toward the enemy pickets. Sensing an opportunity, he charged forward and reached out a hand. As he helped the soldier aboard Vengeance, a Mississippi color sergeant waved his bullet-riddled Stars and Bars. Red mist exploded from the sergeant's knee. Dropping to the ground, he clung to his wooden staff and struggled to keep his regimental colors upright. His distinct, close-set eyes tightened.

The Confederate attack in Duncan Field stalled. Shane escorted the gut-shot soldier toward the rear but couldn't get the wounded Mississippi color sergeant's face out his mind. Placing the dying man beneath a tree, Shane rode back to the battlefield and searched for the battle flag. The wounded sergeant clung to his flag pole and crawled forward. His severed leg lay in the mud behind him.

Shane needed to apply a tourniquet before the color sergeant bled out. Reaching into his saddlebag, he grabbed his three-foot Garrote rope and raced Vengeance across the field. The brave sergeant lifted his head into the air. As he balanced on his flag pole, a sharpshooter's bullet ripped his skull open. A Yankee War Whoop rang out from the sunken thicket.

Shane couldn't let the sergeant's valiant efforts go in vain. Compelled by duty, he spurred his horse and reached out a hand. He grasped the wooden pole a split-second before the flag kissed the ground. Mississippians cheered.

"Lead us, ranger!" A war-weary soldier raised his bayonet. "No guts, no glory."

Shane waved the Stars and Bars with long sweeping movements. Wheeling Vengeance toward the thicket, he left his fate in the hands of God and sounded a fierce rebel yell. As he set out across the killing field, a sharpshooter's bullet held no fear. The Mississippians fixed bayonets and shouted support.

Union soldiers turned tail and ran into the woods. Shane felt invincible and bulletproof. Picking his way around the dead, he led the Gray line across Duncan Field while boldly waving the regimental colors. Union sharpshooters knocked down Mississippians with deadly accuracy. As one soldier fell, the next man heroically stepped up and filled the line.

Arriving at the enemy picket line, Shane rolled Vengeance onto her hind legs and slammed the regiment's battle flag into the mud. The column of Mississippians sounded a rebel yell and charged toward the pickets. Union cannons blasted a deadly barrage of canister fire.

Soldiers melted into the earth. Inside the range of enemy artillery, Shane steered Vengeance through a blasted hole in the pickets and rode into the labyrinth of underbrush. As he hunted for the enemy, a volley of musketry shot through the thicket. Bullets bounced off trees and sounded like a hornet's nest. Dashes of the enemy appeared in the corner of his eye.

As he struggled to maneuver his beloved horse into the brush, a bullet hit his left arm. The shot stung like fire but didn't penetrate his thick-wool jacket.

"To Retreat" trumpeted from the Confederate bugler. Lifting his hooded capote, Shane peeled back his shell jacket and spotted a Minnie ball lodged in his sleeve. As he dug the crushed bullet out of his arm, an artillery shell with a timed-fuse ricocheted off a tree twenty feet away. The iron-casing ball rolled to a stop and exploded. Dozens of deadly musket balls blew through the trees like a hurricane.

Vengeance stumbled forward and let out a high-pitched whinny. As she collapsed, Shane felt a sharp pain in his chest. A silver-dollar sized piece of iron casing protruded from his jacket. Trapped in his stirrups, he rode his loyal and majestic horse to the ground. The thousand-pound ani-

mal rolled onto her side and crushed Shane's knee. Pain
shot through his leg.

Confederate soldiers rushed out of the thicket and onto
Duncan Field. Stuck beneath his horse, Shane clenched his
teeth and pulled the iron casing out of his chest. His exhausted body needed rest. As he paused to admire the forest's natural beauty, a fluffy cottontail rabbit hopped behind
a blown-apart timber. Fearing capture, Shane closed his
eyes and fought the urge to sleep.

Vengeance snorted and cried. Kicking her legs, the beautiful black Appaloosa lifted her head but couldn't muster the
strength to stand. Shane twisted and slid his leg free. His
crushed knee throbbed. As he grabbed his six-shooter and
climbed to his feet, Vengeance stared into his eyes. Blood
pooled around her body. She'd shielded him from the brunt
of the explosion. Musket balls lodged deep inside her chest.

"I'm sorry, girl." Shane hovered over his beloved horse
and choked back tears. "I brought you in here. It's my
fault."

Vengeance deserved to die like a warrior. Her suffering
tormented him. He'd taken her loyalty for granted and reck-
lessly put her in harm's way. Placing his gun to the back of
her skull, he recited an Old Norwegian prayer taught by his
mother.

"'We'll meet again in the glorious Halls of Valhalla.'"
Shane squeezed the trigger and wiped his eyes. "'Where the
brave live forever.'"

CHAPTER 17

Nightmare in a Peach Orchard

Pittsburg Landing, Tennessee, 7:00 p.m., April 6, 1862:

The Confederate's early successes ground into bitter deadlock. Thousands of bloodstained bodies stretched to the horizon. If hell was worse than Shiloh, Shane feared eternal damnation with every fiber of his body. The loss of his beloved Vengeance left him without a horse. His gunshot arm throbbed and his chest wound oozed blood. Separated from his company, he carried his twenty-pound saddle and bags and limped toward the rear on his crushed knee. Constant rain and impending darkness exacerbated his misery.

Shane wandered through the killing fields and prayed the Crawford Boys survived. Sergeant Beavers, Mack, and the Ringo brothers were like a band of brothers. Searching for a safe place to bed down, Shane passed through a peach orchard filled with bloodstained bodies and fell in line with Confederate General Hardee's troops.

US gunboats Lexington and Tyler launched barrages of artillery screaming through the night sky. Settling under an oak tree near the Tennessee River, Shane pulled the hood of his capote over his head and took refuge for the night. His bloodstained clothes clung to his wet battered body. Wild hogs gnawed on the corpses. As he shivered from the cold, thoughts of suicide crept into his mind. Naval bombardment and endless streams of thunderstorms made sleep near impossible.

Screams of suffering soldiers swept through the darkness. Haunted by gory images of death, Shane wondered if his life could be any worse. He never should've allowed himself to get talked into joining the army.

Lightning exposed eerie pictures of vultures circling overhead. Like demons sent from hell, the ravenous birds swooped down and landed on the dead. As their powerful razor-sharp beaks tore flesh from bone, Shane calmed his fears with prayer and tranquil thoughts of home. His weary eyes closed and worries faded. If he survived the war, he'd take care of his mother and never stray far from the Shamrock Ranch.

"Reveille" trumpeted across the peach orchard. Shane rubbed the rain from his face and woke to a sadistic perversion of mankind. Contorted bodies littered the killing fields. Union General Buell and his Army of the Ohio arrived by paddleboat overnight. Eight thousand fresh enemy troops joined the battle. While the sharp crackle of enemy musketry echoed along the Tennessee River, a wounded cavalry horse appeared to drag its rider. Gathering his saddle and belongings, Shane watched the blood-soaked bay approach and shuddered. The rider-less horse dragged its hind leg.

Duncan Field looked like hell on earth. Bombed out artillery and knee-deep craters, filled with dead and dying soldiers, peppered the ground. While the Confederates withdrew from the hard-fought fields surrounding Pittsburg Landing, Shane yearned to return to his regiment. Passing through another orchard, he glanced down and carefully picked his way around the dead. White peach blossoms fell during the night covering the bodies like ominous snowflakes. Approaching a group of dejected officers, he looked to ask directions and spotted a familiar face. The uppity Mississippi captain, who'd ordered him to support the infantry's charge across the field, clutched a bottle of whiskey.

"Sir, we did our damnedest yesterday." Shane lowered his cumbersome saddle and waited for a response. "Sir, can you tell me where the Terry's Texas Rangers are posted?"

The Mississippi captain sipped his whiskey. His eyes were glossed over and hands shook uncontrollably. As he stared into gory field of corpses, Shane saluted and looked to clarify the question. The drunken officer stumbled.

"Sir, where's the Texas Eighth Cavalry? Colonel Wharton's Texas Regiment?" Shane stared at the despondent officer. "Sir, are there any survivors?"

"I'm waiting for my men to return." The captain slurred his words. "Johnny Rogers—Dave Bass—Ben—"

Shane feared the distraught officer had lost his mind. The only things alive in the orchard were vultures. Stepping away from the suicidal man, he eyed the group of officers and looked to excuse himself.

"Stand down, ranger." A shaggy lieutenant with a goatee approached. "You'll have to forgive the captain. He's deeply saddened and drunk. He lost his entire company in the field." His somber voice softened. "Wharton's at a field hospital along Corinth Road. His men took heavy losses. If there's any of 'em left, you should check there. Captain—nooo!" The lieutenant rushed past Shane. "Don't do it."

The distraught Mississippi captain stared into the grisly field of bodies with his pistol pressed against his temple. His gun hand trembled violently. Saluting his fallen soldiers, he stiffened and squeezed the trigger. Blood and tissue exploded from his head. As he collapsed, the lieutenant caught his body and carefully laid him down to earth.

A proud Yankee War Whoop echoed from Pittsburg Landing. Passing a fishpond, Shane cleared his dry throat and longed for a drink. Dead soldiers floated in the water. As he stepped over a headless body and worked his way through the sea of corpses, a dying soldier cried out for his mother. Shane wondered what motivated the Northern Devils to invade the sovereignty of the South?

Surrounded by death and suffering, he stepped over two enemy soldiers and pushed aside a bloated body on the water's edge. The bloodstained water made him gag. Yearning for a drink, he knelt and dipped his palm into the pond. A gory hand with a finger missing locked onto his ankle.

"Water!" A boy soldier with a split-open stomach stared through flaccid eyes. "Please, sir—I want a drink of water."

Shane jerked and leaped back. The dying soldier let go of his leg. Pulling his Colt, he took aim at the enemy and realized the heathen Yankees, he hated so, were young men and boys just like him. His vengeful heart slowed and began to beat with mercy for others.

Thunder roared while rain fell from the heavens. Shane cupped his hands to gather water for the soldier. As he bent down to deliver the drink, the Angel of Death claimed the boy.

೧ঌ৩

Texas Eighth Cavalry bivouac along the Corinth Road, 5:00 p.m., April 7, 1862:

From Mrs. Sarah Bell's peach orchard to Farmer James Fraley's cotton field, twenty-four-thousand soldiers lay dead, wounded, or missing. More Americans died in two days of fighting at Shiloh than all the previous American wars combined. While the Confederate Army of the Mississippi withdrew from the battlefield, Union General Grant reinforced his defenses. Shane feared the Crawford Boys were dead. Hungry and exhausted, he cut through a forest of pine trees and passed the bombed-out shell of the Shiloh Church. Bullet holes pock marked the once pristine walls. As he arrived at the Wharton Ranger bivouac, a group of Archer Grays huddled around crates of supplies marked US Army. The large silhouette of a ranger brightened his mood.

Mack peered over his shoulder. "Frank! We've been worried sick about you. Sergeant Beavers said you'd been killed." He pushed past two rangers and approached with a smile as big as Texas. "You look like hell."

Glancing at a row of captured Union horses, Shane dropped his cumbersome saddle and bags. "I just passed through hell." His eyes scanned the bivouac. "I've been worried about you too. Where're the Ringo brothers?"

Mack wrapped his arms around Shane and lifted him off the ground. The brawny bear hug lasted an awkward thirty seconds. As a half dozen rangers gathered around, Shane searched for any sign of Sergeant Rufus Beavers and the Ringos.

"I bet you're starving." Mack handed over an open can of sardines. "We've got triple rations, tonight. I took this salted fish right outta Grant's hand."

"Balderdash." Shane knew Mack liked to spin a yarn and tossed a headless sardine into his mouth. "Where're the Ringo Brothers?"

"I'm over here, wagon dog!" Jerry shouted from behind the row of captured horses. "Better report to Major Harrison. He's been asking about you."

"I'm glad to see you're still alive and kicking, Ringo." Shane sighed and spit out a sardine tail. "Wish Vengeance was alive to do the same. I lost her."

"Why'd you spit out the tail?" Mack's eyes narrowed. "I eat the bones—and the head if they'd left on there."

"That's nasty!" Shane feared Colonel Wharton had succumbed to his leg wound. "Why's the Jimtown Major in charge?"

"Wharton's hurt real bad—might not make it through the night." Mack picked up Shane's saddle. "He nearly bled out on the battlefield—like General Johnston."

"Hell's bells, Johnston died? I spoke with him yesterday." Shane eyed the group of Archer Grays. "He was shouting encouragement to his troops, acted like his injured knee was just a flesh wound."

A veteran ranger from Waco pushed between two men. "Sergeant Beavers said we're all gonna die tomorrow when Colonel Forrest takes over command."

"Quit bothering, Frank. Honor your word to the Confederacy." Mack placed his hand on Shane's shoulder and steered him away from the disgruntled soldiers. "Come with me." His deep voice softened. "Since our deaf and blind generals are so stupid, why don't we get you a horse and we'll ride on out of here after dark."

Shane wasn't ready to listen to Mack's dribble. "Where's Jimmy?"

"Don't worry—Jimmy's fine." Mack pointed toward Owl Creek. "I sent him down to the stream to fill our canteens."

"What?" Shane shook his head in disgust. "Did you send anyone with him? He's fourteen—enemy's all around us."

"You worry too much. Sound like a woman." Mack shrugged and headed toward the row of captured horses. "That boy is plum lucky. If anyone makes it outta this war alive, it'll be him.

"Does Jerry know you sent his little brother off alone?" Shane wondered about the new regimental commander. "Who in the hell is Colonel Forrest?"

"I ain't never met him." Mack scoffed. "Major Harrison says he's a millionaire, slave trader, and riverboat gambler. Probably just another uptight blowhard officer." He pointed toward a raw-boned mare with an expensive McClellan saddle. "See that Roan over there? It belonged to General Grant."

"Grant would never ride a skinny horse like that." Shane eyed a black stallion and grabbed his saddle from Mack. "That thick-shouldered stallion looks like a general's horse."

"That stallion belonged to a Yankee officer." Mack approached the raw-boned Roan and lifted up the fancy quilted seat. "See the name on the saddle? Says US Grant. I took his damn horse." He pulled a package of sugar cookies and another can of sardines from his jacket. "Where do you think I got all this food? I took it from Grant's tent."

Shane didn't believe a word. "Whatever you say." He approached Jerry and greeted him with a big hug. "Can't believe you let Dodd send Jimmy off for water alone."

Jerry stepped back and glared at Mack. "You made Jimmy fill all those canteens by himself? Why didn't you go with him, lard ass?"

"Quit treating him like a damn child." Mack threw his hands in the air and stormed off. "For crying out loud, it's only been an hour."

Jerry turned toward Shane. "Pick out a horse and we'll go looking for him."

Scanning the livestock, Shane eyed Grant's raw-boned Roan. "If that horse really belonged to Grant, why hasn't Sergeant Beavers tried to sell it."

"Didn't you hear? Rufus got shot." Jerry's voice choked. "He's at the field hospital with Wharton."

Shane felt the joy leave his body. Rufus had a wife and baby back home. Placing his saddle on the thick-shouldered black stallion, he felt lost and feared his own mortality. Half of the original Rangers had died or deserted. He needed to write his mother and apologize before it was too late.

April 7, 1862

Dear Mother,

I'm sick with regret for leaving the Shamrock Ranch. You were right. I was foolish to leave you alone. War changes a man. Mother, I miss you more every day. War is an awful affair. So much death. We fought a mass battle at the Shiloh Methodist Church on a Sunday morning. I've been told Shiloh means a "House of Peace" in Hebrew. For the rest of my life, I'm going to hear and even smell the death and suffering.

Your loving son,
Shane

Please write back and send a package of supplies.
We have nothing. Please let Mary Kelly know that I
think of her, too.

CHAPTER 18

Poker Face

Confederate Field Hospital six miles south of the Shiloh Church, 5:30 a.m., April 8, 1862:

While Grant's army dug in around Pittsburg Landing, General PGT Beauregard took command of the Confederate Army and ordered a full retreat back to Corinth. Colonel Nathan Bedford Forrest mustered the remnants of four Confederate cavalry regiments to check the Union Army's pursuit. Dispatched to Forrest's Cavalry Brigade, Shane and the Crawford Boys camped near a field hospital along the Corinth Road. Two days of fighting left him weary of war. Cussing his wretched life, he sutured his wounded chest with horse hair and feared a third day of fighting would end in his demise.

"Reveille" trumpeted through the woods of Hardin County Tennessee. Wiping the sleep from his eyes, Shane peeled off his itchy bloodstained bandage and picked at his scabbed-over chest.

His crushed knee ached. As he dressed his wounds in fresh cloth bandages, Mack Dodd and the Ringo brothers cleaned their weapons.

The intimidating sound of Yankee war drums pounded in the distance. Colonel Forrest planned to ambush the Union

Fifth Division along Ridge Road. Looking to protect the
Confederate field hospital, he ordered troopers to cover the
narrow road with logs. Shane hated the backbreaking duty.
Working along a wooded ridge, he helped drag timbers
down the hillside onto a log-strewn blockade.

"I ain't no damn lumberjack!" Mack spit a mouthful of
tobacco juice toward the Ringo brothers. "We're supposed
to be killing Yankees, not hauling logs." He picked at an
open blister on his index finger. "If our deaf and blind generals would've let us keep on fighting, Grant would've surrendered."

Jerry chopped an axe blade through a back-cut pine.
"Quit your bitching. It was your idea to join the Confederacy." He pushed the tree toward the road and stepped back.
"Better start hauling timber before Major Harrison flogs
your lard ass."

The fifty-foot pine tree split and cracked. As the trunk
crashed against the muddy hillside, Mack cussed, and his
face turned red as a rooster. Lifting the end of the fallen
timber, he dragged the thousand pound log down the ridge
while howling like a mad man. The Ringo brothers rushed
to get out of his way. Rangers stopped working and stared
in amazement.

Dropping the log on the ten-foot-wide road, Mack turned
toward a group of Tennessee Troopers and pounded his
chest. "Arrrghhh!"

"Holy Moly!" Jimmy approached Shane. "Somebody really set Dodd off. Did you see him drag that big log all by
himself?"

"Dodd's not human," Shane joked. "He's half man and
half beast."

"He smells like a damn donkey." Jerry stepped in front
of his brother and shook his head. "How can anyone be that
strong and that hard headed?"

Shane feared Mack's volatile temper. "I don't know, but
you really pissed him off this time."

"Good. Someone needs to get his attention." Jerry stared

down the hillside. "But I sure as hell ain't telling him nothing."

Major Harrison rode along the ridgeline. "McLean, what's gotten into your men? Private Dodd can't scream and holler like that. It's bad for morale."

"Sir, you tell him." Shane figured Mack was in one of his moods. "When he's hungry and tired, he gets mean and ornery. I've seen him fight a man over a biscuit."

"We don't have time for Dodd's nonsense." Harrison brandished a four-foot-long whip. "General Sherman and his Fifth Division are preparing to attack our army's retreat to Corinth." His tone sharpened. "Ten lashes will get the private to act like a soldier."

The company was demoralized by the loss of men and stunned by the humiliating withdrawal from Shiloh. If Harrison whipped Mack in front of the soldiers, Shane feared Armageddon would breakout among the men. Mack was a crude pain in the ass, but every ranger respected him.

"Sir, Dodd's moody but he's a hard worker." Shane grabbed Harrison's bridle and pointed to the log-covered road. "You saw him lug that timber down the ridge. Would've taken three or four men to do that job. He doesn't deserve to be flogged." His voice deepened. "We both know he's fearless in battle."

"Dodd's gotta be held accountable." Harrison snapped off a warning lash. "A chain is only as strong as its weakest link."

Jerry removed his cavalry jacket. "Sir, Dodd ain't no weak link." He ripped off his shirt and presented his bare back. "If you're gonna flog men for not working, start with me."

The Crawford Boys were like brothers. Shane and his friends ruthlessly harassed each other but no one else better say a word. If the Jimtown major whipped Mack, they'd all end up in hell.

Lowering his whip, Harrison stared down the ridge and sipped his Masonic flask. Mack flipped his middle-finger at a group of Tennessee Troopers. As he pounded his chest and headed up the ridge, Shane looked to diffuse the situation.

"What's your damn problem, Dodd?" Harrison's angry voice attracted the attention of every soldier in earshot. "Your attitude needs an adjustment."

Mack stopped in his tracks and cocked his head. A look of puzzlement covered his face. Rangers along the ridge stopped working and stared in disbelief.

"Sir, I have no problem. I'm a happy soldier." Mack eyed Shane. "Ask Frank or the Ringo brothers, I've been working hard all morning."

"Quit all this nonsense or Frank will receive a beating for your behavior." Harrison brandished his whip. "If that doesn't get your attention, the Archer Grays will face company punishment while you're made to watch."

Mack shook his head. "Sir, why would you make the company suffer for my actions?"

"Because you don't respond to normal discipline." Harrison stood in his stirrups and addressed the rangers. "God commands all of you to give our army a chance to withdraw—even if death awaits us." His voice trembled. "Get back to work. Every damned of you."

∽∂∽

Confederate Field Hospital, 11:30 a.m., April 8, 1862:

A fifty-foot blockade of fallen timber covered Ridge Road. While sympathetic Southerners set up a Cracker Line in a meadow adjacent to the hospital, Shane and the Crawford Boys broke for lunch. His empty stomach and battered body yearned for sustenance. A limited quantity of bread, pan sausage, strawberries, and fresh vegetables were served off a white table cloth. Hungry soldiers ate with their fingers.

Shane didn't want to appear greedy and looked to ration the food. Grabbing a slice of bread, he spotted an older woman working the serving line. He politely tore a circular pan-sausage in half. The prim and proper lady reminded him of his mother. As she offered up the other half of sausage, he shook his head and politely refused the extra ration.

"Thank you for bringing the food, ma'am." Shane missed his mother and her home cooking. "I ain't eaten anything warm in days."

"You're welcome. I wanted to be here today for you fighting men." The woman stared through watery eyes and her voice cracked. "I lost my son and my husband in yesterday's battle."

"Sorry for your loss, ma'am. We'll whip 'em Yankees today for you." Shane thought she even sounded like his mother. "You sure remind me of my ma back home in Texas."

The grieving woman stepped away from the table and broke down. Her body trembled and tears cascaded down her cheeks. As she cried, Shane wished he'd kept his mouth shut.

The ration-issue line stopped serving. A preacher rushed to comfort the upset woman. Her suffering made Shane question his own mortality. He didn't want his mother to grieve for him while she still mourned the loss of his father. Thoughts of returning home crept into his mind.

The Ringo brothers spread a gray horse blanket on top of a grassy knoll. Joining his friends for lunch, Shane bit into his tiny ration of bread and thought about the futility of the impending fight. Colonel Nathan Bedford Forrest and three-hundred Confederate cavalrymen were up against General Sherman's Fifth Division. The suicidal task reminded Shane of the Greek Spartans march from ancient Corinth and the Battle at Thermopylae.

Shane shared the inspiring story with the Ringo brothers. "Two-thousand years ago, King Leonidas and three-hundred fierce Spartan Hoplites were left behind to fight

Xeroxes the Great and a hundred-thousand Persians."

Jerry tossed a morsel of bread into his mouth. "Did the Spartans win?"

"Hell, no! One-hundred-thousand Persians against three-hundred Greeks." Shane raised his eyebrows. "But the Spartan's died honorably. They stalled the mighty Persian Army at Thermopylae, while the Greek nation rallied and won the war." His voice choked. "If we sacrifice ourselves in battle today, General Beauregard and the rest of his army can retreat back to Corinth safely."

"I don't wanna die." Jimmy snatched a bread crumb off the blanket. "I wanna go home and live my life in peace. Can't believe I let Dodd talk me into joining the rangers."

Staring at the war weary cavalrymen in the meadow, Shane realized they'd all be slaughtered for 'The Cause.' Self-sacrifice rang hollow in his mind. The thought of dying in mass combat, so the generals could claim glory felt like a wasted life. He suffered through each day, in hopes of one day punishing his father's killers.

"Anybody wanna play euchre?" Mack approached with an entire loaf of bread under his arm. "We've got a couple of hours to kill before the Yankees get here." His pockets overflowed with fresh carrots and turnips. "Nickel a game?"

"How in hell's name did you get all that extra food?" Shane sat on the horse blanket and wondered. "Did you steal it?"

"Hell, no. I got it off the Cracker Line." Mack gave a smug grin. "Some old lady was crying, so I took a handful of sausages when nobody was looking. Went back through the line twice." His voice scoffed. "Those gray-haired ladies don't remember who's been through."

"Have a little compassion!" Shane's voice trembled. "She lost her son and husband in yesterday's battle."

"Sorry, Frank, I didn't know." Mack shifted the Sharps shotgun strapped to his back and retrieved a deck of playing cards. "Thought she was crying because she was old or something."

"You're gonna get us in trouble." Jerry pointed at Mack's pocketful of food. "Colonel Forrest's Escort Company ain't eaten yet. They're patrolling the Corinth Road." His face twisted in disgust. "When the food runs out, I'll tell the hungry troopers you ate their lunch."

"Let 'er rip!" Mack scoffed at the challenge. "I ain't scared of those high-falutin bastards. Colonel Forrest and his Tennessee Troopers can kiss my ass."

Jerry snatched a sausage out of Mack's hand. "I'll play a hand of euchre, but Frank's my partner. I always lose with you."

"Dodd ain't gonna be my partner. He's terrible." Jimmy folded his arms in protest. "I'm playing with Frank."

"Quit bellyaching, you damn bad egg." Jerry pushed his finger into his little brother's chest. "It's your turn to play on Dodd's team. I played with him last time."

"Get your hand out of my face." Jimmy's eyes narrowed. "You always say you're better than me. Prove it. You play with him." His voiced echoed through a meadow of soldiers. "I'm playing with Frank. He's the best euchre player in the company."

Euchre eased the long spells of camp boredom. Shane didn't consider himself a great player but rarely lost a fair game. Counting player discards and playing patterns took his mind off the war.

"I ain't playing with either of you damn Ringos." Mack began dealing cards. "Frank's gonna be my partner."

A boisterous voice reverberated up the grassy knoll. "Who's the best card player in this company of Texas Rangers?"

Shane snapped his head around. Five Tennessee officers approached on foot. The Elite Escort Company Troopers wore leg gaiters and spotless shell jackets accented with golden buttons. Shane knew he wasn't supposed to be playing cards. If Harrison caught them playing euchre before a fight, they'd all be flogged. Soldiers in the meadow suddenly rushed to attention.

Mack leapt to his feet and saluted. As the Ringo brothers followed suit, Shane folded his cards and climbed to his feet. An intimidating colonel with a collar full of stars and sleeves with yellow-braided Chicken Guts approached. His beady eyes narrowed.

"Is this some kind of Robber's Row?" The colonel rested his hand on a gold-leaf saber handle. "What do you, Texicans got going on up here?"

"No, sir. We're just killing time before we whip 'em Yankees." Shane hoped to avoid company punishment and lied. "Major Harrison allows us to play cards, so I asked my friends to join me in a game."

"I'm Colonel Forrest, and I'll be commanding Harrison's Rangers." Forrest glanced at the cards in Shane's hand and grinned through his thick-pointed goatee. "You men may carry on. Poker calms the soul."

Mack squared his shoulders. "Sir, we ain't playing poker. We're playing euchre."

"Euchre?" Forrest scoffed. "Here in Tennessee, euchre is played by old ladies." He turned to a junior officer with dark shoulder-length hair. "Corporal Trimble, did you know these fearless Texas Rangers we've all heard about play old lady games?"

"No, sir, I didn't know that." The long-haired corporal's face tightened. "Hope they don't fight like old ladies, too."

"Sir, y'all don't play euchre?" Mack cocked his head in astonishment. "Everybody in Texas plays euchre."

Shane expected Colonel Forrest to be uppity like the rest of his Escort Company. Forrest had a confident air but didn't appear uptight like Major Harrison. The Jimtown major viewed gambling as the Devil's vice.

"I'd never have walked up here if I'd known you Texicans were playing old lady games." Forrest pulled a deck of Goodall cards out of his coat pocket and unhooked his fancy gold-leaf saber. "In Tennessee, we play games for men like five-card draw and stud poker." He shuffled the cards like a skillful vaudeville magician. "You Texicans wanna play a quick hand of poker?"

Shane relished the opportunity to play with the colonel, but feared his inexperience. "Yessir, but I've only played euchre."

Forrest motioned for his officers to leave and eyed Corporal Trimble. "Kelly, keep me posted on General Sherman's advance. I wanna know when his advanced guard reaches Ridge Road." He stepped between Shane and Mack. "Damn, you Texicans are tall. Don't be looking down at my cards when the betting starts."

"Sir, I ain't got much money to bet." Shane didn't realize the colonel intended to gamble. "Colonel Wharton used to pay us out of his own pocket, but he got shot. Probably in an ambulance wagon on his way back home to Texas."

"Hush your mouth, boy. Wharton ain't going home." Forrest's beady eyes narrowed. "He'll be back to this regiment before you can scratch your little ass. What's your name, soldier?"

"Frank McLean, sir." Shane wished he'd kept his mouth shut. "Sir, I didn't mean Wharton abandoned us. I meant he wasn't around to loan us money so we can play cards and bet with you."

"I don't want your damn spondulix." Forrest's face tightened. "I've got more money than I could spend in a dozen lifetimes. I bet for sport." He pointed to the horse blanket. "Take a seat. I'm over here to have some fun with my new rangers before we kill some Yankee scum."

Whispers of the poker game shot through the ranks like bullets in a gunfight. The crowd had swollen to over a dozen troopers. Shane admired Forrest's brash demeanor and envied his ability to intimidate men with a wicked glance. While Shane took a seat on the blanket, curious soldiers wandered up the grassy knoll. Mack and the Ringo brothers circled around and took a seat.

"Listen to the rules." Forrest squeezed between Shane and Mack. "You're looking for same-suit straights and like-cards to string together. More pairs and straights you have, the more you bet."

Hoping to gain a playing advantage, Shane studied Forrest's leadership style and looked for insight into his mannerisms. The colonel pulled two old-English court jester cards from the deck. Spectators around the poker game hushed.

"I've added a pair of jokers to be used at your discretion." Forrest held up the colorful double-ended cards and eyed Shane. "What do you know about jokers?"

"Sir, Dodd's the only joker I know." Shane nodded at Mack. "But he ain't too funny."

Mack cocked his head and made a fist. As he glared across the blanket, laughter resonated through the crowd. Shane waited for the amused soldiers to hush.

Forrest placed the two wild cards into the deck. "Did you want to play poker or make childish jokes?"

"Sorry, sir." Shane wished he'd kept his mouth shut. "I'd like to play poker, sir."

"Major Harrison informed me you men were some of the toughest around. Hope I didn't get hoodwinked." Forrest shuffled the cards. "In the game of poker, jokers ain't funny, but they're extremely valuable. They can be used in any suit, run, or rank. A joker can make an average hand great and a great hand unbeatable." He nodded at Mack. "Jokers can save your ass in a bad situation."

"Then I guess I'm a joker." Mack eyed Shane. "I've been saving Frank's ass for years."

Forrest placed the stack of cards in front of Jimmy. "Cut the deck. We'll bet personal items in lieu of cash." He placed his fancy gold-leaf cavalry saber in the middle of the blanket. "I'll start the betting."

Shane didn't have a fancy sword but feared backing out in front of so many soldiers. He felt duped. Colonel Forrest implied they'd play for entertainment not up the ante with each subsequent bet.

Jimmy split the deck and returned the cards.

"Sir, I ain't got nothing as expensive as your saber." Jerry shrugged and lowered his chin. "I'm just a Pie Eater from the country."

"Bet that Texas Star on your hat." Forrest pointed to the four-inch tin star pinned on Jerry's campaign hat. "It can't be bought. It has to be earned through blood and sweat." His eyes widened. "I'd be honored to wage my saber against all of your Texas Stars."

Shane perked up at Forrest's offer. His loyalty lay with his friends not a ten cent token symbol. The Ranger Stars were a gift from Colonel Wharton, who purchased them in Nashville to curry favor. Reaching for the star on his wool-felt campaign hat, Shane cussed his luck. He'd foolishly worn the straw palmetto Mary Kelly had purchased for him in Waco. While Jerry stared at his campaign hat, Mack and Jimmy tossed their Ranger Stars into the pot.

"Colonel, with all due respect." Jerry shook his head. "I ain't much on gambling. I'm gonna sit and watch." He sighed and rubbed his thumb over his Ranger Star. "I was with Colonel Wharton when he purchased these stars. He'd be disappointed in me if I lost it in a card game."

Mack nodded in agreement. "Sir, I better not bet mine."

"Hold it, Private." Forrest's voice deepened. "Once something is placed in the pot, it stays in the pot."

"Sir, I'll bet my star but my hats in my saddlebag." Shane motioned toward a row of picketed horses. "Do you mind if I run and fetch it?"

"Yankees are coming. I ain't got time to wait." Forrest shook his head. "There're already two stars in the pot." He pointed to the black neckerchief around Shane's neck. "If your friends are in agreement, you can bet that cravat."

Shane supposed the offer was fair but took offense to the humiliating demand. His neckerchief hid the jagged inch-wide scar surrounding his throat. He hated the tormented looks and embarrassing questions about his disfigured neck. Staring into the Forrest's beady eyes, he untied his neckerchief and tossed the black cloth into the pot.

Groans circulated through the crowd. A few troopers gawked while others simply turned away. Shane felt insecure and vulnerable. He hated the gang of Jayhawkers and wished he'd never gone into that damn saloon in Austin. His friends would never understand his suffering and emotional toil.

"Those damn Jayhawkers!" Mack's voice trembled. "Frank, we're gonna kill all of 'em sons-of-bitches."

"Put your cravat back on, soldier." Forrest shook his head and grimaced in disgust. "Bet the shirt off your back instead."

"Sir, my bet's been placed." Shane defiantly left his neckerchief on the blanket. "Once an item's placed in the pot it stays in the pot. I ain't ashamed of my past. It's made me who I am."

Forrest cocked his head. "And who exactly is that?"

"Sir, you spoke with Major Harrison before you walked up here." Shane felt his services were being peddled and didn't feel the need to explain. "You know good and well who we are and what we've done. Why else would you play cards with a bunch of Texicans?" His voice trembled. "No amount of money is gonna get me to join your squadron of Elite Escorts."

Yankee war drums echoed through the ridge of fallen timbers. While a dozen spectators looked on, Colonel Forrest ignored General Sherman's approaching Fifth Division. He dealt four hands of five cards, one to himself, and one to Shane, Mack, and Jimmy. Jerry Ringo remained steadfast in his refusal to participate.

Picking up his cards, Shane shuffled through his hand in search of pairs or straight runs. A joker appeared behind a queen of hearts. As he pondered the possibilities, Forrest studied his hand, shook his head, and mumbled to himself.

Shane placed his thumb on an eight of clubs and slid two worthless cards to the edge of his hand. "Sir, how many can I discard?"

"You can discard all five, but you'll need to ante up a

second bet." Forrest pulled a shiny Army Colt from his side holster. "I purchased this pistol last month in Nashville." He pointed to the ivory-handled .36 in Shane's hand-tooled holster. "I'll bet my Colt against your custom gun."

Shane thought they were playing for sport and sensed a rouse. Adrenalin surged through his veins. Kirby's *work* gun held a special purpose. No amount of money could replace the satisfaction of killing his father's murderers with that gun. "Sir, the only way my pa's gun will leave my side is if it's pried out of my dead hand." He squeezed his cards and motioned toward his new black stallion. "I've got two other pistols in my saddlebag I'd be willing to bet."

"I told you once, I don't have time to wait." Forrest pointed at the square and compass engraved on Shane's ivory-handled revolver. "You're a Freemason?"

"Yessir." Shane's voice strengthened with resolve. "I'm gonna use my pa's gun to kill the gang of Jayhawkers who murdered him."

"Then you'd better not risk that pistol." Forrest's beady eyes narrowed. "I don't care for Freemasonry. Bastards got too many rules." He motioned toward Shane's prized Bowie knife. "Toss in that big pig sticker and we've got a deal."

Shane pulled his Bowie from a leather scabbard. "Sir, this knife holds special meaning. Sam Houston presented it to me when I won a shooting contest in Waco."

"Thought you hated Houston?" Mack glared across the blanket. "We're gonna ride to Huntsville this summer and slit the bastard's throat."

"Shut your mouth, or I'll cut your tongue out." Shane didn't want to divulge his true intentions. "Silence is golden. It's time you woke up and learned that."

Shane planned to visit Sam Houston at the conclusion of war and demand answers. Why did Houston conspire to have Kirby murdered? Who else was involved? If he didn't like the big drunk's answers, he'd suffocate Houston with a pillow.

Colonel Forrest sighed and looked like he intended to

fold his hand. His eyes wandered from his cards to his Army Colt. Shane kept his joker, eight of clubs and queen of hearts. Hoping to test the colonel's resolve, he brandished his Bowie and stuck the ten-inch blade into the ground. Forrest's beady eyes widened.

"Sir, I'll take your bet." Shane released his pig sticker and discarded two worthless cards at the colonel's feet. "If you'll fold, your saber stays in the pot."

"I'm out." Jimmy took a deep breath and frowned. "Can't bet my pistol. It's all I own." He tossed his cards on the ground and joined his big brother as a spectator. "Ya'll can fight over my ten-cent star."

"Damn Sunday soldier." Mack eyed Jimmy with disdain. "You're just afraid to face Frank and the colonel. I'm gonna win." He turned and gave Forrest a smug grin. "Unless the colonel's holding a joker or something."

"I ain't got a joker, but there're two in this deck," Forrest mumbled and squeezed the cards in his hand. "I should probably fold this god-awful hand."

Shane assumed the colonel was bluffing. According to Sergeant Beavers, Forrest was a millionaire with the shrewd reputation of a riverboat gambler. If he folded, Shane liked his chances to win everything. Mack Dodd could barely count to ten much less play cards or keep a secret.

"Sir, don't quit. I heard you're rich." Mack shook his head. "At least bet your Army Colt, so you can discard. You might like your new hand."

Shane wanted to cut out Mack's tongue. "Let the colonel fold if he wants too. Shut your mouth until you've placed your bet."

Mack reached behind his back. "You need to shut your mouth, Frank. I got something to bet and I've got a damn good hand too."

"Thanks for telling everyone, dufus." Shane attempted to bluff Forrest into folding his hand. "Now the colonel knows you've got good cards, he'll be afraid to ante up."

A grin climbed the side of Forrest's face. "I didn't say I was folding."

Tennessee Troopers whistled and cheered. A lieutenant gestured a big thumbs up to the colonel. Forrest had no intention of quitting.

Shane needed to change his tact with the colonel. "Sir, do you mind if I reclaim my Bowie for a moment." He glared at Mack. "I feel a need to stick my big-mouth friend with it."

Grabbing his deck of cards, Forrest smothered a laugh. "Your knife stays in the pot." He placed two new cards at Shane's feet. "Take a look at those fresh cards. It might cheer you up."

"No thanks, sir. My hand's already dealt." Shane feared the colonel would read his face and gauge his reaction. "I'll wait until you and Dodd decide to ante up or walk away."

"My hand is a surefire winner. I'm all in." Mack discarded a single card and placed a ten-gauge English percussion shotgun alongside the colonel's saber. "Only one card, please."

"Do you even know the difference between a pair and a flush?" Shane eyed the cumbersome four-foot shotgun. "Dodd is the only man I know who brings a big double-barrel shotgun to lunch when he's already carrying three pistols."

"Come a little closer and you'll see something even funnier." Mack pointed to the ten gauge shotgun. "I'm betting the gun you lent me before riding into Tiny Town." He chuckled with delight and snorted through his nostrils. "Ain't that a side bender?"

Shane wanted to whip the smirk off Mack's face. "You even laugh like a damn pig. Don't expect me to give you anything else."

"I don't need nothing from you—*ever again*." Mack fanned his face with his cards. "Don't be sore, Frank. I'll return your shotgun. Right after I win this pot."

"Texans sure like to hold 'em cards." Forrest placed his

expensive Army Colt in the pot and tossed a pair of cards onto the horse blanket. "I've gotta see what Dodd's holding in his hand that makes him so damn giddy. Must be a joker."

Shane sensed a cheat. While soldiers cheered Forrest's decision, Mack smiled like a fat kid holding a cake. Eying the hand-painted joker in his hand, Shane intended to win both of the colonel's weapons but desired more. He wanted something extra, something every ranger wanted and deserved.

"Sir, if I win this hand and we chase Grant's army back to Pittsburg Landing will you grant this entire regiment furlough?" Shane raised his voice. "Colonel Forrest, take us to revel in New Orleans."

An exuberant spectator seconded the proposition. "Hear! Hear!"

Shane recognized Forrest couldn't grant three-hundred men furlough in the middle of war. But he figured it wouldn't hurt to ask. As he eyed the colonel's reaction, a group of rangers wandered up the knoll. The crowd around the poker game had grown to nearly two-dozen soldiers.

"I like your style, Frank. We could all use a week's furlough." Forrest picked up his deck of cards and addressed the soldiers. "I'll make this regiment a promise. If Frank McLean wins and we chase General Sherman's Fifth Division back to Pittsburg Landing." He eyed a group of troopers and his smile widened. "I'll grant everyone furlough with a dozen of the best whores in Tennessee."

Men erupted into raucous celebration. A boisterous Tennessean danced a jig like a headless chickens. No rational person really believed the colonel, but the perverted promise gave them something to look forward to.

Forrest dealt Mack a single card and then dealt himself two cards. As he placed the deck on the blanket, Shane eyed the two facedown cards at his feet. Holding an eight and a queen of hearts, he needed a like card to place with his joker for a three-of-a-kind.

Mack shrugged. "Colonel Forrest, what happens if I win?"

"If you win." Forrest picked up his two cards and his eyes suddenly widened. "We'll ride on to Washington and steal Lincoln's gold."

A Partisan Ranger shouted his support. "Woohoo! Hang Lincoln from the White House porch."

"Start weeping, boys." Forrest laid down his cards and smirked through his pointed goatee. "Two kings and a joker makes three-of-a-kind."

Tennesseans applauded Forrest's impressive hand. Shane cussed his luck. He needed a near impossible four-of-a-kind to beat the colonel's three kings. Staring at the two facedown cards at his feet, he felt like a loser.

"Poppycock, Colonel!" A trooper slapped his thigh in joyful celebration. "You whipped 'em damn Texicans."

Shane prayed for a pair of eights or queens and divine intervention. His frustration mounted. As he eyed the pair of facedown cards at his feet, sporadic gunfire rang out along the Corinth Road.

"Goddammit!" Mack tossed his cards on the blanket and shook his head. "I'm out. Three kings beats my two eights."

"You bet my ten-gauge shotgun with just a pair of eights." Shane realized only one eight remained in play. "Thought you had a joker, you damn fool."

"I didn't wanna tell Wharton I lost my Ranger Star in a poker game. He'd be disappointed in me." Mack eyed the two facedown cards at Shane's feet. "I got faith in you. You'll beat three-of-a-kind."

Colonel Forrest leaned back and nodded at a trooper. As he confidently stretched out his legs, Shane turned his first card, *Queen of Diamonds*. Adrenaline pumped through his veins. The Ringo brothers cheered. But a pair of queens and a joker didn't beat the colonel's three kings. Everything came down to his final card.

Gambling rivaled the excitement of a running gun battle. Shane needed another queen or the last eight to pair with his joker for a full-house. His heart raced and breathing quickened. As he glanced over his shoulder, Forrest sat stonefaced and bit the nail on his index finger.

"Sir, I like your game of poker." Shane pinched the edge of his last card and stared at the colonel. "It keeps my mind sharp."

Troopers hushed to a whisper. Win or lose, Shane savored every delectable moment. He was hooked on gambling like an addict craves morphine. His mind yearned for the exhilarating high. Jimmy Ringo clung to his big brother.

"Holy molly, Frank. Flip the damn card." Jerry's eyes narrowed. "You're taking forever."

Shane glanced at Jerry and turned the last card. Mack leapt to his feet. As he pumped his massive fist into the air, Jimmy hugged his brother's neck. Rangers around the game roared with applause.

Mack sounded a boisterous Indian whoop. "Whoo hoo!"

Shane had drawn the eight of spades giving him two pairs and a joker. His full-house beat Forrest's three kings. The colonel dropped his head and mumbled under his breath.

"Beginner's luck, sir." Shane reclaimed his black neckerchief and prized Bowie out of the pot. "Who'd of thought I'd have two pairs and a joker?"

"I'll say." Forrest pretended not to care. "It was a great comeback."

Shane intended to make Mack eat his words and cheerfully returned Jimmy's Texas Star. As he pocketed Mack's star, Corporal Kelly Trimble rushed up the grassy hill. The Elite Escort Trooper appeared concerned as he pushed his way through the spectators.

"Colonel Forrest, sir. Scouts report Sherman's advanced cavalry is a mile away on Corinth Road." Trimble had a long face and his voice trembled. "Sir, they're coming after us."

Forrest picked up his cards and climbed to his feet. "Prepare for battle, men. Devils in Blue are coming for you."

Looking to make peace, Shane holstered the colonel's Army Colt and presented his gold-leaf cavalry saber as a gift. "Sir, Texas Rangers shoot to kill. I have no use for your fancy knife."

"Don't patronize me, boy! I'll slit your throat and hang you by your ankles." Forrest's beady eyes narrowed. "If you have no use for my sword, sell it or give it away before I feed you to the damn Yankees."

Shane feared he'd offended the colonel and quickly took back his saber. Corporal Trimble escorted Forrest back down the knoll. Troopers cleared a path and saluted. While Yankee war drums pounded in the distance, a somber mood settled over the soldiers.

Folding his arms, Mack waited for the crowd of Tennesseans to disperse. "Frank, if you don't want Forrest's sword, I'll sure as hell take it."

"You still haven't apologized for betting my shotgun." Shane extended his saber and crouched in a fencer's stance. "*En garde!*" He placed the polished-steel tip to Mack's cheek. "'Neither a borrower nor a lender be.'"

Mack slapped the three-foot blade out of his face. "Point that sword at me again, I'll break it over your head and ram it where the sun don't shine."

Shane slashed his fancy saber like a swashbuckling pirate and lunged forward. As he boldly returned the pointed tip to Mack's face, Prince Hamlet's feigning words dashed through his mind. The Ringo brothers gathered around.

"'To be or not to be?'" Shane flicked his wrist and knocked Mack's campaign hat to the ground. "'Death or suicide...the unfairness of life.'"

Mack picked up his hat. "Speak English! You know I don't understand that fancy Shakespeare talk." He rubbed his thumb over the empty pin holes in the front crown. "Why'd you give Jimmy his Ranger Star back and not me?"

"You said you didn't need anything from me, *not ever again.*" Shane didn't want to lug around Forrest's cumbersome saber during battle. "Apologize for betting my shotgun, and I'll let you carry my sword today."

"Quit being a damn Tender Foot." Mack snatched the saber and metal scabbard. "Give it to me, Frank. I'll wash and wipe down your horse for a week. I want my star back."

Jerry stepped forward. "You ain't getting an apology out of Dodd. He's too hard-headed to admit he's wrong." He grabbed Shane's arm and steered him toward the row of picketed horses. "Let's get mounted up before Colonel Forrest comes back. He's looking for an excuse to flog you."

Shane dangled the Ranger Star in Mack's face. "Think I'll hold onto this ten cent star for a while. Can't buy one...gotta earn it."

"All right, I'm sorry, Frank. I'm sorry I bet your damn shotgun." Mack's voice waned. "Now can I get my star back?"

CHAPTER 19

Ambush in the Fallen Timbers

Confederate Field Hospital, 3:30 p.m., April 8, 1862:

S hane and the Crawford Boys joined Colonel Nathan Bedford Forrest and three hundred Confederate cavalrymen beneath a ridge overlooking a rain soaked cotton field. Five-thousand Union soldiers from General Sherman's Fifth Division marched in a mass parade. Bound by loyalty and friendship, Shane loaded his weapons and prepared to ambush the vastly superior Union Army. The inspirational story of Spartan King Leonidas against the mighty Persian Army rallied his fighting spirit.

Fifty feet of timbers covered Ridge Road. Positioned in the center of the cavalry line, Shane sat atop his new black stallion and guarded the Confederate field hospital. He intended to fight to the death. General Sherman's advanced guard veered down the ten-foot-wide road. While Yankee wagons clamored through the piney woods, Shane squeezed his Colt Walker and sought to gauge the performance of his horse. The thick-shouldered stallion was larger than Vengeance but not as fast or agile.

"Goddamn rebel trash!" A Yankee stared up the ridge. "Be on the lookout for a trap."

Flanked by Mack and the Ringo brothers, Shane spotted

movement on the roadway and strained to see through the overcast sky. His palms sweated and his heart pounded in his chest. Saber-wielding troopers from the Illinois Fourth halted in front of the blockade of timbers. Mack rose in his saddle and stared at the enemy.

Union infantrymen in the rear of the column continued to move forward. While trapped soldiers dropped their muskets and raced to clear the log-strewn blockade, a bottleneck of men and horses blocked the narrow roadway.

Mass hysteria ensued. Enemy troopers funneled through the blockade and rode onto the soggy cotton field. Colonel Forrest suddenly raced his horse down Ridge Road. "To Charge" trumpeted from the Ranger bugler.

Shane and the Crawford Boys charged after the colonel like screaming banshee. Joining three hundred blood-thirsty Confederates, Shane rose in his saddle and his shoulder-length hair bounced in the wind. As he raced his new black stallion, chunks of grass and muck flew through the air. The glorious cavalry charge sent terrified Illinois Fourth cavalrymen scurrying for protection.

Ear-splitting gunfire blasted along Ridge Road. Enemy troopers wheeled their horses and rammed into comrades trapped in the log-strewn blockade. Shane followed a group of Forrest's Elite Escort Guards through an opening in the roadside woods. As he steered beneath the budding spring canopy, trampled bodies littered the muddy pathway. His black stallion thundered through the pine trees like a powerful locomotive. The Union officer who'd owned the animal had trained it well.

Shane fired round after around toward the overcrowded roadway. The acrid smell of gunpowder lingered in the air. Looking to silence Yankee communications, he scanned the trapped soldiers for buglers and color guards. Panicked enemy soldiers cried out for help.

"It's an ambush! Close ranks," a Union officer shouted to his troops. "Kill those damned rebel bushwhackers."

An enemy firing line formed along the roadside. Agonizing screams echoed through the smoky haze. Shane spotted a portly bugler and fired. The twenty-yard shot ripped open the bastard's skull and continued on to kill a soldier standing behind. Packed in tight formation, dead men were held upright and used as human shields. The blur of a fast approaching rider caught Shane's eye.

"Woohoo!" Mack raced out of the haze and fired toward the crowded road. "This is why I joined the rangers— bushwhacking on a grand scale." He reined up and raised three fingers in the air. "I done shot *four*." His voice choked with excitement. "How many do I gotta kill to get my Ranger Star back?"

Eying the firing line on the edge of the meadow, Shane feared for Mack's safety. "If you can make it out of the woods alive, it's yours."

A volley of enemy musketry tore through the pine trees. Bullets bounced off branches and cut down budding twigs. Shane returned gunfire until all three of his pistols were empty. As he searched the thick haze for a safe spot to reload, a Minnie ball whizzed past his head.

"Yee haw!" Mack pulled Colonel Forrest's fancy saber and charged toward the crowded roadway. "I'm gonna find the Ringo brothers."

"Wrong way, Dodd!" Shane screamed at the top of his lungs. "Stop!"

Mack rode into a cloud of gun smoke and disappeared. Shane wheeled his horse to chase after his friend. Out of bullets, he pulled his Bowie knife and rode toward the haze. A loud blast of musketry shot from Ridge Road. His head throbbed and ears rang like church bells.

"Dodd!" Shane searched through the thick haze for his friend. "Dodd, where are you?"

Gunfire and cries of the wounded drowned out any hope of a reply. Shane struggled to see more than thirty feet in any direction. Riding parallel to the roadway, he spotted Elite Escort Corporal Kelly Trimble locked in a saber fight with a Yankee Trooper. Corporal Trimble had escorted

Colonel Forrest from the poker game and appeared over-matched.

Shane gripped his Bowie and circled in for the kill. Maneuvering behind the Yankee trooper, he leaned forward in his saddle and rammed his razor-sharp blade into the soldier's kidney. The trooper gasped and twisted in his saddle. Shane twisted his knife and recoiled to stick the bastard again. As he reared back, the wounded trooper tumbled to the ground and crawled away.

Corporal Trimble pushed back his shoulder length hair. "Colonel Forrest's under attack."

Shane didn't give a damn about the colonel. His allegiance was to himself and his friends. Looking to escape the roadside woods, he spotted the soggy cotton field and noticed a second firing line of enemy soldiers. Infantrymen knelt in front of a standing row and made exiting the woods a deadly task.

Trapped behind the double-row gauntlet of Yankees, Shane felt doomed. A dismounted Texas Ranger wrestled with an infantryman along roadside. The enemy soldier broke free and swung his musket into the ranger's skull. Blood sprayed the air like red mist. Shane recognized the slaughtered ranger but couldn't react in time. Steering alongside the log-strewn blockage, he searched for any sign of his friends.

Thirty feet away, Colonel Forrest fought atop his horse with an old model 1840 heavy cavalry saber. Raising his cumbersome saber, he parried a Yankee trooper's whip-over attack. A searing clang of steel rang out. Forrest's saber slipped from his grasp.

The Yankee trooper raised his sword to finish off Colonel Forrest. Shane didn't have time to charge. Squeezing his Bowie, he rode toward the soldier and tossed his knife. His razor-sharp blade flew end over end and sunk into the bastard's back. The impaled trooper stiffened and dropped his sword.

Shane bumped his black stallion into the trooper's horse.

Grasping the stag-bone handle of his Bowie, he leaned in his saddle and pushed the ten-inch blade deeper. His fist rammed against the soldier's spine. Blood splashed across his fingers. He pulled out the blade and quickly stuck the trooper twice more. While the soldier slithered from his saddle and fell to the ground, Colonel Forrest dismounted to retrieve his scimitar.

Shane wiped his blood-soaked knife across his thigh. "Sir, what are you doing so far in front of the men?"

"Killing Yankees, McLean!" Forrest brandished his heavy cavalry saber. "If I hadn't lost my sword to you, I wouldn't be hindered by this damn wrist-breaker." His eyes narrowed. "Where's my sword you won from me?"

Shane didn't want to answer and scanned the haze for Mack. As he thought about a response, Colonel Forrest placed his foot in a stirrup. A broad-shouldered infantryman dashed out of the haze. The enemy soldier leveled his musket and disappeared behind the colonel.

Shane didn't have a clear view of Forrest's attacker. "Watch your back!"

The Yankee assassin fired his musket. Gun smoke filled the air. Colonel Forrest buckled and grabbed his spine. His spooked horse whinnied. As the brown Bay wheeled around, Forrest struggled to remain in his saddle.

The assassin rushed toward Ridge Road. Shane stood in his stirrups and took aim at the bastard. Squeezing his bloodstained Bowie, he took a deep breath and coiled his arm to throw. The slick blade slipped from his grasp.

Corporal Trimble rode out of the haze with his polished-steel saber raised high overhead. Swooping in behind the Yankee assassin, he twisted in his saddle and unleashed a vicious downward thrust. His three-foot blade sliced straight through the assassin's neck. As the soldier's head rolled backward off his broad shoulders, blood spurted from his throat like a fountain.

Colonel Forrest slumped forward in his saddle. Suffering from a bullet to his spine, he held his lower back and steered toward the double-row gauntlet of Yankee infan-trymen. The Confederate field hospital was a quarter-mile ride through vicious hand to hand fighting on the battlefield.

"Sir, there's an enemy firing line on the edge of the cot-ton field. You'll never make it." Shane intended to use the headless soldier as a human shield. "Wait here, sir."

Placing his Bowie in his scabbard, Shane dragged the headless body toward Colonel Forrest. His crushed knee ached. The broad-shouldered soldier weighed nearly two-hundred pounds. Bracing the headless body against the colonel's horse, he wrapped his arms around the soldier's waist and lifted. The corpse collapsed over his shoulder.

Corporal Trimble leaped from his horse. "Put him down, McLean. Blood's draining out of his neck." His face tight-ened. "It's all over the back of your jacket."

Shane inched the headless body upward. "Help me lift him so the colonel can use him as a human shield."

A loud rebel yell echoed from the battlefield. Corporal Trimble grabbed the soldier's legs and heaved the body up-ward. Forrest draped the corpse around his shoulders and steered toward the field hospital.

"Yah!" Shane swatted Forrest's horse on the rear. "Stay low and ride hard, sir."

The blue infantry jacket on the headless body made Colonel Forrest appear to be a Yankee. Holding the head-less soldier's arms, Forrest steered with one hand and veered toward the battlefield. A barrage of musketry blasted from the enemy firing line. Corporal Trimble's horse crum-bled to the ground.

Shane rushed to his black stallion and stepped into his stirrup. As he mounted his horse, the wounded Illinois Fourth trooper he'd stabbed through the kidney staggered out of the haze. The trooper leveled his three-foot sword and charged.

Reaching for his knife, Shane rose and twisted in his saddle. Mind-numbing pain sliced through his upper but-tocks. His stallion rammed the Yankee bastard.

The jolted trooper pulled his sword out of Shane's backside. "Die, rebel trash!"

Shane spun around and stuck the trooper in the side of the neck. His massive blade laid open the enemy's throat. As the soldier crumbled to the ground, Corporal Trimble stood with his mouth open.

"You killed three soldiers with a knife. That's the damndest thing I've ever seen." Tremble's voice choked with excitement. "I'm gonna tell Colonel Forrest to give you a badge or something."

Shane didn't seek out attention and damn sure didn't want a rise in rank. He did what he had to do to survive and live another day. His actions were a result of preservation of himself and his friends.

He slid forward in his saddle and extended his hand. "Climb aboard, friend. We'll ride outta here together."

While Corporal Tremble leapt onto the stallion, a volley of musketry shot from Ridge Road. Shane prayed the firing line needed to reload and pointed his horse toward the hospital tents. Riding double, he charged his stallion onto battlefield with Corporal Trimble hanging onto his waist. Three-hundred Confederate Troopers fought to hold back Sherman's Fifth Division.

Weaving his horse through the fierce hand to hand fighting, Shane passed in range of the Yankee firing line and lowered his profile. Blood oozed from his stabbed buttock. Enemy muskets blasted. Corporal Trimble gasped and his body went limp. A red mist splashed the back of Shane's neck.

"Hold on!" Shane grabbed the corporal's arm. "We're almost out of range."

Trimble had been shot in the back and skull. His chin slithered down Shane's spine. Slowing his horse, Shane whispered a short prayer and slid his friend to the ground. The corporal had shielded him from certain death.

The headless Yankee soldier lay in the grass. Twenty feet away, Colonel Forrest sat slumped in his saddle. Blood oozed from his gunshot spine and stained his uniform. While Yankee troops massed into defensive positions along Ridge Road, five rangers led fifty prisoners toward the rear.

Shane squeezed his blood-soaked buttock through his pants. His saber wound required sutures. Glancing at the lines of wounded around the surgical tents, he figured on a long wait and potential capture.

Forrest approached on horseback holding his wounded spine. "You saved my ass, McLean!"

"Sir, let me escort you to the ambulances." Shane couldn't believe the colonel hadn't sought treatment. "You've got a musket ball lodged in your spine."

"We can't defend the hospital much longer." Forrest reined up and grimaced in pain. "You still want that week's furlough in New Orleans?"

Shane peeled his bloodstained fingers from his wounded buttock. "Yessir."

"Find some men to round up the livestock and prisoners." Forrest's voice softened. "We're withdrawing to Corinth, to hell with Fallen Timbers."

CHAPTER 20

Siege of Corinth

Mass graves south of Corinth, Mississippi, April, 1862:

Aweek after the Battle of Fallen Timbers, Shane and the Crawford Boys arrived in Corinth with a herd of cattle and dozens of Yankee prisoners. Typhoid and dysentery ran rampant amongst the Confederate troops. Swarms of gnats, ticks, and mosquitoes added to the misery. The overcrowded city maintained a key railroad hub that provided troop transport throughout the Tennessee Valley. Union Major General Henry Halleck combined three federal armies and pursued the Army of the Mississippi. One-hundred-thousand enemy soldiers marched toward the Confederate stronghold of Corinth.

Fifty thousand Confederate soldiers defended the city under siege. Thousands of accompanying cattle, pigs, horses, and pack mules strained the limited sanitation system. Shane struggled to find food and clean water. His malnourished body ached. Forced to work double-duty shifts, he helped construct an eight-foot-high earth mound around the town and tended to the Confederate livestock at night. The strongest souls emerged out of suffering.

Water-borne diseases killed hundreds of animals and soldiers daily. Bodies piled up. Assigned to a burial detail,

Shane worked at the bottom of a mass grave with Mack and the Ringo brothers. Shane covered his nose with his black neckerchief and laid a dead soldier in a row of bodies. The putrid stench of rotting corpses made his eyes water. As he wiped his sweaty forehead, Ranger Privates Groce and Harper carried a bloodstained boy ranger through the thirty-foot trench. Shane didn't trust the surly men. The Archer Grays were notoriously underhanded and informants for Colonel Wharton.

"What a life!" Mack slammed a coal shovel into the waist-deep grave and stepped backward. "Work all day— stable and crib at night." He tripped over a dead soldier's boot and fell to his knees. "Goddammit! Our dumb, deaf, and blind generals are worthless."

Peering over a mound surrounding the gravesite, Shane searched for the duty officer. "Quit your bitching. You talked me into joining the rangers—said we'd be home by Christmas." His voice filled with disgust. "Which one were you talking about, this year or last year?"

Jimmy swatted a fly buzzing around his head. "My father needs me and my brother at home for planting."

"If I don't die of thirst, first." Jerry wiped his sweaty brow and eyed the row of corpses. "Damn its hot today, even the dead are sweating."

Privates Groce and Harper placed the kid soldier in the row of dead soldiers. The bloodstained boy twitched. Shane recognized the soldier but couldn't recall his name. He wondered if the boy could be alive but decided his eyes were playing tricks.

"When did little Leonard die?" Mack shook his head and tossed a shovel full of lime on the Leonard's body. "I just talked to him the other day."

Private Harper smirked and pushed his curly blond hair under his campaign hat. As he walked away, Shane stared across the mass grave and cussed his wretched duty. Six more months of war felt like a lifetime. He leaned on his shovel handle and dreamed of a permanent French Leave.

Jimmy stretched his back. "If Jimtown Major didn't send names of deserters to the Galveston News for publication, I'd have already slipped past the Provost Guards and be halfway home."

"All you men do is cry like girls." Private Groce shouted from across the grave. "Thought Harrison's Elite Rangers were trained killers and cold-blooded assassins."

Rushing his finger to his mouth, Jerry shushed the surly ranger. "Groce, we do what we're trained to do. If that means killing, so be it."

Mack tossed his flat-headed shovel out of the grave and wiped his hands. "Why don't you tell our ignorant officers to quit giving us bad equipment? I can't dig graves with a coal shovel."

"Watch your words." Groce's eyes narrowed. "Officers are doing the best they can."

"I hate losing to the Yankees, but I hate quitting more. It's downright shameful." Mack's voice filled with disgust. "We had Grant's army licked at Shiloh and our cowardly generals stopped us from charging. Now we're gonna have to fight 'em again."

"This time will be different." Shane scoffed. "Three Union Armies against one. We'll be fighting Grant's army, Buell's army and Halleck's army."

"We're all gonna die here." Jerry kicked dirt across the body-filled trench. "Get buried in a grave like this with no markers. Nobody will ever know your name."

"It's a rich man's war and a poor man's fight." Shane eyed Harper and Groce across the grave. "One day you'll all figure that out."

"You're full of it, McLean. You enjoy killing people." Private Groce stared at Leonard's bloodstained body and smirked. "If you weren't killing Yankees, what else would you do?"

Shane glared at pint-sized ranger. "Big words from a little man. I'm not sure what I'd be doing. But you can rest assured, any killing I do will start with you."

Private Groce locked eyes with Shane. "Is that a threat?"

The vile little man rubbed Shane the wrong way. Shane wanted to slit Groce's throat but refrained himself. Jimmy sat against the dirt wall and stared into space.

"Better to die fighting like these men in the grave than suffer the shame and indignity of living in tyranny." Harper shouted across the grave. "When Lincoln and the Yankees invade Texas, they'll rape women, murder children, and kill everyone."

"He's got a point, Frank. Look what happened to you in Austin." Mack's shook his head. "You stood idle and let the bastards kill your father in front of you."

"Damn you, Dodd!" Shane tugged on his black neckerchief and wanted to choke his loud-mouth friend. "You weren't there. It was six against one. What more could I do?"

"I didn't mean you were a coward, Frank." Mack stepped in front of the bloodstained boy-ranger's boot. "I'm sure you done all you could."

Shane bore the guilt of his father's murder every day of his life. "If you *ever* question my manhood again, I'll cut you into so many pieces they'll never find you." He grabbed his stag-boned handle Bowie and lost his composure. "I'm in a damn grave, knee-deep with bodies. What more do you want from me?"

"Sorry, Frank. Didn't mean to make you mad." Mack's voice choked. "You're the meanest and toughest son-of-a-bitch I know. I really am sorry."

Mack rarely apologized. Shane appreciated the kind words but struggled to contain his emotions. He wanted to kill Sam Houston and the Jayhawkers more than he wanted to live. "I hate our ignorant generals too, Dodd. And I don't give a damn about state's rights or slavery." Shane didn't care who heard his litigious words. "I'm bidding my time until I can hunt down Houston and the rest of those bounty hunters." His heart pounded and his voice trembled. "Only reason I ain't escaped this God-forsaken war is because I didn't wanna abandon you and the Ringos."

Leonard's bloodstained face twitched. Shane eyed the boy-ranger and wondered if he'd seen a ghost. As he brandished his Bowie, Leonard sat up and latched onto Mack's ankle. Shane feared for his big friend. Coiling his knife, he squeezed his knife handle and lunged forward.

"Ahh!" Mack sounded a blood-curdling scream and fell on his back. "Ahh....ghost!"

Shane sunk his knife into the Leonard's side. Flesh and blood dripped down his double-edge blade. The boy released Mack's leg and cried out in agony. Shane looked to stick him again. As he twisted his blade to widen the wound and removed his knife, bright red blood stained his fingers. Groce and Harper rushed to Leonard's aid.

"Don't stab him, McLean! It's a joke." Private Harper's voice trembled. "He's alive."

Shane wiped his blood-soaked blade on the toe of his boot. He didn't appreciate the joke or their lack of respect for the dead. Everyone in the grave looked like they'd seen a ghost.

"They put me up to it, Frank!" Leonard grasped his stab wound and cried out. "Someone help me. I'm bleeding real bad."

Leonard arrived with a dozen other men to replace the rangers lost over the winter. Dark blood drained like water from his three-inch gash.

Private Harper dropped to his knees and placed his hand over the boy's knife wound. "Goddammit, McLean! You're one mean son-of-a-bitch." He turned toward Private Groce and his voice trembled. "Bring some bandages. Leonard's gonna bleed out."

"That's a sick damn joke, boy!" Jerry shouted at Leonard. "You scared the hell out of us."

Private Groce leapt out of the grave. As he rushed toward the horses for bandages, Shane lowered his head and pitied the boy-ranger. He feared his knife blade went too deep. His stomach tightened with guilt.

Leonard moaned and cried out. Mack and the Ringo brothers looked on in horror. Shane couldn't look at Lenard and prayed the suffering boy would survive. His nightmares were already haunted by gory images of the dead.

Private Harper's fingers dripped with Leonard's blood. "You're a cold-blooded killer, McLean. Better hope Leonard doesn't die or you'll face a tribunal for murder."

Jerry shook his head. "Leonard shouldn't have jumped up and scared us. Hell, I nearly shot him myself."

"What in hell's going on down there?" A duty officer approached the edge of the grave. "Put that knife away, McLean."

Private Harper pointed at Shane. "Frank, stabbed little Leonard for no reason. He's a damn killer."

"Doc Weston's on his way." The duty officer shrugged. "Put a bandage over the wound. Press down to stop the blood." He pointed at a cart of dead soldiers. "Get back to work. We've got another wagon full of bodies on the way."

Private Harper cradled Leonard's head. "Sir, you ain't gonna do nothing to Frank?"

"I'll make a report and send it to Major Harrison. If the kid dies, McLean will face hanging." The duty officer's eyes narrowed. "If you played a joke like this on me, there'd be one more dead body down there."

"Sir, I can't find my damn shovel to get back to work." Mack pointed a finger at Harper. "He took it."

Harper's face tightened. "I don't have your damn shovel, Dodd."

"Is this it?" The duty officer picked up Mack's coal shovel and tossed into the grave. "Get back to work. A dozen hogs need to be buried before nightfall."

❧❦❧

Archer Gray Camp, May 29, 1862, Corinth, Mississippi:

"'The evil that men do lives after them; the good is often

interred with their bones.'" The boy-ranger Leonard died of fever three days after Shane stabbed him in the side.

Placed under company arrest, Shane faced ranger tribunal when Colonel Wharton recovered from his wounded leg and returned to the regiment. He thought he'd win in a fair trial but didn't want to put his life in the hands of others. Especially when hard feelings were held by all parties involved.

The siege of Corinth maintained the largest deployment of soldiers and weaponry in the history of the Western Hemisphere. An eight-foot earth mound separated one-hundred-thousand Union soldiers from fifty-thousand Confederates. Typhoid and dysentery ravished the troops.

While the afternoon sun cast long shadows, Shane rested inside his pup tent. He could smell the Yankee campfires and lived in constant fear of an attack over the wall. If he didn't escape the city under siege, he would die from dehydration, disease, or an enemy bullet. A quick execution by a hangman's noose seemed like a welcome reprieve.

"Get up, McLean. Old men nap during the day." Major Harrison's deep voice echoed through the canvas tent. "How old are you, sixteen?"

"Seventeen, sir." Shane crawled outside and climbed to his feet. "I'll be eighteen on Fourth of July."

"Sows are near death. Find Dodd and the Ringo brothers and wrangle the hogs to the fishpond." Harrison pulled out his Masonic flask and took a drink. "Have a sip—a small one. There's a shortage of liquor." He tossed the fancy tin container to Shane and his voice deepened. "I'm sending Privates Groce and Harper to keep an eye on you."

Shane despised the surly rangers and feared he'd slit their throats. "Sir, I don't want them watching over me. They're accusing me of murder."

"I ain't taking any chances of you absquatulating. I've lost a dozen soldiers this week." Harrison snatched his whiskey flask. "Water the hogs. That's an order."

Under the watchful eye of Harper and Groce, Shane and

the Crawford Boys grabbed their canteens and led two-dozen pigs to the murky manure-infested watering hole south of town. As he approached the waist-deep pond, his nostrils flared. The water reeked of animal dung.

Thirsty hogs smelled water and made a mad dash to the waist-deep pond. Suffering from the heat and desperate for a drink, Shane stripped naked and tossed his sweat-stained cotton drawers on top of his boots. His parched lips and dry throat yearned for a drink. As he nudged through the thirsty herd, a three-hundred pound sow rammed his leg and knocked him off his feet. Water splashed his overheated body.

Harper and Groce stood watch along the muddy water-line. Shane splashed a handful of foul-smelling pond water in his face. His dry, sunburned lips cracked. As he climbed to his feet, the Ringo brothers waded butt-naked to the center of the pond. Mack filled his canteen with water and took a long drink. Closing his eyes, he choked down the bitter aftertaste while hogs wallowed at the water's edge.

"I wouldn't drink that, Dodd," Private Harper shouted across the pond. "You'll get the Tennessee Quick Step."

"Shut your pie hole!" Mack wiped his mouth and sighed. "I'm so damn thirsty I'd lick this slop right off the ground."

Harper threw his hands in the air. "Just trying to keep you from getting the diarrhea."

"Do yourself a favor and don't talk to any of us." Jerry shook his head. "I hate filthy little liars who kiss up to officers."

"I ain't no liar." Harper pointed at Shane. "Frank murdered little Leonard outta spite."

Jerry spit a mouthful of water. "Hold your tongue!"

Mack gagged and reached into his mouth. "Hell's bells." A mushy dark lump stuck to his finger. "Pig shit."

"Told you so." Harper scoffed. "That's why I get all my water from the creek."

"I'm sick of our second-class status." Jerry pointed toward a lavish Corinth Mansion used as a headquarters. "Officers meeting for the Council of War have fresh water while we're forced to drink from a pond full of pig piss."

Mack wiped his finger around the inside of his mouth and spit. "CSA don't pay us. Don't feed us. And they're gonna try and hang Frank for stabbing that kid." His voice choked. "Harper and Groce should be hung for playing that trick on Frank."

"I've heard enough of this treasonous talk." Groce's eyes narrowed. "Frank killed Leonard, end of story. Keep this up and I'll have all of you arrested and brought before Major Harrison."

"Damn you, Groce! It was an accident." Mack rose out of the water and splashed his way over to the surly Rangers. "Why do you claim Frank killed that boy? Them's fighting words."

Groce looked for protection and stepped behind Harper. Shane knew Mack meant business and rushed to defend the two men. With the death of Leonard, he was already in trouble and didn't want two more problems. A dozen thirsty hogs wallowed snout-deep in the muck along the waterline.

Ramming his knee into the side of a large sow, Mack forced his way through the herd of hogs. "Tell General Beauregard and the rest of the high-falutin officers to kiss my ass. I'll fight as a Partisan Ranger." Mack's foot slipped in the filthy mud. "But I ain't staying here."

He tumbled forward and plunged face-first into a pile of pig manure. As he lifted his head out of the muck, Shane turned his cheek to hide his amusement. Mack didn't handle embarrassment well.

Harper laughed out loud. "Dodd, a greased pig has more grace than you."

Lifting his head out of a pile of pig shit, Mack wiped his mouth and spit. "You two think it's funny?" His hair, cheek and chin were caked in foul smelling manure. "I'm gonna slit both your throats and feed you to the pigs."

Harper and Groce clammed up tighter than Major Harrison's grip on a flask of whiskey. Shane expected fists to fly at any moment. As he splashed naked out of the pond, Mack climbed to his feet and slipped again. Everybody laughed.

Shane cherished his friendship with Mack but feared his volatile temperament. Mack could be kind to a stray dog or homeless child and even cooked for the entire company. But cross him, and he'd slit your throat quicker than a downhill freight train.

"Why are you being nice to those weasels?" Mack eyed Shane with disdain. "They're intending to put a noose around your neck."

A clump of manure dangled from Mack's curly long hair. He pinched the dark spongy lump out of a tangled curl and sniffed his fingers. His face wrinkled in disgust. Shane smothered a laugh.

Jerry pointed at Mack. "Dodd's got pig dung in his hair."

Rushing his finger to his lips, Shane feared Groce and Harper would add further insult. He turned to warn the loathsome rangers, but both men were gone. The Ringo brothers laughed like cackling hyena. Scanning the pine trees around the pond, Shane feared the devious men went to complain to Major Harrison.

"Damn you, Ringo! It ain't funny." Mack threw the piece of manure on the ground and stormed back into the pond. "I've got pig shit in my hair. Ain't never gonna wash out."

Struggling to keep a straight face, Shane waded through the waist-deep water to help his friend. Mack took a deep breath and splashed down under the surface. As he scrubbed his scalp with both hands, clumps of hair and dung floated to the surface. The pond rippled with tiny waves. Popping his head out of the water, he shook his tangled hair and wiped his eyes.

Jimmy shouldered up to his big brother. "Damn, Dodd, you look like a mangy dog scratching for fleas."

Shane grabbed a clump of Mack's hair. "Hold still and I'll help you clean out the dung."

"Frank, we've got to do something." Mack sunk to his

knees and kept his head above water. "Let's desert tonight. Dozens of men already done it. Officers too."

A horse whinnied in the thicket. The sound of approaching riders drew Shane's attention to the woods north of the pond. As he helped Mack wash the pig dung in his hair, a group of ranger officers rode down a pathway through the pine trees.

"What in hell's name is going on here?" Major Harrison's angry voice rang out. "Four naked Rangers bathing each other in the pond."

A roar of laughter sounded from the junior officers. Shane searched for a valid explanation but had none. Fortunately, Major Harrison was a friend and his Freemason sponsor. While pigs wallowed around the water's edge, the ranger officers lined up in a row. Privates Groce and Harper walked alongside the officers.

"McLean, you're an embarrassment to the company." Major Harrison brandished his whip. "Sergeant Beavers gets sent home to recover from his wounds and you Crawford Boys go hog-wild crazy." His eyes narrowed. "Get your asses out of that pond. Front and center!"

A train whistle from the Mobile and Ohio engine sounded in the distance. Slogging out of the water, Shane sensed trouble and rushed to get dressed. As he shouldered up alongside Mack and the Ringo brothers, the row of tight-lipped officers sat atop their horses like a band of righteous critics.

"Major Harrison, sir!" Groce stepped around the Jimtown Major's horse. "Private Dodd needs to be reprimanded for making a threat on our lives. He said he was gonna cut us into pieces and feed us to the hogs."

Mack stepped forward to protest. Shane grabbed Mack's arm and yanked him back into line. He intended to fight Groce's accusations with allegations of his own and indulged his friendship with the Major Harrison.

"Sir, Groce is a damn liar. On the way to the pond, he called you an incompetent intoxicated lush who couldn't lead a bunch of drunkards into a bar." Shane approached the row of horse-mounted officers. "Private Dodd took exception to Groce's comment, so he threatened to cut him up and feed him to the pigs."

"Sir, I did no such thing." Groce shook his head. "McLean and his friends are lying. They killed Leonard for no reason and should be hung in front of the company."

Shane wiped a bead of water from his nose. "Groce, lied about what happened in the grave and he's lying now."

Mack approached Major Harrison. "Sir, on the way down to the pond Groce and Harper referred to you as the Jimtown Major. Lying bastards don't have the balls to say it to your face."

"Harper bragged if Colonel Wharton was in commanded we'd be in Tennessee with the rest of Colonel Forrest's cavalry." Shane grabbed Jerry's arm and presented him to the row of officers. "Ask Ringo if you don't believe me."

"Major Harrison, sir." Private Harper's voice trembled. "We signed up in Brazoria County to fight with Wharton, but you're doing a good job of running the regiment until the colonel returns to active duty."

Harrison pulled his Masonic flask from his jacket and took a long sip. He grimaced and appeared hurt by the accusations of his incompetence. Bad blood and jealousy between officers tore regiments apart. Shane liked Wharton, but his loyalties lay with Harrison.

"Sir, Groce and Harper are out to improve their rank at your expense and potentially my life." Shane pled for reason. "If the tribunal believes their lies, I'll be a dead man."

Jerry flashed a Masonic Hand Sign. "Sir, you know us from the lodge in Waco. We signed-up to fight in the Harrison Rangers. If Brother Dodd threatened to cut up Groce and Harper, he had a good reason."

Harper threw his hands in the air. "Major Harrison, Sir. Those men are lying."

An ear-piercing train whistle silenced Private Harper's rebuttal. Half a mile away, Shane spotted a thick-line of gray smoke spewing from the Mobile and Ohio engine and scanned the train for much needed troop reinforcements. His stomach churned. Passenger cars were devoid of men and supplies. As the engine chugged toward the Corinth Station, a festive drum-roll greeted the empty train. Confederate buglers trumpeted "Dixieland." Soldiers in town cheered. Shane wondered why a vacant train brought such a cheerful response.

"Arrest these two!" Major Harrison pointed to Groce and Harper. "Tie their wrists and hang them over a tree branch. Whip 'em until their minds get right."

Shane sighed. Five junior officers arrested Groce and Harper. The two men kicked and screamed while their hands were bound with hemp rope. Cries of blasphemy and the crack of a whip echoed through the air.

Harrison approached Shane and pointed toward a herd of cattle grazing along the train tracks south of town. "I've got a special duty for you and your men. Beauregard's sneaking the army out of Corinth tonight." His voice softened to a whisper. "You and your men are going to round up the officer's cattle and drive them fifty miles south to Tupelo."

Shane perked up at the news. "Sir, did I hear you right? The entire army's withdrawing from Corinth?"

A grin curled the side of Harrison's mouth. "It's a hoax, McLean. Every time a train rolls into town, infantrymen are under orders to cheer like it's full of reinforcements." He pointed to the bare bones crew of men posted on the earthmound wall separating the armies. "We're gonna keep the campfires lit all night and send off a few cannon volleys every hour. Make the Yankees think we're still here and ready to fight."

Shane recalled a similar ploy used during the Revolutionary War. "Yessir. It worked for General Washington a century ago when he escaped across the frozen Delaware River."

"It's going to work, tonight." Harrison crouched in his saddle and whispered. "Wharton's joining the regiment in

Murfreesboro but the junior officers want to hang you for killing Leonard. Save your hide and ride back home."

Shane didn't want to run from his problems. "Sir, those charges are false. I want to go with you to Tennessee and fight the charges."

Harrison took a sip from his flask and wiped his chin. "If you know what's good for you, Frank, you'll deliver the cattle and then be gone back to Texas."

CHAPTER 21

Corinth Hoax

Corinth, Mississippi, 11:30 p.m., May 29, 1862:

The Confederate Army exodus began at sundown. Wounded soldiers and supplies were loaded onto boxcars and shipped by train to Tupelo.

While volleys of cannon fire soared back and forth over the earth mound wall, trains chugged in and out of Corinth Station. Intending to put his own escape plan into action, Shane and the Crawford Boys rounded up a hundred head of cattle and drove the animals along the train tracks. Moonlight reflected off rows of cross-bearing graves south of town.

Five miles south of Corinth, Shane scanned the piney woods for an escape route to the Shamrock Ranch. Knee-high corn stalks sprouted in an open field. Eager to put his plan into action, he turned in his saddle and eyed Mack and the Ringo brothers.

"It's now or never." Shane sighed. "If we ride all night, we can slip past the rear guards."

"You've got to leave or they'll hang you for Leonard's murder." Mack stared across the moonlit cornfield. "Let's do it."

"Frank, I'm having second thoughts." Jerry reined up

along the train tracks. "I can't go home, my father will dis-own me."

"Damn it, Jerry." Jimmy threw his arms in the air. "I can't go home if you don't go home. Daddy would beat me and turn me in to the authorities."

"I thought y'all were smart." Mack steered toward the Ringo brothers. "This war is a lost cause. Even I got enough horse sense to know when it's time to quit."

Jerry brushed off Mack with a wave of his hand. "Y'all go and return home. When I get to Tupelo, I'll tell 'em we ran into a Yankee patrol and you got captured or something."

Shane stared into the moonlit field. "I understand, Ringo. But they're gonna hang me for Leonard's killing. I gotta leave." He sank his spurs into his new black stallion and steered for home. "'Freedom is the word.'"

"Enough of your fancy Shakespeare talk." Mack raced after Shane. "Wait up, I'm coming with you."

Riding beneath a sky full of stars, Shane charged down a row of corn like an arrow shot from a bow. The leafy stalks quivered under the thunderous power of his stallion. Cattle mooed in the distance. Impressed by Jerry's staunch alle-giance to duty, Shane rode through the middle of the field and glanced over his shoulder. The Ringo brothers' silhou-ettes reflected in the moonlight.

Mack rushed to catch up. "*Freedom* is a good name for your new horse."

Shane liked the name Freedom. As he escaped the scourge of war, the weight of the world lifted from his shoulders. He felt at peace with his inner demons and looked forward to a simple life on the Shamrock Ranch.

A torch light flickered in the woods north of the corn-field. Tracking the ominous light, Shane spotted a proces-sion of riders trailing the flame and steered south. Adrenalin rushed through his veins. He didn't expect a friendly patrol this far south of Corinth. As he attempted to stay one step ahead of the light, a second torch appeared in the thicket south of the field. The patrols circled around and closed in.

"Damn it, Frank." Mack's voice trembled. "We're in big trouble."

In an attempt to outrun the horsemen, Shane steered Freedom due west. A gunshot rang out. He lowered his profile and continued to flee through the middle of the cornfield. If the patrols were Union, he feared intense interrogation and agonizing torture. If captured by a Confederate Cavalry, they'd put a bullet in his head for desertion.

Mack steered alongside Shane. "Confederate Secret Service is gonna hang us."

"Might be slave catchers. Maybe we'll get lucky." Shane liked his chances with a Yankee patrol and slowed his horse to a gallop. "Blue bellies will torture us for information. But they may let us *swallow the dog* and send us home."

"I ain't pledging no allegiance to the Union!" Mack's voice trembled. "Lincoln kills innocent women and children."

A second gun blast echoed through the night sky. As the warning shot whizzed over his head, Shane reined up his black stallion. He thought about returning to the cattle drive but he was surrounded by two patrols. Mack pulled out his pistols and closed rank.

"Put those guns away and let me do the talking." Shane tugged on his black neckerchief and readied his three pistols. "Be prepared to shoot it out."

Mack holstered his weapons. Shane pressed down in his stirrups and wheeled Freedom toward the northern patrol. As he prepared to fight to the death, fifty Confederate Provost Guards circled in. Gold and silver buttons glimmered on their pressed gray uniforms. The elite horsemen patrolled the rear of the lines and shot deserters.

A wild-eyed Provost captain with a thick beard shouted at an officer leading the southern patrol. "Lieutenant C—r—e—w—s, if these deserters run, shoot 'em in the head."

Lieutenant Cruz carried a torch and circled behind his troopers. The sawed-off Tejano officer had dark skin and a thick mustache. Guardsmen moved like gray ghosts in the dark. As the elite horsemen circled around, Shane steered alongside Mack's horse. Freedom snorted and whinnied.

The captain approached with a noose dangling in his hand. Shane twisted in his saddle and steadied his nervous horse. Scanning the torchlight, he looked for a familiar face but saw none. Mack dropped his hand to his side holster and cussed.

"We're hanging deserters." The Provost Captain halted in front of Shane. "What're you rangers doing out here after dark?"

"Sir, we're driving the officers' livestock to Tupelo." Shane pointed toward the herd of cattle grazing along the train tracks and lied. "Our CO ordered us into the field to round up strays."

"Lieutenant Crews, you're from Goliad, Texas." The captain sat up in his saddle and scoffed. "Where do you suppose your fellow Texicans are heading? All alone after dark."

"*Señor*, Burleson." The Tejano Lieutenant replied in a condescending Spanish accent. "These *hombres* ain't real Texicans. They're deserters." His thick mustache twitched. "Sooner we hang these *chiñgos* the better."

Shane feared bullets were about to fly. Scanning the circle of guardsmen, he planned to spring a trap but needed to draw Captain Burleson closer. Mack looked like he'd open fire at any moment.

"Sir, I played cards last month with Colonel Nathan Bedford Forrest. He's out in front of his men like a real leader." Shane took a shot at the Tejano Lieutenant's short stature. "Lieutenant Crews is a half officer who hides in the rear and shoots his fellow soldiers."

Burleson rode closer and dangled his noose in Shane's face. "Ranger, insult one of my officers again, and I'll hang you myself. Arrest these traitors for desertion."

Captain Burleson had no intention of being impartial. As he slipped his hand to his holster, Shane snatched his ivory-handled .36 and sprang his trap like a magician. He aimed the custom eight-inch barrel at the lieutenant's chest and cocked the hammer. Cruz froze in his saddle.

Captain Burleson twitched. Shane reached under his belt and grabbed his Big Colt Walker. As he leveled the barrel at Burleson's forehead, Mack pulled out both his pistols. The guardsmen scrambled for their guns. A high-stakes game of chicken ensued.

"Move an inch, Captain." Shane glared down the barrel of his revolver. "I'll spray your brains all over Lieutenant Crews."

"Men, if he dares shoot me." Burleson held his hands away from his body. "Gun him down like a wild animal and quarter him into pieces."

Shane figured they'd all be damned to hell, but he wanted desperately to return home. As he sat in his saddle, guns were aimed and turned like fans at the slightest movement.

"Captain Burleson, you mean to hang us without a trial." Shane cocked the hammer on his Colt Walker. "I can't let that happen. We're just following orders to take cattle to Tupelo."

"Soldier, you're surrounded by fifty of my troopers." Burleson threw back his shoulders and spoke in a patronizing tone. "Put your pistols down and we'll see about a tribunal." His hand slipped to his side. "I don't negotiate at the barrel of a gun."

"Move again, Captain. I'll blow your damn head-off." Shane's voice hardened with resolve. "I've got nothing to lose."

Mack swiveled his head and aimed his pistols at any threatening movement. Shane didn't want to assassinate Captain Burleson but couldn't hold out forever. If he surrendered, he'd be shot off his horse in a hail of gunfire.

"Drop that pistol, Captain." Jerry Ringo's voice rang out in the darkness. "Or I'll blow a hole in the back of your head the size of Texas."

Shane had no clue Burleson held a pistol by his side.

Staring through the torchlight, he took his eyes off the captain and watched the Ringo brothers approach on horseback. Guardsmen wheeled their mounts and stared through the moonlit field.

Burleson took a deep breath and begrudgingly holstered his gun. Jerry aimed his six-shot Army Colt at the back of the Lieutenant Cruz's head. As Jerry steered behind the Tejano Lieutenant, Jimmy approached with his reins in his teeth and a pistol in each hand.

"I'm a fair minded man." Burleson sat up in his saddle and shouted to his men. "If these Texas Rangers claim they ain't deserters, we'll give them a chance to prove it back in Corinth."

"He's lying, Frank! Shoot him now." Mack spit a mouthful of tobacco on the ground. "They're gonna shoot us in the back. First chance they get."

"Shut up, Dodd. Your hollering is making me nervous." Shane knew Mack was right but kept his Colt Walker aimed at Burleson's head. "Don't want to shoot the captain by accident."

"Sir, we were simply following orders like good soldiers do." Jerry spoke through the darkness. "You can hear the cows and smell the herd. We were ordered to take the officer's cattle to Tupelo."

"Don't waste your breath, Ringo. Save it for the noose." Shane vented his frustration. "They've already made up their minds to hang us. For doing our damn duty."

"Soldier, I'll speak to your C.O." Burleson's angry voice turned icy. "But I sure as hell ain't listening to you until that pistol's out of my face."

"Sir, I'll put down my guns, just as soon as *all* your men put away theirs and ride outta here." Shane pointed to the heard along the tracks. "I'm sure you know about the Hoax, tonight. If we don't deliver that livestock to Tupelo, a lot of important officers are gonna be eating beans and crackers instead of steak."

"Put your guns away, men." Burleson placed his noose across his saddle and eyed Shane. "Ranger, holster your pistols before I change my mind."

The troopers holstered their weapons.

Shane kept his Colt aimed at Captain Burleson's head. "Jerry, you and your brother ride around my rear. Let me know when *all* the soldiers put their guns away."

A haughty smirk scaled the side of Burleson's face. "Soldier, I know Colonel Forrest. He'd never play poker with you."

Mack wheeled his horse. "Captain, I'd beg to disagree." He withdrew Colonel Forrest's gold-leaf handled cavalry saber from his saddle scabbard. "My friend Frank won the colonel's old wrist-breaker last month in a card game."

"Balderdash!" Burleson scoffed. "I've seen the Colonel's saber. Bring me that cheap imitation."

Guardsmen cussed and moved their horses in a threatening manner. Shane braced his boots in his stirrups and stared through the torchlight. As he prepared for a gunfight, Mack maneuvered his horse over to the captain and extended Colonel Forrest's three-foot sword.

Burleson grabbed the fancy saber and ran his gloved finger down the length of the blade. "This is Nathan's sword."

Desperate to return home, Shane offered up an enticement. "Captain Burleson, sir. Let us finish our duty and drive the cattle to Tupelo and you can keep Colonel Forrest's saber."

"Bribing an officer is a hanging offense." Burleson waved his torch in Shane's face. "Get that gun out of my face."

Shane didn't believe bribery was a death sentence. "Sir, if that were so, half the Texas Rangers would be hung from trees. I'm offering the sword as a gift to be returned to Colonel Forrest."

"Sir, Frank helped the colonel escape capture and saved his life." Jerry approached with his brother in tow. "Aren't you going to Tennessee with the other cavalry regiments?

Forrest's in Murfreesboro recovering from a gunshot wound to the spine."

Burleson's eyes narrowed. "I don't offer deals down the barrel of a gun."

Shane lowered his gun. "Sir, I'm sure if you returned Colonel Forrest's sword, he'd be obliged to offer you a position in his elite Escort Company."

"I recon so, Ranger." Burleson turned toward Lieutenant Cruz. "Lee, gather your troopers and escort these men on their cattle drive to Tupelo. Then put 'em on a train to the Eastern Front in Virginia." He placed Forrest's saber in his saddle scabbard. "If they try to absquatulate again, shoot 'em in the head."

Shane gave up the fight and placed his trust in Colonel Burleson. Hell bent on revenge, he holstered his custom Colt Special but vowed to finish his quest for vengeance. He'd made a promise to himself to hunt down and punish Sam Houston and the gang of Jayhawkers. Mary Kelly and a peaceful life on Shamrock Ranch would have to wait.

About the Author

Ian McLean is a freelance writer and member of the Houston Writers Guild. Born in Long Beach, California, Ian graduated from University High School in Waco, Texas. A love of literature led him to Sam Houston State University where he played football and excelled in storytelling. For the past twenty-five years, he has devoted his life to teaching and coaching high school and middle school athletes. In 2010, Ian entered *Legend of Shane McLean* in a HWG writing contest and was named a finalist. His fifth place finish inspired a passion to write. He is a member of the Texas High School Coaches Association and Texas Federation of Teachers. Ian is a husband and proud father of three.

CPSIA information can be obtained
at www.ICGtesting.com
Printed in the USA
FSOW04n1115251116
27800FS